THE WOMEN'S DECAMERON

Julia Voznesenskaya was born and educated in Leningrad. She later studied drama, became a member of the unofficial Cultural Movement, and acquired a considerable reputation as a poet. She was a founder of the first Russian independent Women's Group, *Maria*, but in the late seventies was imprisoned and later exiled for her social and literary activities. In 1980 she was forced to emigrate to West Germany, and she now lives in Munich. She is the subject of the American feature film *Julia's Diary*.

JULIA VOZNESENSKAYA

The Women's Decameron

Translated by W B Linton

Minerva

A Minerva Paperback

THE WOMEN'S DECAMERON

First published as *Damskii Dekameron*
First published in in Great Britain 1986
by Quartet Books Ltd
First paperback edition published 1987
by Methuen London
This Minerva edition published 1990
Reprinted 1991
by Mandarin Paperbacks
Michelin House, 81 Fulham Road, London SW3 6RB

Minerva is an imprint of the Octopus Publishing Group,
a division of Reed International Books Limited

Copyright © 1985 Julia Voznesenskaya
Translation Copyright © 1986 Quartet Books Ltd

A CIP catalogue record for this book
is available from the British Library

ISBN 0 7493 9092 1

Printed in Great Britain
by Cox and Wyman Ltd, Reading, Berks

The Women's Decameron

A book about how ten young women in the same ward of a maternity hospital learn that the building has been placed under quarantine and that they will have to stay confined for another ten days, a prospect which of course hardly fills them with delight. It occurs to one of them to borrow the idea of a certain Florentine writer by the name of Boccaccio and to pass the ten days telling each other various stories about life, men, love and everything that is of concern, in their case, to the woman of today. The suggestion is accepted unanimously and over the course of ten days
100
different stories are told. You will find a summary of their contents in their sub-titles, and if you have the time you will read the stories themselves.

The First Day

With which it all begins, although it must be said that the majority of books known to us begin with the first chapter. Hardly anyone could name a book that began with the last chapter, so that it is not so much this that is significant as the fact that, having agreed to tell each other various stories, the women begin with stories of

First Love

Once women have made up their minds to divulge their most intimate secrets they will inevitably begin with stories about First Love. So now, after a brief introduction which we also recommend you to read, you will start our book with the first story of First Love.

'How is it possible to read in this bedlam!' thought Emma. She turned over on to her stomach, propped the *Decameron* between her elbows, pulled the pillow over her ears and tried to concentrate.

She could already visualize how the play would begin. As they entered the auditorium and spectators would not be met by the usual theatre attendants, but by monks with their cowls drawn down over their eyes; they would check the tickets and show the spectators to their seats in the dark auditorium, lighting the way and pointing out the seat numbers, with old-fashioned lanterns. She would have to call in at the Hermitage, look out a suitable lantern, and draw a sketch of it ... The stage would be open from the very beginning, but lit only by a bluish moon. It would depict a square in Florence with the dark outlines of a fountain and a church door, over which would be the inscription 'Memento Mori' – remember you must die. Every now and then some monks would cross the stage with a cart – the corpse-collectors. And a bell, there must definitely be a bell ringing the whole time – 'For whom the bell tolls'. It was essential that from the very beginning, even before the play started, there should be a feeling of death in the theatre. Against this background ten merry mortals would tell their stories.

Yet it was difficult to believe that it happened like that: plague, death and misery were all around and in the midst of this a company of cavaliers and ladies were amusing each other with romantic and bawdy stories. These women, on the other hand, did not have the plague but a simple skin infection such as frequently occurs in maternity hospitals, and yet look at all the tears and hysterics! Perhaps people were much shallower nowadays. Stupid woman, why were

2

they so impatient? Were they in such a hurry to start the nappy-changing routine? God, the very thought was enough to make you want to give up: thirty liners, thirty nappies and as many swaddling sheets, rain or shine. And each one had to be washed, boiled and ironed on both sides. It could drive you crazy. In the West they had invented disposable nappies and plastic pants long ago. Our people were supposed to be involved in industrial espionage, so why couldn't they steal some useful secret instead of always going for electronics?

'Hey, girls! You could at least take it in turns to whine! The noise is really bugging me. If my milk goes off I'll really freak out!' This outburst came from Zina, a 'woman of no fixed abode' as the doctors described her on their rounds; in other words, a tramp. Nobody came to visit her, and she was in no hurry to leave the hospital.

'If only we had something nice to think about!' sighed Irina, or Irishka as everyone called her, a plump girl who was popular in the ward because of her kind, homely disposition.

And then it suddenly dawned on Emma. She lifted the *Decameron* high above her head so that everyone could see the fat book in its colourful cover. 'Dear mothers! How many of you have read this book?' Naturally about half of them had. 'Well,' continued Emma, 'for those who haven't I'll explain it simply. During a plague ten young men and women leave the city and place themselves in quarantine for ten days, just as they've done to us here. Each day they take it in turns to tell each other different stories about life and love, the tricks that clever lovers play and the tragedies that come from love. How about all of us doing the same?'

That was all they needed. They immediately decided that this was much more interesting than telling endless stories about family problems.

'We should begin at the very beginning!' announced Irishka. 'Let's kick off with stories about first love. Only you must let me go last! I'm much too shy to start the ball rolling!'

'What's there to be shy about?' laughed Zina. 'We're all women, aren't we? We all love with the same part of the body, don't we?'

'And what part did you have in mind?' enquired an

3

attractive blonde with the foreign name Albina, screwing up her eyes.

'She means the heart!' replied Valentina hurriedly on Zina's behalf, just to be on the safe side. Valentina, as it later transpired, was a Party bigwig.

'Oh, the heart!' said Albina, disappointed, and gave a bored yawn. But it was obvious that she was just teasing Valentina and that actually her eyes were sparkling at the idea of all sharing stories.

But Valentina persisted: 'I don't know why the word "love" gets a dirty laugh from some people. In this country love is a matter of national importance, because the family is founded on love and families are the cells that make up the state.'

'Quite right,' said Olga, a worker from the Admiralty shipyard, entering the conversation for the first time. 'I even had two states involved in my first love, the Soviet Union and the German Democratic Republic, so there you are.'

'You don't say? Well, tell us about it, Olga! Tell us!' clamoured the women, sitting up in their beds all ready to listen. So without further ado Olga began the story of her first love.

Story One

by Olga, the shipyard worker, about how a romance in the spirit of internationalism started up between a German shipbuilder and a Soviet worker, a romance which, despite the involvement of two governments, ended in a miscarriage.

'My first love turned out to be a dissident one in some ways. I work at the Admiralty shipyard as a varnisher in the furnishings shop. I make good money, I'm not complaining, but the authorities won't get off my back. If there's a travel pass going, or even a shift up in the queue for a flat, anyone else could get it, but not me. And why not? Because I was engaged to a German. An East German of course, not a real one, but even so . . .

4

'It's ten years since that love affair. They were building the Germans a tanker at our yard. It was a joint Russian-German project, sorry – *Soviet*-German. The Germans built the hull and the engines and we were fitting it out. We were both socialist countries, so there was good socialist competition and the tanker was delivered six months early. Then we spent the next eight months getting rid of the defects. Sometimes the tanker was sent to our yard with its German shipbuilders, sometimes it was shunted back to its home port of Rostock with us still on board repairing the faults. And so we went backwards and forwards between Rostock and Leningrad. There were a lot of young people, we made friends, and some of us fell in love.

'I got to like a mechanic called Peter, or Petya, as we would say. He was clean, nice, serious, and he spoke Russian. The only trouble was, he was a believer. There are still quite a few of them in the GDR, after all they didn't join us so long ago. Maybe that's why when he found out I was pregnant he wouldn't even talk about an abortion, but went rushing off to his superiors to get permission to marry me. They gave him permission, but my bosses wouldn't hear of it. They brought me from the tanker and had me up before their Party committee, union committee, and everything else committee, trying to persuade me and even telling me straight out: "Get an abortion! We'll never let you out anyway. Or persuade your Fritz to settle in the Soviet Union."

'But how was I supposed to do that? Petya had his parents, brothers and sisters in Rostock and a little house with a garden, but I was an orphan living in a dormitory and I had nothing. How was I supposed to drag Petya away from his GDR Germany? What sort of home sweet home could I offer him? So I said to them: "If you can't give me a flat, at least give me a room where we could live together, then I'll try and persuade him."

' "You're a cunning one!" they said, "if we gave everyone flats you'd all be fixing yourselves up with foreigners."

'And they hassled me so much that I miscarried in the fifth month – a boy. The miscarriage wasn't so bad, but I was scared to write to Petya in case he changed his mind about marrying me. He was over there fighting for me, sending documents to different places in Germany and the Soviet

5

Union. But he wasn't getting anywhere because our bosses had obviously agreed among themselves about it. Then, when it came time for me to have the baby Petya sent me a cat-fur coat and such a parcel of things for the baby that all my friends in the dormitory came running to look – everything synthetic! I cried and cried over the baby clothes and thought my life was a wreck.

'Then I got a letter from him saying it was all over between us because I had deceived him. I don't know who wrote to him about the baby. Maybe the neighbours got jealous and copied his address from a letter, or maybe the authorities took charge.

'What then? Well, nothing much. I married a nice guy from the shipyard. He drinks a lot, but otherwise he's OK. Of course you couldn't compare him to Petya. He was an educated German and knew how to treat a woman. All I've got left of Petya is the coat, which never seems to wear out. Sometimes I cry on it: you little bastard, I tell it, why don't you ever get torn or wear out so I can forget you? But I haven't the heart to sell it. All those memories . . .'

'Yes, real cat doesn't wear out . . . ,' said Nelya thoughtfully, a quiet, dark woman who taught music. 'My mother wore a cat-fur coat for the whole war, and there was still enough left to make me a collar.'

'What's so surprising about that?' smiled Olga. 'Four years isn't long for a fur coat. Mine is still as good as new.'

'But you should have seen how my mother used it – that coat has been under the ground, it's been on a bunk in a German concentration camp, and it even hid me from the Fascists.'

'Why don't you tell us about it?' asked Emma.

But there were tears in Nelya's eyes and she shook her head:

'Later, all right? I can't now . . . Later.'

Then Larissa sat up in her bed: 'Then I'll tell you the story of my first love. Do you want me to?'

'Of course!' shouted the women. Larissa had long been a focus of attention in the ward because of her independence and her even disposition. The only people who came to visit her were colleagues from work, and they only came two or three times, but she pretended not to be in the least put out by this. Everyone in the ward was naturally intrigued to know how she came to be so self-reliant and proud.

Larissa thought for a little, then began her story.

Story Two

by Larissa, doctor of biology, about how once upon a time she fell in love passionately, hopelessly and forever, how the love became mutual, how she got rid of a hateful rival, how she thought her beloved was dead and gone, but went on waiting for him until he finally came back, only to lose him again, this time for good; how she waited and waited for him, gave up in the end, and then found out that he was dead; how she hoped to meet someone like her first love, but never did, and eventually decided to become a single parent.

'I fell in love for the first and last time when I was only five years old ... Don't laugh, first hear what sort of love it was. Perhaps you won't feel like laughing when you've heard the whole story.

'It was during the war. My father was in charge of a military aerodrome and my mother was a medical officer. They were both serving in the same unit and were so afraid of losing me in the general chaos of war that they dragged me around with them rather than entrust me to relatives or children's homes. The aerodrome got shifted from place to place as the front line moved, and I was shifted about with it, camouflaged beneath a bundle of clothes and ordered not to move when documents were being checked. And they would hide me whenever the top brass visited the unit. This way I spent the whole of the war in an active unit.

'One time a new pilot came to us straight from flying school. He was the youngest, only eighteen, but of course he seemed grown up to me, even quite old. He was a tall, fair-haired man with a suntanned face and blue eyes, always cheerful and very brave. His name was Volodya, and everyone took to him straightaway. There were several girls in the unit working in the met office and the sick bay, and there was also the telegraphist Rayechka. They all had their eye on Volodka, and this Rayechka girl even had some success. But I got Volodka away from her. Don't laugh, it's true!

'Why that boy – at least now as a forty-year-old woman he seems like a boy – should have got attached to me, the spoilt daughter of the regiment, I just don't know. But we just couldn't get through a day without seeing each other. I would get up in the morning and run straight across to the airmen. They would see me through the window and shout to Volodka: "Your girlfriend's here early today, go and meet her!"

'Volodka would meet me in the doorway, sweep me up in his arms, and only after that would we go to the mess together for breakfast. All the best morsels from Volodka's plate, usually some watery compote of dried fruits, a luxury of the early war years, would be mine by right as his 'girlfriend'. My parents tried to put a stop to this pampering. Once they forbade me to bother him for a whole day. I sat at home and whined. Imagine their surprise when Volodka reported in person to our room, saluted my father in the doorway, and said to him: "Comrade Commander! Request permission to collect my girlfriend; it's time for us to check our aircraft."

'Of course they let me go with Volodka, and the two of us raced happily out to the airfield. Volodka groomed and cared for his machine, a U2 reconnaissance plane, or "bookcase", as his fighter pilot friends used to call it jokingly. He would inspect the engine, tuning and fixing here and there, and I would clamber about the outside with a rag wiping the dust off. When we had finished Volodka would take me into the cockpit and we would do a couple of circuits round the aerodrome. My father permitted that, too. After "work" we used to go to dinner, and the airmen in the mess would ask me: "Well, Lorka, how's your plane?"

' "All in working order!" I would answer importantly.

'One day Volodka had a fight with another pilot over me. I had been playing, and I ran into his room to get a drink. Some of the guys were drinking spirits on the quiet, but they didn't worry about me: Volodka had taught me strict loyalty to friends. I knew what went on in our unit, and in

8

some respects I knew even more than my father. I came into the room, saw that Volodka wasn't there, and asked the first airman I saw for a drink of water. And this idiot, who was already well oiled, gave me a glass of spirits instead of water. I took a big gulp, gasped, then started bawling my head off. Volodka appeared as soon as he heard my screams. He saw straightaway what had happened, took me in his arms and began to force water down me. I didn't understand what was going on and continued to yell. When I had recovered Volodka laid me on his bunk, dragged the offender outside by the shirt-front and beat him up so badly that he went around covered in bruises for a week. My father never found out, of course, and from that time on I became even more convinced that Volodka was my chief protector, even more that my father.

'But then a romance started up between him and this telegraphist, Rayechka. The bitch! I still hate her. They used to meet in the eveing after I had gone to bed. I don't know what happened between them or how long it had been going on, but one day someone said to me as a joke: "Your Volodka is being unfaithful to you with Rayechka."

'My jealousy knew no bounds. I was burning up with hatred and despair, but I was determined to get Volodka away from Rayechka. And I did. You want to know how? I got him away in the direct sense. If I saw Raya coming towards him I would rush at her and yell: "Get lost! He's my boyfriend, not yours!"

'People would reproach me or try to talk to me, but one thing I knew: I wasn't going to let Rayechka near Volodka. Finally my father lost his patience and gave me a thrashing. I even had red strap-marks on my backside. But there was no limit to my female cunning. I ran straight over to Volodka, took down my trousers in front of everyone, showed him my backside and said: "Look what I got because of your stupid Rayechka. And my father says I'll get it again if you go on seeing her."

'My father of course, had put it slightly differently. So what do you think happened? Either Volodka wasn't so very attached to my rival, or she couldn't take all the jokes about our "triangle", with people predicting she would lose, but anyway their romance soon died. After that, if I met Rayechka I would always proudly turn my head away from my defeated rival and never say hello to her.

'What did our love consist of apart from all those silly things? Real love, that's what. When Volodka was not flying we used to walk together in the woods round the aerodrome and go into the nearby villages. I don't remember what we talked about, but our relationship was one of long unbroken chatter. It's hard to imagine now what a youth of eighteen could have found to talk about for hours and days on end with a little girl of five. I only recall the state of clarity, peace, and seriousness during our chats. Sometimes we talked about grasshoppers and their special lives which no one was interested in except Volodka and me; sometimes we talked about the war and the lives of grown-ups. That big boy, whose life had been disrupted by the war like mine, was the only person who could give me back a real childhood – fields, woods, fairy-tales. We even made up our own fairy-tales, inventing stories about things we had seen. And I also remember the feeling of total security, which for some reason I didn't get from my mother and father, but only from Volodka. We often got bombed. The aerodrome was camouflaged as a small wood, but somehow the Fascists found it and then we would have to re-locate. As a war child I used to see wounded and dead people, craters, bombed houses, burnt-out planes. I remember airmen's funerals, when a propeller was put on the grave instead of a cross. But when I was with Volodka I knew for sure that he would protect me from Messerschmidts in the sky and mines on the ground.

'When Volodka went away on a mission – he did aerial reconnaissance photography in his U2 – I would await his return like a little woman. I didn't play, but sat in some corner listening. I could distinguish the engine of Volodka's plane a long way off. Then I would run to the airstrip shouting for joy: "Here comes Volodka!" And I was never wrong.

'One day he didn't return. They reported to my father that they had seen a Fascist Messerschmidt attack Volodka, hit his plane and set fire to it in the air. Everybody heard about it in the unit, including me. They were all sorry – his friends, my parents, and even Rayechka went about with red eyes. But I didn't believe he was dead, and I turned out to be right. I felt cold and lonely without my Volodka. I

10

became sad, but every time they tried to comfort me I would reply: "I am lonely because I'm waiting for Volodka. He'll come back soon."

'Several months passed. Then one winter's day my mother came into the room and said to me: "Hurry, Volodka is here."

'For some reason she didn't look too happy as she said it, but I took no notice. I ran out of the house just as I was, without putting on my coat, and dashed over to the staff bunker. I saw Volodka, and as I rushed up to him someone shouted: "Careful!"

'But I was already in his arms. I felt him stagger as he took hold of me, and someone supported him. Volodka had returned with only one leg, on crutches. And here's another surprising thing which will make you realize this was true love. On that flight Volodka had been so badly burned that when he returned people didn't recognize him at first. His whole face was covered with taut, shiny purple skin and there were several deep, livid scars on his cheeks. But I didn't examine his face to try and recognize him. I just flew into his arms, knowing in my heart that it was him. And once again I remember that feeling of complete peace, love and security as we sat at the table, me in his arms, as he recounted his adventures. I stroked the scars on his face with my finger and asked. "Does this hurt? Does that? What if I kiss it?"

'For that flight Volodka was promoted to captain, and I gave him a new, more solemn name: my Captain Burns. Later everybody started to call him that. A month later he was sent an artificial leg and went back to flying.

'The war with Germany ended, and the time came for me to be parted from Captain Burns, my Volodka. We were going back to Leningrad, and he was being sent to the Far East. As we were separating Volodka said to me: "The war with Japan will end, you will grow up and become a beautiful woman, and then I will find you and you will be my wife."

'I took him at his word, and I can't guarantee that Volodka himself was joking. On the farewell day he didn't talk to anyone except me. As we were leaving and I was being bundled crying into the jeep, he said: "Goodbye, my true sweetheart. Wait for me."

11

'The years passed, and Volodka didn't come back. As I grew older, I became embarrassed to ask my parents about him. I kept quiet and waited. But at sixteen I started my search. My heart told me that Volodka had not forgotten me but was looking for me, too. One thing I couldn't understand: he was the strongest and cleverest of men, so why had he still not found me? I questioned my parents and airmen that we knew, trying to find out what had happened to him. Nobody knew anything. But the flying world is also a small one, and I was sure that sooner or later I would hear about him. And I did . . .

'Do you remember how many secrets came out after the 20th Party Congress? Many people had relatives turn up whose children didn't even know about them, and wives whose husbands had at one time or another disappeared into labour camps found out whether they were alive or dead. My mother, who used to shake her head sadly as she listened to me asking about Volodka, one day sat me down next to her and told me about his terrible fate. For that very same heroic flight which by some miracle Volodka had escaped with his life he was first of all promoted in rank and decorated with the gold star of Hero of the Soviet Union. But later, after they had "shed light on the matter", he was sent to a camp. It turned out that Volodka had landed his plane behind German lines, grabbed his photographic equipment, and made his way back across the front to our side, burnt and with a shattered leg. To begin with he was idolized like a second Maresev, then they decided one was enough. He perished at Kolyma.

'And that's the whole story of my first love. I never had a second one. I looked at the boys of my age, then at the men as I grew older, and not one of them seemed to be a real man by comparison to my Volodka. I never did get married, though I had a few tries. But when it came down to a decision I always said to myself: "No, this one isn't a Volodka either. I'll have to wait a little longer."

'But I never did find a man like him. I received my doctorate and decided it was time to have a family by myself, without a husband. I've now borne my son, Volodka, and I'm going to bring him up by myself.'

'Now I understand why you have so much strength and

confidence,' said Valentina, who worked at the Cultural Directorate of the Leningrad City Soviet's Executive Committee. 'Demanding high standards of others has forced you to demand high standards of yourself and has helped you achieve everything by your own strength. The state will help you with your child of course.

'Thanks a lot!' laughed Larissa. 'I can probably earn the extra five roubles myself.'

'Come off it!' smiled Zina the 'tramp'. 'Five roubles is half a litre, or three small ones.'

They began to joke about what you could buy a baby for five roubles a month: one little shoe, two kilos of butter in a shop or one kilo at the market, a kilo of apples at the market or three in a shop, a quarter of a school uniform or one wheel of a child's tricycle.

The only person who was not laughing at this price list was Natasha, another fairly modern woman, though not as self-assured as Larissa.

'I think, Larissa,' she said, 'that all your strength comes precisely from your insecurity. It happens to a lot of women these days. It's not so much that we're striving to be strong ourselves, but the weakness of the men forces us to be. It's frightening how unmanly they have become. A husband in the home is just another child, only greedier.'

They exchanged some gossip about their husbands, then they suggested that Zina should tell a story.

Story Three

by Zina the tramp, officially designated a 'citizen of no fixed abode', about how a valiant warrior of the Soviet Army suddenly impassioned with tender feelings towards the young Zina enticed her to a rendezvous where he succeeded in making the experience completely mutual, acting in the full spirit of the regulations for forces in the field, and how, after the lovers became separated by circumstances beyond Zina's control, her mother tried in vain to restore her daughter's honour.

'Well, girls my first love was also a military one. There was an engineers' battalion stationed just outside our village. The soldiers would go to the club and they used to run after our girls. Once after the movie a soldier walked back with me, pulled me into the bushes and fucked me good and proper. He was a real strong one, the bastard. But I was afraid to shout. A week later I got up the courage to tell my mother. She rushed to the authorities to complain about the soldier, but he had already vanished into thin air – demobbed apparently. Vasya his name was. Or was it Kolya? No, Vasya, I think. That was my first love!'

The women laughed:
  'Zina! What sort of love is that?'
  'What do you mean? It's the most natural kind. If Larissa over there had been about ten years older d'you think Volodka wouldn't have fucked her? At fifteen she wouldn't have been going round with him catching grasshoppers, but something a bit bigger! You girls were all protected by your parents and never got laid so now you believe all these fairy-tales about love.'
  And Zina turned away angrily. Her neighbour Natasha, who had spoken of men becoming effeminate, sympathized: 'Zina, don't be angry at us or at life. After all, not everyone is destined to have a true first love. And those who do for some reason don't know how to keep it. Otherwise all families would be founded on first love, and that hasn't happened for a long time, if ever. It's my turn now, and I'm going to tell you the story of my first love which I spoiled in the stupidest fashion.'

Story Four

by Natasha the engineer, containing a classic description of love and an account of her cousin's treachery, quite rare in a person so young.

'My first love came neither too early nor too late, but at the most appropriate time – seventeen years old.

14

'I finished the ninth class with top grades, and so that I could have a holiday before beginning the difficult tenth class my parents sent me to Sukhumi for the entire summer, to some distant Georgian relatives. And, so that there should be somebody to look after me, my older cousin Nadenka went as well. She was at medical school, and was another straight A student.

'We were both indoor, academic girls. Apart from school work our only interest was music, and we only did it a little, for ourselves. We were both obedient daughters and even wore pigtails though few people of our age still had them.

'The first thing Nadenka and I did in Sukhumi was to go straight to the hairdresser at the station and have our pigtails cut off and get a boy's style. In other words, we had broken free! True, that was as far as we went. We didn't dare go to dances or the cinema because we had heard lots of stories about Georgians kidnapping Russian girls. And when we went to the beach during the daytime we were accompanied by our Aunt Eteri who vigilantly watched to see that we didn't strike up any beach acquaintances. But the local boys noticed us right away. I don't know what I look like now after having a baby; but then, at seventeen, I was a raving beauty, believe me. And my cousin was just as striking as I was. So when the family used to sit on the balcony to drink tea in the evening, including Nadenka and me, a whole gang of boys would walk up and down past our house. They would strum their guitars and sing songs, and sometimes, if Aunt Eteri wasn't there, they would half jokingly invite us to go for a walk with them. Nadenka and I would sit there frustrated and bored, but we never reacted to their invitations. That really made our aunt happy, but all the time we were just thinking about how to escape.

'Fortune, or rather a misfortune, came to our aid. One day there was a gale and a very rough sea. We went down to the beach in the morning, but our aunt didn't let us swim. Nadenka accepted it, but I started arguing: "Go on, just let us have one little swim, just a little way out! After all, we grew up by the sea, too, we've been swimming like frogs since we were born!"

'Finally our aunt relented and let us go: "But not too far."

'Not too far, indeed! We dived through the first waves and then started swimming out to sea as fast as we could. We had a great time swimming, diving, doing somersaults in the waves, and then it was time to come in. Only we couldn't make it to the beach! We would swim in until we feel the ground under our feet but before we could wade up to the beach we would be knocked over by a wave and thrown on to the rocks. My aunt saw what was happening and rushed down to the water's edge, flapping her arms and squawking like an old hen. This only made things worse, because her panicking made us feel panicky. I could see from Nadenka's face that she was about to start howling, so I said: "Come on, let's swim out to sea again, have a rest and then come back in."

'Out we went to sea, where we swam about again, though not feeling as brave as before. We lay on our backs to get back our strength for coming ashore again. Then we saw two boys go up to my aunt who was frantically pointing at us. They pulled off their shirts and trousers and dived in to rescue us. They explained what we should do. Apparently you had to dive under the waves again, and then, when you were in the shallow part, quickly get up and run up the beach before the next wave knocked you over. We made it to the shore, all holding hands. My aunt thanked our two saviours, but Nadenka and I were in no state even to have a look at them.

'For a punishment we weren't allowed on the beach for two days, but on the third day she felt sorry for us and took us. No sooner were we settled on the sand than the same two boys appeared and went right up to her.

'If you want,' said one of them, 'we will look after your girls in the sea!'

'And on the land!' added the other.

'My aunt gave them a suspicious look, but agreed to let us swim with them. They had saved us, after all! Later she let us go for walks with them. But she made one rule: we could go walking and swimming only during the daytime, and they had to deliver us directly back to her.

'Of course we quickly sorted ourselves out and fell in love, Nadenka with Shalva and me with Amiran. To begin with we went for walks all together, but later we began to separate, agreeing to meet up later so as to reach the house together. And later on still Nadenka and I learned how to climb out of our bedroom window and down the thick grapevine. My aunt was full of praise for us: "My little girls don't run about the streets, like others, they go to bed with the chickens!"

'True, we did go to bed with the chickens, but then we were up and having a good time until the first cock-crow. It was already getting light by the time we climbed back into the house.

'To begin with we just held hands and talked as we walked up and down the boulevard at night. Then one time I was sitting on the rocks by the sea with Amiran, and he suddenly went and kissed me on the cheek. I was so scared I began to howl. Poor fellow, he was walking round and round me wondering how to console me. Then he went into the water right in his trousers and shoes and said: "As long as you go on crying salt tears I shall go on drinking salt water!" And he started scooping up the water with his hand and drinking it, all the time saying: "Foul stuff! This will kill me!"

'I got frightened and shouted: "Stop it! Stop it! I'm not angry any more!"

'But the cunning little devil answered: "I'll stop if you kiss me yourself!"

'I had to give in. And then I began to like it and kissed him as much as he wanted. But nothing more!

'What a wonderful summer that was, I can tell you . . . Amiran took me to all his favourite places he had known since he was a child. We gathered nuts in the mountains, collected shells by the sea, went out in a boat fishing for mackerel. As you might expect, we made plans for the future: he would finish school in another year and would come to Leningrad to study, and every summer we would return here to the sea. He taught me to swim so well that we had a ball every time a storm blew up. I would plunge through the waves like a little dolphin. And I was blossoming more and more each day. Twice that summer I outgrew my bra and had to get a new one.

'The time came for Nadenka and me to return to Leningrad. Amiran and I spent the whole night before our departure sitting by the sea saying goodbye. He couldn't see me off because of Aunt Eteri: she would have thought it intolerable impudence. But no sooner had the train moved off, and Nadenka and I had begun staring glumly out of the window, than there was a knock on our compartment door and in walked Shalva and Amiran with big smiles on their faces. Amiran was holding a jar with some twigs of magnolia blossom – he knew I was crazy about it. You should have seen the stares I got in Leningrad as I walked along the Nevsky with that bouquet, from the Moskovsky Station to where I lived on Ligovka! The boys saw us as far as Adler, and then we parted until the following summer, or so we thought.

'Autumn was already beginning at home, the first yellow leaves were falling. But for me, all I had to do was close my eyes and I could hear the murmur of the sea at night and Amiran's soft voice. And I developed a bad habit – licking my lips. I was doing it to recall his salty kisses. I had that habit for a long time. And the dry magnolia twigs hung over my bed where I had nailed them on to the wall. The flowers had fallen off and the buds had turned dry and brown, but when I pressed my nose against them I could catch a very faint, distant smell of magnolia. Especially if I shut my eyes.

'Amiran and I wrote to each other. He sent me his photograph just after that summer and I carried it around in my school bag. I was not so good at my studies because my mind was always getting carried away, back to the sea.

About three months later, when the snow had already started, Nadenka came to stay with us. I was delighted to see her, immediately carried her off to my room and started showering her with questions: "Well? Does Shalva write to you? Do you miss him a lot?"

'Nadenka gave me a puzzled look: "What are you talking about, Natasha? Not that little summer romance? Don't think about it any more, it wasn't anything serious. Boys in resort towns always court the holidaymakers. Who takes it seriously?"

' "I do. Amiran and I love each other, and it is serious."

'Nadenka burst out laughing and for a long time couldn't control herself.

' "What a little fool you are, Natasha! Don't you realize that nothing will come of it? You're from completely different backgrounds, apart from anything else. Come on, show me the last letter you got from Amiran."

'Like an idiot I obediently pulled the envelope out of my school bag and handed it to her. Nadenka began to read, and smiled. Then she took a red pencil out of my glass and started to mark the mistakes in the letter. I felt the blood rush to my face, but I couldn't stop her – I just watched the red marks appearing on every line like red thorns growing. After Nadenka had disfigured the whole letter she gave it back to me and said: "Now show that letter to your schoolfriends. Boast about the boyfriend you've got."

'Without a word I put the letter back in the school bag, but not in order to show it in class.

'In Amiran's next letter I already noticed all the mistakes myself, and because of the mistakes I no longer followed what he was saying, I could no longer hear his voice in every line. A month later Nadenka appeared again, having given me time to think things over.

' "Well, have you come to your senses? Do you realize you're not suited? Just remember, your parents would never allow you to marry a half-literate Georgian. Wait a bit and you'll see him selling mandarins or mimosa at the Kuznechny Market!"

'Once again she really stung my pride. We had been brought up to think that trade, especially at the market, was an extremely improper and even shameful occupation.

' "Here, let me help you write a farewell letter. We'll write it so that he'll immediately forget all your stupidity."

'And obediently I agreed. What a bitchy letter she dictated to me! I'm not going to tell you what it said, though I remember every line to this day. Its general thrust was: you're getting too big for your boots, boy, keep to your place. You Georgies should stick to your business of growing mandarins for us and making money out of the tourists.

'While Nadenka was dictating this foul stuff to me I secretly decided that on no account would I post the letter, but I would tear it up as soon as she left. But she was too clever for me: she took the letter with her.

' "You might change your mind, so I have to be your big sister and take charge, so you won't get any deeper into this shameful business. Otherwise I'll have to tell your parents everything."

'So that letter was sent to Amiran. He didn't answer, not a word. I took the magnolia twigs off the wall, and just kept one little leaf which I hid in a book. Then that got lost, too.

'About five years later, when Nadenka and I were both

happily married, she said to me one day: "Do you still remember your little summer romance? Do you know, I was head over heels in love with Amiran myself and I was furious that his friend started courting me, and not him. And so I forced you to break it off with him because I couldn't forget him myself. But you can see everything worked out for the best, he really wasn't a match for you."

'I loved my husband, and I still do, but all night after Nadenka's confession I howled into my pillow, hurt at my childish gullibility and stupidity and terrified by the treachery of people. It alienated me from Nadenka forever, and we hardly ever meet now.'

The women expressed amazement at Nadenka's treachery and decided without fail to devote one of the days to stories about the real bitches among women.

Then Valentina, whose turn it was, spoke up: 'Of course it was not good, Natasha, that your cousin gave you those chauvinistic attitudes. Ours is a multi-national state, and you could easily have married a Georgian, no one would have blamed you. But in one respect your cousin was right: you and your boy would hardly have had any common interests and aspirations. And without those you can't build a strong family. Now my first love, my dears, was no fantasy. It was a real, strong feeling based on shared interests and shared work. Listen.'

Story Five

Story Five by Valentina, functionary in the city soviet executive committee, in which she lays down her views, albeit succint, on the healthy Soviet family.

'Pavel Petrovich and I both came to work at the regional committee of the Komsomol (Communist Youth) straight from the institute. He was appointed senior instructor, and I was made his assistant. We worked well together, got to like each other, and then decided to build a healthy Soviet family. Our comrades supported us and began agitating to

20

get us a flat. We got it and were married immediately. Our son has been born, and a daughter is planned for three years' time. We're a happy family, and I think it is because we created it with sober heads, without any illusions.'

After Valentina's short story – which sounded to her audience more like an official report – the women prepared to listen to Albina, an attractive blonde who never stopped making herself up even in the maternity hospital, having brought in with her a whole bag of imported cosmetics.

'Well, Valentina – I don't know your patronymic – you've lectured us about your healthy family,' Albina began, 'but in my opinion a man's as good as his cock. That's what the people say, isn't it, Zina? And also, a real man ought to provide his woman with comforts. In one way I agree with you: all our women's troubles come from our fantasies. But where do the fantasies come from, I would like to know? To put it bluntly, it's because we don't get fucked enough. Take you, for example, Valentina. You look like a proper upperclass type, a typical Party lady with your solid figure and your hair in a bun. But you blush, and your little eyes sparkle even though you try to hide it. You've just tried to give us a lecture on the healthy family . . . But I bet when you're in bed with your husband the conversation isn't about the decisions of the latest plenum, so don't try to tell me they are! And now, girls, I'm going to tell you what a beautiful first love I had, better than your wildest dreams!

Story Six

*Story Six by Albina, Aeroflot airhostess, about how today's gilded youth amuses itself. It includes an explanation of the game of daisy, so popular among that youth, and also
a number of other useful pieces of information about the sexual revolution in the age of advanced socialism. Albina passed through great trials and tribulations in her quest*

21

for love, and the present story may be seen in this context.

'It was New Year. I had just got out of hospital after my latest abortion, and my friends started ringing me up: "Alka, come and see in the New Year with us!"

'I'm a sociable girl, I have stacks of friends, mostly sons and daughters of rich parents, or they're well-off themselves – dealers, hairdressers, girls and fellows from Intourist hotels. The gilded youth, in fact. Of course it would be nice to go out – eating and drinking all the things normally in short supply, dancing, smoking grass, playing daisy or some other game. But actually I wasn't too keen on playing daisy right after an abortion... What? You don't know what grass and daisy are? Well, well, you people are not with it, I can see that. Grass is marijuana, Indian hemp. It's a completely harmless drug, very mild stuff. But you get a good high from it, especially if you're already feeling good, that's called a "kaif" in Russian. And daisy's a young people's game. The girls lie down on the carpet with their heads towards the centre and their legs spread out like daisy petals, and the fellows go round in a circle from one to the other. The trick is for everyone to come at the same time, when the word is given. Only then do you get a real "kaif"!

'Now, what's all the squealing I hear from the kindergarten? If you don't like it I won't go on. I can't stand hypocrisy. I'm sure if I took you to one of those parties you'd be spreading your legs out before you got through the door. If you haven't seen anything of life, then at least listen, you might learn something. So, shall I continue or not? Right, then...

'I decided that first of all I would just look in at one of my friends who had promised to bring a "grandad". And if she served me up a wanker I could ring for a taxi and go to my other friends.

'So I turn up at my friend's place. It's all dark inside, but everything's oh so proper! They're sitting around watching that silly twit Pugachova on TV. I sit down in an armchair and start giving grandad the once-over, but I couldn't see him properly in the dark. He looked like any other man, but his suit was a tailor-made one – I spotted that right away from the shape of it. My friend and her man sat with their arms around each other like a good little married couple. He

22

was the manager of a hotel and through him we used to get to know foreigners. Why? To discuss the international situation of course, isn't it obvious?

'Pugachova finished her whining, and my friend turned on the main light. And then, girls, I fell completely in love with my grandad at first sight! You should have seen his suit, his shirt, his watch – all from over there, everything down to the last button. And not the sort of trash the sailors bring back from abroad, but all the genuine brand name stuff. So I immediately send him a look and a smile, stick out my boobs and go all out for him. And he looks me over carefully, gives a sort of smile and says: "The hostess's bar seems to have dried up rather. We ought to have something for the road."

'My friend goes off to the bar, leaving me feeling shattered. The swine, I think to myself, he didn't even notice me! But I pluck up my courage, get up out of my chair and, showing a leg here and a bum there, off I go to the bar to help my friend bring the glasses to the table. I notice my handsome man is looking approvingly at me. Just what we were aiming for. I go over to the record player, switch it on, and then back I go, swinging my hips to the music. This time he leans right back in his chair to get a better look at me, and he's sizing me up all over. I can feel I've got through to him.

'Well, to cut a long story short, I hooked him, girls. He took me back to his flat, and what a love affair we had! For a start he told me to chuck out all my rags, and he bought me new clothes and shoes and took me off to the Black Sea. After that I went abroad with him. He took me along as his interpreter, even though I didn't speakee-de-English or any of those other lingos. But he made me learn languages, and for that I'll be grateful to him until I die, because now I do foreign flights.

'And if I need to earn a bit more at home, if the worst comes to the worst, I can always find myself a dissident, or I can sometimes even fix up a western cadre. During the three years I was with him I saw the kind of life you could never even dream about, I went to places that they wouldn't even let you look at. And when my time was up – he only accepts girls up to twenty – he didn't abandon me like other bastards do. Instead he set me up in Aeroflot as an

23

airhostess. So now you know how it was with my first love!'

Albina finished her story, leaving some of the women gasping and others laughing. 'Thank you, you've enlightened us! From now on we shall know what the progressive youth mean by love. Good for Albina!'

Only Zina the tramp took Albina's side: 'What are you all squawking about? Maybe the girl got into that scene because she had a bad background; you don't know all her secrets! From the camp I was sent to the virgin lands, and I saw what happened to the clean little Komsomol girls who went out there to work . . .'

Now it was the turn of Galina, a thin, fair-haired, girlish woman who usually lay with her nose buried in a book, but had now livened up after listening attentively to the women's stories, sometimes even jotting something down in a notebook.

Story Seven

by Galina the 'dissident wife', about how a clever little plain Jane, because of her willingness to embark on any adventure for the sake of friendship, finds her happiness in one of the political camps of the Soviet Union –though not, of course, as one of the inmates!

I'm sure you've all heard of dissidents. Well, I happened to marry one. And he was my first love.

'You can see for yourselves that I'm not the type that men go crazy about: skinny, glasses, and in general not exactly God's gift to men . . . well, I was already twenty and had never been kissed, though somehow I didn't think about that sort of thing much. I loved the theatre and poetry, and I was studying at the Academy of Arts, in the architectural institute. Of course I had friends, quite a few in fact. And I had one friend from school called Lyudmila. After starting at the institute we didn't meet so often, but when we did there was always plenty to talk about and we would sit up till all hours.

'We first got friendly in school, and it was because we

both loved poetry. While everyone else was engrossed in Yesenin, and then in Asadov, she and I were getting hold of Tsvetaeva's and Mandelshtam's poetry. And also for some reason we both loved Kipling, and we had our favourite song which we put to music and sang together:

> 'I've never seen a Jaguar
>   Nor yet an Armadill –
> O dilloing in his armour,
>   And I s'pose I never will,
>   Unless I go to Rio
>   These wonders to behold –
>   Roll down – roll down to Rio –
>   Roll really down to Rio!
>   Oh, I'd love to roll to Rio
>   Some day before I'm old!

'One day, when we were already at the institute, I came along to see Lyudmila. She was packing up a parcel and cheerfully singing our song, only with different words:

> 'I've never seen the heroes
>   who proclaim ideas, until
> They get thrown into a prison,
>   And I s'pose I never will,
>   Unless I go to Gulag
>   Those heroes to behold –
>   Roll down – roll down to Gulag –
>   Roll really down to Gulag!
>   Oh, I'd love to roll to Gulag
>   Some day before I'm old!

'Now, before I go on, let's make an agreement: forget what I'm about to tell you straightaway and don't remember it again under any circumstances. I'm not going to blab too much, and I shall change all the names, but it's better to warn you all the same. That applies to you mainly, Valentina. Anyway, I don't know any state secrets, so your Party conscience can rest in peace. Are we agreed? Then I'll continue.

'I was beginning to guess my friend had got tied up with the dissidents. Sometimes she would tell me some piece of

25

news which you couldn't get from the papers; sometimes she would explain what was going on in some book that everyone was talking about but no one could understand properly. She was particularly open about her own views.

'One day I called in to see Lyudmila, and she was sitting in tears at the table, and there was lots of hard-to-get food laid out on the table: smoked sausage, jars of instant coffee, tins of food with foreign labels, even a tin of caviar.

' "What on earth are you doing, Lyudmila," I asked, "sitting crying over such riches? It's not logical."

'Then Lyudmila lifted up her head, looked at me intently and said: "Galka, I think God has sent you to me. Listen, and I'll tell you the story. Do you know about the airliner affair?"

' "Yes, you told me."

' "Well, for the past three years I've been visiting one lad who got a frightful sentence for his part in the affair."

' "Where do you go?"

' "Where? Vladimir, to the central political prison. As his fiancée. He hasn't any relatives and he's not married. I'm trying to get permission to marry him, but they're not giving it yet. Now they've moved him to a camp, it's time for a visit and there's no way I can go. My mother is seriously ill – yesterday she was taken to hospital for an operation. There's no one to go for me, and anyway they wouldn't let anyone else in because I'm the only person listed in his file. You and I look a bit alike – you could go in my place!"

'At first I was completely taken aback. I was frightened, of course: going to a political camp is no joke! But Lyudmila was crying so much, she was so sorry for her man, that I began to waver. She gave me his letters to read, and there was so much gratitude for her concern in them, so much warmth, that I began to feel sorry for him, too. I thought, this guy's going to wait and suffer, and nobody's going to come . . . And Lyudmila and I really did look very alike – as children people even thought we were sisters. Besides it was a kind of romantic idea! So I made up my mind to go.

'Lyudmila was so delighted she nearly gobbled me up. In between kissing me she started telling me what to do, where to go, what to say and who to . . . and a few other details which I'll keep quiet about.

'Making my way out to that God-forsaken Mordovia I felt like a Decembrist's wife. The bags of food made my arms feel as if they would drop off, and as for transport – you take what you can get. The whole situation was unfamiliar. And without Lyudmila's support fear started to get the better of me.

'I found the camp and was even more frightened: it was just like being in a film about the Fascists! Please, Valentina, no comments from you. A camp is a camp, but it doesn't matter whether there is a star over it or a swastika, it's just as horrible for those inside. Don't forget how many of your Party colleagues have been through it. No, I didn't get that out of Solzhenitsyn, though I have read him, too. It was our own Khrushchev who announced it from on high to all the people. Anyhow, the story's about first love, not that.

'They made me out some papers, then led me feeling more dead than alive down a corridor to the meeting room. There was a long table in the middle of this room with chairs down both sides. They told me to sit down and wait. I was left alone, my whole body trembling. What am I supposed to do, I wondered, when my "fiancé" is brought? I know his name and I've seen a photograph of him before he went to camp, so I'll recognize him. But how am I supposed to greet him so that he'll guess straightaway that I'm here instead of Lyudmila? What if he says: "Who's this you've brought to visit me? That's not my fiancée . . ." Or what if they don't bring him, but someone else? What if there's another meeting scheduled in this room? What'll happen if I start calling someone else's brother or husband my fiancé. And apart from that, how am I supposed to greet him: just quite simply, or must I kiss him? I got so worked up about this that I began to sweat all over. I thought, I'm going to ruin this meeting and get put inside with Lyudmila's passport, and then Lyudmila herself will get about ten years. And as soon as I saw the guard bring a tall lad into the room in a "zek" (convict) uniform, I rushed up to him, threw my arms round his neck and screamed:' "Slava, darling! Darling!" and began to kiss him all over. At the same time I whispered in his ear: "I've come instead of Lyudmila on her passport . . ."

'He hugged me, too, looked into my face, blinked his eyes. Then suddenly he pressed me to himself and started kissing me – I nearly fainted. And between the kisses he whispered to me: "Tell Lyudmila that Gek is in hospital in a serious condition. He needs an operation and they're just giving

27

him pain-killers. We're afraid for his life. We need publicity urgently."

'The guard separated us on either side of the table and then sat down nearby to hear what we were going to talk about. But we didn't have anything to talk about. A couple to times I asked about his health, and he asked about mine. We were quiet for a minute or two, and then I had an idea: I would tell him about my actual life at home – that everyone was fine, that my father had managed to get a really good dacha for the summer in Toskovo, on a lake just near a big diving-board, and that we were all going out there in a month's time. Suddenly he livened up and his voice became friendly "Is that Lake Kheppo-Yarvi or the canal?"

' "The peninsula behind the diving-board."

' "Did you specially choose the place where my grand-mother used to live, or was it a coincidence?"

' "A coincidence! Everything happens by coincidence with us! Don't be angry . . ."

' "Why should I be angry, I'm very happy. You've really got much more beautiful since our last meeting."

'I should tell you that although Lyudmila looks like me she is much more interesting and knows how to take care of herself. Beside her I'm a right old blue-stocking . . . So I got embarrassed, but Slava was looking at me with such eyes, right into my heart. Nobody ever looked at me like that before. And also I could see from those eyes that he was a pure person and very deep. My last doubts about whether I was doing the right thing faded away . . .

'Valentina, please! I didn't interrupt your story about your model family. Don't you realize I haven't said a word about politics? We're just talking about love, that's all. Do the rest of you want to listen? Then I'll continue, and you can read a book in the meantime, Valentina.

'I don't remember very well any more what we talked about at our first meeting. The two hours passed. I had come all that distance just for two hours! Slava came up to me again, took me by the shoulders and quietly kissed me once on the cheek and once on the hand. And to me those two last kisses were the most frightening of all.

'They took him away. Of all the food the guard only allowed him to have the apples and a little sausage. And he was quite a kind one; later on other guards didn't even allow that. I had to drag almost everything back again.

'I returned to Leningrad a different person. I gave my report to Lyudmila, told her everything, all about Gek. And then I started dropping in on her almost every day. She was surprised, and I was embarrassed to ask if there was a letter from Slava. Then one day I came to see her and she said to me: "Here's a letter just arrived from Slava. It's for you, I think . . ."

'I took the letter and read: "Dear Lyuda, as soon as I saw you at that last meeting I realized that all my life I have dreamt of meeting a girl like you, someone whose life is governed not by ideas and noble feelings, but by natural kindness and goodness, unbounded and naïve . . ." There were a lot of beautiful words in that letter, and they were all meant for me, not Lyudmila. My friend glanced at me and asked: "Do you think our Slava has found himself a real fiancée?"

' "I don't know yet, but just in case, tell me how to get permission to marry a political prisoner."

'The next time I went to see Slava I travelled on my own passport and I was really afraid that either they wouldn't allow the meeting, or that we would get the same guard or some chief who met me the time before under a different name. But everything worked out well. Three years later we got permission to marry. Andryushka was something else I brought back from one of our meetings. Now his father is in exile, and when my son grows a bit bigger and stronger, then we're going to join him.'

'So that's what you dissidents are like!' exclaimed Irishka, when Galina had finished her story. 'And I thought you were some special sort of people . . .'

'With four ears or something, so they can listen to "enemy voices" better?' laughed Natasha. 'People are people. We have a dissident working with us. He used to be always collecting signatures, but now he's tamed down. Times are different, obviously . . . You either get put inside or you leave, that's what everyone reckons.'

Then the women talked a little longer about the wives of political prisoners, and about whether it was easier for them in the nineteenth century or now. Most of them decided that it was harder in the last century, especially for the aristocratic wives of the Decembrists, because today's women were more used to hardship but not everyone agreed with this.

'I saw this film where these poor Decembrist wives were traipsing about Siberia, all in such huge fur coats that any fashion girl, like Albinka here, would go green with envy. In coats like those you could put up with anything, I can tell you!'

This speech came from Zina the tramp, of course. But suddenly Larissa remembered about Nelya:

'Nelya, perhaps now you'll tell us about your mother? You began talking about her cat-fur coat, I remember.'

'All right, I will. Only it won't be a story about first love, which I didn't experience in the normal sense, but about why I didn't.'

Story Eight

by the music teacher Nelya, in which she describes how she learned first to hate, not love. The author dedicates this novella to the kindest of all Russian poets – Naum Korzhavin, who wrote the poem 'Men Tortured Children', about the children at Auschwitz. Copies of this poem do the rounds in Soviet camps – the author has seen it for herself and recommends all those who are not left indifferent by Nelya's story to get hold of Naum Korzhavin's poetry for themselves.

'I was born in Lvov, just before the war, of a Jewish mother and a Polish father. I always think of myself as a Jew, not because Jewish nationality goes by the mother's line, I just feel that way . . . Anyway, you'll understand later.

'My parents were both musical. The only picture I still have in my mind's eye from that life is of mother playing the piano. Then such a terrible life began that for a long time I regarded that memory as a dream: could life ever really have been so wonderful? The open window, the breeze filling the lace curtain which billows into the room, lightly touching the edge of the piano. And Mother sitting at the piano looking very beautiful in a white dress. Sometimes she

30

turns her smiling face towards me and very slightly nods her head to the music. And just everywhere – on the shiny black lid of the piano, on her white dress, on the yellow floor that smells so nice, little sunbeams are dancing to the music. There are lots of them because there's a big tree swaying outside the window, and its leaves are dancing and the curtain is dancing and I'm dancing in my cot. Of course, I was just holding on to the wooden bars, jumping and squatting, but I remember it as dancing. Some other time I'll tell you how it came out that this was not just a dream . . .

'Well, then. Next the war began, and all my connected memories are linked to it. The Fascists arrived in Lvov and general raids on the Jews began. Our father – mother told me this later when I was older – decided that the best thing for us was to pack up all our things and go to the station in the morning, as all the Jews were being ordered to do. "Us" meant my mother and her three children. I was two years old, my brother Levushka was twelve and my sister Genya was seven. The order for the Jews did not apply to my father, I told you he was Polish . . . Mother began to cry – she was so afraid for the children.

' "Why are you so upset?" asked my father, annoyed. "The Germans are a civilized nation, they won't do you any harm. You will be evacuated to somewhere safe in Germany, and from there you can write to me. Don't forget to tell them immediately that you're a well-known pianist – maybe they'll organize a concert tour for you in Germany. They're cultured people, Basya. I don't understand why you're getting into a panic."

'But father wasn't able to calm her down. She told him she would go to her relatives to find out what they were planning to do, and she rushed over to Uncle Aron for advice.

'Uncle Aron was a very wise man. He quietly told everyone that the only way for a Jew to survive in this situation was to listen carefully to every Fascist order and then do exactly the opposite. When my mother arrived she found all Uncle Aron's family busy packing.

' "You surely don't want to go to the station, too, do you?" she asked in amazement.

' "Not likely!" answered Uncle Aron. "We're going underground."

31

'It turned out that Uncle Aron and a few other brave and resourceful Jews had unearthed from somewhere a plan of Lvov's sewer system and had decided to go down through the pipes to an underground river that flowed through the city. Uncle Aron ordered my mother to collect everything she needed, with as much food as possible, put on warm clothes and come to him that night with the children. He told her not to say anything to my father, but just to explain to him that all the relatives had decided to show up at the station together so as not to get lost on the journey.

'We made our way to Uncle Aron's house at the dead of night. It was dangerous because the patrol was going round the city. Then, together with his family and a few other Jews, we made our way through back gardens to some remote yard. Here the sewage manhole cover had already been removed, and we all lowered ourselves down into it one by one, with the smallest being lifted down by the men. Uncle Aron's old mother who could no longer walk was also lowered down from hand to hand.

'Of our underground life, which continued for several months, I remember little. There was the darkness, the home-made lanterns burning dimly, water dripping everywhere and the revolting smell. And sometimes we could hear the sounds of trams and bells above our heads. The children cried and asked to be let out. I didn't want to stay down there either. Mother said she had to hold me in her arms the whole time: if she merely let go of me for a second I would try to escape from that nasty place. And there were huge rats running around everywhere. They were after our food, and Mother had to hold not just me on her knees, but our sack of food as well. She couldn't trust Levushka or Genya with it because the air was so foul that they kept falling asleep and then the rats would chew the sack. But one day, when we had hardly any food left and Mother had hidden the sack on her breast under her coat, the rats robbed us anyway. Either she had fallen fast asleep or she had lost consciousness briefly, but the rats chewed through her fur coat, then through the sack, and dragged off everything we had left. Mother borrowed a needle from someone and made a patch for her fur coat out of the empty sack. We didn't starve, however, mother continued to wear the fur coat even in the camp where the German women

32

laughed at the way she looked. Yes, in the end the Germans hunted us down with their dogs and took us to Auschwitz. But not everyone. Nine families managed to escape. Apparently they were the only Jews to get out of Lvov.

'We were loaded into railway trucks and taken to Germany. That, of course, was a great blow for all the Jews, except the children who didn't understand anything and were just glad to see the sun. Admittedly, we couldn't look at the light at first – it hurt our eyes – but that passed eventually.

'I won't tell you about the concentration camp. You know more than I do from films and books – I was very small at the time and I don't remember anything myself. One thing I do remember well: how we children, put into the women's barracks together with the mothers, were afraid of men. We had it firmly fixed in our heads that women, not just our own mothers, signified security and men meant terrible danger. They could beat you up, they could kill you on the spot, they could shoot a child like a puppy just because it cried too loud. Worst of all, they could separate you from your mother. The youngest of us were afraid to stay more than a couple of feet from our mothers, we were constantly trying to hold on to their skirts or their hands.

'Levushka was taken away from us to be put in with the men, and we never saw him again. Genya soon fell ill. She was taken to the hospital, and from there to the crematorium. Mother and I were left alone. We were lucky, we survived and even returned to Lvov. But my father had already put his new wife into our flat and they had had a baby. He gave my mother money for the road and advised her to go to Leningrad where she had relatives living. He promised to pay support for me, but she refused: money wasn't worth anything in those days, and she thought she would get a job straightaway in Leningrad as a pianist. It was this kind of naïveté that ultimately destroyed her.

'But here's the other thing I wanted to tell you about Auschwitz. One day our women found out that an order was being drawn up for the liquidation of all Jewish children. There were hardly any of us left anyway; they had gradually liquidated nearly all of us, however much the women tried to protect us. My mother told me never to leave her side, and if I saw a "nice man", it didn't matter who, I was to run to our bunk and crawl under the mattress. I was so skinny that when I lay under the mattress there wasn't even a bump. It was really difficult for my mother to break me of that habit in later years! Even after we were settled in Leningrad and I understood more about things, if ever a strange man came into our room, like the house manager or a neighbour, then without a word I would run to my mother's bed and crawl under the mattress.

'I grew bigger and started going to school. I stopped hiding under the mattress, but my insane terror of men didn't leave me. In school I did excellently in all my subjects except drawing – that class was taught by a male teacher. Whenever the head-teacher passed me in the corridor I would cower into the wall, and if he spoke to me I could never answer a word, and I was so frightened I didn't even hear what he was saying.

'It got better as the years went by. But I could never understand my friends when I was a teenager: how could they experience tender feelings for young men. And if a boy tried to get to know me I immediately pictured him in an SS uniform. Of course, what my mother told me about my father sowed mistrust in me for men, but the most frightening thing was this fixed idea I had acquired in the camp: if any men come you've got to hide, or something terrible will happen.

'Perhaps you're wondering how, with this fear, I still got married. Quite simple. After Mother's death my relatives enabled me to finish at the music school and go to college. Then they began to look for a husband for me so as to get me settled as soon as possible. They were already old, my uncle and aunt, and they wanted to carry out their promise to my mother as quickly as possible, not to abandon me before I could stand on my own two feet. They introduced me to several handsome, bright young men, also Jewish, who wanted to marry a girl from Leningrad. A lot of them liked me, but I cried and refused every time, saying I didn't want to make my family unhappy. One day a friend came to see one of my uncles, a widower of about forty. He wanted to get married, too, and was asking him to find him a calm, kind woman who could take the place of mother for his twelve-year-old daughter. Now this man I was not scared of, and I felt terribly sorry for the little girl: I, too, was twelve when I lost my mother.

'But Boris Nikolaevich didn't notice me, and the girl just sat in the corner listening. When he had gone I plucked up my courage and said to my uncle that there was a man I would marry without any fear. My uncle was amazed and tried to talk me out of it: "You're just a child yourself, so how are you going to bring up a daughter!" – and he refused to encourage the match. But I performed the single heroic deed of my life. The very next time Boris came with his daughter to see my uncle, I called Lenusya into my room and told her straight out who I was and that I wanted to be her mother. Dear Lena burst into tears, threw her arms round me and immediately called me Mama. Well, in three days she had matched me up with her father. And so we began to live together, and my fears soon left me, except that I sometimes, in my sleep . . .'

All the women had become sad listening to Nelya's story, and Irishka was even sobbing into her handkerchief and snuffling through her snub-nose like a baby.

Zina shook her head and said: 'The bastards, the real bastards . . . Of course it's no bed of roses for the little kids in the camps nowadays, but at least they're our people, not Fascists, they don't shoot them at least.'

'What camps are you talking about, Zina?'

'Ours, the Soviet ones with the barracks for little kids. MBUs they're called – Mother and Baby Units. If a zek turns up with her baby or has one in camp, they're sent to the MBU. I'm lucky I'm not doing time right now, otherwise my little daughter would be on prison grub.'

'Will you tell us about women's camps?'

'Oh, not today, girls! Two camps in one day would be too much! Another time. Let Emma tell a story now; this is all her idea so let's listen to her.'

Story Nine

by Emma, theatre director, about how she became the object of a first love.

'I shall tell you how I became the object of a first love, one which was unselfish and, if you like, crazy.

'My first marriage, a student one, was both unsuccessful and brief: we got divorced after a year, thanks to the new laws that had come out to speed up that soul-destroying process. My fellow student and I separated and I immediately married someone else, also an actor, but this time one who used to be well known and was now at the tail end of his glory. Now he's a complete drunkard and has disappeared from my life, but in those days I thought we had a very successful marriage. The only thing that really drove me mad was his perpetual love affairs. As soon as he was given a new part he immediately fell in love with his opposite number. We fought and fought over this, and I decided that the only way to save our marriage was to leave and play in the provinces. I was given a job as director of a newly opened theatre in one of the new towns in Siberia. We packed up and left Leningrad. My husband was tempted by the idea that in the provinces he was sure to get all the leading roles, especially with his wife as director. And so it turned out. The very first thing I put on was *Romeo and Juliet*, and he got the part of Romeo, even though from his age and appearance he was more suited for Falstaff and certainly wasn't up to King Lear. Well, as you can guess, he began studying for the part by falling for Juliet. Our Juliet was a real dish: a young girl just out of drama school, with great big eyes and a slim litte frame. Naturally, she was completely carried away by my clapped-out Romeo, that's why he was attracted to the young ones: a slightly older woman would see through his shallow feeelings straight-away. What came next was absolute hell for me. I would be taking a rehearsal, and my bastard of a husband was quite shamelessly making eyes at his Juliet and squeezing her hand, and meanwhile acting his part badly – not remember-ing his words, all his intonations wrong. I mean, just think, what sort of Romeo is a man of over forty? The actors, the assistant stage manager, the stage hands, all of them could see everything and they were giving me strange looks, some of them sympathetic, but most of them enjoying it and waiting to see what would happen. And I was trying to control myself and put on a good show. In other words, there was a mass of work to do before the end of the first stint, and I was already reaching a state of total nervous exhaustion.

'Then, just as my nerves were about to give out altogether, I suddenly noticed that our scenery painter, Alyosha, who was just a young boy, was looking at me with sad, loving eyes. Life became easier for me. As soon as my geriatric Romeo started up in front of everybody making advances to his silly little Juliet at rehearsal, I would just look at Alyosha, and feel better.

'One day Alyosha stayed behind after rehearsal, waited for me – I always left the theatre last – and declared his love. I didn't say anything, but stroked his cheek and left. But he continued to sit through all the rehearsals, never taking his eyes off me.

'The day of the first performance arrived. My play was a triumph, and the local VIPs threw a banquet for us. And in the middle of the banquet Mr Actor announced that he was leaving me and going off with his Juliet. A fine moment to choose for a family conflict. I was so upset I went for a walk round the town with Alyosha after the banquet, and then went back to the little room he had at the theatre and spent the night with him. From that day things took off. I felt I was giving my husband a bit of his own medicine, and it was doing me good, too. I would look at him and not feel so bad, then I would look at Alyosha and feel even better.

'One day Alyosha asked me: "When are we getting married?"

'I looked at him in surprise and told him that it was impossible.

' "Don't you dare play around with me!" he flared up, "you're not in the theatre now! If you don't agree today to stay with me forever, I'll kill myself."

'I shrugged my shoulders. "Do you want to shoot yourself with a stage pistol? Then good luck to you!" And I left.

'A couple of hours later I arrived at the rehearsal, and Alyosha was not there. Just as well, I thought, now at least I can work in peace. He had begun to get on my nerves with his constant gazing at me, it was putting me off my stroke ... Suddenly our business manager came running in and informed me that Alyosha had been taken to hospital to have his stomach pumped out: he had poisoned himself

37

with sleeping pills. My first thought was "How dare he! He's just making me look ridiculous!"

'One of the younger actors rushed off to the hospital to find out the facts, and I took myself in hand and got on with the rehearsal as if nothing was wrong, though my heart was racing. And in the evening they told me Alyosha was dying, he had taken too much of that revolting stuff. I couldn't bear it any longer, and ran to him. They let me into the ward when they found out I was his boss. He was barely conscious, but he recognized me and his little eyes sparkled. "You won't leave me now will you?" he whispered.

' "Of course not! Of course not!" I replied, though I wondered privately, what I would do with this idiot, how would I get rid of him?

'While Alyosha was ill I managed to get a transfer to Leningrad, and what do you think happened? As soon as he had recovered he resigned from the theatre and came rushing after me.

'From then on it was an absolute nightmare: he had no job in Leningrad, nowhere to live, he was drifting around God knows where and ringing me every day. One day I said to him: "Look, Alyosha, you're not a girl; I haven't seduced you and left you with a baby. You should be ashamed of yourself. Why don't you act like a man!"

'The stupid idiot didn't understand. He said: "If we did have a baby I would keep it and feel better."

'The upshot was that because of all the tension I had to go into a mental hospital. That's what it took to stop Alyosha and make him leave Leningrad. He took fright. And now when I hear stories about girls being seduced and abandoned I sometimes wonder who has the worse time of it, her or him. And do you know, I'd rather be abandoned myself than endure the storm of someone else's love again. Who needs it, this first love! I prefer to see it on stage where the daggers are made of cardboard and the poison is coloured water.'

Some of the women were sympathetic to Alyosha, others to Emma.

They then turned their attention to Irishka, the nice plump girl who worked as a secretary to the director of a milk factory.

Story Ten

by Irishka about a pair of young lovers whose story ends happily.

'I met Seryozha, my husband-to-be, on the beach at the Peter and Paul Fortress. It was a hot day and everyone was swimming, but I had a sore throat. I was sitting on the trunk of a fallen willow right at the water's edge, feeling hot and unhappy. Suddenly a huge black chow bounded up to me and started sniffing me. I'm afraid of strange dogs, so I froze, remembering what my father used to say: "If you are afraid of a dog, try not to move and don't show that you are afraid."

'And then I heard a cheerful voice: "Mishka! What are you doing, frightening such a pretty girl? Look, she's almost as pretty as you are." The dog's owner came up to us and sat down on the tree next to me. "You won't be angry if I sit here while Mishka has a swim?"

' "Sit as long as you like. But why don't you go for a swim with him?"

' "I can't. I've got a sore throat. And why aren't you swimming?"

' "I've got a sore throat, too."

' "Then let's sit together and watch Mishka swimming."

'We sat and watched. Then Mishka ran out of the Neva, rushed up to us and started shaking himself. A whole fountain of water sprayed all over us from his shaggy coat, but we enjoyed it and didn't feel so hot.

' "What's your name?"

' "Ira. What's yours?"

' "Seryozhka. And that's my mother sunbathing over there. Do you want to meet her? Come on."

'We went over to Seryozhka's mother and he said: "Mama, look what a pretty girl Mishka and I found! She's got such pretty eyes, even prettier than Mishka's, don't you think? She has eyes like a cow. Can I marry her?"

'Seryozhka's mother said he could, only later – meantime she was going to treat us to strawberries. She got a jar of strawberries out of her bag and gave it to us. Seryozhka began to select the biggest strawberries and give them to me.

' "Why are you giving me the biggest ones? That's not fair."

' "Because you have a sore throat."

' "But so have you."

' "That doesn't count, I'm stronger and healthier than you and I shall always take care of you. Agreed?"

' "Yes."

'Then I took Seryozhka to meet my older sisters, telling them he was going to marry me, that his mother had given permission. They laughed at me, but not unkindly.

'It was time to go home, and we began to collect up our things.

' "Will you be coming here tomorrow? I walk Mishka every day near that tree."

' "I will if my mother lets me go without my sisters. Or you can ring me; we have a telephone. Remember this number."

'I told Seryozhka our telephone number and he repeated it several times so as not to forget it.

'But the next day I was worse: from the throat it went to my heart, and I was taken to hospital. I lay there crying at the thought that Seryozhka was waiting in vain for me at the tree and feeling sad. And I was also crying over being shaved bald because of my illness, and that I didn't look like Mishka any more. Those were the most miserable days of my life.

'But one day the nurse came into the ward and told me to put on my dressing gown and go out into the corridor: "You've got visitors!"

'That surprised me because my mother had already been to see me that day. But it turned out to be Seryozhka and his mother. When he saw that I had been completely shaved he started howling.

' "You don't look like Mishka any more! They've made you quite ugly!"

'I thought Seryozhka didn't love me any more, and I burst into tears and went back towards the ward. I thought I would die of sadness, but as I approached the doors of the ward, Seryozhka caught up with me.

' "Where are you going? We've brought you some grapes. Mama says they'll make you better right away. Come on!"

'Then, as we sat on a bench in the corridor eating grapes, Seryozhka said to me: "You're not at all pretty now. You look as sorry as a wet kitten.'

'His mother said that he shouldn't go comparing a girl to

different animals all the time, and she wasn't going to let him hurt my feelings. She was as good as her word: for the rest of her life she did nothing but defend me if she felt Seryozhka was hurting me. Only he didn't really hurt me any more, and life proceeded without any more dramatic moments. We sat at the same desk through all our ten years of school, and after school we got married almost immediately. That was my first love. I don't know why I said "was"? It still is . . .'

With this story the first day of our *Women's Decameron* was concluded.

Just at that moment the babies were brought in on trolleys and given to their mothers who set about nursing their tiny sons and daughters. And for the morrow they agreed to tell stories about being seduced and abandoned.

THE SECOND DAY

during which tales are told about those
who have been

Seduced and Abandoned

The second day of the quarantine and of the *The Women's Decameron* began somewhat more cheerfully than the first; from early morning the women were preparing for the evening stories. When evening came, Larissa was the first to tell her story.

Story One

by Larissa, doctor of biology, in which she tries to set the tone for the evening.

'I'll tell you an anecdote which I think gives the key to most stories about people who are seduced and abandoned. Judge for yourselves whether it does or not.

'Two people are lying on the grass in the forest. He is trying to seduce her; she is reluctant, but is giving in.

' "But do you love me, Vanya?"

' "I do, I do!"

' "And you will marry me?"

' "I will, I will!"

' "You won't leave me with a baby?"

' "I won't, I won't!"

' "And you will buy a co-operative flat?"

' "I will, I will!"

' "And you will buy me a fur coat?"

' "I will, I will!"

' "And will you take me to a holiday resort?"

' "I will, I will!"

' "And will you give me an umbrella?"

' "Ugh! What in God's name do you want an umbrella for?" '

43

'That's right,' said Zina the tramp, whose turn it was after Larissa, 'that's just the sort of thing that does happen. I could have begun my tale with the very same anecdote, girls, but seeing as Larissa, got there first I'll take a different line . . .'

Story Two

by Zina the tramp, a tale alike as two peas to her first story, from which one may conclude that a soldier's love is a precarious and unreliable thing. However, we only have in mind a soldier's love for a girl, and not at all his love for his country, the Communist Party, or the ideals of internationalism. No one can accuse us of slandering the Soviet Army, since betrayal of one's bride and betrayal of one's country – they're as different as chalk and cheese, as they say in Odessa.

'We had this girl Klavka living in our village. Oh, she was bad news! She had a whole stream of soldiers after her, but she took real good care of herself. If anyone tried anything, she landed him one on the kisser. The only dowry she had was her virginity. Her father was a drunk, and her mother was an invalid. So she hung on to that virginity with both hands. And so as not to get raped by anyone she wouldn't let anybody walk her home after the movie, but always went home with girlfriends that no one was interested in.

'But, as the saying goes, for every smart arse there's a smart prick. A re-enlisted sergeant from the Ukraine took a fancy to her and made up his mind to have her. He had his little plan all worked out. He started telling her he had his old mum living in the Ukraine, and she had a nice house and garden, but she was getting on and needed a helper . . . Klavka swallowed that one – hook, line and sinker. She let the sergeant walk her home after the dance. But she was careful not to go into the bushes with him. So he outsmarted her – he had her on her parent's feather bed. How? He went and proposed to her. Klavka was glad, and so were her parents – their girl was going down south to the land of plenty. They laid everything on: killed their last sheep, sold

44

the pig, still had to borrow money for vodka, but they gave their daughter a proper wedding. The sergeant suggested signing the papers at home, in the Ukraine. He said there was no point in stamping his army book, because he would have to surrender it in the end; it would be safer in his passport. Klavka herself knew what happened to signatures in army books: along comes demob, and you've got no book and no man.

'They had the wedding, and our sergeant and his young wife started to pack up to go down to his mother's. He buys up a whole lot of suitcases and grabs just about everything he can lay his hands on for Klavka's dowry. He walks round the house looking for something else to put into these new suitcases of his.

' "Mother," he says, "give us this and give us that, it'll be useful for a young couple setting up house."

'He even took the icon off the wall: "That'll be your parental blessing on us."

'All this stuff he sent off on the slow train, and for himself and Klavka he got tickets not just for any old seats, but for a real compartment, and off went our young couple to their happy new life. The rest of us girls envied Klavka as we saw her off: "Good for you, girl! You're a smart one!"

'But we envied her a bit too soon. A couple of days later Klavka's mother gets a telegram: "Mama, send money. Find out Mikhail's address from his unit. I lost him on the journey."

'Everyone in the village started laughing when Klavka's mother began showing people the telegram. But they genuinely felt sorry for the girl and gave her Mikhail's address in the unit. I don't know where on earth Klavka's mother found the money – the wedding had cleaned her out completely.

'A month later a final letter arrives from our clever Klavka. She writes that she found the village where Mikhail lived, some kind people showed her the house. Only she's met at the house by a young woman with a bouncing two-year-old in her arms. Klavka bursts into tears and starts telling her how Mikhail deceived her, but this other woman, as soon as she twigs who it is standing in front of her, grabs a rake and chases Klavka out of the yard.

'So there, as you put it, was someone "seduced and

abandoned" in our village. And no one knows where she is now. Maybe she started going downhill like me, had her fill of camp food, and now she's tramping it. Or maybe she just snuffed it, I don't know.'

Next it was Natasha's turn to tell a story, but she opened with a warning: 'The story that I am about to tell you is very similar to Zina's, but it has a different ending, a happy one. But take note, my friends, that in order for the story of my seduced and abandoned girl to turn out well in the end an improbable chain of circumstances was necessary.'

Story Three

by Natasha the engineer, which ends with a wedding, for the simple reason that great naïveté was met with equally great wisdom.

'There was a young female draughtsman called Sveta Paramonova working in our design office. A really pretty girl, but incredibly naïve. She believed, for example, that Bird's Milk sweets really were made from bird's milk. People used to tease her and say: "Little Svetochka, fed on bird's milk!"

'One day a nice guy from Yerevan in Armenia turned up to work with us for a period. He began to court Sveta, and not without success, as we could see. What a picture they were together! Sveta was all white and fluffy like a dandelion clock, and he was a handsome Caucasian with fine dark eyes. He was insanely jealous while courting her, flashing his eyes at everyone. Then he promised the silly girl he was going home to tell his parents to prepare for the wedding, and off he went, leaving Sveta knocked up. She waited and waited: well, Rafik had said he was coming, so she would just have to be patient. Who could say, she said, how long it would take him to talk it all over with his parents and prepare for the wedding?

'Anyway, while Rafik was "getting ready for the wedding", Sveta was safely delivered of a little boy. As soon as she was strong again she got ready to leave. "Don't be silly!" we told her. "You're a mother now, you can't be so trusting, you're not just responsible for yourself. Where do you think you're going with that baby?"

'But she wouldn't listen.

' "What if he's ill or something awful has happened?"

'She went off to Yerevan without even knowing the address. A month later we get a wedding photo: Sveta and Rafik beaming away as if this was how the wedding had been planned all along.

' "Incredible!" the people in our section said. "Was our Sveta really cleverer than we thought? How on earth did she manage to put the pressure on that lad?"

'In the summer one of our group went to Armenia on holiday and decided to call in on Sveta. Then the whole story came out.

'Apparently she had located Rafik's parents and simply turned up with her baby on their doorstep, asking where Rafik was. They told her he had been sent to work in Moscow.

' "And who might you be?"

' "I'm his wife, and this is baby Rafik, his son. Pleased to meet you both. You must be the grandparents."

'The old people didn't know what to say. But Sveta wasn't bothered a bit.

' "I'm so glad to have found you! What happened to Rafik? Was he sent off on such a long assignment, or did he get ill? Why couldn't he come and get us?"

'That mother of Rafik's turned out to be a wise woman. She took her grandson, carried him into the house, fed her uninvited daughter-in-law, and at supper got the whole story from her, blow by blow. She realized the sort of child she was dealing with, and she told the old man.

'A month later Rafik comes back, and in the garden there are tables set out and guests sitting waiting.

' "What's this, Mama? Sister's wedding, or something?"

' "No, Son, yours."

'At this point the old man comes out of the house and goes up to him with the happy Sveta! The silly girl rushes up to him, hugs him and cries: "Why didn't you write to tell me about all your illnesses and official trips, I was so worried! If it had gone on a bit longer I would have begun to have doubts!"

47

'At these words the old man shook his finger at Rafik as if to say, see for yourself the sort of child you wanted to deceive!

'So Sveta never did find out that she had been seduced and abandoned. Good on her!'

After Natasha, it was the turn of Valentina whom the others had started to call the Party bigwig behind her back. They all turned towards her rather apprehensively: was she going to give them another moral lecture? But on this occasion their fears proved groundless.

Story Four

by Valentina the bigwig. It is one of those fantastic 'exit'
stories, though it must be said that all stories about
emigration from the Soviet Union are completely
fantastic.

'Do you know, the workers' deputies sometimes have to deal with cases that are so strange that most people don't even know they happen at all. For example, how would you establish fatherhood if a man was married, had children, but died, and some woman tried to prove that she had his child after his death. Such cases do not often crop up in our practice, and they nearly always remain unresolved even if they try to sort them out in a court of law. It is so difficult to prove anything that even the courts find themselves at a dead end. But there was one such case that was resolved both positively and quickly.

'An old woman came to us and said:"My son has died, and now a student at the philological faculty of the university is about to have his child. We would like our grandson to have our son's name and be registered. Can you do that?"

'We replied that we could, but if there was a widow she would have to confirm that her late husband was unfaithful and slept with this particular woman, and that she would have no objection to one more child receiving a pension on his behalf.

'Next day a young woman came along and said: "Yes, I know that is my husband's child. I don't mind him being given the same name as my children."

'Our workers were all amazed at such generosity, but they asked for more witnesses all the same. And the witnesses duly appeared – residents of the flat where the deceased used to live. Yes, they confirmed, in the absence of his wife he brought citizen So-and-so along and in front of them all in the kitchen he promised to get a divorce and marry her. They saw him give her money and one day they saw her bring a set of dishes in a box as a present for him – in other words, they were sharing possessions. Well, then the janitor of the building presented himself and confirmed the statements that the deceased had gone here and there and carried this and that – so in the end we had to register the fatherhood. Just then the baby was born.

'All the papers were drawn up properly, and we were all amazed at the maturity and generosity of Soviet people. Here a man has seduced a woman and so tragically abandoned her, but she has had a son and given him the father's name, and she's going to receive a good pension for him, not just five roubles as a single parent. And all this because those around her turned out to be good, honest, genuine people.

'A month later we discovered that the "seduced and abandoned" girl had taken her whole gang of brand new relatives and emigrated with them to Israel. It turned out that just before the birth she had got an exit visa, so they all immediately drew up the papers! Whether her child was really from the dead man we will unfortunately never know. Later we tried to prosecute the janitor and the neighbours for perjury – but just try to prove anything. They all managed to escape responsibility. We are often reminded of that incident so as to keep us vigilant.'

Hardly had Valentina finished than she was pounced upon by Galina who had come to look on Valentina with mistrust.

'Excuse me, Valentina!' she exclaimed, 'but do you have any grounds for thinking that the baby was not the dead man's son?'

'Well, of course! I'm telling you, they all beat it to Israel, they just vanished!'

'And what's wrong with that?'

'The fact that they jumped on the bandwagon like that, hitching themselves to the baby and that "seduced and abandoned" girl – do you think that's honest?'

'So they wanted to leave, but they couldn't have just got a visa, bought a plane ticket and flown off, could they?'

'If they had been given permission, then of course no one would have stopped them.'

'And do you think Israel might not give them permission to enter?'

'What's Israel got to do with it? *We* might not give permission on grounds of state security.'

'Thank you, Valentina, you have just told us a wonderful story, even though it was a thoroughly anti-Soviet one.'

Everyone smiled at this unexpected conclusion. But nobody felt like talking politics, so they asked Albina, whose turn was next, to begin her story.

Story Five

by Albina, airhostess, being a Soviet version of Nabokov's
Lolita.

For a start Albina turned straightaway to the dissident wife, Galina, and asked: 'You, Galya, have you ever read Nabokov's banned novel *Lolita*?'

'Yes, I have. But it isn't banned, it's just printed in the West. The author has lived over there for a long time now.'

'Well, it ought to be banned!'

'This coming from you, Albina? I'm surprised that you're embarrassed by things in books when you practise them yourself in real life.'

'In real life nothing would embarrass me, it's true. But I would ban that book for its lies, not for its sex. That book, girls, is about this healthy prick who describes with great relish how he murdered a girl's mother so she wouldn't prevent him enjoying the girl, and then how he ruined the girl's life and finally murdered her too.'

'Albina, what are you talking about? The hero didn't murder the mother or the daughter. He killed Lolita's lover out of jealousy, and the mother and daughter died accidentally: one was run over by a car, and the other died in childbirth.'

'That's what he says, and you're so simple you believe him. You have to read between the lines! Maybe he deliberately slipped the mother his diary where he had written that he was after the girl and had married the old fool just for that reason. In my opinion, Galina, that fellow had everything worked out ten moves ahead. He even wanted to drown her, but it didn't work.'

'All right, let's say he did. But what about Lolita herself? Didn't she die in childbirth?'

'Oh, Galina, you're so slow! How many hours were you in labour?'

'I didn't count. Three or four probably. What about it?'

'Just this. If someone had been screwing you with his fat smelly cock since you were ten years old and all your insides were twisted up, you wouldn't have got off so lightly. They spent three days dragging my little girl out of me, and they even wanted to do a Caesarean. If it was up to me I would take your Nabokov and all the men who go after children and pull off all their equipment with red-hot pincers! And the first one would be the swine who did a Lolita on me . . . I hate him!'

Albina's face was flushed and contorted, and tears were starting from her eyes, spoiling her eye-shadow. Galina rushed over to her, sat on her bed and hugged her.

'Calm down, Albinochka! You might lose your milk. There's no need to tell us, you don't have to remember it.'

'How can I not remember it . . . Even when I'm dying I shall remember it. But the story's a short one, there's hardly anything to tell. That Nabokov obviously wanted to make a packet of money, so he spread his filth over a whole book, smearing the pages with sperm. And you silly little intellectuals sigh over it as if it were spread with honey. I've heard your little discussions, I've been in cultured society. But in real life everything is so simple and there's so little to tell that all that's left is to hang myself out of spite for men and all you lot.'

Albina blew her nose, wiped her eyes, got her breath back and started her story.

'My mother was also stupid, like Lolita's. My father had left us and we were living together on her pay just outside Leningrad in a village called Tolmachovo, near Luga. My mother was a schoolteacher.

'I was a really pretty child, it was terrible! We would be walking down the street, my mother and I, and people were always staring or coming up to us. We liked it. As I look back on it, my mother's one joy was that her daughter was such a doll. Living with Mother I did well for the first few years at school. Afterwards everything went downhill, but that comes later . . .

'Do you girls remember how that craze for figure skating started up? All the parents had this one ambition, to get their children into a figure skating school and turn them all into Blackbeardskys and Whitearsovas. My mother bought me some skates and began taking me into Leningrad to the Sunday figure skating class. I really took to it, like a duck to water. If it hadn't been for that swine Kayur I might have become a champion, skating all round those Europe places instead of serving fruit juice with a smile in an aeroplane.

'So, about Kayur. One day this famous trainer who had already launched many talented skaters, came to our ice-rink. He watched everyone skating and chose me.

' "That little girl definitely has talent. But she needs to study systematically, and with a more experienced trainer. Her basic qualities and technique are unusually good."

'Technique? Bullshit! Both my mother and my teacher swallowed that one, and I certainly did. So he spins us along a bit more: "For the sake of your daughter's future you should move to Leningrad. There's no time to lose. Every month of training now means years of success in the future."

'He let my mother get nice and flustered and upset, then he says: "You try to get an exchange with someone in Leningrad, and I'll have a word with my wife: I think she'll agree to let Albinochka stay with us for the time being and study under me at the sports school."

'I was already his "Albinochka", and we were almost trying to kiss his hands for such kindness. Kindness? Bullshit!

'I'm sorry about the bad language, girls – I haven't got this out of my system yet. And I don't think I ever will. You just listen to what that swine did to me.

'He certainly did have a wife. Only she was a visiting one, just for appearances. I don't know how he got her to play that role at his place, but she definitely was not really his wife. My mother and I never suspected anything. We arrived at Kayur's and this madam greeted us like honoured guests: "Ah, child! Ah, my dear!"

'They gave us all sorts of delicacies, and my mother even agreed to a glass of vodka. And all the time she was sitting on the edge of her chair trembling for my future. Kayur got straight down to business and spelled it all out to us: "There's no point in her going home again, it would be wasting time. She'll go to the school tomorrow and we'll start the training. Allochka, get the girl's room ready!"

'This phoney wife of his, Allochka, took me along to show me my future room. I didn't know at the time that it was to be my prison for three whole years. Not even a prison, a torture chamber. I went into that little room and was so happy I nearly pissed my pants: everything was lovely and new, the furniture was like toy furniture, there was a little bed just for me with a big imported doll sitting on it waiting for me.

'I said goodbye to my mother, and she left. Kayur then said to Alla: "The girl is tired, put her to bed. When she gets undressed have a look at her muscles and let me know if everything is OK."

'That trash was just working for him the whole time. I got undressed in front of her in my new room, she looked me over, felt my arms and legs and said: "I don't know if you'll be all right or not, my dear. It seems to me your leg muscles are a bit tight. Or perhaps I'm mistaken? . . ."

'As if she was thinking it over, the swine. My heart stopped: did that mean I wouldn't be a champion? I looked at her with big eyes and was just about to start bawling. But she stroked me on the head and comforted me: "Don't worry, Semyon Ilich is a very good trainer. Perhaps all is not lost. Shall I call him to have a look for himself.

'Stupid me, I was delighted at the idea: "Oh yes! Please get him!"

'They certainly had it all thought out, all worked out!

'Kayur appeared in his dressing gown, his crooked hairy legs sticking out.

' "Well, what's up then?"

'Alla told him about my legs, acting as if she had doubts. He began to feel my legs, my bum, and a couple of times he stroked my pussy.

' "Yes," he said, "we'll have to work on this a bit. It'll all depend on Albinochka herself: if she takes her training seriously, then all the faults can be smoothed out gradually. Will you do your best, child?"

' "Yes, uncle Semyon!" I said with tears in my eyes.

'He took me in his arms as if to comfort me, put me on his bare knee, covered me with his dressing gown and squeezed me to himself. Comforting me! And Alla was standing right there stroking me on the head and saying something soothing – all to distract my attention, as I realize now. What he was doing under that dressing gown I had no idea at the time. But when I read your *Lolita* it suddenly dawned on me: he was jerking himself off on me, it's quite obvious!

'But tell me, girls, where do women like that Allochka of his come from? She's the one I can't forgive. Do what you like with your man, this is the twentieth century, the age of progress, but why play a dirty trick like that on a stupid kid?

'It gets even worse. Do you think he just raped me and left it at that? No way! That wasn't his style. He understood full well that I would have complained to my mother, and she could have had him in court. And a beauty of a sentence they would have given him, the bastard. But he was much more subtle and clever. He fixed it so that he had his way with me for two years and I hadn't a clue what he was doing! And not just him alone, his friend too.

'You don't believe me? Then listen. The next day he and I went off to the sports school. It had a rink with artificial ice, and boys and girls were skating on it. Kayur put me on the ice straightaway to show me to the other trainers who were all impressed by my performance. Then Kayur winked at one of them: "What do you think, Vitya, are her leg muscles a bit taut? Alla says there's little hope for her."

'This conversation went on so that only I could hear it – there were no other trainers around when they were talking. They ordered me to skate a bit more and do an arabesque. Vitya watched and said: "Yes, not much good. I can see you'll need to work on her a lot."

'He called one girl over and asked her to show what she could do. That girl was a great skater, she spun like a top and she could go right down on the ice doing the splits.

' "Do you remember her?" said Vitya. "She was a pretty hopeless case, too, and now look!"

'So then Kayur said to him: "Come round to my place after work and we'll have a go at Albina."

'And he said: "Why not! She's obviously a talented kid, we ought to do something to save the situation."

'Well, haven't you guessed what they did to me yet? They had me undress, felt me, looked at me, then they told me to sit on the table and open my legs.

' "Aha!" said Vitya, supposedly the more experienced trainer. "Here's where it's all taut! She needs a small operation to free the ligaments."

'And in front of me they began to discuss whether to put me in hospital for the operation or whether to try and deal with it themselves. They were saying that in the hospital the doctors were experienced enough, but they might touch too many ligaments, and that would be the end of all hopes of a sporting career. They could do it better themselves, but they didn't have a legal right. Here I burst out crying, I was so upset, and I begged them: "Uncle Semyon, Uncle Vitya! Do it yourselves! I won't tell anyone, not even Mama."

'Well, they performed the Women's World Figure Skating Champion operation on me: one's holding me and kissing me as if to calm me down, and the other's screwing away down there, turning me inside out. They took it in turns. Blood goes all over the table and on to the floor. I'm crying but bearing it, and I'm hanging on to their hands and pressing up against them, the bastards, so it won't hurt so much. While one is torturing me the other is kissing and slobbering and stroking me. I don't know how many times they had me, they only stopped when I began to lose consciousness. Kayur carried me to the bath, washed me down, and then put me in bed. I fell asleep crying, but in the hopes that now everything was all right.

'The next day Kayur didn't take me to school, he told me to stay in bed and "rest after the operation", while he himself went off to his training. He was back for dinner together with Vitya – to check if the patient was getting better. Can you guess how they checked? Yes, on the same table again, only this time there wasn't so much blood. But it still hurt just as much. And there was always that pain, I always had to grit my teeth, I, the future world champion. Later they used to call this "massaging of taut ligaments". They would say quite openly during a training session: "Did you give Albinochka a massage? She doesn't seem to be doing the splits very well. I'll drop in today and give her one myself."

'But of course they taught me to skate as well, and I made great progress. They were good trainers in that sense.

'For two years those bastards tricked me like that, and I stuck it out. Then one time we went to some heats, because by then I was already taking part in big competitions. It just so happened that Kayur wasn't able to have me with him in his room, though everyone looked upon him as some sort of relative of mine. I was put into a room with that same girl that Vitya had shown us the first day. I remembered they had said that she had had taut ligaments and had also needed an operation. So I asked her: "They operated on your ligaments too, didn't they? Mine still hurt, you know. Only I'm afraid to tell Kayur in case he throws me out of the school. How are yours?"

'That girl, Katya, had understood everything long ago; she had been told by someone who had got the treatment even before her. And she was the one who revealed to me what they had actually done to me and were still doing. And she added: "Only don't go telling anyone, or Kayur and Vitya will sling us out and that'll be the end of figure skating for us. We'll just have to put up with it! Vitya says eventually I'll even get to enjoy it. I don't believe him, but I'm going to hang in there because I love the ice. And as soon as I become a champion I'll get myself a new trainer who won't torment me. A woman preferably."

'Being an idiot I told Kayur all about my conversation with Katya as soon as we got back to Leningrad. And I asked him not to do that to me any more because it always hurt. It didn't frighten him at all that I understood everything. In fact he was glad, the beast.

' "Seeing that you know everything, now we can vary our 'massage'. Then it won't hurt you so much."

'And we did. Perhaps some of his tricks were less painful than others, but now I began to want to hang myself.

'Finally I could stand it no longer and ran home to my mother. I was afraid to tell her, so I just explained that I didn't want to do figure skating any more, I was fed up with it and I didn't feel well. Kayur came for me and persuaded my mother that I was just being temperamental. He shoved me weeping into his car and drove me off.

'I thought and thought about how to get away from him, and finally had an idea. At all the important performances I started to fall down on the ice and act lame. Or in front of everyone I would suddenly hold my stomach and scream: "Ow, it hurts! My whole insides hurt as if I'd been jabbed with a stick!"

'Kayur would shake with fear and anger and try to persuade me to stop this circus act, promising me fame and everything on earth. But I kept right on. In the end he couldn't take any more and took me back to my mother. He didn't care, he could find a thousand other girls like me longing to be world champions!

'At home with my mother I gradually began to recover, but my stomach hurt for a long time and I would have nightmares about Kayur and Vitya. Even now I occasionally dream of their ugly twisted mugs and filthy laughter: "Massage time! Massage time!"

'Galya, you say that your Nabokov didn't kill Lolita's mother? Well, do you know how Kayur and Vitya killed my mother? Quite simply. One night I was dreaming about them again, and I started crying really loud in my sleep. My mother came running in and took me in her arms, and I snuggled up to her and in my half-asleep state told her everything. She did her best to comfort me, tucked me in and went quietly out of the room. And the next day a neighbour took me along to the mortuary: there lay my mother – dead, they had pulled her out of the river Luga.'

At this point Albina, whose voice had begun to tremble some time ago, broke down buried her face in her pillow, her shoulders shaking with sobs. Galya went and sat next to her and began to stroke her back to calm her down. And Zina the tramp shook her head and growled: 'Men are capable of just about anything – as if there weren't enough *women* to go round!'

As soon as she had calmed Albina down Galya took her turn to tell a story.

Story Six

by Galina the dissident, romantic, sentimental, and in somewhat nostalgic vein, about her grandfather and his fiancée.

'I had prepared a completely different story for you, not the one I'm going to tell you now. It was a sad one, too, like almost all such stories. But I think we've had enough sadness for today, and it just so happens I've remembered a 'seduced and abandoned' story that ended in the happy return of the seducer. And that seducer was my grandfather.

'I seem to have dissidence in my blood. My grandfather was in the White Guard and left for the West through the Crimea. There he married my grandmother, a professor's daughter, and my mother was born. After the war they decided to return to this country. They were thrown in prison, of course, and my mother was put in a special children's home. Then my grandparents were let out and he was even given the chance to teach at university – times had changed. He came back from camp as healthy as when he had gone in. He always did have an iron constitution. But his wife just came out, met up with him, admired me, her granddaughter (though I don't know what there was to admire about me), and soon afterwards announced: "Well, that's it. Now I can die in peace."

And she did. She had got very tired in the camps and she didn't seem to want to live any longer – she just hadn't got the strength.

At first my grandfather missed her badly and went to the cemetery almost every day. Then he went back to work. All our relatives, including my parents, all started competing to find him a wife. He was a very interesting man, attractive in every way: tall and completely white-haired, but with a manly face and cheerful look. And no camp was ever able to knock the stuffing out of a White Guard officer. He was over sixty at that time, but women of thirty were taking an interest. He even had a lover, the professor of his department, but nothing ever came of it. Grandfather used to say she had a lot of intelligence and strength, but not an ounce of femininity. So they broke up

'Grandfather retired and went to stay with our relatives in Kiev to have a look at the places of his youth. Suddenly we got a telegram from Kiev: "Meet such-and-such a train. Arriving with fiancée."

'We went to the Moscovsky Station on the appointed day to meet the betrothed couple. We were fascinated to see what sort of fiancée he had found himself. She was bound to be something out of the ordinary, because he had as many girlfriends as he wanted in Leningrad.

'The Kiev train drew in, and out of the carriage stepped my grandfather, and next to him a tiny grey-haired old lady. Grandfather brought her over to us: "Let me introduce you all. This is Nadenka, my fiancée from the year nineteen nineteen."

'We thought Grandfather was joking, but then we found out that it was all true. It turned out that when he was still a young officer he had fallen for this young girl, Nadenka, and proposed to her. The wedding day was already fixed, when suddenly the order came through for his immediate departure from Kiev. Nadenka was beside herself with grief, but they were both absolutely convinced that the civil war would end any day, and that they would meet up again and get married. And so, in this conviction, my grandfather seduced Nadenka. He had ever afterwards felt guilty towards her and in every church he would confess his sin and pray to God that his "crime", as he called it, hadn't ruined her life. And basically he had gone to Kiev to revisit the place of their love.

'Then Nadenka told how after our grandfather had disappeared she just could not forget him. She managed to adapt to a new life, got married, had children and grandchildren, but every year on the anniversary of their farewell she would come to the bank of the Dnieper where they had said goodbye, and where, in a summer-house in the old park, she had given herself to him. As the years passed this area had got built up, but part of the park survived, as by some

59

miracle did the summer-house. Nadezhda Yakovlevna assured us that the only reason she stayed in Kiev was so that she could go to that spot every year on "their special day".

'So imagine their meeting. Dear old Grandfather arrived in Kiev in a sad, romantic mood and went to look for the place where he bade farewell to his fiancée. The first thing that struck him as miraculous was that he found that little corner of the park, changed, but not so changed that he couldn't recognize it. Suddenly he saw a summer-house – the very one! True, it was leaning a bit, and some of the steps had crumbled away. He went into the summer-house, and there sat an old woman with white hair looking thoughtfully at the Dnieper.

' "Forgive me, am I disturbing you?" asked my grandfather, preparing to sit down on the other seat, the empty one. But the old woman suddenly stared at him, got up from her seat and said quite calmly: "So you've come back, Volodechka."

'I'm amazed the old man didn't have a heart attack on the spot! I asked them: "Did you hug and kiss?"

'And Grandfather replied: "My dear! I recognized Nadenka instantly, she had hardly changed at all – so how could I help taking her into my arms after being separated for so many years? We were seventeen and twenty once more."

'And you know, I have to admit I have never known a married couple more in love. Grandfather felt so young he went back to teaching. I'll tell you of one incident as an example of how they were together.

'Grandfather and Nadenka were living near the university. I was visiting them one evening and decided to stay the night and go to classes the next morning with Grandfather. The Academy of Arts where I was a student then was right near the philological faculty where my grandfather gave his lectures. We had breakfast next morning and were getting ready to leave. Time was running out and we were in a hurry. My grandfather stood in the hallway, waiting for something.

' "Nadenka, we're leaving!"

' "Yes, yes! just coming!"

'She was busy doing something in her room. Grandfather hopped nervously from one foot to the other.

' "Nadenka, darling, we're going to be late!"

' "Coming, Volodechka!"

'I thought she was going to give him some money, or bring out some papers – something like that. But suddenly I saw Nadenka waltzing out of the room, and Grandfather bending down to her, giving her his forehead. She crossed him, stood on tiptoe to kiss him, and whispered: "The Lord keep you."

'And with that my grandfather went calmly off to his lectures. That was their rule: he would never leave the house unless she crossed him first. They were both convinced that the reason it took them so long to meet up again was that they had forgotten to cross each other when they said goodbye that day.'

The story of Galina's grandfather helped the women to get over Albina's depressing tale. Their faces all brightened up, the warmth returned to their eyes.

Story Seven

by the worker Olga, about a woman in love who was quick-witted enough to turn general male drunkenness to her own advantage.

'We had one of those seduced and abandoned girls in our workshop, and she was so smart she could have given all yours a hundred points lead and still overtaken them.

'She was called Lyuba Kuzenkova, a real dishy girl from the posh suburbs, all bursting with health. A joiner from our shop, Pashka Mitrokhin, started to go after her. And he got her to sleep with him before the registry office. As soon as he had slept with her he started turning up his nose.

' "What sort of girl are you," he goes, "if you give the first man who promises to marry you a leg-over? What sort of wife would you make? I don't trust you to be a decent woman, and that's all there is to it!"

'Now this Pashka Mitrokhin was quite a drinker, every pay-day he would get pissed out of his mind even before he left the factory. Anyway, time passed since he had told her where to get off, and then along came pay-day. Pashka as usual found a cosy corner of the changing room and started drinking with his mates. But Lyuba was busy doing something nearby, and kept her eye on them. Once they were pretty sloshed Lyuba suddenly appeared with a half-litre and said: "How about another drink, boys?"

'That was fine by them. They drank it, and then Lyuba pulled a second bottle out of her bag: "Another slug?"

'They didn't refuse. By this time Pashka was well away, so Lyuba steered him to the entrance, called for a taxi and took him home to her place. She undressed him and put him to bed with her.

'Next morning Pashka woke up and said: "What am I doing with you again, Lyubka? I'm through with you for good."

'Ever so gently she answered: "I don't know why you latched on to me, Pashenka. You must have been missing me." And she gave him some pickles, a quick glass for his hangover, and even a nice hot cutlet. That seemed to help his hangover. Then she took him by the hand and off they went to the factory. Then she really played it cool: she didn't approach him, she didn't look at him, and it was just as if she didn't know anyone called Pashka Mitrokhin. But actually she was waiting for next pay-day. Then it was the same story all over again. And that was how it went after that: every pay-day Pashka drank all he could hold, Lyuba took him back to her place, sobered him up in the morning and brought him to work. That went on for several months.

Then one day – no Lyuba. Pashka's drinking away and looking all round to see where she is. And Lyuba's sitting at home with everything set up as usual: the pickles are ready, so's the vodka, and the cutlets are fried. In comes lover-boy. Lyuba acts quite calm and does everything as usual: puts him to bed, next morning tidies him up nicely and brings him to work. Come the next pay-day, her beloved Pashenka turns up automatically, but in the morning she doesn't give him pickles or vodka, but an ultimatum: "It's up to you, friend Pashenka: either we go right now to the registry office and put in our application, and then afterwards come back and celebrate the thing properly – I've got some brandy waiting in the fridge, and I got the day off for both of us from the foreman – or you can go somewhere else to get sobered up."

'Pashka reckoned that putting in an application was one thing, but signing was quite a different kettle of fish. "I agree," he says.

Lyuba gets a taxi, and in an hour they're back again and at the table. They were booked to sign in twenty days' time. When the day came round Pashka remembered and avoided Lyuba. But she didn't seem bothered, and she didn't react at all. Pashka was relieved and thought, she's obviously forgotten or changed her mind. When the next pay-day and drinking session came round, there was Lyuba again with her half-litre: "A bit more, Pashenka?"

'Afterwards she took him home as usual, and in the morning she said: "Let's go to the registry office and put in our application again, seeing as we didn't get round to signing last time."

'Pashka already knew that was not dangerous, so he agreed. She brought him slightly boozed-up to the registry office. He was not watching what was going on and was only listening with half an ear to what Lyuba and the registry office women were whispering about. They took their passports, did this, did that, slapped a stamp in them and gave them back: "Congratulations comrades! You are now legally married!"

'Even then Pashka didn't really take it in, he just wanted to get back to the brandy in Lyuba's fridge ...

'How did Lyuba swing it so that they signed the papers? Dead simple. That time Pashka wriggled out of signing because he was sober, she dashed over to the registry office during the break and told them her fiancé was ill, and would they postpone the signing for another ten days or so, in other words, exactly to next pay-day. Why should they care? They postponed it. That's how our Lyuba got her Pashka Mitrokhin and became Lyuba Mitrokhina. And they have the same system going as when they started: twice a month Pashka drinks and Lyuba sobers him up. But on the other days she doesn't give him a drop.

' "Don't you go disturbing my peace and quiet," she says, "I sacrificed half my nerves for it!"

'But it's OK, they get on all right. They'll survive.'

The women had a good laugh over the story of the quick-witted Lyuba and the luckless Pashka and prepared to listen to Nelya.

Story Eight

by the music teacher Nelya, being a further development of the theme begun by Albina in her tale of the villainous trainer, from which one may conclude that teachers who abuse their power over female pupils are to be encountered more frequently than one would wish.

'You know, I can't get Albina's story out of my head. My joy at giving birth to a little girl is tinged with sadness. I have no idea how I'll protect her from such horrors. Bringing up a girl is just as bad as going through the jungle with her: you can't let her out of your sight for a minute or she'll be torn to pieces! They talk of equal rights for men and women. What equal rights? What are we – people, or just bait for predators? I don't know. I'm sorry, but I've just remembered a story similar to the one Albina told, quite horrific.

'The director of our music school had set his sights on teaching at the conservatoire. He tried for a long time, and finally a real chance cropped up and they promised him a post for the next academic year. Then it turned out that one of the female students he had seduced – he was a past master at that – had got pregnant. He himself was married. So what do you think this guy did to avoid a scandal?

'He invited his student to have a holiday with him on the Black Sea before putting in for a divorce – or so he told her. The night before they were due to leave, he took her along to meet a friend of his, a gynaecologist – another swine like himself. They slipped something in her drink to send her to sleep, then gave her pain-killing injection, and in that state the gynaecologist performed an abortion on her.

'In the morning our director woke her up and took her half asleep to the airport, boarded the plane with her and took her off for the promised holiday. She felt there was something not quite right about having secretions in the third month, and pain too, but she put it down to the flight and the recent upheavals. They spent their holiday native style: they pitched their tent right on the beach somewhere near Koktebel and had their meals in local restaurants. When they got home he was brief and to the point: "We're through. There's nothing between us – there never was and never will be. Goodbye, and thanks for a lovely time. And if you are thinking of slandering me you can kiss the school goodbye."

'In tears the girl ran to her teacher and told her everything, and she took the matter straight to the party bureau. Both of them were carpeted, and the director was asked: "Have you just been to the Crimea with this student, as she claims?"

' "Certainly not! I was at a sanatorium at Tskhaltubo. Here's my travel document." And he put his travel document on the table, filled out and stamped – he'd got himself one ahead of time. And how could the girl prove that their tent had stood on some deserted beach? Then they told her to go to a consultant and get a certificate of pregnancy. She went to the doctor who, of course, informed her: "You're not pregnant at all!"

'The poor girl practically went out of her mind. She was expelled from the school for slander. She went home to Vologda covered in shame, her name ruined. Shortly afterwards, she poisoned herself. It was impossible to save her.

'Several years passed. Then that same gynaecologist tried the same nasty business – and blew it. During the investigation he confessed he had done several abortions like that, and he named all his clients. It was such a VIP set of people that our director was a mere shrimp among them. They reminded him at the trial that he had been the cause of a suicide. He was given three years, but for some reason one of our teachers met him a year later in Omsk. In a music school again, by the way, though as an ordinary teacher. In other words, the cat was among the pigeons again. The bigger names weren't even prosecuted. Evidently they were given reprimands at Party headquarters, and that was considered enough.

'Yes, it's frightening to give birth to little girls and let them loose in that jungle. But then is it any better to have a boy if he's going to grow into a monster like that.' After all, our director and that gynaecologist, they must have had mothers too, mustn't they? What turned them into animals?'

'Ye-es,' said Olga thoughtfully, 'it's awful when a man is nothing more than a support for his own prick.'

And Zina the tramp asked, not speaking to anyone in particular: 'I wonder, girls, if there's a single woman on

65

this earth that no one has ever tried to rape. Perhaps some real ugly mug . . . but then appearances don't count for much in the dark.'

Everyone was quiet for a moment. No one in the ward claimed there were any exceptions. Then Zina continued: 'Right then, martyrs, for our next session let's tell how they tried to rape us, OK?'

But Albina protested: 'I've had enough of this depressing stuff. Let's have something more cheerful next time.'

Zina screwed up her eyes: 'Like your daisy, for example?'

'Well?' challenged Albina, 'why not about daisy, or this whole thing will turn sour. Let's tell about the sex we've had in funny situations. Well, what do you say? Have we got what it takes to reveal all?'

They laughed, and then decided to risk making this the theme for the following evening. But there were still two stories left about the seduced and abandoned, so they all turned to Emma and prepared to listen to another theatre story.

Story Nine

by the theatre director Emma, in which the role of seduced and abandoned is played, as on the first occasion, by a man who gets his just deserts.

This story didn't happen to me, but to someone I knew well.

'Yura was a talented journalist and a great theatre-lover. He somehow managed to fall for a woman with three children, each one smaller than the last. That was also a first love, like Alyosha was for me. And the woman was also older than him, and certainly more experienced. Either her husband left her with the three little kids, or she herself left him, I don't know which. This woman really latched on to Yura and very soon seduced him.

'One fine day he found himself the father of three charming little children. Six months later he was suing for alimony. The woman had abandoned him with the three children and disappeared off the face of the earth. And since criminal investigation never did locate her, our single father is receiving state aid and bringing up his three charges diligently and responsibly. Only occasionally, if he's had a glass or two, does he complain: "Show me the unfortunate girl who has been seduced, given three children in six months, and then abandoned! I'll marry her immediately! Meanwhile I'm more unhappy than all those girls put together and just try to prove I'm not!"

The tenth and final story of the evening was told by the general favourite, Irishka.

Story Ten

by plump Irishka in which, once again, it was a man who nearly ended up seduced and abandoned, to the general satisfaction of the ladies.

'I also know a funny story along the same lines, said Irishka, who had been highly amused by Emma's story. 'It happened to my elder sister Tatyana who's a geologist. Well, she spent the whole of one summer on the same field trip as a boy who was also a geologist and also from Leningrad, and in the autumn she came back pregnant by him.

'At first everything was fine. Tanya didn't even seem to me to be thinking so much about whether he would marry her or not, as about the baby. She got advice from doctors, hunted down the necessary books, even got hold of Spock for a hundred roubles on the black market. In other words, she was getting ready to be a very responsible mother. And she continued to see Leva as if nothing was up.

'One day he came to see her and started this long conversation about how she ought to have an abortion, because it would be better if he did postgraduate work first and then started a family. The conversation was going on in our flat, because at the time we were both still living with our parents. I was sitting in the little room next door doing my homework, and I could hear everything: there was no door between our two little rooms, just a curtain.

'Tanya heard him out attentively and then said: "I realize, Leva, that you don't need a wife and child just now. But I've already done the thinking for both of us, me and my child, and I've decided that perhaps he doesn't need a father like you. We can get on very well without you."

' "What do you mean? I'm the father of the future child, so how can you solve questions like that without me?"

' "And how are you going to prove you are its father, Levushka? By the fact that your career is dearer to you than the life of a child that already exists, and dearer than the health of the mother? No, lover-boy, off you go and do your postgrad course, and while you're about it go to hell too. We'll manage without you."

'And she chucked him out. Well, after that the wretched Leva simply blocked our telephone line with his calls, and for days on end he hung around under our windows. But Tanya stuck to her guns: "Don't call me, don't bother me – just get out of my life. It's not good for me to be upset at the moment. We don't need a father like you!"

'Of course, she cried every night, I could hear her. Then one day Leva came to our place, literally burst into Tanya's room, thumped his fist on the table and demanded: "What right do you have to play around with me like this? Why are you tormenting the father of your future children? Get dressed, we're going to get married."

'And that was that – they went straight along and put in their application. But even now at the least spot of trouble Tanya reminds him: "Don't forget that Gulka and I accepted you into our family, otherwise you'd be living all alone!"

'Gulka is their daughter – my niece.'

With this t!. second day of *The Women's Decameron* ended, and the stories about the seduced and abandoned were over. For the morrow it was resolved to tell stories about sex in ridiculous situations.

Meanwhile the nurses brought the babies, and, forgetting about everything else in the world, our storytellers set about feeding them.

THE THIRD DAY

in which are recounted stories about

Sex in Farcical Situations

Story One

by Larissa, doctor of biology, who, like last time, got off lightly with an anecdote – which seemed to have become a rule with her.

'I'll tell you an anecdote from the war years. I may well have heard it as a child, but of course I understood it only much later.

'In one detachment of partisans the stores had run out. So one guy offered to go off to his own village and get some food from his wife. It was winter. He got on to his skis and set off. Next day he returned with a sack. He sat down by the fire and took out a chunk of lard.

' "Well, lads, I came up to my hut in the night time and I knocked on the window. The wife came out on to the porch. Whoever guesses the very first thing I did gets a bit of lard."

The partisans started guessing: "Hugged and kissed her?"
' "No."
' "Asked how the children were?"
' "No."
' "Asked for something to eat?"
' "No."
'Then one man said: "You fucked her right there on the porch!"
' "Right, you got it. Have a piece of lard. And whoever guesses what I did next gets a couple of pickles."
'They began guessing what he did next.
' "Now you asked about the children?"
' "No."
' "Went into the house?"
' "No."

70

' "Looked about to see if there was any danger?"

' "No."

'Once again the same man's deep voice came: "You fucked her again."

' "Right. Take your two pickles. And whoever guesses what I did next gets a bottle of moonshine!"

'All the partisans shouted in chorus: "Fucked her again!"

' "Wrong. I took off my skis."

It was now Zina the tramp's turn, but she was laughing so much over the anecdote that she asked instead to go last.

Natasha volunteered to go next because her story fitted in with the anecdote.

Story Two

by the engineer Natasha, testifying to the fact that in peace time even the partisan's method of lovemaking can be put to shame and outstripped.

'My husband got interested in photography. That, I can assure you, is no joy for a wife. Apart from the fact that I can't get into the bathroom at night, that all the windows are plastered with drying photographs, that the bottles of chemicals make the whole kitchen stink, I even have to serve as his model!

'A few years ago he became interested in "nude life" pictures and took me naked in all sorts of romantic poses: as a mermaid on a river bank, or a lizard on a stone. He fantasized to his heart's content. Often he would take me into the forest for these sessions. Once he was preparing a study called "Spring". We arrived in the forest in early spring, with snow still on the ground and just the very first little leaves appearing. He selected a suitable place among some birch trees and while I stood naked and shivering, he looked around for a place to put me. "Over there under the birch there's a suitable hump, stand on it!" he said.

'I went up to it and had a look. "Vitya! That's not a hump, It's an ant-hill. Ants scare the hell out of me!"

' "Don't be silly, they're still asleep."

'So I got up on to the ant-hill. At first there were no ants to be seen, but they soon came to life under my feet and started crawling up my legs.

' "Vitya! They're crawling over me and biting me!"

' "Hold on a minute! I've got a great shot! Just a couple more and I'm through!"

'I danced up and down with him swearing at me: "What's the matter, can't you stick it out for the sake of art?"

'I yelled and jumped down off that "hump" because those ants had reached certain parts that it is not nice to mention by name in other company, not this company of course!

'Another time he had another idea for a nude study, this time called "Winter". He took a bottle of vodka in his knapsack to warm me up after the session, and a warm blanket to wrap me up in immediately, and we set off into the forest on our skis. He found a suitable place among some huge snowdrifts and white trees, ordered me to get undressed and stand among them on my skis, which I did. There he was, taking photographs, clicking away and growling with satisfaction: "Brilliant!"

'He clicked away half a film, with me shouting at him from my spot: "That's enough! Give me a break, will you?"

'At this point Vitya rushed up to me on his skis, took the bottle of vodka out of his knapsack, threw the blanket round me and rubbed me down with it, all the time saying: "Well done my beauty! That'll be a fantastic work!"

'I got warmed up a little, at least the worst chills were over.

' "Give me my clothes, Vitya! Quickly!"

' "No, don't get dressed yet."

' "Wha-at? More photographs?"

' "No, not this time."

'Then he performed what the partisan had done, without taking off his skis ...

'The study "Winter" took first prize at the regional amateur photographers' exhibition. Now it hangs on our sitting-room wall, together with the first prize certificate: the snowy forest, the snow-drifts, and among them the delicate outline of a white female body – the symbol of winter. Sometimes Vitya and I look at that photograph and have a laugh as we recall our "study on skis". Now when I get home I shall tell him Larissa's anecdote straightaway!'

It was now the turn of Valentina to tell a story. She was obviously embarrassed to begin and sat in bed playing with her long pigtail, the hairdo she had adopted for the maternity hospital instead of her usual fancy topknot.

Story Three

by Valentina, the bigwig, revealing the mystery of Khrushchev's downfall.

'Now you women, especially you, Galina, keep giving me suspicious looks as though I wasn't a normal woman but a Communist Manifesto in a skirt. Well I take offence at that, I really do. Don't think that we people working in the upper echelons haven't noticed how the people's attitude towards us has changed. You ride in the tram and you hear someone say: "Why are you pushing, are you a communist or something." Or in a shop someone says: "Get in the queue, communists aren't allowed to go to the front here. You should have gone to the front in the war!"

'But there are decent people among us, just as anywhere else, and we know how to have a joke, too. So I'm going to tell the story of how I had intimate relations with Nikita Sergeevich Khrushchev on the eve of his downfall. You didn't expect that, did you? Only please, if you're going to repeat this to anyone else, don't mention me by name or the town where I live. Agreed? Right, listen.

'My husband and I often get sent to the provinces to check on local work. We try to arrange it so that we go together: it's better for the peace of mind, and it saves money. One time we were sent to a certain regional centre. We arrived, and there was some sort of sporting festival going on, so all the hotels were fully booked and all the dormitories in town full. The chairman of the regional soviet invited us to stay with him. We spent a week in the passage of his flat, and there were no opportunities for us to fulfil our marital obligations. I was all right, I can last out, but Pavel was climbing the wall. Well, I thought to myself,

73

we've got to find a solution to this one. The wife of the chairman of the regional executive committee was in charge of the local club. So I said to her: "Masha, don't you have some quiet little room in the club where my husband and I could spend an hour or so together?"

'So Masha gave me the keys to the club and told me where to find a room with a sofa. Pavel and I set off. We went into the club and looked for the room where the sofa was supposed to be. Pavel could hardly last out another minute. I opened a door: wrong one. There was no sofa, but a lot of picture frames, posters, and portraits leaning against the wall – it was obviously an artist's studio. My husband threw his coat down on the floor, me on to the coat, and got to work. He's working away, putting his heart and soul in to it, and I'm having a pretty good time too ... Suddenly – crash! a sort of shield thing falls right on top of us. He stops for a moment, looks round, tries to shake the shield off his back, but it won't come off, it just rocks up and down with his movements.

' "To hell with it!" barks my husband, "let it stay there!" and like a tortoise beneath its shell finishes his business under the shield. Only then did he throw it off, got to his feet, did himself up, and then took hold of the shield to put it back in its place. Suddenly he burst out laughing: "Valentina, look who you've been making love with today!"

'I looked – it was a portrait of our General Secretary, Nikita Sergeevich Khrushchev.

'Don't laugh yet, women. Next morning we suddenly have continuous music playing – you know, just as if some important statesman had died. My husband jokes in a whisper: "Valentina! What if the General Secretary died after having it off with you? You're quite hot stuff, you know, and he's no spring chicken any more ..."

'They went on churning out the music and torturing the citizens, and then they announced Khrushchev's removal from office. Can you imagine how hard it was for us to keep a straight face at that news?'

Valentina finished her story amid general merriment.

'So, we have a terrorist among us!' laughed Galina the dissident, noticeably warming towards Valentina.

Valentina turned redder than the Soviet flag, but the

women's laughter obviously delighted her.

Now Albina began her story.

Story Four

*by the airhostess Albina, about how with Albina's help an
American agent got his leg over three KGB men.*

'I once worked for a while at the Hotel Europa. In what
position, you ask, Zina? In all positions. I was working with
foreigners. There were ten of us girls, each with a telephone,
and when we were needed they contacted us directly and
told us exactly when to be there. Of course, the guys from
the KGB were watching everything. In fact we were
invaluable to them: we would entertain our clients if their
room needed to be searched or the tape changed in the tape
recorder, by getting them into conversation and all that sort
of stuff. We weren't paid by the KGB – the foreign client
took care of all the bills. And you didn't argue with those
KGB guys: step out of line, and you were out on the street!
We already have loads of prostitutes on the streets, and I for
one was not turned on by the idea of doing business with
our own general public: they're either drunkards, or savages,
or they're people on business trips with no money. Not at all
like a clean little foreigner in a de luxe suite, complete with
restaurant, gifts, and European manners! But, of course, we
were all on the KGB's books and had signed a pledge to carry
out all their requests. And we did – that goes without
saying.

'One day our porter summoned me: "There's an important
assignment for you, Albinochka," he whispered. "Go to
room 13, they'll give you your instructions there."

'Room 13 was the KGB's headquarters; that was where
they kept their equipment and sat when they were on duty.
I went in. There was an important looking type sitting
there, I'd never seen him in the hotel before; and with him
there were three young, robust secret policemen. The first
type scowled at me: "That one?"

'I answered by lowering my eyes and looking rather
bashful. After all, I know what these guys go for. He

mumbled: "All right, maybe she'll do. I still think Captain Lebedeva would have been more suitable . . . We ought to increase the size of her group so that we don't get these gaps and have to send out the first person we can get hold of on important assignments. Well, give the girl her instructions."

'They explained the job to me: an important American had arrived and was staying for one day. They needed to search his baggage, but he didn't leave his room for more than half an hour at a time. So I had to sit down next to him at supper and keep him in the restaurant as long as possible. Meanwhile these three guys would search the room. I was shown a photograph of the client and told to remember it and toddle along to the restaurant. He was supposed to appear for dinner quite soon. I nodded, gave the old guy another smile to be on the safe side, and floated down to the restaurant.

'The head waiter immediately came up to me in the restaurant, led me over to an empty table, sat me down and started suggesting in French a "light supper, not too burdensome, good for the figure", at the same time nodding at the next table, which was also empty, to indicate that that's where he was going to put my client. He just brought a bit of supper for appearances, the swine: cheese, olives, and a glass of wine. I could have had a better meal off my own lipstick. Well, I sat there, sipping my wine and waiting. Half an hour later my client appeared, a handsome type. I could see there were obviously no flies on him and quickly decided there was no point in acting the Soviet society lady with him – he would cotton on straightaway that I was a plant. So I decided to be brazen and get him that way: I stared at him, and when he looked up at me I gave him the most obvious wink from behind my glass. He laughed and beckoned me over. I got up, bluffed my way over to his table, bent down to him and said: "Is Monsieur feeling lonely?"

'Then something happened that I didn't expect at all. Without saying a word he chucks a ten-rouble note on to the table, grabs me by the hand and leads me out of the restaurant. I signal to the head waiter who's gone as white as a sheet and is mouthing at me to stop him. But how are you supposed to stop the sort who doesn't go for frills, but just drags you straight up to his room to get on with it. As we were leaving the restaurant I noticed the head waiter rush over to a telephone in the corner to warn the people who were digging around in the room. He must have got to them in time: we came into the room, and there was no one there. My client picked me up, slung me on to the bed, and started tearing off his own clothes. I came crashing down on to the bed and almost yelled out: my bum had landed on some hard lump. I felt around quietly and realized that it was in fact someone's head. Obviously the KGB guy had crawled under the bed. My client jumped on to the bed, we began making love, and I could feel with my bum that it wasn't just one head under the bed, but three: the lumps kept popping up in different places. There clearly wasn't room for them under there, they didn't know where to stick their heads. I can't imagine what it was like for them while we bounced around on the bed. Afterwards he got up and went into the bathroom. I opened the door into the corridor and whispered to the guys stuck under the bed: "Get out quick while he's having a shower!"

'The three of them scrambled out from under the bed, each one angrier than the last. "Just you wait, you bitch!" they hissed, "you'll do time for betraying your country!" And out they went . . .

'Well, of course, they couldn't pin any betrayal on me – they didn't have a reason. But that was the end of my work at the Europa. I wasn't particulary sorry, because two or three months later all our girls were given the boot. I think a KGB brigade took their place so that they wouldn't have any more funny business like they had with me. I saw that Captain Lebedeva earlier on. She was OK, a pretty mug and everything. They wouldn't have made her captain for nothing. But I don't envy her; we're in the same business, but she's there because of her rank and I'm my own boss. But that American I was with – I don't know whether he was a spy or not, but we screwed three KGB guys and that was a real "kaif" for me. I can't stand those types, girls, and I think we all feel the same. They're always trying to get something out of you cheap, and if anything happens they turn up their noses as if we were worse scum than them. We pinch the clients' papers, learn our lines and have conversation with them, take them wherever we're told, and the only reward we get is that we don't get chucked out of the hotel. But these guys get the medals, the pay, the respect. Look at all the films about the secret police. But not one about how many girls slog their guts out for each secret policeman! That's why I'm glad we really screwed them. Justice was done at least once!'

Albina's story provoked many questions from the women: what sort of equipment was in the rooms for foreigners, do they ever guess that they are under KGB surveillance, and so on. Albina did indeed prove to be very well informed about these matters, and everyone listened attentively, especially Galina who then told her story.

Story Five

by Galina the dissident, containing one of the very many methods of passing information from camp to the outside.

'This happened at my third meeting with Slava, after we had already been married in the camp. I came to see him for three days as usual, bringing food and greetings from friends. I was taken into the meeting room. I was beside myself with happiness. I tried to give that little cell a homely look: I put flowers into a jar and laid the fruit out on the table, and kept looking at the door and listening for footsteps in the corridor. Finally they brought him in. What those first minutes of a camp meeting are like I can't convey to you, much as I would like to, because I was never able to remember them afterwards – it was always total loss of consciousness from joy and pity.

'Later, when Slavik and I had calmed down a bit and recovered, and I had had time to feed him up a bit, I noticed that he was worried by something

' "What's happened, darling?"

' "Well, it's just that I've not been able to get a certain message out because there's a really fierce son-of-a-bitch on duty today."

' "But don't you know it by heart?"

78

' "I do, but you won't be able to learn it in three days. There haven't been any meetings for a long time and a lot of information has piled up."

' "Well, can't I write it down if you tell me it?"

' "How are you going to write it down here? We both know that these meeting rooms are watched. And you'd need to do at least four pages in small writing."

' "Well, let's think of something."

'Basically, what we thought up was this. We would get up in the morning, have a quick snack, and then get back into bed. I let down my hair – you can see it's quite thick, lay on top of my husband and shook my head so that my hair covered both our heads, and under that cover I wrote, leaning on Slava's chest while he dictated. It was hard to write: not just because I had to fit a huge amount of information on four small exercise book pages of squared paper, but also because Slava was rocking me up and down so that our love-making would look more authentic. Of course, they looked in at us from time to time, but they didn't suspect us of anything except sexual prowess. In fact, when I was leaving the camp after the three days, they could have searched me from top to bottom if they'd had any suspicions, but none of them even thought of frisking me.

'Apart from the politics, I also brought our little son away from that meeting!'

The women laughed at the ruses of the dissidents, and Olga remarked: 'So your son was made under dictation? Well, he'll be politically minded like his parents . . . There's no hurry, nothing sensible is going to happen in Russia before our children grow up. So, now I'll tell you how my husband and I arranged things when we were living in the dormitory.'

Story Six

by the worker Olga, about how she and her husband lacked the opportunity to lead a normal married life, until a brainwave released them from their misery.

'I've already told you that I married a workmate from our yard. Well . . . They gave us a wedding at the yard, a Komsomol one in the Red Corner. After the wedding was over Misha and I had nowhere to go, nowhere to take our wedding presents – a coffee service and bed linen. We were both living in the same dormitory, only he was in the men's section and I was in the women's. One day went by, two days, a week – and we were as good as unmarried: we met after work, went to the cinema together or the park of culture and rest, or just visited friends. Everything was fine – only one thing was missing: a double bed. In the park we hugged and kissed until our bones ached and our lips were swollen, then we would return gloomily to our separate rooms in the dormitory. The management promised to find us a room, but you could be drawing an old age pension and they'd still be promising. It was a real hell for us.

'In our dormitory, we had a TV which the women had clubbed together to buy. One day it went on the blink and started showing nothing but snowflakes. Just then Misha came in to get me. He looked at the screen and said: "Something's wrong with the aerial, I'll go up on to the roof."

'Off he went, with me after him. We climbed out of the attic window on to the roof, and Misha immediately saw what was wrong and fixed the aerial. I sat nearby, watching him work. He finished the job and sat down next to me. And there we stayed admiring the view of the town in the evening: lights all around down below, the air above almost as clean as in the countryside, and best of all – no one else around. As we sat there, Misha said to me: "This is the first time we've been together away from people. What better time and place to start our married life!"

'He threw off his jacket, tucked it under me, and for the first time we felt like husband and wife together. It was terrific! Nobody next to us or through the wall, just the trams tinkling below and the stars twinkling above.

'And that was how it went from that day on: as soon as it got dark Misha came knocking at my door, and I was always ready. I would grab my blanket which was in a bag under my bed, and we would go up to the attic, and then to our place on the roof. We both became calmer and more cheerful. The only thing we were sorry about was that summer would soon be over, and then where? But, in fact, our bliss ended even sooner.

'One day I was standing in our communal kitchen frying potatoes for Misha and me. We had planned to eat in my room and then go up... Into the kitchen came our cleaning woman, Shura. I should tell you that she lived right up near the roof; the door to her cubby-hole was next to the attic door. So she appeared and in front of the whole kitchen announced: "Oh, it's you, Olga! I've been wanting to have a word with you for a long time. Explain something to me, my dear. What you and your husband do above my head on the roof I know full well, I was young myself once. But why does it make such a din, like two skeletons having it off on a sheet of metal? That's what I can't understand. You look quite chubby, so where do you get all those bones from? The first time I heard it I was going to see the doctor and tell him I heard thunder all evening when the sky was clear. Then I saw the little love-nest on the roof!"

'All the women in the dormitory almost split their sides when they heard all this. It was a laugh for them, but tears for me. Misha and I didn't go up on the roof any more, we stuck it out till spring, when the yard finally gave us a room. A nice room, fiften square metres. Now at least I have somewhere to take my son.'

On hearing Olga's story the women expressed sympathy for all such homeless married couples, and Valentina said that in their executive committee they were trying to decide whether young married couples caught in the act in doorways by the militia and voluntary police, should be deemed to have committed a public order offence. So far they hadn't reached a decision.

Nelya added that even in communal flats these things were quite complicated, and she told her own story as evidence.

Story Seven

by the music teacher Nelya, adding an unexpected Leningrad detail to Galsworthy's Forsyte Saga.

'One could say that Borya and I did not have a problem with living quarters. We had a furniture problem.

'Borya swapped rooms with my uncle who lived through the wall from me. On his ten metres we put Lenusya and were happy: not many people can give their child a separate corner. We slept in my room which was also our common room. During the daytime Lenusya spent most of the time with us, only going to her room to do her homework or go to bed. Our family life settled down happily in no time, except that a problem arose with the sofa. After our wedding we bought a stylish convertible sofa, and it turned out to be musical. At first Borya joked: "Just like the mistress of the house!"

'But it became no joking matter. Through the other wall lived my aunt, an old maid. She was good-natured, but terribly inquisitive about everything to do with marital relations. The walls in the flat were thin, plywood virtually. If my aunt coughed, we could hear it. In the daytime if Borya sneezed, my aunt would shout through the wall: "Bless you, Boris!"

'So how were we supposed to conduct our conjugal life on a musical sofa with such thin walls? And yet we found a solution – Borya thought it up. In the evening we sent Lenusya off to bed in her room, then we turned the TV on loud and played our own symphony on the sofa to the noise of the TV.

'One time they started to broadcast *The Forsyte Saga*, a serial in several parts. We switched on the TV and as we opened out our sofa so as to make love the serial was just beginning. The next day I was walking down the corridor when my aunt stopped me and asked: "How did last night's episode end, dear? I didn't see it all because I fell asleep."

'I hadn't seen any of it so I had to tell her I had fallen asleep too.

' "Well, it doesn't matter," she replied. "When Boris gets back from work I'll ask him."

'I had to run out and ring up some friends from a telephone box to find out who saw the film that night and how it ended, so that I could warn Borya in time. Neither of us wanted to offend my aunt, or let her little mind do overtime.'

It was now Emma's turn, and she began her story.

Story Eight

by the theatre director Emma, on the question of how difficult it is for innovations in theatrical production to be accepted on a conservative stage.

'I'll tell you about how the artist Alyosha and I – you remember, I told you about him on the first day? – accidentally introduced an innovative moment into a Shakespeare play.

'It was at one of the first performances of *Romeo and Juliet*. The fever pitch of the first night had died down, certain details had needed smoothing out, but on the whole the play had come off well and was running successfully. Young spectators were cramming the hall, coming in from neighbouring towns and from a large building site not far away. And that was the time when my romance with Alyosha was at its height. He was having his first serious relationship with a woman, and the boy had completely lost his head, and so had I, for that matter. We would exchange a look in the middle of the day, and immediately rush off to his place or to mine, there was no stopping us. Sometimes we made it right there in the theatre somewhere. And that's how we very nearly came unstuck.

'Like all young directors I couldn't do without innovations. The scene where Romeo and Juliet say goodbye after their wedding night I had them play against a background of Juliet's dishevelled bed. The artistic council tried to make me at least have the bed made up, but I insisted on the "loving disorder". So, the performance was just approaching this scene when Alyosha and I were seized by another amorous fever. We had a revolving stage, so the scenery was prepared in advance on the revolving part. We decided to make use of Juliet's bed, which at that moment was behind the scenes in darkness. We threw ourselves on to the bed and forgot about the world. The previous act ended, the lights went down on the stage and the scene change began. I had another innovation, too: the scene changes took place with the curtain up. The stage was dark, and in the darkness the spectator could just make out the scenery of the next scene. Well, as you have already guessed, the stage started moving, and Alyosha and I solemnly came out on stage, lying on Juliet's bed. The young spectators went wild with delight and began to applaud, but our props man was horrified and instead of quietly lowering the curtain he pressed the wrong button and with a clank and a crash the iron safety curtain came down. But the young Soviet spectators had got the message: they were being kept away from freedom of speech in theatrical art by the iron curtain! At this point such an ovation began as I have never heard before or after at any of my plays. Alyosha and I hopped off Juliet's bed in the dark and ran for it! Fortunately no one recognized us and I even gave a general reprimand after the play, holding "whoever it was" up to shame! Well, what else could I do?

'The legend of my innovation even reached Leningrad, but in Leningrad I told our theatre-lovers the truth about what had happened. And what do you think, Goga Tovstonogova really took a fancy to that trick and they copied it in the theatre on Liteyny, although somewhat toned down: in a play about students, when the hero and heroine are alone in their tent, two spots of light have intercourse on the backdrop. Very impressive. But of course we were much more daring in our play.'

Story Nine

by Irishka, who like the others suffered from problems with living conditions, till she managed to find a way out of the situation.

'When my husband and I were married we didn't have our own place either. We had to live with my sister, her husband and daughter, and our mother. Six people in a room of thirty-two square metres. They wouldn't register my husband with us because he was already registered in his dormitory, which gave us six metres each and they didn't even put us on the waiting list. They just said: "Find a swop!"

'But where are you going to find someone who'll swop two rooms for one? You'd have to throw in a lot of money, and how were we to find that? We weren't too bothered in the daytime because we all got on well together. But it was hard at night, as you can understand. And so Seryozha and I came up with a way of being alone together at least once a week, on Sundays. We bought my niece a tricycle. As soon as my mother had gone off to the kitchen to cook dinner, we popped my niece on to her tricycle and into the corridor, and got down to business. So did my sister and her husband; they were behind a cupboard, we were behind a screen. We were all adults, so we managed somehow to get used to it and not be embarrassed. The main thing was that we didn't have either Mum or Gulka in the room.

'It was a big flat, and everybody was unusually good about children. Kids would be racing up and down the corridor on bikes for days on end and no one said anything; and even if there was a collision, the children weren't scolded. It was the children themselves who soon revealed the secret of this general tolerance. I was coming out of the bathroom one morning in my dressing gown and little Vovochka, the neighbour's little boy, came running up to me: "Aunt Ira, are you going back to bed with Uncle Seryozha now?"

' "Why do you ask that, Vovochka?"

' "Because my parents have just gone to bed, and so have Yura's, so I thought Gulya would be coming out to play on her trike." '

'Life's such a bag of shit!' exclaimed Olga after Irishka's story. 'It's not life, it's one long anecdote! But you've got to laugh to survive, haven't you?'

On the whole almost everyone agreed with her. The women sighed a little, and then recalled that Zina the tramp had not yet told her story. They asked her to begin, which she did.

Story Ten

by Zina the tramp, a story by her own definition 'funny as hell', though for some reason nobody laughed except Zina herself, and she laughed without mirth.

'Something happened to me, girls, that was as funny as hell, about nine months ago with this pigeon I met. It all started

85

when they let me out of camp at the end of my time. I'd done a year near here in Sablino for "infringement of passport regulations". When they let me go they gave me a certificate of release and ten roubles for the road, but I had nowhere to go. There was no way I could go back to my mother in the country. That road was closed the first time I landed in the zone: they found out about it in the village and the woman gave my mother a hard time and all the tongues were wagging over me. I couldn't settle in Leningrad, the place was already crawling with people like me with nowhere to live. But I stopped off here anyway and decided to visit some of my old mates. Maybe they'll help me out, I thought. But that was a dead end. Some were inside themselves, others turned their noses up at me. I wandered around like that for a day, spent the night on Moskovsky Station, and next day I just didn't know where to go. I thought of calling on one old lady I knew who lived on Kryukov Canal. I knocked at her door, and the neighbours said: "The old lady's dead, they burried her a month ago."

'I came away from there, and walked along the canal thinking, why don't I just hop straight into the water? The ice looks nice and thin, so I'll probably go through! I was quite envious that my old lady friend had finished all her suffering, while I had to hang around for God knows how long. I leaned over the railing looking at the dark ice, and my head felt heavier and heavier, just like there was a big rock growing inside it. It kept pulling me down towards the water, and I held on to the railing so as not to get pulled in. Suddenly I heard bells ringing close by, ever so pure sounding, like waking up on a bright morning. And my head seemed to get lighter. I turned and walked away from the water, looking about to see where the church was where the bells were ringing. I saw a bell-tower above the trees, blue and gold, and started walking towards it. I saw a little old woman going in the same direction, then a second and a third . . . I joined up with one of them and asked: "Hey, Gran, what's going on in the church today?"

' "Don't you know? Today is Holy Thursday, the people are going to confession. Are you without the cross, that you don't know that?"

'I sure was without the cross, my cross got ripped off five years ago when the militia picked me up drunk. I always meant to get a new one, but never got round to it. I couldn't remember when I was last in a church. Well Zinka, I thought, the water can wait; first pop into the church, and then the Kryukov Canal won't be so scary.

'I must have stuck out like a sore thumb going into God's Temple; I couldn't even remember how to cross myself, let alone pray. So I reckoned I would just follow my old woman and do whatever she did and go wherever she went. She bought a candle, so I bought two: I had a cartload of sins, so I should have bought the whole crate. But the only crates I ever bought were crates of vodka when we went around with the gang . . .

'My old woman went off to the left where there was a whole crowd of people standing, and above them a priest was going on about something. I set myself up there too, and started listening. But I didn't get much of it, because my head still felt weak and that rock was still buzzing away inside, though it had got a bit lighter. Next to me the old woman whispered: "Father, I have sinned!", crossed herself and bowed down. I copied her, because I was a sinner too, so I bowed down and crossed myself.

'I can't remember anything about the service, but it didn't seem anything like in our village when we still had a church. And then suddenly I heard the priest forgiving us all our sins! I asked my old woman: "What's going on, Gran? How can he forgive all our sins together? We've all got different sins, yours are like a pea, and mine are probably the size of a mountain . . ."

' "Never mind, dear! We are all equal before the Lord, that's why the confession was a general one. Did you repent and say 'Father, I have sinned'? Well, you are forgiven. Now come with me to communion."

'I followed the old woman and took communion. I stood there rooted to the spot, even forgetting to tell the priest my name.

' "What is your name?"

' "Zinka . . ."

' "Before the Lord you are Zinaida, so do not grieve the saint whose name you bear! Zinaida, servant of God, I give you the sacrament of communion . . ."

'So I took communion. When I walked back, feeling warm inside from the wine, that's when it got to me. Down I went on to my knees, in floods of tears. Whether it was the communion wine that went to my head, or just that my soul was all turned inside out, I don't know. I knelt there, crying away, and old women walked round me, not touching me, saying: "See how sincerely she prays!"

'I lifted up my head, and there was the Virgin and Child painted on an icon above me. She was looking as if she felt sorry for me. So I complained to her: "Why doesn't your Son give me any sort of life, a woman's life or a man's life? You ought to tell Him . . ."

'The service ended and everyone left the church, including me. I came out and sat down on a little seat in the churchyard, and I wiped away my stupid tears. Then the same little old woman sat down beside me. "I've been looking at you, dear, and I see things are bad for you. You could tell me about it, perhaps I can help you."

'Well, her kind words got to me and I gave her the whole story. So my old woman said to me: "I'm alone, I have my own house in Luga. Come to me tomorrow. I'll register you with me, and then we'll see if we can find you a job. Why should a Christian soul perish in the Kryukov Canal! I'm staying with my sister today, but I'll be going home tomorrow morning, so you come in time for dinner. Remember this address."

'The old woman gave me her address, I memorized it, and we split up.

'Don't be annoyed that it's such a long story, girls. The funny part begins soon.

'Me and the old woman split up, and I thought I'd go to Luga right then. Better to spend the night on the station there than have the pigs bothering me here. I bought myself a French loaf at the baker's, a bottle of kefir at the dairy, and two hundred grams of sausage at the grocer's, and with that I went off to the station. I got in the train, laid out all my stuff on the table, and started eating. I hadn't eaten anything for a day so I was famished. The train was almost empty. No one tried to sit near me, I had that look about me. But at the first stop, still in Leningrad, this bearded type got in and came straight over to me.

' "Excuse me, is this seat free?"

' "Help yourself . . ."

I looked quickly at him, and knew at once he was another

zek, same as me. His black coat hung on him like a sack, his face was white as chalk, and he had this really short hair sticking out under his cap.

' "I see you're just out of the zone too?"

'He smiled. "Quite correct, I have just been released from prison."

'Oho, I think, prison! Must be some big-time operator – he talks more like an academic than a zek. I shoved my bread and sausage over towards him and started drinking the bottle of milk.

' "There you are, have something!"

' "Oh, no, thank you. I'm not hungry."

' "Not good enough for you? Go on, eat! Look how skinny you are, you look like death warmed up. If you're not hungry, then just keep me company!"

' "All right, just to keep you company."

'He broke off a piece of bread put a tiny bit of sausage on it, and ate it, all neat and tidy.

' "How long ago did you get out of the zone?" he asked.

' "Yesterday."

' "And where are you staying?"

' "Nowhere."

' "What do you mean? Where are you going now?"

'What a day! I started confessing in the morning, and now I couldn't stop: I told him everything, didn't keep anything back. But this time no crying, I keep my cool in front of a man. Only when I got to the bit about the church a couple of tears came. I could see his eyes looked a bit wet too. And when I finished my story he said: "You know, there's no point in spending the night on the station, it's dangerous with your camp papers. If it doesn't embarrass you, I invite you to come and stay with me. It's a bit cramped, one little room, but the flat has a bath. You can wash, rest, and then tomorrow go happily off to your old woman."

'Of course I was happy about this break. Not that I felt like running around with a man on a day like this, but I certainly didn't want to end up with the militia!

'We got to Luga and he took me to his place. His room was small all right, more like a little boxroom. One wall was nothing but shelves, and the books went right up to the ceiling; the other wall had the sofa and table, and that's all there was. His clothes hung on nails in the corner. He sat me down on the sofa and went off to run the bath and make tea.

'Well, girls, I had a good scrub and soak after the camp, and I felt I'd been born again. I did my washing at the same time, of course. After that we sat down together and had tea and a long heart-to-heart. Funny thing: I'm an uneducated tramp, and he's got brains and was inside just because of his education. For the truth, in other words. Once for three years, then he did eight. The last couple of years he did in a penalty isolator – he didn't get on with the bosses. And I'm giving him my life story, from childhood on, just as though I had to give a full confession instead of this morning's general one. So we listened to each other and felt sorry for each other till night-time. I've never been so open with a man before, and we didn't even have vodka, just tea...Come bedtime, he beds down in the corner on his camp jacket and puts a coat over him, and even though I objected, he put me to bed on his sofa on clean sheets. And still we went on talking. I don't even remember what we talked about. It wasn't happy talk, it was all about life. But I could feel tears of joy collecting in my heart like a bucket filling up. Then I said to him: "Why do you have to sleep down there in the corner? You may be brainy and all, but to me you're still a zek, so let's drop the formalities. Come on over here. Or I'll feel hurt."

'He got into bed with me and I put my arms round him, and I felt so sorry for the two of us that I started blubbering like a baby. I don't even remember what happened between us then. Only it was good with him, girls, just like there had never been anyone before him. And I remember his eyes were wet too, it wasn't just me that turned on the waterworks. Funny, isn't it? You don't think it's funny yet? Well, wait, now comes the real laugh.

'We got up in the morning, and he suddenly said: "Forgive me Zina, I should have said this to you yesterday. But since things have turned out the way they have I'll say it now. I want you to be my wife."

' "Are you crazy? Just think who you are and who I am!"

' "But he covers my mouth with his hand and kisses me on the eyes.

' "You don't know yourself who you are. I know better than you, and that's why I'm asking you to be my wife."

'I couldn't follow his brainy argument at all. I thought he was out of his mind. It was all so wacky... Then he had to go to work, and he says to me: "Zina, can you cook dinner for us today? Here's some money, and the shop is in the next building. Here's the key to my room, here's the flat key. I'll warn my neighbour that my wife has arrived, so make yourself at home. I'll be back at five."

'He just tipped all that on my head and left for work. Well, I sat there for a while, then I went into the kitchen to meet the neighbour. It was OK, she was nice to me, showed me where his kitchen table was, explained where the shop was, and the market. I went to both, then I rolled up my sleeves and started on the housework. While dinner was cooking I washed his floor, found his clothes and washed them too. Then I had a bite to eat and sat down to wait for him to get back from work. I waited and waited, and then I suddenly realized I had to get away from there. He was a good man, I couldn't go fouling up his life. I grabbed my bag, chucked the keys on the table and I was out through the door. And just as I banged the door behind me I remembered I'd left the piece of paper with the old woman's address on the table, because I was showing it to him the day before. I rang the neighbour's bell but she must have been out somewhere. So I walked to the station and the same evening I left Luga and went to Vologda where I had a friend from our village working on a building site. And that is the funny story I wanted to tell you.'

'Yes... I'll die laughing...', said Olga, shaking her head. 'Unless you dreamed that whole thing up to make an interesting story, you're a hopeless idiot to run away from a man like that! What must he have thought of you when he got back?'

'What should he think? I left him his dinner in the kitchen, borshch and cutlets. I put the change from the shop and the market on the table where he would see it. He couldn't think anything bad of me.'

'Zina, was his name Igor Mikhaylovich?' asked Galina.

'Yes! But how did you know? I didn't say his name.'

'It's just that I know that man well. I still wouldn't have been quite sure if you hadn't said when he'd been

91

in camp. When you did, I knew exactly who you were talking about. Aren't you sorry now that you left him?'

'Why should I be? I've got a son now, I'm just about a family.'

'Wait a moment!' said Albina, jumping up on her bed. 'You started off by saying that all this was nine months ago. So your son is from that night, is he?'

'So?'

'Oh, you fool!'

Galina looked steadily at Zina.

'By the way, Zina, Igor is still living alone.'

Zina suddenly jumped out of bed and seized her dressing gown and cigarettes. 'Go to hell, girls! I wanted to tell you about some of the crazy types there are and give you something to laugh at, and you ... Well, I'm off for a smoke. To hell with these stories of ours!'

And Zina went to the corridor, singing loudly and defiantly:

> 'Leningrad jail
> Is a well-worn stair!
> I was nicked by Article
> One Four Four!'

And with this song ended the third day of *The Women's Decameron*.

THE FOURTH DAY

which is devoted to

Bitches

The morning of the fourth day commenced with the arrival of the duty cleaning woman, Fedosya Polikarpovna, complete with bucket, cloth and mop to begin washing the ward floor. Out of the pocket of her gown stuck a grey cloth which she passed along the backs of the beds and over the stools. All the time she kept grumbling at the women: 'Look how they just lie around! They've brought more poverty into the world and yet they're happy ... And I've got to clean up after them for seventy roubles ...'

The women got the message and passed Fedosya three roubles. The grumbling stopped, but so did the cleaning: the sly old fox immediately gathered up her equipment and set off to do the next ward.

'The bitch! Where do people like that come from?' sighed Emma.

'Life makes them that way,' replied Zina the tramp.

'The perfect prelude for this evening!' said Larissa. 'Why don't we tell stories about all the real bitches we've known?'

So the day passed, and when evening came, Larissa was the first to tell her story.

Story One

by Larissa. An anecdote again, but this time an ancient Chinese one, from which one may conclude that the bitch is both a historical and a universal phenomenon.

'The peasant Li was working in the paddy field. Suddenly he saw a crowd of people from his village approaching, waving their arms and shouting something. Li raised his head, sighed and continued working. The villagers ran up to him and shouted: "Are you deaf? Your wife went into the forest to collect brushwood and a tiger attacked her!"

' "Well, it's his own fault. The tiger attacked her – let him get out of it himself. I've got to get this paddy finished before my wife gets back or she'll tear me to pieces." '

'The Chinese have a strong brand of bitchiness!' commented Zina. 'But I'll tell you, girls – men are mostly to blame for women turning that way. Now I'll tell you about two of my friends who were in the zone with me.'

Story Two

by Zina about two rivals who eliminated the object of their rivalry.

'We had two girls in our zone who had been accomplices together. They both got three years and both worked as cleaners in the camp hospital. Before their crime, they were studying to be doctors at a medical institute. Only now they'll never be doctors because they used their medical knowledge for wicked female revenge. Here's their story.

'They got friendly as students and shared everything. You know what student life is like – one of them soon got a boyfriend who declared his love for her, wanted to marry her and all the rest. Soon the other girl got her own lover, and she was getting ready to go to the registry office too. The two girls lived in a student hostel and took turns to meet their boyfriends, because to save money they only had one smart pair of shoes between them. In the evening they would tell each other how they spent the time with their lovers.

'Well, to come to the point, they both got themselves pregnant about the same time. They were both healthy girls, and they wanted to go ahead and have babies. And then one told the other her boyfriend was asking her to get an abortion; he was trying to get her to wait before having a child because he said this wasn't the time. It was the same story with the other girl. But what really surprised the two friends was that their boyfriends both said exactly the same words to them about the abortion. So one said to the other: "Listen. There's something funny going on here: our boyfriends both have the same name, they say the same things to both of us, and we take turns to go out with them. I'm getting suspicious: have we both got the same boyfriend?"

'They decided to check it out. One set off to meet him in her going-out shoes, and the other followed in her slippers. And it turned out, my friends, that it was this one smart guy leading them both by the nose! They were sad, they cried, and then they went off together to get their abortions. After they'd got over the worst, they plotted their revenge.

' "What sort of justice is that? We have to do all the suffering and he goes on wagging his tail!"

'So they decided to get that deceiver and shorten his tail for him. They planned it all together, and got everything ready. One of them invited him over and slipped some sleeping stuff in his vodka. Then the other turned up and together they laid their lover-boy out and castrated him according to all the rules of medical science. The trial caused something of a sensation. The victim was sobbing away in court, but the public was laughing. The girls admitted it all, but showed no remorse. They were lucky that both the judge and the prosecutor were women, or they wouldn't have got off with three years!

'What surprised us all in the zone was that those two never fell out, before or after the trial. So what makes a fellow stronger than a woman? His tail, you think? No-o! It's because of the endless battle we women fight among ourselves. A man's power and freedom come from our lack of unity! If we stuck closer together and respected each other more, you'd see, he'd soon tuck that tail of his between his legs!'

'Basically that's true, Zina,' remarked Natasha. 'Female solidarity is a rare thing. But then you've got to hold on to your man. For instance, it's not my fault that my husband is handsome and women are attracted to him. He hasn't been unfaithful to me yet, I know that for sure. But how many times he's been on the verge of it! And what a lot of nervous energy it cost me to get him away from that verge at the moment of danger! And not by force – you can't get him by force, you have to use intelligence, subtlety, and, if you like, this bitchiness we're talking about. I'll tell you about just one episode from our life when I had to become a bitch, which surprises me even to this day.'

Story Three

by the engineer Natasha, about how much tact, wisdom and bitchiness she was obliged to display in order to hold on to her husband.

'We had been married for four years at the time. We were living happily with our son in a two-room co-operative flat. But we had our marital scenes as well. Because I was young I wasn't able to stop them straightaway, but got carried away. I would throw a tantrum, burst into tears and run home to my mother. She would take pity on me, comfort me, and then my husband would come to take me home. I would go back feeling as proud as a queen, thinking, "I really know how to handle my man! He's terrified to lose me!" But it was just by walking out like that I very nearly lost *him*.

'One day we quarrelled over something trivial. It was summer, and I had another two weeks' holiday to go. I grabbed Seryozhka and went off to stay with my mother in her dacha. She and I had lots of "women's talk" and she lent a hand with Seryozhka. On the third day I started looking out of the window and wondering why Vitya wasn't coming to get us. But there was no sign of him. I decided to ring up some friends of ours. Vitya usually ran round to them for consolation when I nagged him too much. I had to walk more than two kilometres to the station for a telephone. Olya answered and told me: "If you don't want to lose your husband, you'd better come back quick. He's already got a girlfriend, some sort of artist. It's Avgust's birthday tomorrow and he's thinking of bringing her. That's why Avgust was embarrassed to invite you. But since you've rung and I've told you what's what, you must definitely come as well."

'I went back to the dacha, reported everything and, of course, cried. But my mother said to me: "Well, my dear,

97

your childhood's over. Now your married life is beginning in earnest. Up to now it's all been childish games, that's why I have treated you like a child who has to be humoured. Now I'm going to give you different advice. Whatever happens, under no circumstances make a scene or demand explanations! And if your rival really does present a serious threat, then get to know her immediately."

'I was horrified: "What? Get to know her? I'll scratch her eyes out!"

' "And you'll lose your husband," she answered wisely. "Leave tomorrow, only don't go home, go straight to the birthday party. Here's some money: get your hair done if you like. I would give you money for a new dress, but it will be better if you slip into the house when Viktor is still at work and put on his favourite dress. Is there one?"

'I thought for a moment and said: "It isn't a proper dress, but an old sarafan that's lying around here somewhere. I was wearing it when we went on a picnic together and he first declared his love for me."

' "That's perfect! You go and find your sarafan. I'll wash it and iron it, and you go to bed and have a good night's sleep. You've got to look good tomorrow. And you can leave Seryozhka with me, he would only get in your way now."

'I went to bed, but was in a state of total panic and cried myself to sleep. I didn't see how an old sarafan could do any good. I wanted to appear at the party in some flashy outfit and really make an impression. But deep down I felt that my mother was right, not me. I decided to try doing exactly what she said. I got up late next morning because no one woke me. The sarafan hung on the chair all nice and fresh, and next to it a basket of flowers and apples – a present for the birthday boy. I put on the sarafan, picked up the basket, looked at myself in the mirror – and rushed to kiss my mother.

' "I don't really need to get my hair done, so I?'

' "Aha, you're catching on! Well, God make you a wise woman quickly."

'I was late for the party on purpose. I rang Olya from the bus stop and asked if Vitya and his flame had arrived yet. She said they hadn't. I had to kill an hour sitting in the square opposite their house. Finally I saw my husband walking along with some dark-haired beauty in jeans and a stylish suede jacket, so I waited another whole hour and then went to the party myself.

'I went into Olya's sitting room, and it was absolute pandemonium in there, with everybody sitting at the table shouting to each other and all the different conversations going on at once. Everyone was dressed to kill, and I looked like Cinderella.

' "I'm sorry I didn't have time to change," I said. "I've come straight from our dacha."

'The effect was devastating. My friends all came rushing over to pay me compliments. The birthday boy was a little embarrassed, but took my apples and put them in the middle of the table and said: "Just look how beautiful they are!"

'Then he sat me down right next to him and started chatting me up. And on my other side Olga was whispering in my ear: "Well, sister, you've really done youself proud today. You look as fresh as a morning rose."

'And with her head she pointed towards my husband and his beauty. I didn't bat an eyelid but my heart was pounding.

'After a while, the tables were moved back to the sides and the dancing began. Avgust and I went first, and he put on a waltz specially. After Avgust, men that I knew, and some that I didn't, came to invite me one after the other. Out of the corner of my eye I noticed Vitya looking at me more and more, although he didn't budge from his ladyfriend. I got tired of dancing, and as I sat down on the sofa to rest, Vitya came up to me: "Am I permitted to invite you to dance with me, beautiful country girl?"

'And I answered very gently: "Oh, Vitya, I'm sorry, I'm so tired! Later, all right, darling?"

'But a couple of minutes later I was dancing again with Avgust. I could see my rival looking rather stunned, gazing after me. She was sitting alone already – my husband was off somewhere else talking to his friends about the photograph he had brought and put up on the wall as a birthday present. Suddenly I had an idea: I asked Avgust to take me over to the empty chair next to my rival at the end of the dance. He was surprised, but he did it. I sat down, then I said to him: "Avgust, dear, could you bring me something cold to drink? Would you like something?"

'This I said directly to her. She gave a start and answered

nervously: "Yes, thank you . . . I'd love something . . ."

'Avgust brought us a bottle of lemonade and two glasses. Now I could start a conversation. I asked her if she'd known Avgust and Olya for long.

' "No," she said, blushing, "Viktor only introduced me to them a couple of days ago . . ."

'I didn't react and pretended everything was fine. I even bailed her out rather unkindly: "You got to know Viktor through your love of art, I suppose?"

' "Yes, I came to try and get into the Academy of Arts, but I didn't get a place. I'm going to try again next year."

' "And do you like my husband's work?"

' "His photography? Yes, it's . . . interesting."

'Here I looked surprised and exclaimed sharply: "Interesting? Is that all? But his lyricism is practically unique. Surely you, as an artist, can recognize a genius when you see one?"

'I really laid it on, even blushing myself at my own blatant flattery. When I had finally finished my passionate monologue, she replied: "Oh, forgive me! I probably just don't know his work very well . . ."

'So I called my husband: "Vitya! Come over here!"

'He came over to us looking worried – he was wondering what we'd been talking about.

' "Vitya, why don't you show Sasha your work? You just must invite her round and show her everything you have!"

'Vitya was relieved.

' "Of course, why not? Come round some time, Sasha."

'But I forced the issue: "Why put it off till later? Sasha and I have just had such an interesting conversation about your photography that I want to show her everything as soon as possible. Let's go straight back to our place from here. Our son is at the dacha just now, so you can spend the night with us. He's got so many photographs that there's enough to fill the whole of tomorrow." And the stupid girl, after making a few lame excuses, agreed to come. Vitya looked at me rather surprised, and I could sense that he was beginning to feel rather ashamed at my openness – inviting my rival to my own house!

'Till the early hours of the morning we bored that Sasha stiff with Vitya's photographs: I showed enough enthusiasm for both of us and kept asking him to show us more and more, which of course pleased him no end. Sasha was trying to stifle her little yawns, and became thoroughly sick of his photographic creations. But he was too stupid to notice this, and kept laying out his masterpieces on the floor in front of us, loving all the attention. The photographs were all of me – sometimes wearing nothing but what I came into this world in. We went to bed in the small hours. As soon as Vitya and I were in bed together he started up about our quarrel, trying to apologize, but I just yawned and whispered: "It's all right, Vityusha, I've forgotten about it already! Do you know how much there was to do in the garden at the dacha? Sorry, darling, but I'm just exhausted!"

'And I turned away towards the wall. Vitya tossed and turned, grunted a bit, and went to sleep.

'The next morning I made him show her the rest of the photographs, which really wiped the smile off poor Sasha's face: she looked as if she'd had a mouthful of lemon. Only after that did I go to the kitchen to make the breakfast, whispering to her as I went: "Now do you see you are dealing with a genius of artistic photography?"

'I went away to make breakfast, knowing that my words would be passed straight on to Vitya. So they were. Vitya came out to me in the kitchen and said: "Why are you boasting like that about my photographs in front of a stange woman. You never gave me such good advertisements before."

'And I said to him so innocently:

' "Well, why would I talk like that to people who know nothing about art? She's an artist, she ought to realize who she's dealing with."

'My Vitya just glowed with pleasure.

'It turned out at breakfast that Sasha still hadn't found a permanent room in Leningrad. So I announced: "We still have two weeks off, and my mum doesn't want to part with her grandson. Stay with us, Sashenka!"

'The poor girl was confused, but pleased: it's no easy job renting a room in Leningrad! But Vitya frowned, he didn't go for the idea: he's not the sort of person who likes to get up to mischief in his own house. But he had to agree.

'Then life really began to get interesting! I was looking after my rival like a best friend, and Vitya started to get jealous because I was paying less attention to him. And he was cooling off towards her daily, by the hour even. She was a young girl, and beautiful, you can't deny that. But a stranger in your house is still a stanger, with habits that certainly don't always fit in with what you've settled into over five years. She left her shoes in the middle of the hall and her stockings in the bathroom. I didn't clear anything up, and it was driving Vitya up the wall.

' "You ought to tell her not to scatter her rags all over the house!"

'I tried to soothe him: "Be patient, Vityusha, she's our guest."

'And I could see that he was now really doing little more than tolerate her. I'm still ashamed of one particular incident. Sasha had come from Sverdlovsk where there was a terrible food shortage. She was saying that butter and meat were being issued on ration cards. On one occasion when we were having dinner together without Vitya I noticed her stealthily eating butter out of the butter dish with her spoon. I pushed the butter dish over to her and said:"Have as much as you like, Sashenka! What a touching extravagance, it's lovely to watch, like a child indulging itself!"

'And from that day on I carefully put the butter dish in front of her place with a teaspoon next to it. She took the bait, poor little fish, and even licked the spoon. And Vitya, I could see, was disgusted at this "touching extravagance".

'Well, their romance ended with Vitya saying to me one day: "Do what you want, Natasha, but I can't take any more. One of us has to go, me or her."

'Bingo! For that long-awaited day I had already fixed up a room for Sasha at the other side of town through some friends – so that I could time Vitya just in case, to see if he was going to see her or not. Sasha left, and my husband and I began a second honeymoon. Every day I heard the same thing from him: "It's so nice not to have anyone staying!"

'So, my dears, that's how I came to be a bitch. And, as you see, it worked.'

Natasha finished her story and looked round at the women in some embarrassment to see if any of them would condemn her. But everyone agreed that Sasha had got what she deserved – she should not have been chasing after other people's husbands. But Valentina laughed and said quietly: 'You were lucky, you know, Natasha. It could have all ended differently.'

And she began her story.

Story Four

*by Valentina the bigwig, completely different from the
one just recounted by Natasha.*

'I had a friend called Tamarochka. She worked for a Leningrad journal as a typist and sometimes wrote poetry herself. A real little St Petersburg intellectual, very elegant, very pretty, and stuffed full of literature since childhood. She was a thin, pale little thing, but that suited her. For some reason we made friends, even though we were very different. Her parents had brought her up very strictly, but Tamarochka herself was a very trendy girl: if she fell in love with someone she would immediately start to live with him without giving the matter a thought. No, she didn't have a bad reputation, just liberated ideas. She was in no hurry to get married; what attracted her was the romance of meetings, the affairs, and then the break-ups and the suffering. She lived on it.

'Anyway, for one of her many affairs she fell in love a bit more seriously than usual. She started talking about a house and family. Well, I thought, the girl is coming to her senses, and about time too. I only wanted the best for her, but she didn't listen to me much. Deep down she considered me bourgeois, I could see that. And she also felt that as a woman I was less than zero compared to her! That suited her down to the ground: she felt that my "earthiness", as she unashamedly called it, merely highlighted her refined spirituality. And that was the thing that really finished her, poor dear.

'My husband was once sent away on an official trip for a whole month. It was during the summer. I was lonely without him, naturally. It was depressing to be in the flat alone, but if I had gone to the dacha alone it would have been even more depressing. One day I was moaning to Tamarochka about it, and she said to me: "Valyusha, how fortunate! Yurik and I have nowhere to live, we can't find a room. Why don't we move in with you for a month? It'll be more cheerful for you, and I can gradually get him used to family life and home sweet home."

' "But Tamarochka, somebody else's home isn't necessarily sweet. And it would be awkward: after all, I'm a young woman, too – what if he starts looking at me and you get jealous?"

'Here my Tamarochka smiled quietly. And she did it in such a way that that faint smile cut me to the bone. I could just hear her saying, "Jealous of you? Look at yourself in the mirror, country bumpkin." But aloud she said something quite different: "Oh, Valyusha! I'm not in the least bit worried about that. You're not his type at all. He's an artist, from a St Petersburg family of artists and connoisseurs. So it's a completely different mentality!"

' "Well, all right, bring your mentality along. Only don't complain to me if anything happens!"

'I was pretending to joke, but actually I was thinking, Just you wait, my little friend!

'The next day she moved in with her friend. She brought a suitcase full of clothes and a bag of poetry, and he had canvases and paints. I let them have my husband's study. I hardly changed anything in the room, but one thing I did deliberately. It's true, I am a country girl, that is, both my parents came from the country and managed to make their way in the town, where I was born. But we never lost our ties with the country, and we used to go to relatives near Vologda every year for holidays. And the peasant women there gave me all sorts of lace. You should have seen the way they made lace down there! It's not the same any more, they just make shoddy stuff and send it all abroad. My grandmother went on making lace till she went blind and she gave me a huge lace bedspread, incredibly beautiful. It was grey, of unbleached thread, and it had a very simple design: a field with a little country boy feeding some geese, and nearby a little girl making a garland. Grandmother originally made it for her own dowry, and then gave it to me. I kept it in a cupboard. My husband wouldn't let me put it on the bed because it was old-fashioned. So now I decided to test whether Tamarochka's artist had any feel for simple beauty, or whether he was just into the modern stuff like her. I hung the bedspread on the wall like a carpet. The wallpaper in our study was an imported wood-grain pattern and went just perfectly with the lace. I also took down the nylon curtains and instead hung another of grandmother's presents – home-made lace curtains. They had a design on them, too: a forest in winter with snow-flakes woven into it. I also got hold of a large earthenware pot that I used for making pickles for my husband's snacks. I put this in the room instead of a vase. I was going to go to the market specially to get some flowers, then I changed my mind. I had just been at the dacha, and I had brought back two sunflowers. I had hung them up in the kitchen to ripen. They hadn't yet withered, they had just started to go a bit soft. I stuck them in the pot. Luckily the stems were long – I had left them long so as to be able to hang them up. When I had finished all this the result was a bright little country nook in place of the standard man's study.

'My guests appeared. First Tamarochka looked into the nook and turned up her thin little nose: "Oh, Valyusha, we ought to clear all this away!"

'I shrugged my shoulders: "It's up to you, dear, you're the one who's living there . . ."

'But actually I was waiting to see what the artist would say. You couldn't tell by looking at him: a lanky type, with lanky hair too, fair, and blue eyes. And he didn't say anything, just gave his name – Yury. I said to him: "Go through to your room and make yourself at home."

'He nodded and walked past me silently. I listened from the big room to hear if he'd notice anything or not. It turned out even better than I thought. All I heard was a quiet gasp.

'So they settled in with me. I even forgot my grudge against Tamarochka and didn't plan any more dirty tricks. Grandmother's lace was enough for me. Anyway, I had a lot of my own work to do, I couldn't be looking after guests the whole time. They took care of themselves, I took care of myself. Only once I tested out my powers on Yurik. One Saturday morning I didn't set off early to the dacha as usual, I decided to wash my hair first. My hair is blonde, but it's like the mane of a horse, I have no end of trouble with it. I boiled up some dried camomile to rinse it with after washing it. The smell went right through the house, like a summer countryside. I washed my hair, rinsed it, and sat down in front of the television with it all hanging down loose, so it would dry quicker. *Travel Club* just happened to be on, and I love that programme. Tamarochka and Yurik also came out of their room and sat down to watch. Yurik was looking around and sniffing – he smelt the camomile. Suddenly he took a piece of my hair and lifted it to his face.

' "I kept wondering where that smell was coming from, and it turns out it's your hair! What do you wash it with, what shampoo do you use?"

' "It's not shampoo, it's ordinary camomile."

' "Wonderful smell. I never thought hair could smell so good. Tamarochka, you ought to wash your hair with camomile, too."

' "Tamarochka shrugged her shoulders. And I said quite simply, without thinking: "No, camomile isn't suitable for brunettes. Stinging nettles would suit Tamarochka better."

'Yurik laughed: "That's true! She has a rather stinging nettle character, so they'd go well together."

'Tamarochka flared up, so I tried to get out of it.

' "Well, it doesn't have to be stinging nettles, though it gives a pleasant shade and it strengthens the roots. You could also use mint, marsh tea or thyme. I'm on my way to Irinovka – I'll pick some suitable herbs for you, if you like."

' "Do you pick the herbs and dry them yourself? This is the first time in my life I've come across a real herbalist."

'Poor Tamarochka was so jealous she had to go and make a catty remark: "Those are Valyusha's remnants of country life coming out."

'She wanted to hurt me. But it had a different effect. I am patient, but I have my limits. It's best not to get my back up.

' "Yes, Tamarochka's right. One of my grandmothers was a bit of a sorceress: she knew about plants and she knew various evil spells, and she taught me some. I could charm your beloved, Tamarochka. D'you want me to?"

' "Rubbish!" she said, but Yurik looked at me wide-eyed. No wonder! What modern intelligent man doesn't dream of meeting a witch! He was really excited now.

' "Valya, take us with you to Irinovka. We're fascinated by your plants. And I'll paint your portrait for you, if you want."

' "Well, it's up to Tamara."

'I went to the kitchen to put some food together for the dacha, thinking they'd never go with me – Tamarochka was not that stupid. But she suddenly appeared behind me in the kitchen and said: "Valyusha, perhaps Yurik and I really could come to your dacha for a couple of days? He's a bit on edge recently. I'm afraid our relationship may break up. So a bit of nature, lyricism . . . Shall we go together?"

'Believe me, I felt sorry for her. So sorry that I told her right out: "Tamarochka, you know me, I don't play games with men, it's not my way; I'm quite happy with my own. But surely you can see for yourself your artist is attracted to me? I don't need that, and you certainly don't."

' "So, let's go! He'll be with me the whole time there."

' "That's what you think now. You forget that every little bush knows me in Irinovka, every tree's my friend. I'm the boss there, Tamarochka, everything there is mine. And your darling Yurik will be mine, too."

' "Valyusha, I don't wish to hurt you, but you do have the most absurd notions. You two are totally different sorts of people!"

' "That's why I am a threat to you, because we are so different. Anyway, if you want to take the risk, take it. It's all the same to me, I don't need your Yurik one little bit."

' "That's fine, then! Let's go, shall we?"

' "Let's go!"

'And off we went, like three fools, to my Irinovka. What I did there I don't need to pass on to you. My grandmother, the herbalist and spell-weaver, would certainly have recognized me as her granddaughter. Actually, I don't know or remember all that much of what she told me as a child, but now that I needed it I turned into a real witch. We arrived at dinner time, and I looked up at the sky and for no apparent reason said: "We won't go for a walk this evening – there's going to be a thick fog."

'Tamarochka and Yurik didn't believe me: "Why should there be a fog?"

'And I joked: "I'm going to call for one, I need it for the flowers, they're all dying in this heat."

'Evening came and, just like in the song, "the fog came down on the empty field . . ." They still asked to go for a walk. I took them through the forest in the fog. I played with them: sometimes I left them alone, sometimes I appeared unexpectedly – on my home ground I don't trip over a single stone, even in the fog. Yurik regarded this as something

107

miraculous. When we got back only my cheeks were red, because I was used to this. But Tamarochka had gone pale, she was blue with cold, and all her lustre had vanished. I put on the samovar to warm her up. Again Yurik couldn't get over it: "How marvellous! The samovar on the terrace, and the garden shrouded in fog. I must do a picture of them. You don't see these things any more but they're so Russian . . .'

'In the morning I got up at five as usual. I decided to pick some strawberries for breakfast. I have a lot to them at the dacha. I don't grow them in beds, but along the paths – it's prettier and they give more berries that way. I collected a whole sieve-full and walked back along the path to the house. I was barefoot, and I'd just thrown a long skirt on over my nightdress. I hadn't even done my hair, and it was hanging down as far as it could go. Suddenly I looked up: Yurik was standing on the porch admiring me. And how could he help it – a witch, if ever there was one!

' "Valyusha, I've never been in the forest in the early morning. Let's go for a walk and you can tell me about plants."

' "I have to get dressed and do my hair."

' "For heaven's sake, there's no need! Let's go as we are."

'Well, I thought, let's go, if that's what he wants . . .

'I took him through the forest glades and told him about medicinal plants and plants for casting spells. Personally, I don't believe in either, except perhaps for washing my hair or spicing up food. But I told him what I knew from my grandmother. He listened with bated breath. I could see his eyes were completely wild and he was going to kiss me at any moment. Oh no, I thought, that I don't need! I turned off the path and led him through the bog. There's no point kissing in a bog – there's nowhere to lie down. I jumped very skilfully from hump to hump, but he, poor sod, fell in and got his jeans wet up to the knees. Never mind, hang in there, it was you who wanted to go chasing witches through the forest! I led him around like that for a couple of hours, then I had pity on him and took him back to the house, still through the bog. He was so happy the bog was finished, and I just pushed the shrubbery aside and showed him the house. And on the terrace sat poor, lonely Tamarochka, wondering what had happened to us.

'Well, it would take too long to say how that day passed.

Even I was ready to lose my head, and Yurik had already lost his completely. Tamarochka had bad luck in everything: she got a sunburn, and she landed in a wasps' nest and got stung under the eye. As to her mood, what can one say – they don't come any worse. I felt terribly sorry for her, after all she was my friend; but I had to teach her a lesson.

'To cut a long story short, our trip ended tragically for Tamarochka. Although Yurik finally realized he wasn't going to make it with me, he still didn't want to be with Tamarochka any more. When we got back to the town he immediately packed his things and vanished out of my life and hers. But he did do a portrait of me, from memory: just as I was then, barefoot, in a crumpled nightdress with an old skirt over it, picking some plants in the forest. It's called "The Young Witch". Tamarochka took me to his show after we had made it up together.

'And do you know why she renewed her friendship with me? To learn "witchery" from me. But how can it be learnt when I don't know myself how anything works with me? A woman needs a special gift and aptitude for both witchery and bitchiness. But too much intelligence kills both. I know for myself, if I give a couple of lectures about the international situation even my own husband gets bored with me in bed.'

The women approved Valentina's story, but advised her strongly not to overdo things and neglect her own husband.

Albina then began her story.

Story Five

by Albina the airhostess, about how she was a bitch, not out of self-interest or rivalry, but purely by natural inclination.

'This happened after I had finished my spell of loose living and started to work as an airhostess on the international circuit. I got friendly with a navigating officer called Grishenka. We both flew the same TU. He was from the provinces, a plain little kid. Short, eyes like little buttons and a body like a turnip. Not a patch on the other pilots who had all done a lot of foreign flying and picked up fancy Western manners. He had his eye on me as soon as I came on board, and although in general I can take pretty good care of myself, I felt I needed a bit of protection at first, so I played along.

'Basically our love took place in the air. I would take round the sweets and mineral water, and return to the little service cubicle. Then Grishenka would come from the flight deck, we would turf my mate out and get down to business. We had our share of adventures, but we were lucky and always got away with it. One time I forgot to switch off the microphone. We began to make love together, and it was all going out on the PA system. Luckily it was a delegation of Frenchmen. They're a sexually enlightened nation; they were listening to the racket and lapping it up. Afterwards I came out to serve the lunches, and I couldn't understand what was going on: everyone was smiling and complimenting me. And there was a little old man sitting in the back row. He called me over and whispered in Russian: "Mademoiselle! Please, if you retire with your friend again, could you possibly leave the microphone on again? It gave me tremendous pleasure, it has been the best flight of my life!"

'But I soon got fed up with Grishenka. Our characters were very different; he was always trying to make me more modest, blushing at every little thing I said. He was an incredible bore, always lecturing me. Well, he gave me one lecture too many.

' "Look, turnip," I said to him one day, "if you're such a little prude why don't you propose to me, instead of doing all these immodest things with me? And the more immodest they are, the more pleasure you get out of doing them. Your modesty is all in your head, isn't it, Grishenka?"

' "No, I don't love you enough to marry you," he explained. "And marriage would be immoral without love."

'So even now he was serving me up morals, the little jerk. Well, I sent him packing, and soon I had another pilot who was more interesting and didn't have any moral hang-ups. But I still continued in the same aircrew with Grishenka. I paid him zero attention, he sighed a bit, and then got over it.

And suddenly I found out he was having an affair with a dispatcher at our airport. I went along to have a look out of curiosity. Well, I saw my turnip had found himself a swede to suit him: a dumb little thing, round, and with eyes like buttons, just like him. I laughed at Grishenka's luck and was about to leave the dispatchers' room, when suddenly I felt something stir inside me, a sort of darkness that crept up from my stomach to my eyes and started ringing in my ears. After it had gone away I was left with a cold, clear determination – to pull up that swede and dump it. I went over to her, sat down on a chair beside her, put my elbows on her desk and looked her right in the eye. I said nothing, and I could feel that my eyes were really terrifying and wild.

' "What is it? Who are you? What do you want?" The girl just didn't know what was up.

'Then I said to her in a very quiet voice: "Do not go near Grishenka any more. I will allow you to ask him just once who Albina is. You'll see how scared he gets and then you'll understand. And if that's not enough for you, ask anybody about Galya Klimova. If you disobey me, you have yourself to blame. That is my last word. You have been warned."

'I threw those words into her scared little mug and left. I walked out of the room, and my own heart was thumping away. Later I came to myself and I thought: "Why did I have to go and do that? What was the point?"

'I could think of no answer.

'That Galya Klimova I'd threatened her with was one of our airhostesses who got burnt with acid by a jealous girlfriend. I hardly knew her, it was just the first thing that came into my head.

'The very next day I found out that Grishenka's new love had resigned at short notice and disappeared into thin air.

'During the next flight Grishenka came to our cubby-hole, asked the other airhostess to leave for a moment, then took me by the hand and said: "Forgive me, Albina, I didn't realize you felt so strongly about me."

'I looked at him in surprise and didn't understand what he was talking about – I had already forgotten about his little cadre at the dispatchers' room. I shrugged my shoulders and walked out.

'So poor old Grishenka got nothing for his pains and

111

ended up with neither of us. And if you ask me why I had to go and do that I can't give you an answer. I don't know myself. There's obviously some special woman's devil sitting inside us, and he takes us over at such times.

It was Galya the dissident's turn to tell a story. 'You know, Albina, I think the devil you were talking about is perhaps bisexual. Listen to this story about a friend of mine who was possessed by the same devil.'

Story Six

by Galina from which it becomes clear that men and women have very different conceptions about bitchiness.

'I had some friends, a husband and wife called Hermann and Tonya. They had seven years together, then Hermann suddenly took it into his head to chuck Tonya. He fixed himself up with a friend. And it just so happened that this girl of his also turned out to be an old friend of mine. I watched the whole affair and for the time being didn't interfere. Tonya was clever, she realized she couldn't be with Hermann any more. She grieved for a while, then she began to look for a replacement. She had a friend from childhood who had been in love with her since schooldays; well, she latched on to him. They met, they went out together, they went to the cinema. Hermann spent night and day with Zhenya, his new found love. Zhenya knew about Tonya, but she'd lost her head over Hermann and only listened to him.

'And then one evening Hermann came rushing over to see me, absolutely furious. "Well, now I've discovered what sort of wife I have!" he declared even before getting through the door. "I'm not putting up with that any more, I've got to have a divorce."

' "What's happened? What are you so up tight about?"

' "Just imagine, I come out into the street and what do I see? There's my faithful wife, or rather, my once faithful wife, walking along with some guy. They're looking into each other's eyes, and he's even got his hand on her shoulder. I go up to them, remove his little hand from her little shoulder and say: 'Allow me to introduce myself: I am this lady's husband. And now allow me to suggest that you get lost, go to hell, and don't show your face in these parts again!' The guy looks at Tonya and asks: 'Is this really your husband?' My wife gets very confused and starts stammering: 'Yes, it is . . . But I can explain everything!' He says to her: 'I don't need any explanations!' He turns on his heel and marches off. And the little fool goes rushing after him. How do you like that?'

'He was so angry he was all red in the face. Then I said to him: "Listen, Hermann, what if I ring Tonya up right now and give her Zhenya's address, so that she can go there and remove your little hand from someone else's little shoulder, too?"

'He was dumbfounded for a moment, then he grabbed his hat and coat and rushed to the door. As he was going out he turned round and hissed: "You're a bitch, Galina!"

'So you see, that's how I too became a bitch.'

'Yes, men certainly have a double standard,' laughed Emma. 'Here's how their logic runs: "Did she let you?" "No, what about you?" "No. What a whore!" '

'Yes,' said Olga. 'Husbands can be swine and wives can be bitches, but you'll never find a worse swine or bitch than a mother who takes a dislike to her son's wife! Now listen to another story from our shipyard.'

Story Seven

by Olga, from which it does indeed follow that the very best bitches are to be found among mothers-in-law.

'We had a woman called Masha Klyazmina working with us. She was one of those production heroes, but a good person, quite harmless. She'd had a hard life: she had to bring up her son alone because her husband was killed in the war. And what she wouldn't do for her Yegorushka wasn't worth talking about. She sacrificed everything for his education, and managed to get him trained as an engineer. They both worked with us at the Admiralty shipyard: the mother in the shop with dirt up to her ears, and the son – a white-collar worker – all neat and tidy in shirt and tie. Of course she washed and ironed his shirts for him. Sometimes it was quite embarrassing going to the dinner room: the mother would be in her dirty overalls, munching away on bread cutlets with the rest of us in the canteen, and her little boy would be sitting eating schnitzel next door in the room for white-collar workers, with white tablecloths and waitresses. But Masha would peep into their room and announce proudly to us: "My boy's sitting with the director!"

'Actually, Yegor, Masha's son, was a good kid; he got on with the workers well and he knew his stuff. But it was too much motherly love that was his ruin: he lost his wife and child, and he lost his mind too and landed up in the loony bin.

'He took a fancy to a draughtsman called Shura. She was a nice, quiet girl. But she was from a simple family and didn't have any higher education. The son went to his mother and said he wanted to marry Shura. But she would have none of it: "Is that the best you could find? She doesn't even have a diploma, and they're such a simple family! She's not our kind!"

'To listen to her you'd think she was from the gentry herself. But Yegor insisted. He threatened to leave Leningrad and go to the north with Shura, so his mother gave in. But privately she told us: "Never mind, let him have his way. Marriages don't last long these days. If he's going to go sleeping around, it's better for him to be married. Then they'll get divorced and Yegorushka will find himself a wife that's good enough for him. He's not stupid, he'll see that Shurka's as common as dirt!"

'When Yegor and Shura got married the yard gave them a two-room flat with his mother, since she was an honoured worker and he was a young engineer. The three of them lived together. We all thought Masha would calm down and accept things. Shura had a really sweet nature, and was always giving in to her. But it made no difference – Masha hadn't changed her mind at all, she was just waiting for them to get divorced. But soon a baby was born and that made Masha even worse. She started taking out all her hatred on the innocent little kid. Her own grandson! Who ever heard of such a thing? She wouldn't even use his name, she just referred to him as the brat or the mongrel. Shura just couldn't take it, she started asking Yegor if they could move. First he was against it – she was his mother, after all! But then he saw there would never be any peace with Masha, and he put in for an exchange. Then she went rushing round the yard to all the different committees, screaming blue murder: "Help! My son and daughter-in-law are driving me out of house and home!"

'They had Yegor up before them, made him feel guilty and tried to persuade him to change his mind about the exchange. In the end he backed down and withdrew his application. But Masha got her teeth into her daughter-in-law and wouldn't let the poor girl alone: "You're the one who's setting him against his mother, damn you!"

'Shura couldn't stand it and moved out to our dormitory at the yard. But that wasn't enough for Masha. She found out that Yegor was going along there every day trying to get Shura to come home. So, very quickly, without telling Yegor, she signed Shura and the baby out of her own flat and then set the militia on to her, telling them: "She's living in the dormitory without registration!"

'The militia went to the head of the dormitory, who came to Shura and said: "I'm sorry, I'm powerless against the militia. You'll have to go back to your husband, the militia's pestering us about it."

'Shura ended up on the street. But she was still very weak, her nerves were all shot. Well, she took her baby and jumped off the Lieutenant Schmidt Bridge into the Neva. They couldn't save her. Yegor Nikolaich went to pieces and ended up in the loony bin. He had treatment for a year, now they've let him out. He's started work again, but he's not the same as he was before: he's quiet, and he goes about the yard like a shadow. He left his mother and took a room. And do you think all this got through to Masha? Not at all! She's turned completely grey and she's gone a bit up top now, but she's still sticking to her old line: "The doctors will cure Yegorushka, and I'll find him a girl with a diploma and lots of money. Do you think I skimped and saved all my life for nothing, getting him educated?"

'So there's how one fool destroyed a whole family. But when you come to think about it, you've got to feel sorry for

Masha too. The older women there say that until Yegor finished at the institute Masha never once ate in the yard canteen; she would bring her piece of bread and jam or margarine and nibble it in a corner of the cloakroom. She wouldn't even spend fifty copecks on her own dinner or get herself a bottle of kefir at the buffet! Don't you think that's a tragedy too?'

'Well,' said Nelya, whose turn it was after Olga, 'I think the biggest bitches are ex-wives. We had one living in our flat.'

Story Eight

by the music teacher Nelya, asserting that ex-wives are among the worst bitches towards their ex-husbands, though without insisting that this is a general rule.

'We had a husband, wife and son living in our flat. Quite frankly, she was not the most peaceable character. Anyway, they got divorced. As usual, the son stayed with his mother. The father wanted to see his son, but she wouldn't let him in the door: "You're no father to us now," she said. "You're nothing but a supplier of alimony, and everybody despises people like you. Your job is to keep the money coming in on time, otherwise we'll throw you in jail. You have no other rights or duties towards us."

'Meanwhile the boy was growing up, and he didn't know his father. One day I overheard mother and son talking in the kitchen: "Mama, who's my father?"

' "Your father's a bastard!"

'Finally the father decided to go to court and demand the right to see the child. The court granted him a two-hour meeting every Sunday. Do you think she let her son have even one meeting with his father? Not on your life! He would ring – she hung up on him. He would come – they were not at home. Every Sunday she would leave with him in the morning and take him out to the country.

'The father couldn't take any more of this, so he went back to the court. They imposed a thirty-rouble fine on her

116

for obstructing meetings between father and son. So what did that bitch do? You'll never guess!

'I came back from work one day and saw moving men carrying chairs out of Anna Pavlovna's room – that was his ex-wife's name.

' "What's happening, Anna," I asked, "are you moving?"
' "No," she answered, "I've sold my suite."

'Next day some people arrived and carted off her carpet, then the TV. Later we found out that Anna Pavlovna had sold everything she could, didn't pay the fine, then when the bailiff arrived to take an inventory of her possessions the flat was empty! Meanwhile Anna quickly married some elderly officer, an old flame of hers, and left with him without, of course, saying goodbye to her ex-husband. I don't know whether he's given up on the boy or whether he's still looking for him. But he has to continue to pay child support, which the court is keeping on account.'

The women were divided in their opinions about this fighter for mothers' rights: some sympathized with the unhappy father, others considered he had got what he deserved. The discussion dragged on, and to cut it short Emma asked for their attention and began her story.

Story Nine

by the director Emma, being yet another self-critical account of the narrator's own bitchiness.

'I have met many bitches in my life, but the one I know best is me so I shall tell you about myself.

'My ex-husband, that tireless ageing celebrity, gave me hundreds of reasons for being bitchy towards the women of his choice. I hated them all one after the other as they appeared on the stage of his life. I will tell you of a couple of incidents and try to convey what I felt at the time and analyse the actual mechanism of my bitchiness.

'The first is about that young Juliet he had an affair with in Siberia. At first I tried to run my rival down. They say that is the least productive form of jealousy. True, if you do

117

it crudely, right between the eyes, and that much I quickly realized. Then I started to operate more cautiously. Since my husband never admitted to his relationship with her in so many words, it gave me the opportunity to attribute my criticisms of her to other people and then be surprised if he stuck up for her.

' "You know, dear, for some reason everyone keeps saying Juliet is bow-legged. Of course she is a bit, but I don't think it's at all noticeable from the audience!"

'You can imagine that after I'd said that my husband spent the next three days examining Juliet's legs, and finally he began to think there was something wrong with them, expecially if "everyone keeps saying" so. The next thing I criticized on behalf of everyone else was her eyes – "she has bulging eyes, and one of them is squint" – then the way she did her hair, then the way she dressed. The sign of my success was that our Juliet, who was a perfectly pretty girl in every way, started to change her hairdo and clothes and to use too much make-up. I once came across her in the lavatory standing in front of the mirror in tears.

' "What's the matter?"

' "People are saying one of my eyes is bigger than the other, and I keep looking at them and I can't tell if it's the right or the left . . ."

'And I just listened to her with malicious pleasure.

'But the way I finally split them up was not so trivial, it was more subtle. I began to praise her acting, again on behalf of the others: "Why does everybody praise that Juliet of yours and say that she eclipses you, and that next to her you look more like her father, Capulet, than Romeo? What rubbish!"

'That really made an impression on him. He began to get irritated at Juliet. When I realized I was on to a good thing I finished Juliet off altogether. I wrote a letter to the local paper as if from an anonymous admirer, praising her acting to the skies, and adding at the end: "It is a pity that the man playing Romeo, an excellent actor from the capital, fails next to Juliet merely because of his age."

'That was the end of their romance.

'For a while my husband and I made it up and were back together again, but then the second act of this play began. The actress was replaced by a girl working at the buffet in our theatre. She was a fresh little Siberian girl, and of course she couldn't resist the visiting celebrity. The old goat would even jump out to flirt with her during the intervals wearing his stage costume – that had a devastating effect on the girl: she had friends and neighbours among the audience, and they could all see how successful she was. She would stand behind the counter blushing like the Snow Maiden and sparkling like a Christmas tree.

'I lost my cool again at first: "How could you lower yourself like that? What do you talk to her about?"

' "I find things to talk about. And don't you dare say anything bad about her, it's not kind!"

' "Not kind?! the main thing is that I'm talking about her at all. This may be the big moment of her life. Just imagine: I, a director from Leningrad, have taken an interest in an uncultured little provincial girl. What difference does it make whether what I say is good or bad?"

'These conversations would make him furious, and me even more so. So many times I wanted to control myself, but I just couldn't do it. But the more heated and malicious my words became, the colder I grew inside, until that intolerable fire of hatred gave way to a total emptiness. The hardest thing at that time was to keep going. But I had to keep going because I was holding the theatre together. Everyone realized this, including my dear little husband, when I finally cracked, chucked everything in and left: the company fell apart, and he just scraped a job organizing amateur entertainment at a regional club.

'Anyway, I managed to take care of the buffet girl too, and very simply. I went over to them one evening just before the end of the interval, while she was cooing at him over the bar, as if I needed to tell my husband something before the next act. I made some comment, pretty sternly too, showing both him and the girl who was boss in the world of theatre. He got really angry, but had to control himself, and the little buffet girl just listened to us with her mouth wide open. Then the first bell went and he had to go. I turned to the girl and said: "Don't worry, Anechka, you'll get used to it! If you really do have talent and ought to go on the stage, then first of all you'll have to learn what's what in the theatre. Oh, what am I saying! My husband asked me not to say anything yet about his plans for your future in the theatre, even to you! Please don't tell him I said anything."

'I walked away. And that did it. The poor girl began to imagine the glitter of the footlights, the sound of applause, the posters. And the main thing was she was so close to it all. She had obviously come straight from the schoolroom to the buffet and had naturally fallen in love with the theatre, that poison. And of course she couldn't help revealing her dreams to my husband in her simplicity. My husband may have been a dirty old man, not to mince words, but he knew something about acting and he did have talent. He could see the girl was a non-starter: she had legs like barrels, she was about twenty kilos overweight, and her accent and diction were positively barbaric. And her timid hopes that he would help her drove him into a fury.

'And do you know, my dears, what stopped me doing this sort of thing, in spite of all my success in destroying rivals? It was the fact that I expended so much nervous energy on it. After I had succeeded I would either feel completely drained for a long time or I would become hysterical, even when it was all over and my husband was coming back to me. And one time I got to thinking about this, and I realized that the bitch in me was destroying me more than anyone else, that I could not lead a creative life with this, that it was a sort of drug addiction that destroys a woman. Since then I have felt very sorry for women who are bogged down in this sort of devilry – they haven't the strength for anything else any more. If a relationship has got so bad that it has turned the woman into a bitch, then the best thing she can do is to get out. Because she won't be able to stop herself or change.'

After Emma it was Irishka's turn, and so she began.

Story Ten

by the secretary Irishka, about how a loving mother turned into a bitchy mother-in-law.

'This story happened to my friend Alla. The father had left her and her mother, and the two of them lived in a small

120

room in a communal flat. They were poor: the mother was a hairdresser, but she loved and spoiled Alla. Alla grew up, finished technical school, started working, and then got a boyfriend – a young naval officer, handsome, clever and head over heels in love with Alla. He sailed in warships, so his registered address was the ship. After they got married they started living at Alla's place, in the same room as the mother. Everything went all right to begin with, the mother seemed to accept her son-in-law and even like him. But then we began to notice that our friend Alla was looking unhappy and nervous.

'"What's the matter with you? Things not going well with your husband?"

'"No, everything's fine with my husband. But my mother's giving us a hard time."

'"How?"

'Alla just waved her hand. But then she opened up to me privately. For some reason her mother had started to be jealous of their intimate life. They just had the one room, so they used a cupboard to partition off the mother's area with her bed, and they themselves slept on a folding sofa. They would go to bed at night and wait for the mother to fall asleep. But she developed this habit: she would turn over a few times, and then start snoring as if she had fallen asleep. But as soon as the young couple got down to business she would get up and come out from behind her partition and begin looking for a headache pill, or a drink of water, or something else. She would complain she couldn't get to sleep! She was deliberately ruining their life together. They started looking for a room. But you try to rent a room in Leningrad – you can't find one, and even if you could, no amount of money would be enough. And on top of it all Alla got pregnant, and no one is going to give you a room if you're expecting a baby, as you know yourselves.

'Alla tried to have a talk with her mother, but she pretended not to understand what she was talking about: "I've lived without a husband for fifteen years, I don't understand what your problem is!"

'It all ended very sadly for them. The husband took Alla to the maternity hospital, waited nearby until she had given birth to a boy, and ran happily home with a bottle of brandy to congratulate the grandmother on the birth of her

121

grandson! They finished the bottle, he went to bed, his mother-in-law went behind her cupboard. But during the night she climbed into her son-in law's bed, can you imagine that? He was half asleep and drunk, so he got on top of her ... Then he let out a yell, jumped up and ran for it! And so Alla's whole family life collapsed: her husband was so ashamed he wouldn't show his face again, though he sends good money for the little boy. And Alla turned grey with grief.'

The women decided that this brand of bitchiness was hard to beat. After a short discussion they resolved for the next day to tell stories about unfaithful husbands and wives. Then Emma laid down a condition: 'Since we all trust each other let's make an agreement: If any of us have actually been unfaithful to our husbands, let's tell about it without trying to conceal anything!'

'But if there hasn't been any unfaithfulness, just a nasty, unjustified jealousy, then can we tell about that?' asked Irishka.

So it was decided that if there had been no infidelity, only jealousy, then such stories could be told, too.

So ended the fourth day.

THE FIFTH DAY

given to stories about
Infidelity and Jealousy

All day our storytellers kept giving each other sly glances, trying to guess who would be confessing that evening to having broken their vows of marital fidelity.

Evening came and the stories began. As usual, Larissa went first.

Story One

by the doctor of biology, Larissa, in which she defines in the form of an anecdote two kinds of female infidelity.

'Since I do not have a husband, and never did have one, I have not had anyone to be unfaithful to or jealous of. So I offer you an anecdote instead.

'A communal flat. Two women, neighbours, meet in the corridor. One is carrying a sheet and a pillow towards the front door and crying.

' "Why are you so upset, Marya Ivanovna, and where are you taking those bedclothes?"

' "Oh, I've just committed adultery on them and I'm taking them out to the dustbin so as not to be reminded of my sin."

' "Well, my dear, if I started chucking out everything I'd committed adultery on, I'd have nothing left in the room except the lampshade. Even that, come to think of it ... That Ivan Ivanych is such a joker, he really is!" '

The women had a good laugh, then turned to Zina, whose turn it was next.

Story Two

*by Zina the tramp, which in almost every detail
resembles the drama of Othello, Iago and Desdemona,
only in a camp variant.*

'We had a couple of dykes – lesbians – in our zone; the butch
one was Natashka Kuznetsova, nicknamed Natan, and her
wife was Ninka Semirechnaya. Their love was really strong,
it gave you the creeps; they wouldn't even go on the march
off to work without being together. Natan guarded her wife
and was jealous as hell of her – I mean, she would beat her
up if any of the other butch dykes even looked at her. But
Ninka stayed faithful to her, she never got hitched up with
the others. She was scared to. And still Natan would throw a
scene with her for the tiniest reason. Of course they lived
together as a couple, they ate together and slept together
like man and wife. At night they would hang a sheet in front
of the bunk and make love to their hearts' content; you
could hear the squeaking all round the barrack room.
Everyone knew about it, but the camp authorities didn't
touch them because Ninka was a good seamstress – she did
twice the norm on a sewing machine – and Natan was a
sewing machine mechanic, and they couldn't do without
her. Whenever the work plan depended on dykes the
authorities would turn a blind eye to their love-making.
Their ID would be marked with a blue stripe, which meant a
zek was into forbidden "women's love", and that was the end
of it. They didn't try to re-educate them. In return the butch
ones would try and go over the norm themselves and force
the other zeks to do the same. You just had to look around
the zone, and every time you saw a gang boss it was either a
butch or a female dyke. And even the detachment chiefs
and officers who had been working at the camp for a long
time ended up getting into "women's love". Their menfolk
had left them because they couldn't stick their fascist ways,
so they switched over to zek love.

'Anyway, here's what happened to our inseparable pair,
Natan and Ninka. A butch dyke called Tsygan was brought
to our zone from a teenage zone. Tsygan was quite small,
she looked like a black sparrow, but a real fucker even so.
She went through all the female dykes in the zone one after
the other, and Ninka was the only one who stayed faithful

to her Natan. This was like a slap in the face to Tsygan: she had to try that one too so as to get known as the chief dyke of the zone. She kept trying to chat Ninka up, but she wouldn't give in and even threatened to tell Natan on her. And Natan was twice the size of Tsygan, with shoulders like a man. She had been acting the man since she was fifteen, and she came to the zone at fourteen, so by now she looked completely male. No breasts at all, but those shoulders – Jesus!

'So this Tsygan thought up a way of splitting up Ninka and Natan; nobody had ever played such a dirty trick in our zone. Like any good husband, Natan used to give Ninka various presents: she would barter for a neck scarf, a little towel, a bra. And Ninka used to go around in this beautiful blue neck scarf that Natan had given her. You would go into the sewing shop, and you could see the scarf way over in the distance shining like a cornflower in the field! One day Ninka lost her blue scarf. She looked for it all over the place, but it was gone. Oh, well, she thought, the crumb snatchers have nicked it, that's the camp thieves. It was just before the November 7th holiday, October Revolution Day. Everyone in the zone was getting ready for it, dressing up. There was going to be a concert at the club and dancing afterwards. Ninka put on a different scarf, a red one. Natan noticed and asked: "Why didn't you put on the blue one?"

'Ninka should have told her straight out that she'd lost the scarf, but she was scared Natan would get mad and start laying into her for not looking after her special present. So she lied: "Oh, I'm tired of it, I wear it every day at work. I want to wear something red today because of the holiday."

'So all the zeks go piling into the club. We sit there waiting for the show to begin. In comes the political deputy and starts giving us this lecture. What a drag! All that political bullshit! We had to sit through that first. Then the camp choir comes on to the stage with benches. They set up the benches in two rows, climb up on to them and start singing that song, "Buchenwald Alarm". Remember how it goes?

'People of the world, stand up?
They're ringing the bells in Buchenwald.

'It's a good song for zeks, very popular in the camps. And

the authorities like it because it's a political song. Anyway, they're singing, "People of the world, stand up," and suddenly we see Natan getting up from her chair, leaning forward and staring at the leader. The leader is Tsygan, and round her gipsy neck is tied Ninka's blue scarf. Just as if she's announcing to the whole zone, See, I've had her too! Natan grabs Ninka by the arm and hisses at her: "Outside!"

'Ninka immediately starts crying and refusing to go out, and the authorities sitting in the front row and the zeks with cushy jobs – the priduroks – start looking in their direction. But Natan is white with rage and refuses to give in: "Come outside, you slut!"

'So Ninka goes outside with her. Then one of the women says: "We'd better go after them. Natan will murder her Ninka!"

'But others said: "Let her! It's not our affair, we shouldn't get involved in someone else's family drama."

'It's true, you don't usually do that in the zone. So we stayed for the rest of the show. They announced the interval between the concert and the dance, so we came out of the club for a smoke and a stretch. The whole zone was in a state of alarm, with guards rushing around the place yelling. There was a crowd of people near the hospital. It turned out Natan had stabbed Ninka because of the blue scarf. They grabbed hold of her and dragged her off to the penalty isolator, otherwise she would have knifed Tsygan too.

'Ninka pulled through, the doctors sewed her up. But Tsygan knew things didn't look good for her: Natan would get out in fifteen days, find out the truth, and put a knife in her. So Tsygan tried to run away. They caught her, of course: they tracked her down with the dogs. She was given an extra two years and sent off to prison – that was Tsygan's only way to escape the knife. Natan got out of the isolator and walked up and down under the hospital windows singing:

' "Women's love is over!
I tell you once more:
I don't need your promises,
All I ask for
Is, before we say goodbye,
You look me in the eye!"

'In other words, she was making a big drama about getting Ninka to come clean. Well, when she found out about Tsygan she believed that Ninka had been faithful to her. Only, Natan herself didn't wait for Ninka to get out of hospital, she started up with a new little gipsy that had just arrived with a shipment from the south. "I can't go for long without a woman," she would say.

'That's a butch dyke for you.'

'A very interesting variant of *Othello*,' said Emma after listening to Zina the tramp's story. 'From what you say, life in the camp is never dull.'

'That's true enough! You don't get bored in the zone! Provided you survive . . .' replied Zina.

Now it was Natasha's turn to tell a story. She hesitated, looked embarrassed, then finally burst out: 'All right, women! Since we have this agreement I'll tell you the secret of how I betrayed my husband. Only it was his own fault!'

'OK, OK!' laughed Albina, 'we'll sort out whose fault it was; first tell us the story!'

Story Three

by the engineer Natasha, who was sincerely convinced that her husband forced her into infidelity by his overweening jealousy, and that of her own accord she would never, never have done it!

'I had an old friend called Antosha: we were in the same year together. A wonderful man, good-looking and good fun. At one time Antosha tried to get involved with me, but I just looked on him as my friend. No, more than a friend – a brother. And if he kissed me when we met, as people did at school, to me that was like kissing a girlfriend. I told Antosha all my girlish secrets, and when my future husband appeared on the horizon I told Antosha everything about that, down to the last detail. Quite simply, Antosha was like a best girlfriend to me. I got married, and soon after that Antosha got married too, and our friendship continued.

My husband had his male friends from schooldays, and I had Antosha. At first he was surprised at our friendship, then he gradually began to get jealous.

' "I can't believe there was nothing between you!" he would say. "How can you be so close?"

'And I would try to reason with him: "Nonsense! If there had been something we would have separated long ago. We're just good friends, can't you understand that?"

'But my Vitya wouldn't relax, and started scowling at Antosha more and more. One day Antosha said to me: "Maybe I shouldn't see you any more? Your husband keeps giving me dirty looks."

'But I was so hurt by the idea that Antosha might be taken away from me that I felt like crying. I persuaded Antosha to take no notice. And so as not to irritate my husband I started meeting Antosha more and more often away from home. If something happened or I had some ideas I wanted to share with my friend, I would ring up Antosha at work and arrange to meet him at a café. Then I would have to deceive my husband and say I had been at a meeting, or seeing a girlfriend. But now I had a secret, and I could see that my husband sensed it. One day Antosha invited us for his birthday. My husband announced: "I'm not going, and it would be best if you didn't go either."

'I tried to make him see that it wouldn't be nice of me not to go to my best friend's birthday party. So then my dear husband said: "All right, go then. But don't come back here for the night. You can stay there!"

' "Don't be ridiculous!" I said. "Antosha's married, so how can I stay there?"

'So the little fool said to me: "Well, how have you managed it up to now?"

'I lost my temper: "I see! Very well, then! I shall go to the birthday party and I shall not come back until tomorrow. Of that you can be sure."

'I threw some clothes on and ran out of the house, slamming the door behind me. I got to Antosha's, wished him a happy birthday, sat down at the table with the other guests and pretended I was having a fantastic time. And all the time I was thinking, What am I going to do? If I come home late at night there'll be a scene. If I don't go home there'll be a scene too. But I had to teach my little husband a

129

lesson, which meant I had to go somewhere for the night; only not to my mother – he would soon find me there and then it would start all over again. Well, you might say I was in luck. The doorbell suddenly rang, and there was Antosha's brother who lived in Moscow. He was on a business trip to Leningrad, and he'd come to his brother's birthday party. His name was Kirill, and we had known each other from way back. In fact this Kirill had also been after me once. I found out that he was staying at a hotel, and I decided there and then to spend the night with him. Why with him particularly? Well, because I didn't feel like ruining Antosha's life, and I was fond of his wife; whereas Kirill was a bachelor. So I began flirting with him. But so subtly that none of the guests noticed, not even Antosha. But Kirill realized straightaway that I was ready for anything. And after supper he offered to see me home. He wanted to get a taxi immediately, but I suggested going for a walk.

'We were walking along the snowy street arm in arm, and I was so terrified, the snow looked black; it's no joke, being unfaithful to your husband for the first time! We got to Nevsky Prospect, and then it was a question of either turning towards my place or towards the hotel where Kirill was staying. I slowed down on purpose to give him the chance to take the initiative. He seized it and asked: "Perhaps we could just sit for a while in the hotel restaurant?"

'I agreed. We sat drinking some sort of dry wine. I felt sick, but I smiled and chattered away so as to look cheerful. But Kirill saw my embarrassment, and this got him even more wound up. Well, we sat and sat, but finally I felt I had to do something, because I couldn't take much more of it. So I said: "Let's pay the bill and go to your room."

'Kirill was surprised that I was so decisive. He hurriedly paid, and we went to his room. As we were going up the stairs I lost my nerve completely and wanted to run away. But I controlled myself. I realized I might not get another chance like this, where the timing was so perfect!

'We went into the room. It was bare and unlived-in. The ashtray smelt of cigarette ends even though it was empty. The light was yellow and unfriendly. I stopped in the middle of the room and said to Kirill: "Well? Why aren't you undressing me?"

'He came up to me and took off my coat. That was all

right. But when he touched the zip on my dress I felt as if I had been struck by lightning. Strange, cold hands – br-r!

' "Turn round," I said, "I'll undress myself."

'I got undressed and darted under the covers, shivering to myself. Kirill lit a cigarette and sat down beside me: "Can you please explain why you had to do all this?"

'Here I burst into tears and told him everything. Kirill shook his head: "So that's it! And what am I supposed to do? Sit all night in the armchair keeping guard over you? No thanks, these little pranks have to be punished."

'He turned off the light and got into bed with me. I immediately turned towards the wall and huddled up into a little ball, locking my hands under my knees so that he would get me! He tried to turn me over, but I wouldn't let him. I thought I would lie next to him like that the whole night – what could he do to me? And then in the morning I would go home with a clear conscience, having kept myself untouched and at the same time punished my husband. But Kirill turned out to be more crafty than me. He started to stroke my hair very, very gently and whisper tender things to me; then he went on and on about how he had loved me when we were students. I unclasped my hands, straightened my legs out and turned towards him, and then he got me and tore into me like there was no tomorrow. Vitya never did that even after we'd been apart for some time. I had hardly had time to recover when it was all over. For him, that is, not for me. I lay next to him feeling I had been spat on.

'That's it, I thought, I shall leave here and throw myself under a tram. I lay there and cried quietly. His smell was unfamiliar, the hairs on his legs were prickly, and it was cramped and unpleasant lying next to him. Morning had to come sooner or later. But Kirill rested a little, then once again began to stroke me and kiss me and talk to me. I enjoyed it more the second time, and the third time I even felt like stroking his coarse hair, and his smell seemed more homely. By morning, my dears, I was head over heels in love with Kirill! And I didn't feel any guilt, all I felt was that I didn't want the night to end. We spent nearly the whole day in bed together, and only got up towards evening. We had supper in the restaurant, and then he took me home in a taxi. I climbed the stairs to my flat, surprised to find I felt no fear or regret. I went in, and my husband was sitting in front of the television.

' "Well?" he asked. "Satisfied?"

' "Yes," I replied, "you asked for it yourself."

'Then he suddenly said: "So now relax. And don't imagine you succeeded in playing on my nerves. I rang Antosha, and his wife told me you had left with a girlfriend."

'So in the end my infidelity didn't work. Kirill left, I didn't feel like seeing him again. But my Vitya did seem to change a bit: he didn't pull the Othello act on me any more. So I still don't know whether he guessed the truth, or whether intuition warned him that it was dangerous to be jealous of me.'

Emma looked intently at Natasha: 'Tell me, Natasha, did this Kirill look like his brother Antosha?'

'Like two peas in a pod! They were brothers, after all.'

'Well, there's the answer to your infidelity. The person you really wanted to sleep with was Antosha, but you were afraid to. So you got yourself a substitute. That's why you enjoyed the infidelity and had peace of mind afterwards: you achieved what you had unconsciously been wanting for years and years, only you had been hiding it from yourself.'

'Oh, no, that's impossible!' exclaimed Natasha, but she went as red as a beetroot.

'Of course that's it!' laughed Valentina. 'You might as well admit it to yourself. And it was good that you got it out of your system, otherwise your nerves would have gone to pieces. Now you look at me, women: you couldn't imagine anyone looking more healthy, could you? But there was a time when I almost reached the point of total nervous exhaustion, and all it needed to get me back together again was to betray my husband just one little time. Shall I tell you about it?'

'Yes!'

Story Four

by the bigwig Valentina, describing one method of preserving one's sanity and stability.

132

'My husband had a childhood friend called Kostya. It was years and years before I got to know him; all I ever heard were the stories my husband told about him – how clever he was, how gifted, what a wonderful friend. I was dying to see him. This Kostya had a fantastic career, working abroad and occasionally coming to Moscow. When he did my husband would rush down to see him. I was burning with curiosity to know what sort of person he was. Whenever my husband went down to see him I would get very restless thinking about this mysterious man. I pictured him as a sort of Shtirlits from *Seventeen Moments of Spring*, our version of James Bond, one of those handsome secret agents with sad eyes.

'One day Pavlik got a letter from Kostya, read it and started dancing around with it in his hand. "Kostya's coming to stay with us! For three whole days!"

'Well, that started something! Pavlik turned the whole executive committee commissariat upside down collecting food for his friend. He made me bake some pies, saying: "Kostya loves Russian cooking!"

'I rushed back from work every day to traipse round the shops and do the housework, and at night I lay awake trying to imagine this legendary Kostya. Finally our long-awaited guest arrived. I nearly fainted when he walked in: he was like Shtirlits from the film to the last detail – firm jaw, sad eyes, everything! He looked at me and gasped: "Well, Pavel, you certainly picked yourself a Russian beauty! You don't find girls like that abroad, except possibly in Bavaria, but they lack the Russian spark! There's no denying it, she's a beauty!"

'I was completely thrown, but replied boldly: "If that's the case, why do you hang around abroad all the time? If you lived here we would soon find you a girl to suit your taste."

' "No . . . I'm a bachelor by conviction."

' "And by profession!" added my spouse. Kostya gave a dry laugh and nodded: "Yes, perhaps by profession, too."

'This convinced me even more that Kostya was a secret agent. It was all so romantic!

'Well, he stayed three days with us. Most of the time he talked to my husband, or they went for walks together. I just hovered round the table and cooked their breakfasts, dinners and suppers. I was hurt that Kostya didn't take

133

much notice of me, but what could I do?

'The three days flew by. Kostya obviously enjoyed his stay and as he was leaving he took my hand and kissed it, and said: "I've been a fool to sit around in hotels on my visits home. If my hostess has no objection, I will stay with you more often."

' "You will always be very welcome," I replied.

'And that is what happened from then on: every year or so Kostya would appear. It was always a great occasion for my husband, but a torment for me. I knew there was no point in looking longingly at him. I was no match for him, and anyway his friendship with Pavlik was a genuine one and he wasn't about to play a dirty trick like that on his friend. All the same, I felt that Kostya was attracted to me, secretly. Maybe he didn't even realize it himself, but I noticed. I would be walking out of the room to go to the kitchen, and I could feel his eyes burning into my back. Women can sense these things, we can feel it with our whole body. I began to get into such a state that it's frightening even to recall it. For a month before Kostya's arrival I wouldn't get a good night's sleep for thinking about it. I absolutely exhausted myself over him, I just can't tell you. And all the time I kept thinking: "Am I never going to have even one night with him?"

'Pavel and I already had a child by that time, we had a good family life, but when Kostya came to stay, I would go into a fever. Once it happened that just after he arrived my husband had to go on an urgent trip. They had one day together, and the next day Pavlik left and Kostya also started packing to leave. But I said to him: "Why do you have to go rushing off? Stay with us a bit longer. The pies need eating up!"

'He gave me an intent look – and stayed. That night I was the one who went to him where he was sleeping in my husband's study. Although he was expecting it, I knew that, he tried to put up some resistance: "You're mad, Valya! What about Pavel?"

' "I've been waiting for this night for five years. I only want one night, Pavel can have all the rest."

'And what a night it was, my dears! As we had intercourse I could feel five years of unhappiness and longing pouring out of every cell of my body into Kostya. I felt more and more relieved, until by morning I felt completely purged of this illicit love of mine. It had left me. I looked at Kostya, and his eyes had dark shadows round them, and dark desire burning in them. His first words to me in the morning were: "I'll never forget you, Valentina."

' "I know. You won't. But I can forget you now. Now you won't destroy my life."

' "Wasn't it good with me?"

' "It was good, Kostenka. It was better than it's ever been with my husband. But that was nothing to do with you, it was all to do with my own foolish thoughts. Now that's gone. It's finished, I'm cured of you. Off you go abroad now, and remember Valya's Night, and I'll get on with the business of living. Here, with Pavlik."

'He understood. In the doorway he gave me a bone-crushing hug and again said: "I'll never forget you!"

'And he left. For good. He never came to see us again, saying in letters to Pavlik that work prevented him coming. Now it's easy for me to remember him; I remember him, smile at my own boldness, and get on with life.'

'Good for you, Valentina! I like you better every day, even if you do fall in love with spies.'

This remark came from Albina, whose turn it was now to tell a story.

'I would never dare do a thing like that,' sighed Galina.

'That's why you're so skinny,' said Albina, laughing. 'You're all eaten up inside by morals. Give me Valya's health any day rather than your morality. And now I'm going to tell you about a crafty fellow who fixed things so he could betray his wife and have it off with me.'

Story Five

by the airhostess Albina, being a nice example of male cunning in promiscuity.

'I once got to know the head of a railway restaurant car; basically I made friends with him so as to get some new

135

clothes. Winter was round the corner, and I had no coat or boots. I operate according to the proverb that a woman is well dressed when she dresses on credit and undresses for cash. Lev wasn't a bad-looking guy – he was rich, too. I slept with him a few times, and then he had to go and spoil it all by falling hopelessly in love with me. So much so that he couldn't go for a single day without me.

' "Oh, Albinochka," he would say, "I would marry you if it weren't for my wife."

'The mystery about his wife was quite simple: she worked for the Department for Combating the Theft of Socialist Property. A terrifying old witch, and sterile too. Lev married her by voluntary compulsion, rather like the way we all go off to do Saturday work: you don't have to go, it's up to you, but ... He came up against her through some shady business he was involved in, so she gave him the option: either go to jail, or come to the registry office. The poor guy, instead of a definite stretch in camp he opted for indefinite hard labour with a wife he didn't love. He would get his relief on the side, but even though he was a real hardened pro he longed for love, to have a permanent woman to be with him. So he latched on to me.

' "How can we fix it so that we don't have to separate, and don't get caught by my wife?" Lev Borisych would ask after each night with me.

'Then he came up with an idea. He started buying me a return ticket to the last stop for every journey he was on. And not just a seat, but a whole two-berth compartment – so no one would bother us. First he wanted to set me up as a waitress in the restaurant car, but I refused – that sort of job is not for me, I know what these guys get up to when they travel. Even on the plane they sometimes do such disgusting things you feel dirty for a week. And anyway, that jealous old witch used to see Lev off every time he travelled, and she could have got suspicious.

'And so our love affair on wheels began. I got on to the train in Leningrad like any other passenger, only I would be looking out of the window watching the ogre hovering around my lover further down the platform, casting her beady eye on all the female attendants to see if any of them were young and pretty. I would settle down in my compartment and relax – after all, I was travelling alone. Then

136

Lev Borisych would appear and we would start to make love to the click of the wheels. When we got back, his little wife would be there, waiting.

'I travelled about with him like that for six months; I had my southern suntan the whole winter, it was great. And to be honest, although I don't like to admit it, I sort of grew accustomed to him. One day I just couldn't help myself, I said to him: "Levushka, why don't you give up all your shady business, leave your beauty behind, and we'll go away somewhere together?"

' "No, Albinochka, I fear her more than I would fear landmines in the war: a mine explodes once, but that bitch is capable of shredding me alive for the rest of my life. No, we'll just have to hang on . . ."

'Are you wondering how it ended? Well, how could it end? I got fed up traipsing around in trains, so I chucked him. But there's one thought that still bothers me: what if it wasn't so much that he was scared of his witch, but that he was scared of losing his cushy job? For myself I know, girls, that the only sort of man who can stop me hating him is the one who is willing to take a lot of suffering on himself and lose everything for me. But most of them are just interested in having a good time, so it's up to us to have a good time too, while we can . . .'

After some discussion about whether men in general are capable of making great sacrifices for the sake of women, they all reached the conclusion that Albina in particular was hardly likely to find her hero. And they suggested to Galya, whose turn it was, that she should tell her story.

Story Six

by the dissident wife Galina. Set against a background of everyday complications of life in a progressive society, it tells how, in the house of her best friend, she viewed with horror all the signs of marital betrayal.

'I have already told you that I have a very close friend called

Lyudka, who was in fact the one who brought Slavik and me together. She also had her "dissident romance": the man she loved had done seven years in camps. First they corresponded – Lyudka wrote to almost all the political prisoners, sending them parcels and knitting them warm underwear. They even called her the "dissident sister". Then Garik was let out, they met up, fell in love, and got married. It was a very happy marriage; I always used to look at them and think: "Soon Slavik will be free, and it will be the same with us."

'I was eager to learn from Lyudka – watching how she ran the household and how she treated her Garik – I was getting ready for my own future happiness. And when my friends and I discussed family life at work, I would say that I knew the ideal couple and I told them about Lyudka and Garik.

'Then one day, to my horror I realized that my dear Lyudka was blatantly betraying her Garik. This is how it happened. One day I dropped in on Lyudka without warning, just to see how she was. I rang the doorbell and heard Lyudka rushing down the corridor. She threw the door open – her face was shining, her eyes sparkling. But when she saw it was me her expression changed: "Oh, it's you, Galka. Well, come on in."

'I went into the room, and from the doorway I saw the table was laid with cold snacks and a bottle of vodka.

' "Are you expecting people?" I asked.

'She seemed to me to get a bit embarrassed, and answered: "Not people, a person. Listen, Galka, tell me what you came about, and go away, all right? I'm in a terrible hurry."

'She kept on looking at the clock and was obviously very nervous. Well, I stayed a couple of minutes, asked to borrow some book, and left. I was walking home thinking to myself in amazement, who could Lyudka be expecting like that? Maybe one of her prisoners has been let out, but then why does she hide it from me? I was even rather offended.

'A couple of days later I called in again – to return the book, and I found everything the same: the table laid, Lyudka rushing to the door, only now she didn't look so happy, her eyes were red. Obviously her long-awaited guest just wasn't showing up. Curiosity got the better of me, and next day I called in again without warning. Lyudka let me in, went and sat down in the corner of the sofa, and looked at me. She was playing with her fingers, she was nervous, her eyes were red from crying. And then I realized that before my eyes some love drama was taking place. And I had thought Lyudka the ideal wife! But, to be on the safe side, I cautiously asked: "Lyudka, are you still waiting for someone?"

'She nodded, and the tears started rolling down her cheeks.

' "And he doesn't come?"

' "No . . ."

' "Then to hell with him! If he doesn't come, forget him!"

' "I can't do that, Galochka! My whole world depends on him!"

'She snatched a cushion from the sofa, buried her face in it and started sobbing. I was aghast: Lyudka, my little Lyudka, what have you come to, what have you done? And who can I trust now if even my Lyudka, with such a wonderful husband, is eating her heart out over some prick?

'The door suddenly opened and in walked Garik. He saw the table laid, Lyudka crying, me looking bewildered – and no reaction at all. He went over to Lyudka and stroked her hair: "He still hasn't come?"

'Lyudka shook her head and sobbed even louder. Now I didn't know what was going on at all.

' "Well, who is it you're waiting for, for heaven's sake?" I yelled in desperation.

' "Who, who . . .?" answered Lyudka. "The plumber!"

' "I'm being serious."

' "So am I! The lavatory's been leaking for more than a week, I can't keep the floor clean, I've had to take time off work and count it as my holiday, and every day they tell me in the accommodation office: 'Just wait, he'll certainly be there tomorrow!' Our plumber's just a drunk and he's on one of his bouts right now; and there are no other plumbers. I've saved up some vodka to sober him up as soon as he gets here. But he just doesn't show up, he just doesn't show up . . ."

'And she started sobbing bitterly.

'I, meanwhile, had a fit of the giggles and started to laugh like a lunatic. When I had calmed down I explained to Garik and Lyudka that I thought I had witnessed some kind of moral tragedy watching her wait, as I'd supposed, for her lover . . .

' "What an idiot!" said Lyudka. "I would never have waited for Garik the way I've been waiting for the plumber – life is intolerable without him!"

Of course, the women immediately recalled stories of their own interminable waits for plumbers, electricians, fridge repair men, etc. Natasha told how she had waited for two years for builders to come and fix her flat, and Irishka told how a dressmaker had taken so long to make her a mini skirt that the fashion had changed from mini to maxi and she had had to give the dress to her neighbour in the end, so that she could alter it for her little girl to wear.

Now it was Olga's turn to tell a story.

Story Seven

by the worker Olga, testifying to the fact that husbands sometimes only notice their wives' infidelity when they want to.

'You know what surprises me, Galina? That you straightaway suspected your bosom friend of being unfaithful. Not that I blame you – we women are like that, that's the one thing we see. But what really surprises me is men! Even if a man's wife is not looking at other men he drives her up the wall with his jealousy, nagging at her over every little thing. Either she gave someone a funny look, or she sat down in the wrong place, or she suddenly puts on her new dress – who for, why? But then if the wife really is unfaithful, the husband weighs up the situation very carefully: is there any point in noticing her unfaithfulness, or is it better not to?

'We had a master craftsman called Anton working at the yard. He was no kid, but he was still a bachelor. He was certainly no oil painting – huge body, face like a big round football, and nothing very masculine about him. The more mature women didn't even look at him, so he went after the younger ones who came to the yard from the country. He went on like that for quite a while, changing his girls like others change their socks, and he was quite convinced, poor

140

guy, that the younger and less experienced the girl was, the easier it was for him to handle her. And that was just where fate played him a dirty trick.

'A girl called Raymonda Zamoshkina came to us from somewhere near Pskov. The names they give girls in the country these days! Barely fit for cows. Juliet, Silviya, Raymonda. Well, we had to call her something so we called her Rayka. As long as Rayka was still shy she was all right, pretty tame. That was of course when Anton made his move, and asked her to marry him. What was the girl supposed to do? She had no option: you could sleep on dormitory mattresses until you were bruised all over waiting for them to give you a room. The only solution was to get a husband, and here one had presented himself. Like a prayer answered. They got married and started living together. For about a year Rayka controlled herself, then she went to town, opening her legs for anything in trousers. There was nothing private about it – she had open sex right there at the yard, at her place of work. There was a joinery next to our furniture shop, full of young guys, and she was laid by all of them one after the other.

Come dinner break or the end of the shift, our Anton Semyonych would be walking about the joinery, all pale, looking for his wife. He knew exactly what was going on but he refused to take it in. For example, Rayka would be coming out of the shower room, and a young joiner would be coming along behing her doing up his trousers. But as if he couldn't see the guy right in front of him, Anton would just say to her: "Have you had your wash, Rayechka? Well, let's go home."

'The worst time was when he actually caught Rayka in the act. This was in the break between shifts. She was in the joinery, lying on a heap of sawdust with Zhenka, the joiners' brigadier, on top of her. They were going at it great guns, and he walked quietly up to them and politely asked: "What are you two doing here?"

'Rayka, who had almost reached orgasm, looked at him furiously from underneath her lover and answered: "Can't you see? We're fucking!"

'Poor Anton turned round and went back to his office. Rayka finished her business with Zhenka, pulled down her dress, straightened her hair, and off she went. She came into the office as if nothing had happened and said: "Let's go home, Antosha!"

'But he sat there staring at his desk, and didn't answer. He felt terrible. Then the little bitch said to him: "You didn't really think me and Zhenka were having a fuck in the sawdust, did you? I was just joking! We were fooling around, wrestling, trying to see who was stronger. Come on, get up, let's go home, it's time for supper."

'Anton got up quietly and followed his wife home, and he never mentioned what happened in the joinery. He believed her. He didn't believe his own eyes, but he believed her words – not the words that just came out of her in the heat of the moment, but her outright lies. So in a way that's what he wanted, and that's what he deserved.'

Next it was Nelya's turn, and she began her story.

Story Eight

by the music teacher Nelya, in which Soviet workmen make another appearance.

'Both the last two stories prompt me to tell you first an anecdote, and then a story from my own experience.

'First the anecdote, which Olga reminded me of – about men's attitude to adultery and what makes them suspect adultery. Two old friends meet, both of them recently married. One asks the other if his young wife is being unfaithful to him, and says: "I strongly suspect my wife is having it off with some gardener. Every time I come home there are fresh flowers on the table and a whole botanical garden on the window sills. What else could it be unless she has a lover who works with flowers? My heart tells me she's being unfaithful."

'The other one sighs and says: "I also have some suspicions that my wife is having it off with an electrician."

'His friend is surprised: "How did you work that one out? Do you find new light fittings appearing every day?"

' "No. You see, one day I came home from work an hour early and my wife was at home, and there was an electrician

142

in bed next to her. So then I began to suspect she might be having it off with this electrician."

'So much for the anecdote; now for the true-life story, as they say. We once had a short circuit in our kitchen: the wire goes along inside the wall, but the kitchen wall is damp. We needed someone to call for the electrician, but there was no one to do it. The old people in the flat were all down with flu, and the younger ones were all working. You had to send for one early in the morning, otherwise you would never be able to find anyone. I had a concert at the music school that day. Well, I got all dressed up and ran down to the accommodation office before going to work to call for the electrician. As luck would have it, the electrician was there. A fresh-faced type with the kind of eyes that undress you.

' "We've got a short circuit inside the wall, we need a new wire," I told him.

'He gave a sort of dirty laugh and replied: "Well, for a beauty like you we can always find a wire. I'll be there at five."

'He didn't really say anything, it was just normal male humour, but somehow I didn't care for it. I quickly left and forgot all about it.

'I got home around five, and soon there was a ring at the doorbell and there stood the electrician. I hadn't even had time to change, and went to the door in my dressing gown. He was standing on the doorstep, looking playfully at me and smiling quietly. I said to him: "Come in, I'll show you where the emergency is."

'He replied: "I already know where you have your emergencies. Let's get it sorted out!"

'I shrugged my shoulders and took him into the kitchen. I opened the door for him, and he suddenly stared at me and said: "But this is the kitchen!"

' "Yes, of course it is. Look, the wall's all black – a short circuit!"

'He looked at me in amazement, laughed and said: "So you really did have an emergency? So why did you have to get all dressed up to fetch me?"

' "What's that got to do with you? I got dressed up to go to work because I had a concert today . . ."

'Here he chucked his tool bag down and started gouging

away at the wall. He never looked at me again. I could see the lad had started to work on the job, so I went back to my room. When he had finished he called me in.

'I checked that everything was in order, and asked: "How much?"

'He smiled and said: "What for? The state pays me for the cable. I thought you were calling me for a different emergency. For my own cable I always charge ten roubles. If ever you feel like it, I'm always ready."

'Then I realized how our electrician supplemented his wages! Since that time, if ever we need to call someone for repairs I always send my husband.'

The women were amazed at the electrician with his second job, especially Albina: 'And such a modest charge, too! Like the cheapest little scrubber at the Moskovsky Station! He's obviously doing it mainly to satisfy his own needs. But it's nice to hear that even in that we're catching up with the rotten West!'

'Why, do they have that sort of thing?'

'Male prostitutes? Take your pick! I even read that they had special brothels for women. You go along, choose your man and have the time of your life – if you can afford it, that is. Of course, maybe it's just our newspapers talking rubbish again, I don't know . . .'

'How revolting!' exclaimed Irishka.

'And when it's all done in private – isn't that just as revolting?'

And everyone agreed with Albina that secret prostitution was no better than doing it openly, after which Emma began her story.

Story Nine

by the director Emma, not so much on the assigned topic of infidelity or jealousy, as an answer to a question that bothers many Soviet women.

'I shall tell you about how the blondes of one provincial town were unfaithful to their husbands. Why the blondes particularly? Well, listen.

'This took place in a southern town, but I shan't mention its name – you never know who has friends or relatives living there! After divorcing my husband I worked in this town as director of the theatre, and I was very much in evidence, as one might say. I had a whole string of admirers, but I also had one good friend, the head of the town's cultural directorate. At one time we were on the same course in drama school, but then he decided to go on to a different stage – the Party stage – and he moved up pretty fast. But when I arrived in his town to work he remembered our friendship of student years and decided to look after me. He made me director straightaway, wangled me a flat, in other words he helped me in every way. And completely unselfishly, even though he was a terrible womanizer and had been ever since student days.

'My first winter approached, and I could see it was going to be quite a severe one; even though the town was in the south, it was in the mountains, and had a continental climate: the summers were hot, but the winters were freezing cold. I hadn't bargained for that. I had sold my Siberian fur coat when I left my husband, and now I had nothing to wear. I would scuttle to the theatre and back again in a fancy suede coat, reckoning it would be a fortnight at the most before I came down with pneumonia. I had to get some new clothes, something warm. That was the time when sheepskin coats had just come into fashion, and all the rich beauties of the town were swaggering around in them. So I thought, I must get one too, I'm as good as they are. Even some of our actresses had got themselves sheepskins. I asked this one and that one. "Where did you get your sheepskin?"

'They all said some other town, as if they'd all agreed on a story. One said Odessa, another said Moscow, a third said Riga. But the sheepskins were all the same style, that's what surprised me. I turned to my friend for help: "Listen, Gogi, I'm absolutely freezing. Could you help me to get a sheepskin?"

'He practically jumped out of his skin.

' "What! You, a sheepskin! No way, forget it! Have what you like, but not that. I could lay on a car if you like, then you could drive to the theatre."

' "What do you mean, Gogi? Why do I want a car, I can't

145

even drive. I want a sheepskin, I'm frozen."

' "No, you're not getting any sheepskin from me. You're a decent woman, we used to share our last bottle of kefir before our stipends came in, you're like a sister to me – you're not getting a sheepskin!"

'But he wouldn't say why. I decided it must be some stupid local idea that women who went around in sheepskins weren't decent. Then I found out accidentally. It turned out that my friend Gogi, like all Caucasians, was crazy about blondes and considered it a matter of honour to sample every worthwhile blonde in the town. Even in drama school he liked to say that you couldn't hope to sleep with all the blondes, but you should at least aim for that. Down here there weren't so many blondes; it was a southern town and there were far more dark-haired beauties. Gogi used to seduce his blondes with sheepskins supplied by someone he knew in the Western Ukraine where they were produced. In the end he had provided just about all of them with sheepskins, including the wives of the local leadership, actresses, teachers at the college and doctors. And only the few initiated, including me eventually, knew that if a blonde was wearing a sheepskin it meant it was from Gogi. Incidentally, many of the blondes in sheepskins were the wives of very high-up people – the prosecutor's wife, the wife of the secretary of the local Party committee. Their husbands could easily have got them a sheepskin themselves. But no, not one of them could resist, they all had to have their sheepskin from Gogi. I used to tease him afterwards: "You're lucky there aren't many blondes here, what if you liked brunettes. That would be pretty expensive!"

'Gogi would clutch his head, pretending to panic: "Inside a year one of two things would come to an end: either the sheepskins at my friend's factory, or me!"

Now it was the turn of the last narrator, Irishka. She immediately bowled everybody over: 'I shall tell you how I was unfaithful to my Seryozhenka three times in a row.'

'You? But you two are so much in love!'

'That's exactly why. Listen.'

Story Ten

by the plump Irishka, about how she was unfaithful to her husband in order to be 'like everyone else'.

'I was living happily with Seryozha, and suddenly I made a new friend, Sonya. She was pretty as a doll, but what a bitch! She started to nag me, saying I knew nothing about life or about men, and all because Seryozha was the only man I'd ever known.

' "Have you even kissed anyone else?" she asked me one day.

' "Yes. Relatives, friends."

' "But other men?"

' "Of course not! Why should I?"

' "So you don't even know what your Seryozha's like compared to other men. Maybe he's not your type at all, and you don't even know it."

'And she began to explain about sexual incompatibility. I objected: "But my husband and I enjoy each other a lot, we don't get out of bed at all on Sundays if we can possibly avoid it."

' "Well, there you are!" she said. "With somebody else you might not get out of bed for a whole week. You don't know anyone else. You're like a blind kitten; you snuggle up to your Seryozha and you're content."

'And she went on nagging me so much that it started to get to me. What if she's right, I thought, and there is somebody better than Seryozha, without my knowing? These thoughts gave me no peace, they kept on and on. I would go to the cinema, see a handsome film star and think: if I were to kiss him, would it be better than Seryozha? I would lie in bed with my husband, imagining it wasn't him and trying to think how I would feel. I even began to lose weight over all this, can you imagine? It was that bad.

'So once when Seryozha went off on a trip I made up my mind to be unfaithful to him, and prove something to Sonya into the bargain. Deep down, I felt sure Seryozha was an ace performer. And I was right . . .

'Don't interrupt, I'll tell you everything in good time. I started to think about where I would find a suitable object for my adultery? And then I had an idea. I selected three candidates: one a variety singer that drove all the girls crazy; the second an actor from the Comedy Theatre, not anything special to look at, but really famous; and the third a non-conformist artist who had even had an exhibition in America. I found out their addresses and sent all three a letter: "I wish to commit adultery with you. Please do not refuse my request, I need this urgently for the sake of my family happiness."

'In each letter I enclosed my photograph and telephone number. All three called me straightaway, and I arranged to meet them on three consecutive days. And what do you think? Not one of them could begin to compete with Seryozha, not one! I took great pleasure in informing Sonya of this. And when Seryozha got back from his trip I made him happy and then told him everything and even suggested he go off with some other woman and then tell me who was better, me or the other woman. But he said it was quite unnecessary since he had slept with several women before we were married and had concluded that I was by far the best in bed.

'Only, I sometimes think he just said that so that I wouldn't keep on at him. What do you think?'

The women laughed at Irishka's escapades. No one actually believed her, but they pretended to. Then Emma asked, to be polite: 'And did you discover any new sensations in your research?'

'Well, they really tried to please me. I explained the whole thing to them and what they had to do. Only they put too much effort into it, whereas Seryozha puts his heart into it. That's why they couldn't compete.'

'So you're not such a fool after all, Irishka. You may be naïve, but you have a certain wisdom,' Larissa decided diplomatically. 'But any more stupid ideas like that and you'll end up in real trouble.'

'Why should I? I'm satisfied now. Of course I fell out with Sonya. Who knows what she might have put me up to next.'

The women were still laughing over Irishka's 'therapy' when it was time for sleep. And so ended the fifth day.

THE SIXTH DAY

in which the women recount stories of

Rapists and their Victims

On the morning of the sixth day Zina the tramp reminded the others: 'Hey, women! We promised to tell stories about men trying to rape us, didn't we? Have you forgotten?'

'I'd rather you hadn't reminded us,' grumbled Olga.

But no one suggested a different topic, so they fixed on that one.

Evening came, the babies were settled down, and Larissa began her story.

Story One

by the biologist Larissa. It explains why she was well on the way to becoming a dissident when things took a different twist.

'I would be happy to get off with telling an anecdote as usual, but we're not just here to amuse ourselves. The subject is a serious one and I offer for your consideration my own sad experience.

'In this story, Galina, I crossed paths with your dissident circle. There's nothing unusual in that among Leningrad intellectuals; almost all of them have a friend who is a dissident, or a friend of a friend. And there's nothing surprising about the fact that since I couldn't find myself a hero like Volodka, I should turn in the end to those heroes of our time, the dissidents. That was quite easy in the late sixties, since people were always collecting signatures for petitions in support of this one or that one who was suffering persecution. It all seems to have become much quieter and more serious now, but in those days it was quite

150

trendy to have links with the dissidents. My chosen dissident was called Volodya. My sympathy for him may well have started because of his name: half my admirers and lovers have been Volodyas. He was a happy, sociable guy, and a real brainbox; he knew European languages and quite a lot about literature – not just *samizdat* literature. He had done time in a camp, and in the famous Vladimir prison where he was on close terms with Bukovsky and Ginzburg. In other words, he was quite a celebrity.

'As often happened with us women who loved our dissidents but couldn't get time to sleep with them enough, I got deeply involved in his work. I would be signing things, running errands for him, and at night working my fingers to the bone typing samizdat. And it seemed as if my life had begun to take on a new meaning. It was nothing to do with the politics, of course, but it was a growing conviction that I had found my second Volodka. It was a difficult process, so difficult and complicated that in order to get myself sorted out I started writing poetry. I remember comparing myself to a snowdrift with a snowdrop growing through the middle of it – or something of the sort. It was stupid, I agree, but I was happy.

'It was also hard for me because I was used to dominating, and I was having to learn to submit, since that had become my image of happiness. Now I know I wouldn't swap my independence for any happiness, but I had to pay dearly for this knowledge . . .

'I trusted my new Volodya blindly – who else did I have to trust? He was tried and tested according to all the standards of contemporary social morality – dissident morality, of course. His camp friends recounted legends about their friendship with him. He came through both his trials – he was in prison twice – completely unbroken, it was like water off a duck's back. And he never even told me that it was hard inside, in prison. Because of my love for him I even experienced being arrested and held for several hours, and I can tell you, my dears, it's frightening to be under arrest and interrogation for even one hour. Very frightening.

'We were arrested together during a demonstration. Yes, I even marched in a demonstration with him. I'm amazed even now that I wasn't thrown out of my graduate course. They arrested us on Senate Square, shoved us into police

151

cars and took us to the station. On the way Volodya held my hand tightly and whispered instructions on how to behave under questioning, what I should say and so on. Basically he was trying to assure me I had nothing to fear, and that I would certainly be freed. About himself he didn't have the same certainty: they had a file on him and it was always hanging over his head. So, just in case, he gave me my COs – contingency orders: go back to his place, hide his papers, inform various people, but mainly the West. I dreamed of visiting him in prison, bringing food parcels, and I smiled in the darkness of the police car: it was a bitter sort of happiness, but it was happiness! And no wonder: I had at last found a real man . . .

'After we had got to the police station the KGB men arrived, looked at all our papers and questioned us. I just kept quiet, I was afraid that I would say too much out of inexperience.

'Some of us were let out after two hours, others, including Volodya, were given fifteen days. Visits weren't allowed but I succeeded in getting a parcel to him at the prison on Kalyayev Street. When those two weeks were over and Volodya was released, he began to trust me even more, and I fell deeper and deeper in love with him. But ours was a troubled romance: every day as I came home towards his place I used to be afraid he had been taken; he also felt his arrest was imminent, and so he tried to get as much done as possible. He began to bring me more and more into the work, introducing me to the right people and teaching me all about conspiracy. The KGB started to watch me, too: I frequently noticed suspicious shadows following me – an indistinguishable pair of young bull-necks in identical raincoats who just wouldn't leave me alone.

'One evening I stayed with Volodya long after midnight, helping him draw up a petition for some people recently arrested for samizdat.

' "Volodya! I think I'd better move off home."

' "Stay with me. We ought to get this finished tonight, you never know what might happen tomorrow."

' "I can't possibly! I didn't say anything to my mother, and she'll have a fit if I don't appear before morning. I ought to go home, even though it is already two a.m. Have you got any money for a taxi? I didn't bring any with me."

' "You know I'm completely cleaned out."

' "Then come with me so I don't have to walk through the streets alone."

' "I'm sorry, I just can't. I've got to finish this document, these people are in great danger. You don't have very far to go!"

' "I'm still scared. I'm constantly being followed, either by one man or a couple."

' "So what can they do to you? They're your best protection against muggers!"

'And he laughed. Don't be surprised that I can remember the whole conversation word for word: it was our last conversation, almost. Later we exchanged only a few words of goodbye.

'Well, I continued asking him to see me home, and he began to lose his temper: "Really, Lara, you certainly pick your moments to act the nervous little girl. Give it a rest, can't you?"

'I felt really wounded, but I didn't let it show – I just kissed him and left. Gorokhovaya Street was pitch dark and empty and I started hurrying down it to get as fast as possible to Sadovaya Street where there was a bit more light. Suddenly I heard footsteps behind me. The snow was crunching. I foolishly turned into the first side street, thinking that if it was just a chance passer-by he would walk on past, then I could relax and hurry on home. But the footsteps turned into the side street after me, and became faster, gaining on me. I looked round: it was a guy in a fur jacket, his face half hidden by a scarf that was wound round it. He suddenly grabbed me, covered my mouth with a huge gloved hand, and pulled me into an entrance. Here he turned me towards him, crushed me up against the wall, ripped my coat open so violently that all the buttons went flying into the snow like walnuts, and tore my dress right down the front. Luckily I had tights over my knickers. He still held my mouth with one hand, and with the other he felt between my legs. He was grinding his teeth, furious that I wasn't completely naked. His whole body shook with rage – it was vile! I seized my chance to sink my teeth into his hand. He let out a yell and for a second released me: I ran for my life down the side street but he came after me again. Then I had an idea; I don't know how it came to me I was in such a state of terror. I turned into the first courtyard I came to, looked round all the windows to see if any of them had a light on. I saw a light on the first floor and yelled for all I was worth: "Volodya! Volodya! Come quickly! There's a rapist after me!"

'He stopped dead in his tracks. And I just stood there as if help really was on the way. I shouted again: "Volodya, hurry!"

' "Oh, sod it!" he growled, and made a run for it.

'I went into the first doorway and pressed myself against the wall, shivering. I stood there for a while, terrified he would come back. Then I cautiously came out, crossed the yard, and looked up and down the street. No one. I closed my torn dress, pulled my coat together and dragged myself home. I hadn't the strength to run any more. I got home, slipped into the bath to get warm and sob my heart out. Then I went to bed. And that was the end of my "dissident romance".

'You can take offence if you like, Galina, but I'll tell you straight out: of course your friends and brothers in arms are wonderful people, even, if you like, heroes in their own way. But men they are not. Not even they have been spared by the times.'

Galina did not try to argue, but commented: 'Larissa, you're judging by one particular case. I actually know the man you mean. He really would lay down his life for humanity, but for his neighbour he wouldn't lift a finger. Have you met his mother?'

'Yes. A wonderful woman.'

'And do you know where she worked?'

'Isn't she retired?'

'Yes, officially she is. But so that her son can give himself completely to his work his retired mother is still working as a stoker in a boiler house.'

'Is that because she sympathizes with his views?' asked Valentina.

'I don't know. Probably she's just a good mother, and he's taking advantage of her without even realizing it.'

Larissa shrugged her shoulders: 'It doesn't matter to me any more. I have my son, I don't need anyone else. I'm going to try and bring him up to be the sort of man I've always pictured. And then let my daughter-in-law

154

kiss my hand! Can you imagine, I hate the bitch already!'

The women laughed at Larissa's jealousy, and then Zina began to tell her story.

Story Two

by Zina the tramp. The reader will recall that her life as a woman began with rape. It also continued under the constant threat of rape. But here Zina describes the rape of a man by men.

'Well, girls, I'm not going to bore you with all my gripes against men – it would take too long, and there aren't the words to describe all I've suffered. I can't even remember myself which times I was raped and when I did it willingly so as not to get raped – just to have a bit of peace. It happened in prison, it happened in the transit camps, and whenever I was on the road there was never a week went by when some drunken tramp didn't come climbing on top of me for a screw. In our sort of life that's not considered either a sin or something to be afraid of. I've been in the shit for so long – I've been about as low as you can get. Life has twisted me like a clock spring – no prick could screw me up any more than I am already!

'It's the little girls I'm sorry for that have to go through this when they're pure and innocent. And sometimes it happens to boys. And that's what I'm going to tell you – how I once felt the most terrible pity for a boy, and how that boy paid for all the sins of the male sex. Listen.

'It was at the Vologda transit prison. They didn't sort the women out, we were just all put in cells together; some were on their way to the zone, others had only just been arrested and their investigation was just beginning. There were under-age girls and old zeks going off for their sixth or eighth stretch, all in the same cell. All getting experience of life and fleas from each other. Same with the men in their cells. A typical transit prison!

'There was a healthy, bossy woman in our cell who had been head of a meat combine. Having worked in grub, she was pretty well fed. She used to turn her nose up at us:

155

"You're trash! Roadside paupers! You live small and you steal small! My husband always taught me if you're going to steal, you steal a million, if you're going to love, love a princess. And I lived like a princess. I'll do my stretch, of course, whatever I have to, then I'll come out and start again."

' "Then you'll be in for another stretch, Antonina," the women told her.

'She laughed: "Not me! Me and my husband and son will be more careful next time, we've learnt our lesson!"

'Her husband and son were in the same prison, in fact on the same floor as us. They used to talk to each other during exercise and send messages to each other through the gruel ladlers. We asked her how old her son was: "Nineteen. So what? He's got to learn about life so he doesn't get trodden on by other people later." And she burst into song, as if to show how well she'd survive.

'A cheerful woman is a great thing to have in your cell, but there was something malicious about Antonina's good spirits. She was always scornful and saying vile things to the other women. In fact she didn't have a good word for anyone except her son and her husband.

'We were once talking about life in the zone. As usual Antonina took over the conversation, even though she'd never even had a sniff of a zone: "If all men are enemies in life, then it's even more true in camp. Outside I walked all over people to get to the good life, and in the zone I shall do the same to get out! I shall do deals with the authorities, I'll take the younger ones as lovers and bribe the older ones."

'Then an old zek called Makhanya said to her: "Don't sing too soon, little bird. Remember where you are. Prison doesn't like upstarts, it likes cautious ones."

'In fact prison soon tamed her. So much that even Makhanya felt sorry for her.

'The prison was being used for zeks on their way from Koma to Siberia to work on the gas pipeline they had started building for the Germans. They were the worst type, all long-termers – men let out for a time to work on construction sites. Some were criminals, others just riff-raff, but all were dangerous. The prison was bursting at the seams and not a day passed without some terrible fight or row. After one of these flare-ups, ten of the offenders were thrown in the cell where Antonina's son was. And the very first night the whole lot of them raped the boy. First he screamed for his mother and father to save him. Antonina heard him and banged on the iron door till her hands bled. But in vain. After a while, the screams in the cell stopped and everything went quiet. Antonina slid down the door on to the floor, grabbed herself by the hair and sat there moaning. She went on moaning for hours, there was no end to it. And do you know, as we sat there, we saw her hair turn white, right before our eyes.

'Next morning mother and son were both carted off to the prison hospital: he was taken to surgery to be sewn up, and she was taken to the shrinks. She'd gone completely crazy.

'Then Makhanya said to us: "If you ask me, comrades, Antonina ruined her son herself. Not by landing him in prison with her, but by not teaching him how to live with people. He must have done something stupid in the cell. Prison doesn't like the pushy types, it soon breaks their horns."'

The women were horrified by this story, and some expressed amazement: 'Do you really get that between men – rape?'

'Yes,' answered Zina. 'And once a man's been worked over like that he's no longer considered a man in the zone. No one will sit down at table with him or lie near him. And if anyone feels like it they'll take him behind the barracks, turn him round and fuck him in the arse. They're called Mashkas, those men, and they're the most miserable wretches in the zone.'

'And the men who do that to them? Aren't they despised too?'

'No, they're admired for doing that. It's just like between a man and a woman outside: they both fuck, but she's a whore and he's a great guy.'

'Oh, Zina!' sighed Olga, 'and I thought you were going to tell us how justice was done, how life punished at least one man for all the women who have been raped. To hear about a boy being raped is no comfort for us.'

'Wait, Olga! It'll soon be my turn,' said Valentina. 'I'll comfort you. Just be patient! Now you begin your story,

157

Natasha, or Olga will get very upset waiting for justice to be done.'

So Natasha began her tale.

Story Three

by the engineer, Natasha, about a danger that she managed to escape in early childhood thanks to the fact that she had already been partially enlightened by the boy next door.

'I have never been properly raped, thank God. I have, of course, had the usual trouble on the street after dark, but it has usually been men propositioning me rather than displaying aggressive intentions. But something happened to me when I was a child that did almost end badly for me. It was Vitka, my neighbour's son, who helped to save me from being raped. He was in the second year at school, he lived in flat 31, and he was the scourge of my childhood.

'I was a small child, and I just couldn't reach the doorbell to our flat. But the door was next the window on the stairs, so I worked out a way of climbing up on to the window sill and from there reaching across to ring the bell. But at that point trouble was always just round the corner – that Vitka boy. However quietly I tried to go up to the window and climb up on to the window sill, he always managed to be watching me: I think he just spent the whole day looking through his own keyhole, waiting for me to come. As soon as I was on the window sill he would run out of his flat, rush up to me, dive under my skirt and put his hand on my pussy. I would try to kick him away and punch him on the head, and he would give a dirty laugh and run back into his flat before my parents saw him. I would cry, but when my parents asked me what was the matter I wouldn't say anything. Well, they thought someone had been nasty to me when I was playing, and took no notice of it.

'I didn't actually understand why Vitka did that to me, but I felt it was somehow an insult to me, and at the same time something bad. He became a kind of nightmare for me. I was longing to grow up and take revenge on him, and I longed even more to grow big enough to reach the bell as soon as possible, so that I wouldn't have to climb up on the window sill any more. With my feet on the ground, I never felt afraid of Vitka, I never let him get near me. The worst thing was he would always jump out at the very moment I had to stand with my legs apart to keep my balance.

'But, as it turned out, it was through Vitka that I escaped a far greater danger. I was playing one day in the sandpit in the garden next to our house and a man came up to me and asked me if I would like him to show me a trick. I said I would. He took a little glass bottle of water out of his pocket, and there was a funny little coloured man floating in the water. The man pressed down on the cork and the little man in the bottle started spinning and bobbing up and down. Then he let me try, and the same thing happened. I liked the trick, and he said to me: "Come to my place, I've got lots of tricks like that at home. And you can keep the little man."

'I was delighted, and since I liked the man I let him take me by the hand away from the house. He brought me to his place on a different street. He led me into his room and told me to talk every so quietly because there was a big bad dog next door, and he might hear me and try to get me. This also seemed to me interesting and mysterious. He started putting out all sorts of fascinating toys in front of me, all wonderful things I had never seen before: a little Chinaman with a nodding head, a little snake made of tiny stones that looked just like a real live one, a little duck made of fluffy yellow fur that bowed its head. I remember those toys were all the sort that you had to touch with your finger to make them work. Then he took out his penis and asked me if I'd ever seen a toy like that. I said I hadn't, but that I didn't like that toy. He said: "Well, you just touch it with your finger and see what happens."

'I touched his penis and it jumped up under my hand. I liked that. But when he squatted in front of me and put his hand up between my legs just the way Vitka did, I got angry, slapped his hand and screamed at him: "You horrible man! You tricked me! I want to go home!"

'He got scared at this, jumped up, took me out of his flat and down to the corner of our street. I never saw him again. So thanks to Vitya, I was spared much worse miseries.

Remember I was much younger than Albina, when she had her terrible experience. I sometimes wonder if these monsters have any age limit below which they don't go?'

Valentina spoke up at this point: 'I can satisfy your curiosity, Natasha. In practice there's no limit. A father was brought to trial in our region for raping his two-month-old daughter when he was drunk.'

The women gasped.

'Was he shot?'

'No, they just put him in prison, even though the prosecutor demanded execution. But the most striking thing about the trial was the way the wife behaved. She shouted at the judge and the prosecutor: "I've lost a daughter! Do you want to take my husband from me as well?" '

'I can't believe it!' exclaimed Emma.

Here Galina gave a humourless laugh: 'I can give you a theatrical answer: "There are more things in heaven and earth than are dreamt of by our prosecutors, Horatio." I've heard stories from Slava and his friends who have been in the camps, that are enough to make you lose your faith in humanity. So many crimes are committed for revenge, or for other unworthy motives – money, for instance – that it makes me think we've got ourselves rather too bogged down in sexual matters. Man does not live either by the sordid or the elevated feelings alone. Doesn't money, for example, play a vital role in our lives? Let's set aside tomorrow for that – a simple everyday topic. Agreed? Now over to you, Valentina: where is this long-awaited revenge on rapists that you promised us? We're all ears.'

Story Four

by Valentina, describing revenge on a rapist.

'This happened last winter. An old friend of ours, a major in the militia who lived and worked in the town of Pushkin, invited us to his birthday party. My husband went there straight from work, but I got delayed at a meeting and left later on, about eight o'clock. I came out on to the station square at Pushkin, and there was not a single taxi or bus to be seen. There was quite a frost too, and I didn't fancy standing around waiting for a bus in the square while people were already having a good time drinking to the birthday boy. So I decided to go there on foot, especially as our friend Arkady lived not too far away. The only thing I hadn't reckoned on was having to go through the park, something I'd rather not do in the dark.

'I was scurrying along through the park, and suddenly I heard footsteps behind me, and a suspicious crunch of snow. I looked round, and saw a man gaining on me: his jacket was open, his face red, his eyes white. Well, I said to myself, either I've had it, or my astrakhan coat has. He ran up to me, grabbed me by the coat, but instead of pulling it off me he dived underneath it, fumbling for my tits. At the same time he threw me down behind a bush at the edge of the path. I started yelling, but he growled right into my face: "Scream all you like! My mates are just over there drinking in that hut. It'll be a feast for them to have some pussy together."

'Disgusting creature, he was even laughing. But I stopped shouting, and tried in vain to defend myself with my arms and legs. The coat got in the way, my cap came down over my eyes and I couldn't see a thing. Meanwhile he took out his prick, and started poking it at me. It was hard and stiff like a chair leg. I tried pushing it away with my hand, but he kept ramming it inside my torn knickers.

'Here, at this most interesting moment, I have to make a small digression. As I told you before, I was wearing a grey astrakhan coat. Everything else was imported: French boots – only after a lot of string-pulling, a fluffy fox-fur cap and even the mittens came from Canada. In other words, I was dressed like a real lady. There was only one thing out of place: my Canadian mittens were attached to my coat sleeves by bits of thread. I knew I had a habit of losing gloves and mittens but these were from Andryusha, so I sacrificed fashion for the memory of a dear friend and sewed them on with waxed thread. And it was one of those mittens that saved me.

'There was I, struggling away with him for all I was worth,

thrashing about in the snow, trying to push the cap off my eyes, but my strength was going, I felt I was suffocating and that my heart was coming up to my throat, when suddenly he let out a wild yell: "Let go! Let go, you bitch!"

'He gave a wrench, and yelled even louder. "Let go!" he bellowed.

'I couldn't understand who'd got hold of who. Then I felt him pulling my hand towards him for some reason, towards his unbuttoned trousers. When I yanked my hand back, he let out such an animal scream that I got scared the guys in the hut would hear.

' "Keep the noise down!" I said, still trying to understand why he was asking me to let him go, and not the other way round. He wasn't gripping me by the hands any more, but he kept pulling my right hand toward his crotch. I pushed my cap back off my eyes with my left hand, sat up in the snow, and looked to see what the hell was up. And godfathers! I can see it yet! The thread of my mitten had wound itself in a tight knot round his balls. I struggled to my knees and barked at him: "All right, get up. You've had your little game. Now if you don't play my game I'll have your balls off right now!"

'He got up obediently, holding on to his property with both hands. The tears were streaming down his cheeks, but he wasn't yelling any more, just moaning a little.

' "Let me go!" he begged. "I was just having a bit of fun!"

' "And now I'm having a bit of fun. Let's go."

'I led him out on to the path and along it. At arm's length, just in case he should come to his senses and start bashing me about with his maulers.

' "What the hell is it anyway, that thing you're strangling me with?" he asked.

' "It is a special anti-rapist device from Canada. You've heard of handcuffs – these are prick-cuffs. Try to get away and your balls drop off."

'I was talking like that, but actually I was scared: what if he didn't believe me, what if he managed to get out of it? Then what vengeance he'd exact!

' "Where are you taking me?"

' "Come on, keep walking!" I shouted, pulling at the thread.

'But I was getting panicky, wondering how I was going to

get away from him. It was just like the joke about the bear: "I've caught a bear!" "Well, bring him here." "He won't come!" "Then come here yourself." "He won't let me go!" But I suddenly remembered about his friends that he was threatening me with. It was terrifying, but I decided to risk it.

'"Right," I said, "you've learnt your lesson, now I'll release you. Only I can't deal with these prick-cuffs single-handed. Your friends will have to help me."

'"Can't you do it yourself?" he protested.

'"No. They're programmed to sound an alarm when the victim screams."

'"All right, let's go . . ." he grunted.

'And he took me to the hut, where his friends really were drinking vodka in the frosty snow.

'"I've brought your friend back," I told them. "Has anyone got a pen-knife?"

'They looked at us wide-eyed: my hand was you know where, and they didn't know what was going on. One of them searched in his pockets and produced a knife. Then my assailant opened out his jacket and there he was in all his glory – on a string, with a mitten dangling down under his balls. I can't describe what happened next – but they rolled about on top of each other in helpless laughter. They released the victim by cutting the thread, and looked at me full of admiration. "What a woman! Wouldn't want to meet you on a dark night!"

'When that idiot saw that my anti-rape device was really a mitten on a string, he just sat down on the bench and buried his head between his knees in shame.

'Well, I didn't stop to wait for him to recover, I just ran quickly like the wind to my friend's house.

The women laughed and laughed, and Albina hugged Valentina for what she called that 'heroic deed'.

It took a long time for them to settle down but finally Albina began her story.

Story Five

by the airhostess Albina, which tells how she fell into the hands of a sadist, and how she waited in vain for help.

'I am very sorry I cannot tell you something to make you laugh as Valentina has done. You probably think that after what happened to me as a child, no rapists held any terrors for me. You are wrong. In fact, quite the reverse. True, I had a ball with whoever I wanted to, but at the least hint of force I was off like a shot. My men friends knew that, and they were very careful to behave themselves with me. All the same I did get into trouble, and I was so hurt by it that I couldn't relax until I had taken revenge to satisfy my sinful soul.

'Here's how it happened. There was this guy, a real mummy's boy to look at. We got to know each other at dances, went to restaurants and cinemas, that sort of thing. I was planning to get closer to him, so to speak, but he hastened events and that was the end of a beautiful friendship.

'He announced to me one day that the next day was his birthday, that he was having some friends and wanted me to come.

'I agreed, and he wrote his address down for me and told me what time to come.

'Next day I got all dressed up, bought a cake to give him, and presented myself on his doorstep like little Red Riding Hood. I rang the bell. He opened the door to me wearing the most informal clothes – a track suit. It was all quiet and empty in the flat, not a whiff of a party and no guests to be seen.

' "Where is everyone?"

' "They're coming later. We'll have a little time to ourselves first."

'I gave him the cake and went through into the room. He had a separate flat – two rooms, so it was obvious he didn't live there alone. There was a terrible mess everywhere, odd bits of clothing lying around, and shoes – all women's shoes.

' "Who's been throwing all this women's junk around the place?"

' "My wife went off on holiday today."

' "Aha, now I understand. Your wife goes off to her holiday resort in the morning, and you invite me to spend the evening alone with you for your birthday? Why give me all this bull? When I want to have it off with you, I'll decide the time and place."

164

'As soon as he heard that he started pawing me, but I slapped him on the hand. "Get your maulers off! I can't stand deceitful men. Fetch my coat. Your birthday is postponed until you understand how to do business with me."

'Even then I wasn't planning to give him the push completely. He was actually my type. A real angel face with cherub lips and doll's eyes. I've always liked men where the masculine side doesn't come right out and hit you, where there's nothing crude on the outside and their sexuality is not obvious. Well, this one seemed just that kind, all innocent. But I can't stick a lot of lying just for the sake of a night in the sack.

'I made my way towards the door, but he jumped ahead of me, locked the door, and then came at me. I pushed him away: "Are you crazy? You'd like some rough stuff, eh? I'll knock the snot out of you first!"

'"We'll see about that," he answered, and his eyes became evil slits, like those of an angry cat, and suddenly he pounced on me using karate chops. He may have looked a skinny weakling but his hands were strong as iron. He drove me into the corner until I was bent double and didn't have the breath to scream. Then he threw me on to the floor and started to kick me with his boots on the breasts and between the legs. Now I started screaming in earnest. I knew they could hear me because I could hear music coming through the wall. But the music was turned up, obviously to drown my screams. There was going to be no help from the neighbours. Then I managed somehow to pull off one of my shoes and hurl it at the window. The window broke, and the shoe went flying out. Now I could hear the voices of the old men playing dominoes at a table: they had seen me when I came past, had looked me up and down when I came into the courtyard. These were the people I was counting on now. "Help! Murder! Rape!" I screamed as loud as I could.

'The voices outside went silent. They've gone to get the militia, I thought, or they're coming straight here to the flat. But no one ever did come to my aid, and that angelic looking sadist finished beating me up, and as he raped me, he pinched my breasts till they were black and blue and tore out chunks of my hair. As he neared orgasm he grabbed my throat with both hands and squeezed it in time to his coming.

'In the end he let me get dressed, gave me his wife's old shoes so I wouldn't have to go barefoot, and shoved me out of the door.

'The next day I could hardly lift my head off the pillow: my face, my head, my body – all bruised and battered. I telephoned to work and took a week off at my own expense. I gave them some story about a relative being on her death-bed somewhere, and that I had to take the plane and go to her. But actually it was me lying there half dead, choking with pain and weeping in humiliation.

'I stayed in bed till I felt better, then I went to try and bring charges against that creep. They sent me to the investigator. Anokhin was his name. He told me he would open a case provided there were witnesses. I told him how the "witnesses" through the wall and outside in the yard had reacted. He laughed: "Typical. That's the reason most rape cases are not followed up: the witnesses refuse to help the investigation." He advised me to go to the house myself and talk to the people there, and maybe I would find someone with a little more courage.

'That's what I did. I went there, and in a short time I had visited all that creep's neighbours living on his staircase, and I had met the janitor and found out the addresses of all the old-age pensioners and women who spent the day sitting on their bums minding other people's business. But they all refused to help. Some lied that they hadn't heard anything anyway, others said they had heard something but hadn't seen anything, and therefore couldn't testify. Others simply refused to talk to me, saying: "It's none of our business!"

'One old bitch even got angry: "We would never go to court as witnesses! We're a decent family!"

'There was a general living in the flat where I had heard the loud music. He came to the door in his uniform and invited me right into his flat. I told him who I was and what I wanted. I pinned all my hopes on him: someone who had been in the war couldn't be a coward! But do you know what that bastard said to me? "Respectable girls do not get into situations where they can be raped. Nobody will rape my daughter!"

'Those words of his really finished me off, they hurt so much. Later on I got my revenge both on him and that sadistic creep, but I'll tell you about that another time. Basically, my campaign produced only one useful thing: the janitor gave me back my shoe which she had found in the yard the next morning: "I could see it was an expensive shoe, so I picked it up, thinking someone might come asking for it."

'I went back to the investigator, told him what progress I had made, and asked him to have me physically examined. He said he wouldn't do it: "If I open a case and it doesn't get solved, I'll get a reprimand. It's better not to start it at all."

'I realized he was not going to help me either, and I left feeling battered on all sides, so much so that I wanted to do myself in. I didn't, of course, and now I'm glad I didn't. It was best in the end.'

'And how will you get your revenge on him?' asked the women.

'Well and truly. He's still paying for that birthday even now, and he can expect more in the future, although not from me. Right now it makes me sick to think about it so I'll tell you the rest some other time, girls.'

'A good idea,' said Valentina. 'We keep talking about our women's troubles and humiliations but we sometimes get our own back, so let's talk about that on one of the remaining days.'

This was agreed, and the responsibility for telling a story now passed to Galina.

Story Six

by the dissident Galina, recounting how she was subjected to crude violence for the sins of others.

'My misfortune occurred through my own stupidity, through not trusting people: I made enemies where I should have found friends.

'I was travelling from Moscow to visit Slava late one autumn. My train was running ten minutes late, and those ten minutes were crucial. The point was that, according to

167

the timetable, my train got into Potma only twenty minutes before the local train left for Barashevo, where Slava's camp was. In those twenty minutes I had to get down off one train with my heavy bags and knapsack, cross over all the lines – and there must have been about twenty of them – by a long, long overhead footbridge, go down the other side and walk another several hundred metres to get to the platform for the local "cuckoo", which is what they called the train to the camp. Anyway, I was obviously running late for the cuckoo, but I couldn't afford to miss it under any circumstances: the visit was arranged for the next day, and if I didn't make the train I wouldn't get to Barashevo in the morning, and no one would arrange a meeting for me after dinner. I would lose a day, and then we would have two instead of three. Or they might cancel the meeting altogether. It was unfair that everything might be ruined for ten minutes.

'I leapt out of the Moscow train and ran across the overhead bridge. I was dragging my bags along, with the knapsack banging me in the back, gasping for breath and drenched in sweat. Halfway across the bridge I saw the cuckoo passing slowly underneath me: three passenger cars and one for prisoners, with windows on only one side. I dropped my bags, threw the knapsack down, sat on it and burst into tears. After I calmed down a bit I decided I would try and hitch a lift by road. There wasn't much traffic but I stood and waved my arms. A few covered lorries passed with guards in the cabs – zeks being taken to or from work. They weren't going to stop for me, of course. Suddenly an ordinary lorry with some sort of barrels in the back stopped. The driver, a young guy, stuck his head out of the cab and asked: "Where to?"

' "Barashevo."

' "Get in!"

'I climbed into the cab, somehow squeezing all my gear in too, and off we went.

'As we were driving along he glanced at my bags: "You been to Moscow?"

' "Yes."

' "Went to get stocked up, did you?"

'Here I ought to have told the truth and said I was going to visit my husband in camp, and nothing would have happened. But I was scared that if he found out I was a stranger here something bad might happen. So I pretended I was local – my biggest mistake: "Yes, I went to Moscow to do some shopping. It's easier to get food there."

'He accepted my story.

' "Of course. And where do you live? At Barashevo?"

'I had to say I did, because I didn't know any places in Mordovia apart from Barashevo and Potma.

' "Yes, I do."

'It didn't occur to me that the only people living in Barashevo, as in all places near camps, especially political ones, are those connected with the camp.

' "Do you work there yourself, or do you have a husband working there?"

'And again, not sensing the danger, I said: "My husband."

' "Now I understand, Madam," said the driver, and the conversation stopped. This suited me, I was thinking about my own things, about my meeting with Slava. We drove in silence for an hour, two hours. It was dark already. Then the driver suddenly said to me: "Look, dearie, I don't feel like driving any more, I'm tired. I've got a friend just along the road here. He's a watchman at a timber yard, and he lives there, too. We'll spend the night with him, and then I'll get you to Barashevo early in the morning."

'Well, there was no point in arguing. I didn't mind where I spent the night, at Barashevo or on the road, as long as I got there in the morning in time for the meeting. We came to his friend's place. It was pretty desolate, with a long fence and a watchman's hut nearby. I was expecting his friend would have a family house with a wife who would fix me up for the night properly. But it turned out that the hut only had two little rooms: one, a sort of office with charts on the wall, a desk, some benches and an iron stove; and the other, just a little cubby-hole with a bunk – I saw that later. We went in, I put my bags in the corner and sat down on the bench close to the stove to get warmed up: there had been a constant draught in the lorry, and my feet were frozen. I didn't like the look of my driver's friend at all: unclean, unshaven, his padded jacket was all torn.

'The driver brought two bottles of vodka from the lorry, put them on the table and said to his friend: "And her ladyship has brought us some food from Moscow. Come on, dearie, turn out your precious stuff!"

'I got out a piece of sausage, some cheese, and three oranges. "There you are. I'm sorry I can't spare any more."

' "Well, thanks anyway. I only hope you'll be more generous with other things."

'They drank vodka, and I asked for some tea. We sat drinking. They were talking about their things, I was thinking about mine, but a nasty feeling of foreboding crept into my heart.

'They finished one bottle, and the lorry driver said: "Let's get some sleep, and we'll finish the other one afterwards. Maybe madam will get more talkative then, and chuck in some more snacks."

'He got up from the bench, went over to the door into the second room and kicked it open: "S'il vous plait, Madame, as they say in high society. Please get undressed and lie down."

'I went in, and I could only see one bed, so I asked: "Where are you going to sleep, then? Or is there another room here?"

' "Why such luxury? Stepa and me'll take it in turns, we're used to it." And he started to undress, grinning all over his face. At last I understood.

' "What's your game?"

' "You'll see soon enough. I don't mount women with my clothes on."

'He suddenly seized me by the shoulders and threw me on to the bunk. I started crying and begging him to let me go and not touch me. He gripped me by the throat and hissed: "Belt up, and don't bother to struggle, or I'll finish you off and drag you out to the forest like a hunk of carrion and leave you there for the wolves!"

'And his voice was full of such bitter, bitter hatred for me that I just froze in horror: never in my life had I encountered such hatred. I screamed in terror but he rammed a pillow in my face.

' "Belt up, or I'll smother you!"

'He did his business quickly and as though it repelled him. And that, too, I found incomprehensible, humiliating, and frightening. He immediately got up, dressed himself, and opened the door to the other room.

' "Stepan, I've finished with her. Your turn now."

'Here I leapt up, tried to gather up my clothes, screaming all the while: "Rapists!"

'The driver laughed: "That's right, lady! Me and Stepan have heard all that from people like your husband before, we've been through that."

'Then Stepan suddenly said: "Leave her alone, Kolya. I'm not really in the mood for a pig's wife today. Why don't you just take her up to the road, and someone will pick her up. Just watch she doesn't remember the road and your number plate. Otherwise she'll bring a few more guests, and it'll be a lot of bother."

' "All right. Only first I'll take a look through her bags. I have to have something for my labours! I didn't do her for free!" Here he grabbed my bags and started tipping everything out on to the table. I stood there waiting, indifferently watching this plunder; I was past caring. He arranged everything in two piles, saying: "That's for us, that's for the pigs, that's for us . . ." He picked up a piece of lard and a package of garlic and looked at me in amazement: "Why are you bringing garlic and lard to Barashevo all the way from Moscow? Has your own run out before the winter starts? You people always had enough of this sort of stuff, you always help yourselves out of the zeks' parcels when you run out . . ."

'So now, since it didn't matter any longer, I told the truth: "I'm taking it to my husband in the camp."

' "What?! You mean he's inside?"

' "Yes."

' "So you're not a pig's wife?"

'I shook my head.

' "And your husband's a zek?"

'I nodded.

' "Wait . . . Why did you lie and say you lived in Barashevo? Only pigs live there . . ."

' "I thought it would be safer to say I was local."

'Then that lorry driver, Kolya, put his hands to his head: "Oh, you stupid, stupid fool! What have you gone and done, and what have you made me do? I've offended my brother zek's wife!"

'He came up to me, took me by the shoulders, looked into my eyes, and tears were even running down his cheeks. "Forgive me, dear lady, forgive me! You led me astray yourself, I treated you like a pig's wife, not because I felt any desire, but out of hate for them . . . Can you forgive me?"

'I could see they were not drunken tears but sincere ones. I realized that everything that had happened to me had not been meant for me. And of course that made me burst into tears again. Stepan was trying to comfort us both: "All right, kids! It was a mistake, you didn't mean to offend her. Now you forgive him, or he'll be eating his heart out. And forgive me, too, for the things I said."

'Well, girls, I did forgive them. Not immediately, it's true, but I did in the end. And I cried myself to sleep on that same bed. There was nowhere else to sleep, and my legs were giving way under me from all I had been through. In the morning Kolya the driver woke me up and took me right to the camp. As he said goodbye he asked me not to say anything to my husband. "Get over it on your own, don't upset him. And forgive me again."

'Naturally I said nothing to Slava. I decided to bury it deep in my own heart and cope with it alone.

'Three days later, when our visit was over and I had set off to catch the "cuckoo" again, I caught sight of Kolya's lorry not far from the camp: he was waiting for me, so that he could take me to Potma to get the Moscow train. He had been there since early morning – he wanted to make up in some small way for hurting me.'

The person who took this story most to heart was, of course, Zina – she even began to cry. But she felt sorry, not so much for Galina as for the driver, Kolya, who had got into such a predicament. 'It's a good thing you understood him and forgave him, or he might have done something to himself.'

'Yes, he even confessed to me, as we were driving along, that that had been his first thought. OK, enough said, it's still depressing to think about. You tell a story now, Olga!'

Story Seven

by the worker Olga, containing an agonizing discussion about which shift is the safest for a single woman to work.

172

'My husband and I received a one-room flat in a new house beyond Avtovo. You know Avtovo, don't you? Well, just beyond if they've built this new development the other side of the forest. Avtovo ends, then comes this small forest, then our houses. You know what a development is like when it's not yet finished: some houses have people living in them, others are empty boxes with no windows or doors. There's mud everywhere, ditches, all sorts of construction equipment, little huts. Horrible.

'We had our house-warming party. My husband took a week's unpaid leave to get the flat in good order: re-laying some of the floors, re-hanging some of the doors so they would shut properly, filling in cracks in the window frames. Anyone who has moved into a new house knows the sort of thing I mean. Well, he was working in the house, but I had to go to work – we couldn't last out long anyway without his wages. At that time I had to do the evening shift. Alone. Before, we had always gone together, working in the same shop and on the same shift.

'It happened the very first evening when I came back after midnight on the last bus, got out at the last stop, and had to walk through the forest. It's small enough, but it's scary all the same. Right from the bus stop two types started following me. That's good, I thought, in my simple way, it won't be so frightening. All the other people that got off the bus had gone in their different directions, and there were just the three of us left. They even asked if they could take my arm so I wouldn't trip.

'I agreed and even thanked them; it really was quite dangerous in the dark, you couldn't see where you were treading. They took me firmly by the arms, and off we went. They didn't say anything, and their silence suddenly made me worried: it would be better if they were chattering away, I thought, talking any old rubbish. When we got into the forest one of them covered my mouth, the other grabbed me by the legs, and they dragged me into the bushes like a carcass of mutton. But I was lucky that during the day bulldozers and heavy lorries had been going along this road and had churned it up completely: the one that was covering my mouth and pulling me by the shoulders stumbled and twisted his ankle. He dropped me right on my head, gave a cry and took hold of his foot. The other one dragged me another couple of yards along the ground, and then the one who was sitting nursing his foot called to him: "Forget about the bitch! Help me!"

'Isn't that something? On top of everything else, I was a bitch too! So the other one let me go, and I picked myself up and ran.

'I got home, told my husband what had happened and made a big fuss about it. But he said to me: "Olga, you can't stop working. We'll never make it. Perhaps you could ask to be put on a different shift?"

'That's what I did. I told our brigadier and she put me on the night shift. "Your husband can see you off to work, and coming home in the morning won't be dangerous."

'So I started doing nights. I did my first night, then as I was coming back in the bus some time between six and seven in the morning, I noticed as we got towards the last stop that the buses coming towards us were all full of people, but almost everyone had got off mine by the time we reached Avtovo. I would have to tramp the forest alone again!

'I wasn't the only person to get out of the bus; once again there were some men, three or four of them. But this time I crossed over the road to where people were waiting to take the bus in the other direction, and waited until the men had disappeared into the forest. Then I ran home alone. But what do you think? I got through the forest safely, without even stumbling, flying like the wind. But when I came out into the empty space, this guy suddenly leapt out of an empty half-finished house and pulled me into the dark doorway! I landed him one on the mouth with my shopping bag, tore myself free and ran and ran! I got home, sobbing: "What am I to do? I can't go on like this! And I don't want to!"

'My husband tried to calm me down and persuade me to try going on to the day shift. I did. But in the morning crush in the bus I had my purse snatched out of my bag! I'd had about enough.

'At this point I dug my heels in and made my husband leave the flat as it was until our summer leave. We started going to work together, and I had no further adventures to cope with.'

'What about the poor single factory girls who do night shifts and evening shifts, walking through the dark –

174

they're the ones I really feel sorry for,' said Larissa. 'Even a married woman has a hard enough time from those night predators, let alone the young girls!'

'The least the authorities could do is free women from the night shift,' said Nelya. 'Though that alone wouldn't solve the problem. Sex crimes are also committed in broad daylight. Listen to what I have to tell you.'

Story Eight

by the teacher Nelya, about how she was raped a few yards from her husband.

'My husband doesn't know about this, and I hope he'll never find out. You know how Boris and I met, and how his daughter Lenusya brought us together. But there was another reason why we understood each other very quickly and fell in love. Boris had also been in a prison camp during the war, and he only got out alive because the Russian soldiers who were captured with him didn't let on to the Germans that he was Jewish. He's not at all Jewish to look at, in fact he looks more like a German – a real blue-eyed blonde.

'What Boris had gone through damaged him physically, rather than emotionally the way it damaged me. Four years ago he had a heart attack. I already thought I was going to lose him, but fortunately he was spared. He was discharged from the hospital, and we went to the country so that he could get his strength back in the fresh air. That's when it happened.

'Boris still couldn't move about very well, he walked with a stick like an old man. Not far from the village there was a lake with trees growing round it. We used to leave home in the morning before it got too hot, walk to the lake, and spend the whole day there until the heat died down again and Boris and I could make our way back. We took rugs, food, and books with us. Boris spent most of the time lying in a nut grove in the shade, reading. I used to swim in the lake, pick mushrooms, and generally recover from all the anxieties of his illness. I would also gather brushwood by the lake and make a bonfire to boil the tea and fry the mushrooms. Each day Borya got more perky, the bluish colour acquired in hospital gradually disappeared from his face, and his eyes got brighter. Sometimes I lay down next to him and he put his hand on my breast. But that was all, we couldn't risk anything else.

'One day I was walking along near the lake gathering the last bilberries. Borya and I called to each other from time to time and if I went up on to a little hill I could see him through the trees in the nut grove. He lay in the grass quietly, reading a book.

'Suddenly someone jumped on me from behind.

'He threw me down, and started kissing me. My first instinct was to shout to Borya, but then in a flash I pictured Borya running to help me, forgetting his stick and clutching at his heart. I imagined him throwing himself into a fight with this frenzied rapist – and this alone made me submit. I even whispered to that bastard: "Just keep it quiet, for God's sake!"

'And just as silently I let him get away. Then I got up, went down to the lake, got into the water and began to swim. I tried not to cry so that Borya wouldn't ask why my eyes were red. And that's the whole story.

'And then what?' asked Albina. 'What did you do then?'

'Then? I cooked Borya's soup and fed him.'

'And then?' persisted Albina. She was sitting up in bed staring at Nelya with big eyes. 'Did you know where the boy lived?'

'Yes, I knew.'

'And you kept quiet?'

'Of course. Because of Borya.'

'And you didn't even want to go away from there?'

'I couldn't. Borya was recovering really well, and if we had moved to a different place our money would have run out before the end of my leave.'

'I think that's ridiculous!' said Albina.

'And I think it's heroic,' retorted Larissa calmly. The women agreed.

'Why don't we talk one of these evenings about women's heroism,' suggested Emma, 'about the courage

176

that they often show in life.'

'Agreed!' Larissa replied for all of them. 'But now you, Emma, have to tell us a story on the assigned topic. We're waiting!'

Story Nine

by the theatre director Emma, about a rape committed against her without the use of force.

'This is a story about why I decided to become a director and how I succeeded.

'I have loved the theatre since childhood. If you recall, on the first day I didn't tell a story about my first love, but about an artist who was in love with me. That was because my true first love was the theatre. And even now I wouldn't swap that love for any other. Men I have betrayed, the theatre – never. Although once I came within a hair's breadth.

'I've had a gift for acting since I was a child, and it wasn't long before it was noticed: from twelve years old I was in the drama circle at the Pioneers' Palace, and I always played the leading roles. I got into drama school quite easily, even though the competition was horrific: something like a hundred and fifty candidates for every place. I got through the first year, and then the incident I am going to tell you about happened.

'How many of you have seen the film *The Girl from the Forest*? Yes, nearly all of you. Well, don't you recognize me, have I aged so much? You're right, I'm the one who played Natasha, the woodman's daughter. And this is how I got the part. The film people came to our institute and started selecting girls from the drama course to audition for the lead role. I was one of those taken. We were each given a scene to play which was recorded on video. The director looked through the tapes and chose me and one other girl, someone from the third year. She obviously had more acting experience than me, but I looked the part more.

'The director, Gektor Fedoseev, gave us both the script to read through, so that we could get into the part better, then he ordered us to do one more screen test. After that he invited me to the studio for a talk. The invitation came in a splendid letter to the institute. I was delighted – I had won – or so I thought. I got dressed up, had my hair done, and reported. He received me in his study, sat me down in an armchair and said: "Now, my dear. It's very complicated. You're both good, I like you both, but you both come just a fraction short of the part – there's a slight lack of temperament."

'And he began this long speech about what female temperament was and how one got it and that its absence could be detected in even the most placid role.

'You've probably guessed already? but I didn't catch on immediately, even though I had already slept around a bit by that time. But Gektor was patient, he kept on playing the same old tune, till I finally cottoned on to what he was after, which was that I should give myself to him right there, as evidence of my temperament!

'When he realized I had cottoned on he started speaking quite plainly: "You understand, I do not intend to rape or force you. But if you are serious about this part, then here's the sofa, and here's the key to the door. I'm not hurrying you, I'm putting the key here on the table. Sit and think it over. And if you decide – lock the door yourself."

'Well, what can I tell you, my dear friends? You've seen the film, so you know I got the part. And now you know how I got it. After I had started shooting I came face to face one day with my defeated rival. She looked me in the eye, laughed and said: "There's an old joke in the theatre: the way to success is through the director's couch."

'I realized that that girl had been stronger than me and had not yielded. But I got the part.

'Gektor didn't bother me during the shooting. He was actually a bit of a wimp with women, once was enough for him. And yet his secret complex was precisely about being a rapist. His wife was really hideous, a real fat-arsed toad. She was nicknamed Empress Bum at the studio. At one time *his* road to success lay through Empress Bum's bed – she was the director's daughter. So now he was taking it out on young little actresses.

'I found the acting difficult: I had a heroic part to play, but I felt like a prostitute. It came hard, that first part. That was when I made up my mind not to remain in acting, but to try and become a director. And I did, as you see. It's an ill wind . . .'

The women talked about how life on the stage is not one long holiday, as it sometimes seems from a distance. And they discussed at some length what the director had said about 'not intending to rape or use force'.

'Typical male logic!' observed Larissa. 'Just like Olga's rapists shouting that she was a "bitch".'

Inasmuch as they had all finished their confessions with the exception of Irishka, she hastened to tell her story.

Story Ten

by the secretary Irina, recounting how she contrived not only to escape being raped, but also to re-educate her attacker.

'This is what happened to me. I was coming home rather late one evening after work. Seryozha and I live in a high-rise flat at the end of Moskovsky Prospect, by the Chisel. What? You don't know the Chisel? It's a new monument to the defenders of Leningrad. The sculptor is famous, but he's heaped up a pile of stuff that nobody can make head or tail of, he's just blocked off the whole street with a load of masterpieces. And sticking right up out of the middle of the heap is this long granite contraption with its top cut off at an angle. So the people living in our area have nicknamed it the Chisel. And some people give it even less respectable names, but I won't say what because Nelya's here – she's Jewish and might take offence.

'Anyway, just before you get to this Chisel, there are two twenty-storey buildings, one on each side of the avenue, and Seryozha and I live in one of them, on the eighth floor.

'I got into the lift late one evening, and a young guy came in after me. He immediately pressed the button for the twenty-second floor. I looked at him in surprise: no one

179

lives on the twenty-second floor, that's the attic. I was about to press my button, but he took me by the hand and didn't let me: "You're coming up with me."

' "And what for?"

' "You know quite well . . ."

'I could see he was still wet behind the ears, but he had a tight grip on me and I knew I would have to use all my female cunning to get away from him. So I began a conversation with him: "You ought to be ashamed of yourself, a nice boy like you. Any girl would be happy to be fucked by you, and here you are running after strange women in the lift, dragging them up to the attic. Some pleasure – the attic, where it stinks of cat's piss!"

' "No girl would go with me, so don't try to sweet talk me."

' "Why wouldn't they?"

' "Because I'm at training school and I live in a dormitory and I've got no money."

' "So what? True love doesn't depend on money. Anyway, isn't there enough grass in the forest for you?"

'The lift was now passing the eighth floor.

' "And I've got spots all over my face. What girl would want to go with me?"

' "So what? Two little pimples! But those eyes of yours are so expressive!"

'His eyes really were expressive: they expressed his desire, his fear, his curiosity – I've never seen such idiotic eyes in my life.

' "You're just saying that! . . ." He was slightly embarrassed at my compliment, and was not holding on to my hands so tightly. Here I contrived to brush against all the buttons with my elbow, hoping that at least one would get pressed. And just in time, too: the lift had arrived at the twenty-second floor. It stopped, the door opened, and the lad tried to get me out by force.

' "Wait!" I shouted. "I haven't told you how to get rid of your pimples yet!" At the same time I was bracing my leg against the wall of the lift next to the door so that he couldn't get me out. Then the door closed and the lift started to go down – it worked when I pressed the buttons with my elbow. "All right," I said to the lad, "let me go now. Your experiment was a failure. Someone has called the lift."

'He had already realized that, he'd let me go and turned pale.

' "Don't be afraid!" I told him. "I'm not going to hand you over to the militia or tell people. I feel sorry for you. Think about what I've said. Force doesn't suit you, I'm telling you as a woman. If I didn't have a husband I'd arrange to meet you myself."

' "It's bad . . .," he muttered, and he hid his face in his collar. I couldn't tell whether he was ashamed of himself, or just humiliated at having failed.

'The lift kept stopping at every other floor because I had pushed just about all the buttons. I didn't wait for the eighth floor, I got out early and walked down to my floor: I didn't want to stay with him in the lift.

'But that wasn't the end of the story. One day my husband and I were travelling on the metro, and at one stop in got that very same lad – with a girl on his arm. He recognized me and went as red as a lobster. I indicated the girl with my eyes: well? He nodded: fine! Then he did a nice thing: he walked past us down the car as if he was trying to get closer to the door, and as he got level with me he said: "Excuse me, please!"

'My husband and I let him past, and he looked me right in the face and quietly said: "Thank you very much!"

'As if he was thanking me for letting him get past. But I knew what he was really thanking me for . . . I never met him again.'

Irishka's story consoled everybody, though not as much as Valentina's story about the mittens. For the morrow they agreed to tell stories connected with money – how much in life depends on it? And so they prepared for sleep and the sixth day of *The Women's Decameron* ended.

THE SEVENTH DAY

which is devoted to **MONEY** and related matters

Story One

*by the biologist Larissa, about a copper five-copeck piece
which turned out to be invaluable, even though there is
not much one can buy with it.*

'I have never had any great problems over money. At
twenty-five I got a job as a junior research worker after I had
finished my post-graduate course, and started with quite a
good salary. My mother was a doctor, my father was
building aerodromes all over the country, and later had
something to do with building space centres. No, not
Baikonur, there are one or two others, but that's not our
subject . . . When I announced to my parents that I didn't
intend to get married, but that I wanted to have a baby and
live alone, it was a real blow for them and it took them a
long time to get over it. But they got used to the idea, and
they helped me to buy a co-operative flat with just one
room. When my son gets a bit bigger I shall swap it for a
two-room flat. I have already started putting money aside. I
don't stint myself over anything, although I must admit I
don't have any particular needs. I travel abroad at the state's
expense as part of the exchange of scientific information, I
have holidays wherever I please, I'm not interested in
diamonds, and I don't need a car – it's too much hassle. So I
have enough money, and I've even got some saved up for a
rainy day. But what gives me the greatest feeling of security
is the fact that I am dependent on no one.

'But there was one incident in my life when my fate hung
on a five-copeck piece, when I, an atheist, prayed to God for a
five-copeck piece – and God sent me one. There's just no way
to explain the incident except by intervention from above.

183

'It was when I was still on my post-graduate course. I was doing genetics, a subject that had only recently changed from being the "harlot of bourgeois science" to being a "progressive field of Soviet biology". Repressed geneticists, those that were still alive, were rehabilitated, brought back into science, and promoted. But not all of them. I heard that in one autonomous republic which was absolutely full of camps there was one of these "non-returners" teaching biology at the university and doing genetics on the side on the very subject that interested me most: the possibility of predicting genetic deviations in the development of the foetus in the first months of pregnancy. I decided on the impossible: to get that obstinate old man as my supervisor. Everyone said that there was no chance, that it was his Leningrad colleagues that had betrayed him at the time and got him put in prison, and that was why he refused ever to come to our city, even when he was invited to meetings with foreign scientists.

'I wrote the old man a letter. He didn't reply. I wrote him a second letter, enclosing the main points of my dissertation, with copies of the chapters that were already finished. And I asked him for just one thing – to allow me to come out to his backwoods and talk to him. And he agreed. I packed up and set off, full of excitement and fears, as if I was going to meet my first lover.

'The place he had chosen to spend the rest of his life, or rather, that others had chosen for him in 1937, couldn't have been more depressing: out of the train window was taiga, taiga, endless taiga, and every ten kilometres or so there was a camp fence, and watchtowers. They must have been modern criminal camps, not political ones. And there were suspicious-looking individuals drifting up and down the carriages, in grey padded jackets and with short-cropped hair. The passengers were saying there had been an amnesty for criminals recently, and we'd better mind our things. My things consisted of just one athletics bag and a small bag with my documents and money. What could be easier to look after? But I wasn't able to. They both got pinched. I lost my money, my institute pass, my dissertation, my scientific articles. The train was just about to arrive, and what was I to do? I had no idea. Luckily I still had my passport and a five-rouble note in my jacket pocket. I decided to get by somehow; I was determined not to go back home empty-handed. I could at least try!

'I soon tracked down my scholarly idol at the university. A crusty old man. We talked in the break between lectures and he gave me an appointment for ten o'clock the next morning in his lab.

'I left the university with a feeling of impending doom: in ten minutes of conversation I had not seen a flicker of a smile on his face. In fact he looked at me more with suspicion, and was reluctant to agree to a meeting, first of all suggesting that we talk right there in the corridor. But I insisted on at least half an hour. So now, as I came out, I began to wonder how I was going to get out of this situation. Nobody would send me copies of my dissertation and articles, even if I sent a telegram, which meant I would have to rely entirely on the outcome of my talk with him, assuming it was a serious talk. Apart from that there were everyday problems to worry about: how was I to get home, how was I to recover my stolen pass, and how was I to get by with this last five-rouble note?

'I went to the militia by the railway station and told them which train I had been on, which coach, and showed them my ticket. I asked them to forward my papers and pass immediately, if they turned up: sometimes a thief will leave them where they can be found, just keeping the money and other articles for himself. They promised to do that, and I must say that two weeks later they actually did send my bag to Leningrad with my papers and pass. The thief had left it just inside the door of the train, and if I'd just thought to ask the guards about it I wouldn't have had to report to the old man empty-handed.

'I went into the post office and sent my parents a telegram asking them to send money urgently to the poste restante there, then I went to the hotel. I took a bed in the general room for a rouble and a half, which, as usual, had to be paid in advance. There were six strange women in the room, and I had to prepare myself and collect my thoughts for tomorrow's meeting. What was I to do? I went out and walked round the streets for an hour and a half or so. It was cold. Then I went into a café to get warm, ordered coffee and a cake and sat for an hour over it. The waitresses started giving me dirty looks, so I had to order something else.

185

Then I went to the cinema and saw a detective film; I was watching the film, but thinking about my own problems. And even that place of shelter I had to leave when the show came to an end. I didn't have any more money to go anywhere else, so with the very last of it I bought a packet of cigarettes and went back to the hotel. I went to bed early, but couldn't get to sleep; I was tossng and turning, worrying till the early hours. The result was that I very stupidly overslept the next morning – you see, I didn't have my alarm clock with me! I woke up at nine thirty, and it was a half-hour's walk to the university! I didn't even have five copecks for the bus after traipsing round the town the day before. God, what was I going to do? I leapt up, smoothed down my hair somehow, but felt on the brink of despair: why did this have to happen?

'I rushed out into the street. The bus stop for the university was just outside the hotel, and the bus was about to leave. It was as if something gave me a shove: I flew into the bus as the doors were closing. Well, I thought, for once in my life I'll ride free!

'I sat there, not noticing anything round about me or outside the window; I was completely absorbed in my own fears. And suddenly, about one stop from the university, I saw my old man getting in at the front of the bus. He was straight as a ram-rod, and in the morning light his face was grey and unsmiling, and there wasn't a sign of life in his eyes. He got in and sat down on the front seat, facing towards me, but I was at the other end of the bus and he hadn't seen me. I sat there and wondered whether to go over to him. Then I decided there was no point, since he hadn't noticed me. I better just report to his office as we agreed.

'And then to my horror I saw that an inspector had got on to the bus together with my old man, a market wench kind of woman, and that she had started checking tickets. That was it, the ultimate disaster! I sat there, feeling the world crumble about me. What a fool I was! Why couldn't I have saved at least one five-copeck piece yesterday? Any moment now the inspector would reach me and raise hell. And what would he think of me? That I just came here on a spree, or something? No dissertation, no work, no nothing – and the inspector even catching me without a bus ticket . . .

'I felt I could burst into tears at any moment, and the only reason I was controlling myself was that it wouldn't help matters. She was coming closer and closer, checking the tickets, and it was a long stop, so I couldn't jump out, I was trapped.

'Then I started to pray: "O Lord! Unknown world-forming force! Send me salvation, not for my sake, but in the name of science. After all, they've been saying down here that to acknowledge genetics is to acknowledge your existence. So, even in the name of that, O Creator of genes and chromosomes, send me a five-copeck piece!"

'But it was too late, too late ... Inexorably, like a tank, the inspector came towards me. In my panic I turned away and looked out of the window. And suddenly I saw a five-copeck piece stuck behind the rubber strip lining the window, a dark, copper, real live coin! I grabbed it, jumped up from my seat, quickly dropped it into the machine and tore off a ticket. I felt immediate relief, as if a great shadow had departed from me, and I calmly walked down the bus towards the inspector and the front door where my idol was sitting. And he was looking at me – he had noticed. I floated past the inspector, like a little cloud past a cliff, nonchalantly handing her my ticket as I passed. And there was the stop.

'The old man and I got out of the bus together, and he even got down first and gave me his hand to help me down. We walked along the street towards the university, and he suddenly asked: "Tell me honestly, why did you put your five copecks in the machine at the very last minute, when the inspector was about to catch you? Do you always try to save money like that?"

'So I told him the whole truth. He had a good laugh over my prayer to the "unknown world-forming force", but he said there was certainly something in that, some grain of truth – otherwise where could the five-copeck piece have come from? I didn't expect him to be capable of much cheerfulness. The long and short of it was that we arrived at his lab firm friends. It only remains for me to add that to this day he still supervises all my research work, although he never did leave his little hole. I go to him.

'And I can tell you quite truthfully that I have never suffered so much over money as I did then, and I have never been so delighted to find some money as I was to find that five-copeck piece.'

'So, now we've found out something else about you, Larissa!' smiled Emma when the story was over.

'Yes, Larochka, don't you try getting away with anecdotes any more,' said Albina. 'Why do you have to put up a shield and hide behind it? We're not dangerous. I, for one, respect your independence. I even envy you, if you must know.'

'Well, don't be in such a hurry to envy me. Our *Women's Decameron* isn't finished yet – you'll hear quite a bit more from me . . . Now let's hear Zina. Zina, you were in a camp. There must have been some people there for really terrible crimes over money?'

'Quite a few,' said Zina with a wave of the hand.

'Then tell us a really lurid story.'

'All right, I'll try.'

Story Two

by Zina the tramp, which she herself considered the most terrible of all the stories she had heard while in the camp.

'There was a mother and daughter in our zone, one was eighteen, the other thirty-six. They were both being dried out – forcibly of course. They were in for murder, and they both accused each other of doing it. They were kept in different sections because if they had come together the feathers would have gone flying. They were great fighters.

'The other zeks told me their story, and this is what it was. They lived in a workers' settlement, where the people are brought in from outside and they're never sober: they all drink, and they drink the whole time. The mother shacked up with different men, took to drink as a teenager, had her baby when she was pissed out of her mind, and didn't even know who the father was. When this story happened they had a man living with them that they shared. The mother was more or less a complete alcoholic, and the daughter was not far behind.

'One day the man turns up with his pay packet. This gives them an excuse to have a blast, friends are invited and all hell breaks loose. Everyone's boozing away and sleeping

188

with anyone they want. By the second night the vodka and the money run out, the guests go home, but the mother and daughter aren't satisfied – they want more vodka so as to get completely pissed. Suddenly one of them remembers that the man ought to have a pay packet for the thirteenth month as well. They start hassling him: "Where's your thirteenth pay packet? Come on, cough up!"

'He's pretty sloshed, but he mutters: "They haven't paid it yet."

'And he turns over and goes back to sleep.

'So the mother sends the daughter to the neighbour next door who works with the man, to find out if the thirteenth has been paid out yet. She hops next door, then comes right back: "Yes, it has!"

'They start leaning on the man: "Where's the money? Why are you hiding it?"

'They drag him off the bed, frisk him, and because they can't find anything they start hitting him. He just growls. Then one of them, only we don't know which, suggests torturing him to find out where he's hidden the money. That's what all the argument was about in the zone: who thought of it first? Each one blamed the other.

'They tie the man up and start torturing him. First they beat the poor bloke with a strap. Even though he's sloshed he tells them: "You won't get my money even if you burn me alive!"

'So those little devils start to burn him, with cigarettes. He still won't tell them where he's hidden the money. Then they say to him: "If you don't give us the money we'll start sawing through your legs, and we'll saw them right off."

'Then the drunken idiot blows his top, too: "Saw away! My father was a partisan, so I'm not afraid of torture! Fetch your saw!" And he goes back to sleep again.

'They brought a two-man saw from the shed, heaved the man back on to the bed, pulled the bed out into the middle of the room, got on each side of him and started sawing. Perhaps they were just trying to give him a scare at first, and then the booze just turned them into animals – I don't know, so I'll tell you no lies. The saw brought him round, and he started growling: "They sawed my pop's leg off in the forest. They made him drunk, then they sawed it off so it wouldn't rot. Pop took it, and I can take it, too."

'And he didn't say any more, but just lay there like a partisan till they had sawn both his legs clean off. Then he lost consciousness, and they realized they were not going to get any sense out of him, he was hardly about to say much, so they gave up on him. They covered him with a blanket and put cushions against his legs to soak up the blood. Then they started searching the place for the money. And they found it, too: behind the cupboard. They bought some more vodka. And while the daughter was off buying it, the mother pulled the man out on to the balcony and covered him with rags, like a sort of bundle. And she forgot about him, just as if he wasn't there. The daughter came back with the vodka, saw the man wasn't there, and asked: "Where is he?"

'And the mother answered: "I don't know. He left probably . . ."

'The daughter still had a bit of sense in her head: "How could he leave? His legs are sawn off."

'"How should I know? He's a cunning man, he managed it somehow."

'Then they washed up the blood together, cooked some potatoes and invited the guests back. They all boozed another couple of days. If anyone asked about the man, they answered that he had got fed up and left altogether. That was quite normal, no one asked any more questions. A couple of times people came by from work, saw there was a blast going on and went away again.

'Then one woman got sick with the drink, but the toilet was full, so she went out on to the balcony to puke. She leant over the railing, did it right on to the street, then stood waiting to recover a bit. Presently she noticed a heap of rags in the corner of the balcony covered in snow, and she could just make out a good man's shoe sticking out on one side. "Why do they have almost new shoes lying about on the balcony covered in snow?" she wondered. She gave the shoe a tug, and a whole leg came away with it. That sobered her up right away. She went back into the room, didn't say anything to anybody, quickly said goodbye and pretended to go home. But actually she went to the militia.

'They took them both, and they carted off the "partisan's" body, too. The examination said the man had lived a few hours, then bled to death and froze.

'That's what two women did when they were drunk, and what one man suffered because of money.'

This horrific story upset Olga in particular: 'How the people drink, it's awful! And there's no knowing what they will do when they're drunk. Our husbands will go on drinking another ten years or so, then they'll die and we'll be left alone.'

'But women drink too, don't they? You've just heard the story yourself,' said Valentina. 'Yes, they certainly do, and how! And every year more and more women are becoming alcoholics. There are a great many drying-out places for women now, whereas quite recently there was only one for the whole country, in Murmansk. And people in other cities were horrified to hear of that one. And now what's it like? Every decent town has not one, but several.'

'Even the children are drinking, that's the most frightening thing of all!' said Irishka.

'It's time to suggest a new slogan,' laughed the dissident's wife Galina. ' "Communism is Soviet power plus alcoholization of the whole country".'

They chatted a bit more, bemoaned the state of affairs, and then suggested Natasha should tell a story. 'Only please, Natashenka,' begged Irishka, 'something happy; my spine is still crawling!'

'All right. Zina reminded me of one story that is also to do with a thirteenth pay packet. I'll try to get your minds off gloomy things.'

Story Three

by the engineer Natasha, about the thirteenth pay packet and a statue of Lenin.

'The year when the thirteenth pay packet was introduced I had already finished at the institute and was working as an engineer at a factory. It was an old factory, with traditions and many seasoned workers, and the general atmosphere was better than in most factories. But in the workshop I was

191

sent to there was one unpleasant individual who spoilt everything – the Party organizer. For union officials he would pick men like himself, then he would quietly get rid of the good, but non-political, craftsmen and push his own croneys into their places. The workers got no peace from him: he was always demanding some super-conscientiousness from them, or dreaming up new socialist obligations, or devising "initiatives" which of course didn't improve the work, but sounded impressive. Our shop was always being written up in the factory paper, and sometimes an article would even appear in *Leningradskaya Pravda*. The Party organizer used to cut out these articles and keep them, hoping they would pave his way to higher things.

'So when the announcement came about the thirteenth pay packet, the Party organizer started to blackmail the workers with this wage that still hadn't been paid out, just as if he was going to pay it out of his own pocket. He was always going on about it at meetings: "The state realizes that the consciousness of our workers does not unfortunately always rise above the level of material interests, and is therefore introducing the thirteenth pay packet. So look upon it as a concession to your lack of conscientiousness!"

'But although he shouted at every corner about his Party duty – by which he meant, of course, urging the workers to do better – he himself didn't display any particular personal conscientiousness with regard to the state: he got reduced-rate travel passes to the sanatorium for himself and his whole family at the union's expense, and he got our workers to fix up his flat for him, and during working hours, too. Once when the wages were being given out, the young cashier gave him three roubles too little by mistake; well, the row went on for three days and the poor girl was nearly sacked.

'So he started to hassle the workers over this charity payment, the thirteenth pay packet, all the time on the look-out for anyone skiving or being late or insubordinate. At the least little thing he would go to the bosses and nag at them to cancel the man's thirteenth pay packet. And the bosses were a bit scared of him, so they would give in to him. The workers were angry, and the shop foremen could see that production was suffering from his Party enthusiasm, but there was nothing they could do about it – it was ideology! You merely had to contradict him, and he would fire such a political torpedo at you that you would never hear the end of it.

'One of the craftsmen in our shop was an elderly woman called Yuliya Konstantinovna. As a girl she had been a nurse at the front lines during the war, she had been decorated, and in peacetime her style of conduct was bold and independent. The Party organizer would have got rid of her long ago, but the production of a whole section depended on her, and the factory management valued her highly. This Yuliya Konstantinovna saw that the workers detested the Party organizer and had even started to drift away from our shop. So she decided to side with the workers and rid them of that monster. She must have had a secret agreement with the best workers, because they were the first to support her, and then the others all followed. Here's what she thought up to bring the Party organizer down.

'There was a small park in our factory yard, with a fountain and some benches round it. Yuliya agreed with the workers to suggest one of those "initiatives" that the Party organizer was so fond of: that everyone should contribute his thirteenth pay packet to replace the fountain with a statue of Lenin – as a token of gratitude to the state and our party for that very thirteenth pay packet.

'We were all eagerly awaiting the annual shop meeting. Normally, when these meetings are announced the workers, especially the women, try to find ways of getting out of them. The meetings are held after work, and to stop unconscientious workers from running off they close the main gates for that period. But every fence has gaps in it, and our women would get through the factory fences and escape from the meetings and the world peace rallies either to go home or to queue for food. But every single person showed up at this meeting. They all wanted to see how Yulia's daring campaign against the Party organizer would end. And although nobody had money to spare and they had lots of room in their pockets for a thirteenth pay packet, no one regretted losing it if they could get rid of that drag of a Party organizer. And anyway, he had already deprived half the workers of at least some of the money, if not all of it. He had put pressure on the brigadiers, the craftsmen and the shop foreman to make sure that not a single breach of discipline went unpunished. So the workers had nothing to lose, and the craftsmen and brigadiers were sensible and decided to forego their thirteenth pay packets, because they had had as much as they could take, too: they had been in charge of production before, and now they had become little boys and girls running errands for the Party organizer.

'Finally the meeting got started. The shop foreman went up to the rostrum and emptied his figures all over us: plan, over-plan, over-fulfilment, under-fulfilment, etc., etc., then he gathered up his papers and went back to his seat. The Party organizer clambered up to the rostrum and began giving us all this guff about how the Party had shown its great concern for all workers by giving them the thirteenth pay packet, but that certain unconscientious workers . . . and so on, and so forth . . .

'After the Party organizer, Yuliya took the floor, coming up to the front and quite unhurriedly repeating everything the Party organizer had just said: the Party . . . the government . . . the government . . . the Party . . . In fact, winter had passed, summer had come – thank you, Party, for this! We were amazed to hear her giving us the same old bull, and wondered if she had lost her nerve at the last moment. She went on and on, and kept looking at the door and the clock. The Party organizer, who was chairing the meeting, tapped his glass with his pencil: "Time, Yuliya Konstantinovna!"

'She gave him a sweet smile, nodded, and went on talking, this time giving nothing but quotations from Lenin: "As Lenin said, as Vladimir Ilyich observed . . ."

'The Party organizer gave a sigh, but couldn't do anything: he wouldn't risk interrupting a speaker who was spouting Lenin quotes.

'As Yuilya was spinning out her Leniniana the door opened and a journalist and a photographer walked solemnly into the hall, followed by a very pleased-looking editor of the factory paper. The editor hurried over to the Party organizer, bent down to him and whispered so that everyone in the hall could hear: "From *Leningradskaya Pravda*!"

'Delighted, the Party organizer bowed and opened his arms: "Welcome!"

'At the same time he winked and waved at Yuliya to wind up her speech. She just smiled and in a loud voice announced: "And so, in the light of all that has been said, a group of workers, engineers and technicians in our shop has decided as a sign of gratitude to the Party and the government to decline the first thirteenth pay packet, and with the money put up a monument to Lenin in the factory park in place of the fountain."

'When they heard the words they had been waiting so long for, the hall burst into loud applause. Yuliya paused briefly for the ovation, and then continued: "We are sure that we shall be supported by our administration, and above all by our respected Party organizer, Vasily Ivanovich!"

'She turned towards the praesidium and with a smile invited the Party organizer to take her place: "We await your reply, Vasily Ivanovich!"

'Half the praesidium were smiling – those who already knew about Yuliya's idea. The other half, the Party organizer's cronies, detected his displeasure and started shrugging their shoulders in a negative way.

'Our Vasily Ivanovich went up to the rostrum and began: "I don't know who allowed this independent act. Who permitted this rash initiative? Was it approved by anyone? The Party committee cannot support such half-baked initiatives. First we have to discuss everything with comrades, and co-ordinate with higher bodies."

'Then the floor was taken by Alik Bochagin, the Komsomol leader, who was already in the know: "I am surprised at you, Vasily Ivanovich. I did not expect to hear such things from a senior Party comrade! What do you mean by 'independent'? Surely, real initiative has to be independent, and not fabricated in the quietness of the study, as sometimes still happens! We members of the Komsomol fully support the initiative of the workers of our shop and we undertake in addition to clear the site for the monument to Vladimir Ilyich! Long live the monument to the eternally living Lenin in place of the fountains of bureaucracy!"

'This rot was spouted in the style of the militant twenties, but the meeting liked it and laughed and clapped. Now the Party organizer could not possibly bury the initiative! His own personal money was in peril, his own thirteenth, and so were the bonuses of his hangers-on. The journalist was beside himself with joy: "What copy! This will be in tomorrow's paper!"

'He was running round the hall interviewing people, and the photographer was taking flashes, while the Party organizer was standing in a huddle with his people, and we could hear a rumble of discontent coming from them. One of them could be heard to say: "We'll have to ring the regional committee tomorrow, they can sort it out there – we can't have initiatives just starting themselves up like this! The state offers these people something, and they refuse it!"

'The next day *Leningradskaya Pravda* ran an article about our initiative, with the following final paragraph: "It is a great pity that the workers' initiative did not meet with the necessary understanding from the one quarter which seemingly ought to have given it the fullest support – the Party organization of the workshop."

'Our Party organizer fell, and his place was soon taken by Alik Bochagin. He was a pretty good windbag, but he knew what was what and he was more careful with the workers.

'The statue of Lenin was put up in the park, and the factory people nicknamed it the Monument to Ilyich and Konstantinovna, meaning, of course, not Lenin's wife, Nadezhda Konstantinovna Krupskaya, but our own Yuliya Konstantinovna.'

Story Four

by the bigwig Valentina, strangely enough about dissidents and a KGB man.

'Now, my friends, I'm going to tell you a confidential story about dissidents and CIA money. No, don't get indignant yet, Galina, first hear me out. I heard this story first hand from the KGB investigator who was involved. Only please, if you should feel like telling it to anyone else, don't mention my name! I won't give you the investigator's name, and I don't recall any of the dissidents' names. For some reason I just remember the names of an exile's two daughters – Dasha and Sasha. Anyway, that's not important. Even without the names you can tell us, Galya, if the story sounds plausible.

'The story was told me by a friend of mine who worked for a short time in the KGB. I shall call him Yevgeny, but that is not his real name, I have just chosen it for the story.

'Yevgeny, graduated from the law faculty of Leningrad University and was invited to work in the KGB. He became a junior investigator, which quite simply means an errand boy. But then he got one case which caused him to leave the KGB and start working as a defence lawyer. I once asked him why he had turned down such a brilliant career. And this is what he told me, but I repeat – it's highly confidential!

'A tourist arrived in Leningrad from West Germany and met with a dissident. The KGB were absolutely certain that she had brought him money. And Yevgeny was given the job of tracking down the money to see where it went. They had already decided that the money was from the CIA, and it was only a question of proving that the person who received it was either using it for anti-Soviet activities or passing it on to somebody else for the same purpose. Yevgeny had the right to intercept the suspect's outgoing mail, so he quickly established that the day after the German tourist had left he sent fifty roubles to some exile living in Irkutsk province.

'Yevgeny flew to Irkutsk province and soon found the exile. He was living in a small hut on the bank of a river in the taiga with his wife and two girls, Sasha and Dasha. Yevgeny walked round the area, questioned the local KGB people and the neighbours, and checked the post office. And it turned out that as soon as he had received the money the exile had sent it to Vorkuta.

'Yevgeny had to fly to Vorkuta. He got there, found some ex-con who had done twenty years and was on his last legs with TB, and didn't have a single tooth in his mouth. And no money: he had received the fifty roubles, and without even leaving the post office had sent it straight off to some woman exile in Chita province.

'Yevgeny tried to meet this woman in Chita province, but she refused to talk to him. But he discovered the fate of the money without questioning her: she had sent it to the Ukraine.

'Yevgeny flew to the Ukraine, cursing these dissidents who had hatched such a plot that in order to track down the fifty roubles he had spent ten times as much in government

197

money flying backwards and forwards, not to mention other expenses.

'In the Ukraine the local KGB officials met Yevgeny and told him that the addressee had just been released from a strict regime camp, had received the money, but had sent it off on the same day . . . to Irkutsk province.

'Can you imagine what sort of mood Yevgeny was in as he flew back to Irkutsk? It so happened that he got there ahead of the mail, and arrived at the post office just as they were writing out a notification for the exile. He presented his credentials and installed himself behind the counter as though he was sorting mail, so that he could watch for the exile to come for his money.

'He appeared with his wife and two girls. He received the money and, without leaving the post office, immediately started conferring with his wife and daughter over whom to send the money to, who needed it most. And then Yevgeny realized that there was no mystery about those fifty roubles: people were just sending them to each other, considering that others' needs were greater than their own. He didn't bother to follow up where the money went next, but returned to Leningrad and found a respectable excuse for leaving the KGB. They let him go because he was only doing a course with them and didn't know much.

'Well, Galina? Does that sound a likely tale?'

Galina, who had listened to Valentina with shining eyes, said that it was not only likely, but that she could name all the participants in that story except the Ukrainian: 'At least half the people in political camps are Ukrainian, so it's impossible to guess who that was. Of the rest, I will name just Yegor Davydov, who lived in the town of Tulun in Irkutsk province. His wife is called Lyora, and his girls are indeed Dasha and Sasha. I'm not afraid to give their names because they are already in Germany, in Munich. And from there they are helping their friends. Now they'll send me some money or some things, perhaps, by a German tourist, and a new Yevgeny from the KGB will open a new file about CIA money! They'll write a lot of disgraceful things in the papers and they'll knock together some TV film and call it *Hirelings of the CIA* or *They Sold*

Themselves for Dollars. I hope, at least, that if you see anything like that you won't believe it. Thank you, Valentina!'

And all the women were delighted that the ice finally seemed to have melted between Valentina and Galina.

'All right, you two representatives of warring classes, that's enough declarations of love!' said Albina with a note of jealousy in her voice. 'Now it's my turn. I'm going to spoil the effect of your idyllic picture by telling a story about love of money.'

Story Five

by the airhostess Albina, affording a description of all the glitter and squalor of Russian courtesans.

'For starters, an anecdote. About the late Minister of Culture, Yekaterina Furtseva. Furtseva is sitting with her fellow ministers, one woman among a lot of men. The conversation gets on to the subject of whether there is still any prostitution in the Soviet Union. Furtseva says: "We don't have prostitution any more because that is a relic of capitalism and was finished long ago."

'The other ministers laugh: "What do you mean, there's no prostitution, when all our women sell themselves?"

' "What, all of them, even your Minister of Culture?"

' "Yes, comrade minister."

' "And how much do you think I'm worth?"

' "Well, taking into account your age and complexion on the one hand, and your high position on the other, I might give a hundred roubles."

' "Is that all?!"

' "You see, Katya, you're haggling already."

'That was the anecdote. Now I shall tell you what really happens. I can't start with the prostitutes that serve the very top people, because I haven't actually been with them.

'Next in line come the underground millionaires, and I have had dealings with them. Not for long, admittedly, and when I was really young. They like the girls to be really

199

almost little girls, after eighteen they're considered to be old women and ready for general circulation. So that's when I served them. The chauffeur would arrive and say: "Get ready, we're leaving in half an hour. Put on this, and that."

'I would get ready, climb into the car, and we would usually drive out to someone's dacha. There would be guests there, wine, entertainment – and us as an extra snack. For an evening like that I would get up to five hundred roubles, depending on who the guest was and where he came from. The Georgians paid best of all, the Ukrainians worst. Guests from the Baltic states were a bit stingy, but they treated the girls in a classy way, because they were almost Westerners themselves. If you went "out" a few times like that you could sit back and not work for a year.

'After that come the call-girls. I was never a call-girl, but I had friends who were. They spend nearly the whole day sitting at home waiting for customers to ring. The customers are usually rich and important people who value their reputation or are scared of their wives. A client will ring up, often someone the girl has never met before, and invite her to a hotel. A call-girl gets thirty to fifty roubles for a night – if she has a good class of clientele.

'Hotel girls get about the same, but their life is harder: they have to work with foreigners, and under surveillance. But then there's always the chance of getting some good presents, and even establishing a contact for the future. Some of our hotel girls have managed to hook themselves foreigners who married them and took them back abroad with them. Of course they never dreamed their wives were ex-prostitutes working under the auspices of the hotel management, the militia and the KGB. It was always made out to be a pleasant meeting by chance in the hotel restaurant or foyer. Although, think for yourselves, what Soviet girl is going to be dining alone in the restaurant of the Astoria or the Europa? What a load of rubbish!

'You've got the same system in the hotels for our own people, only the guests are a bit more modest: you won't often get more than thirty roubles, unless you happen to get Georgians again. Those fellows always know how to pay! You can't stop a Georgian living in style.

'There's all sorts of different domestic prostitution. Sometimes you'll get a "girl" who's pushing fifty, but she has a solid clientele built up over many years. They're the sort it's good to be able to go to when a man wants to get away from his wife. They serve people they know really well, they give them set days and it's almost a family life. Even money is treated like in a family. For example, my friend used to give hers credit if they were having money problems. And the reverse happens: if she needs a new fur coat she'll take all the money to buy one and then sleep with the fellow for free for six months, or however long it takes.

'Next we have to go out on the street. That's something I've never done, walk the streets. Our girls used to scare each other with stories about the streets: "You'll end up at Moskovsky Station for a fiver a time!"

'They've got their own categories there too. There's the taxi girl – that's still not too bad. The girl agrees with the taxi driver, and he cruises round the stations with her choosing customers for her. And he's carrying vodka in the boot, for a bit extra. Taxi girls get about ten roubles.

'Have you ever walked past Moskovsky Station at night? Some time around midnight? You try it. Such beauties you will see there – they've got everything except a broken nose. These will go with anybody for a fiver. Some go back to their own place, some do it in doorways.

'Women trade for the same price at Gostiny Dvor and other large department stores. I knew a married one once; her husband worked at a factory, and they had two little kids. And every day she went out to do her trade and served two or three customers. In doorways. She would bring home ten or fifteen roubles and be happy.

'I don't know anything about the port girls that serve the sailors, so I won't lie. They're probably more expensive than at the station, but cheaper than the ones at the hotels.

'Boys come dearer than girls in all these categories. Discrimination again, girls! They gather in the little park opposite the Pushkin Theatre, "Katka's Park" – there's a statue of Catherine the Great there. Well, have you had enough? So have I. I can't think of anything more terrible on money. Maybe Zina can add something.'

The first to react to Albina's story was Zina: 'I don't know anything about the girls who get big money from men, but I've met the ones that hang around the stations and ports. Do you know the smallest price I've ever heard of a woman charging a man?'

'What?'

'One rouble.'

The women gasped.

'And that's not all. A rouble is money. But in the morning outside the beer bars the alcoholics give themselves for a mug of beer, that's precisely twenty-two copecks. There. And now, Galya, you tell us something about your beautiful life, where the people give each other their very last copeck.'

'No, Zina. I've got another story prepared about money, which doesn't have anything particularly to do with dissidents. I'm going to tell you about my mother-in-law.'

Story Six

by the dissident Galina, about how her relations with her mother-in-law became established and how, although she had received only a small amount of money from her, she ended up owing her a debt that could never be repaid.

'Slavik's mother had him when she was over forty. An afterthought, as they say. People say they're not always a success; I don't know, but my Slavik was certainly a success!

'We got married in the camp, and during that visit he said to me: "Galochka, I have my mother living in Leningrad. I've written to her about you. You ought to go and see her, get to know her. She's quite poorly, she hardly ever goes out."

'He gave me the address, and the day after I got back from Mordovia I called on Anna Nikolayevna. That was his mother's name. She lived at the end of Sadovaya Street, on Pokrovka. I arrived, rang the bell, and the neighbour answered the door. She took me through the flat and showed me Anna Nikolayevna's room. I knocked, and immediately heard: "Come in, Galina!"

'Scared stiff, I opened the door and saw a thin little old woman, completely grey. She was sitting in a large, worn armchair wrapped in a fluffy grey shawl.

' "Come in, sit down. Well, how was your trip? And how is Slavik?"

' "He's well, everything is all right with him at the moment. But how did you guess it was me?"

' "I've been expecting you," she replied simply. "Slavik wrote to me about you, and I've been waiting for you. I was just wondering why my little daughter-in-law didn't come and show herself to me, when suddenly I heard strange footsteps, and guessed who it was. Not many people come to see me. My sister and the nurse – that's all the visitors I have."

'Anna Nikolayevna and I drank tea together, and I told her about my trip and how we had been registered at the camp. I also told her about myself and my family.

' "How did your parents take it, you having a boyfriend in a camp?"

' "Oh, all right, I think . . ."

' "Don't your rush them. Slavik will get out and then maybe they'll love him. But don't rush your parents. It's not so nice for them either, having a son-in-law behind barbed wire. You can't explain that to everybody, and everybody will want to know who their daughter has married."

'I fell for Anna Nikolayevna at this first meeting. I felt drawn towards her, especially when anything unpleasant happened. I would go to her, we would make tea, chat about this and that, talk about Slavik – and I would feel better.

'But at home things weren't working out too well for me. My parents started disapproving of me as soon as I announced I had a boyfriend in a camp. And when they found out I was expecting a baby things got really bad between us. So I decided to move out. But where to? Anna Nikolayevna had a minute little room; you couldn't even fit a second bed in, and Slavik used to sleep on a camp bed. So how could I fit in there with a baby? I decided to rent a room. I looked around for a long time and finally found one; but it was expensive – forty roubles. Quite a chunk out of my eighty-five a month. And I still needed to put some by for visits and parcels. In fact, it became quite a struggle to live. One good thing was that I found a room close to Anna Nikolayevna, on Fontanka. I was always popping in to see her.

'My own mother tried to get me to have an abortion, but I wouldn't hear of it. I wasn't feeling very well at all. The baby was growing inside me, but I was eating worse than before I was pregnant. Financially I just wasn't making it. I didn't take any money from my parents, even though they offered – my pride, you see. And I began to get dejected and absent-minded. With all my poverty I even started mislaying money as well. I would put it down somewhere at home, and then I couldn't find it. I was moaning one time to Anna Nikolayevna about this latest misfortune of mine, and she told me to keep a purse: "You're always putting your money in your handbag or in your pocket, so it doesn't really know where it belongs."

'And then I began to notice that I was quite often coming upon money underneath a glove in my coat pocket, or right at the bottom of my handbag, and the notes were not folded over in two, the way I always did it, but in four. I put that down to my absent-mindedness, too, and to the general upheaval in my life.

'But those three- and five-rouble notes were a real life-saver to me. My only worry was that this losing money and then finding it again in unexpected places was becoming a habit with me.

'One day, when I was in the sixth month, I came to see Anna Nikolayevna and found she was much worse, and couldn't even get up. I waited till the doctor came, and after she had examined her I followed her out into the corridor and asked: "Doctor, how is she? Is it very serious?"

' "Well, what can I say to you? We're not going to give her a new heart, and the old one is worn out. There's nothing more to be done, you'll have to prepare for the worst. We could keep her going on medication for a year at the most, but then . . ."

' "Maybe she could go to hospital?"

' "Just try getting a person of her age, a pensioner, into hospital! You'd have to have an awful lot of pull. An ambulance will come for her when she's really bad. Otherwise . . . No, don't even bother trying!"

'I pictured Anna Nikolayevna not lasting until Slavik came back, and it made me burst into tears, I couldn't help it. But I controlled myself so that she wouldn't be able to guess from my face what the doctor had told me.

'I went back into the room and my mother-in-law said to me: "Don't grieve about me, Galochka. I shall die in peace now that I know Slavik is not alone. But I would have liked to see my grandson ... Now stop whimpering, and go to the shops for me instead. There's my bag, and the purse is inside."

'I took the bag, listened to what I had to buy, and set off. In the grocer I picked up milk, curds and cheese, but when I opened the purse to pay at the till I couldn't believe it: all the paper money was lying in the purse neatly folded into four, just like all the threes and fives I had been finding. And yet she only received a pension of forty-five roubles. You can work out what sort of pie she was breaking crumbs off for me.

'Then I went to the baker for bread, and by this time the tears were running down my cheeks. And like a child I was daydreaming that a miracle would happen, she would get well again, and then Slavik would come back. We would both work and buy her a warm, light fur coat and very warm winter boots. She never went out in the winter because her padded winter coat was too heavy for her to wear. And I consoled myself with this dream.

'But she died quite recently, when I had just started my maternity leave. We never did buy her a fur coat. And I never did call her Mama, except to myself – I was always too shy. She left money in a little envelope with "For Galina" written on it. It was all that was left from her pension, all she had saved up by the end of her life – twenty-eight roubles, eighty copecks. And then I had to spend it all on the funeral, because that's expensive. I just kept one fiver, and I'm not going to spend it, however hard things get. No, it's not one of the notes she left me, it's quite a different fiver. Just before going into labour I was sorting through my summer things and I found it in my jacket pocket: she must have slipped it in during the summer. When Slavik gets out I'll give it to him.'

The story of Galina's mother-in-law moved everyone deeply, and the women comforted Galya herself as best they could, for she had concluded her story in tears.

When she had calmed down, Olga began her story.

Story Seven

by the worker Olga. This story brings us back to the war, when not only heroic exploits were performed, but crimes were committed as well.

'I actually come from the country, near Tikhvin. I didn't come to work at the shipyard in Leningrad until I was eighteen; before that I was just an ordinary country girl.

'They say that every Russian village has its village idiot or madman. I don't know about other villages, but ours had this old woman called Moneybags Nyurka. Why she was given that nickname I shall tell you right now. Her real name was Antonova.

'When I knew Moneybags Nyurka she already hardly looked human any more. She went about in rags and tatters, in winter she would find a corner in people's huts to stay in, and in summer she just lived in the forest near the village. She was frightening; the children were scared of her, and they teased her and were unkind to her. This is the story they told about her.

'The evacuees from the Leningrad siege were brought through our village. They were apparently on their way to Siberia, but the really sick ones were taken off the train and left with us. I think the same happened at other stations along the way, too. They were distributed round the different huts without the owners even being asked. The order was simply given to settle the evacuees. But as for feeding them, the authorities didn't show any concern about that, and we couldn't even get bread for them on their cards. It was very hard.

'But these people had escaped from the Germans, and they were determined not to die now they were free. So one way or the other they survived. The stronger ones started working on the collective farm. Nobody needed their city education, but their hands could be used, even if they were weak. Others who could hardly walk swapped their town things for bread, potatoes, and milk for their children. Our women felt very sorry for the kiddies from Leningrad. If anyone had a cow they would sit the evacuated children at the same table as their own and shove spuds and milk at them, telling them to eat it while it lasted! But there were

206

some people who took advantage of other people's misfortune and grew rich on it. They did their best to barter the last rags out of the siege people.

'When it came to grasping and greed, Nyurka Antonova took the prize. She didn't wait for the siege people to come to her to barter, oh no! She would take her basket, put eggs, lard, and a bottle of milk in it and set off round the houses.

' "Have you got any foxes living with you?" she would ask. "Foxes" was her name for the siege people, because she said they had been smoked out of their holes in Leningrad, and she wanted to show she didn't care a rap for what people said about her cheating and greed. She would go into a hut where there were lodgers billeted and say to them: "Want to do some bartering? Well then, let's see what you've got!"

'She wouldn't take any of the things they offered her.

' "Show me everything you brought with you! I'll do the choosing!"

'The people had no choice, they had to let Nyurka at their things, and she would look at them and feel them and then name her prices. She would haggle, and the people were too weak and tired to put up a fight; they would see the food and agree to anything.

'Nyurka went on robbing people like that until she had a whole hut full of possessions: high-heeled fashion shoes, astrakhan coats, felt boots, fur collars. She even got herself a whole pile of hats! Our women would laugh at her: "What do you need their city hats for, Nyurka? Are you going to make a scarecrow for your vegetable patch?"

'And Nyurka used to reply: "I'm going to get rich on those scum who ran away instead of defending their city, and then I'm going to apply to live in Leningrad myself. Then the hats will come in useful."

'That was her plan.

'Apart from the rags, Nyurka sold food for cash, too. Those poor siege people, she just ripped them off, it was daylight robbery. And then she would boast: "I've got enough money to paper my walls with, just like a city house! I've got enough to last me to the grave, and there'll be enough left over to last my son for the rest of his life, too."

'Nyurka herself also had a lodger, a young woman with a child, a little girl. She had no one to turn to, so Nyurka stripped her of every copeck. They say the lodger was a clean young girl, and she got rid of all the cockroaches and bedbugs from Nyurka's hut. Only the flies were left. And then someone sent Nyurka some strips of paper soaked in fly poison. She would put one of the bits of papers in a saucer of water, with a tiny piece of sugar on top: the flies would land on it and die. But the Leningrad girl was scared her daughter might get some sort of infection from the flies. One day the little girl happened to see the sugar in the saucer of fly poison. She ate the sugar and licked the saucer clean, and immediately started to double up with stomach pains. The mother rushed to Nyurka.

' "Give me some milk for my child!" she said. "She's poisoned herself!"

'But Nyurka said: "You pay me first!"

'She rushed over to her trunk and pushed out everything she had left. But Nyurka already knew every piece of junk she had, and turned up her nose at it: "There's nothing worth choosing there. Just give me the whole lot for a jar of milk, or your little girl will die!"

'She gave her everything, right down to the last stocking. Then she gave the child milk and water to drink and saved her life. After that incident our women said to Nyurka: "You'll pay for what you've done to the evacuees, Nyurka! If men don't punish you, God will."

'And that's what did happen.

'Fate tested Nyurka for a long time. First it was through her son. She wanted to save her son from going to the front, and she paid a lot of money, saying he was epileptic. But in the end they demanded such a big bribe that she decided her son wasn't worth all that money and told him to get ready to go to the front. It was the last year of the war.

' "Maybe he'll be all right!" she said. "And he ought to visit Germany and get some trophies."

'Her son didn't even make it to the front: his train was bombed. She was sad for a while, but it didn't make her any kinder to others, she kept trying to grab whatever she saw. Her husband didn't come back from the front either, and she took that quite calmly, too: "With all my riches I'll find myself another, and I'll have a new son!"

'Then the money reform finished her off. After the war they had this reform when all the money was replaced almost overnight. Nyurka couldn't exchange her hoards of money because she hadn't kept it in the savings bank, but hidden away in her cellar where no one would find it. So when her money suddenly turned into scraps of paper she just cracked. She came out of her house early the next morning, hung the fur coats and dresses on her apple trees, arranged all the shoes in a row by the gate, hung the underwear and silk stockings on the fence, and then went back into her hut. All the people gathered round and started to gossip: "Has Nyurka gone round the bend?"

'They decided to go into her hut and see how she was. They went in and found her papering the walls with her money and singing songs. The woman really had gone out of her mind.

'Nyurka wasn't frightening to look at, and the people would have felt sorry for her just like you felt sorry for the drunks lying under the fence and the fellows with shell-shock and the village idiots. But she would never let people forget what it was that drove her barmy. In winter and summer she was all right, but when autumn came and the leaves started falling off the trees, that's when Nyurka's madness showed itself. She would wander through the village and the forest collecting leaves and arranging them in little bundles. Then she would tie the bundles up with thread or string or anything else she could get hold of and hide them in secret places. And she would keep looking over her shoulder and repeating: "Now I've got lots of nice money again! Now I've got all my nice money back!"

'But the people remembered how it used to be. That's why they gave her the nickname Moneybags Nyurka.'

The women pondered over Olga's story. Most of them were from Leningrad and every Leningrad family had lost someone in the siege. Their faces became sad.

Now it was Nelya's turn to tell a story; she apologized that hers was not a happy one either, and then began.

Story Eight

by the music teacher Nelya, about how a passion for collecting pictures of the country's leaders can help some people, but harm others.

'I worked for a time giving music lessons at a nursery school. I had the intermediate group, little children of four and five years old. These toddlers were always being told about Lenin, the Party, and other things that children either don't understand at all or understand too literally. The teacher in charge of the intermediate group was particularly enthusiastic in her ideological teaching, and she would frequently interrupt my little songs with her pronouncements: "When he was a little boy Grandpa Lenin used to sing folk songs too. Now children, who knows what children's folk songs Grandpa Lenin used to sing when he was a child?"

'And one of the toddlers would invariably answer: " 'Oppressed by Bondage Dire'!"

'So many times I asked her not to interrupt my lessons, but all to no avail.

' "I'm telling the children about Lenin! That's the most important thing they can know about, even in music!"

'Well, what can you say to a woman like that? Once she thought up an idiotic competition for the children: they had to look around at home and see who could find the most pictures of Lenin in old newspapers and magazines and bring them to school. The children all did their best, cutting out pictures and bringing them in. Then they stuck these little pictures in special scrapbooks. The teacher accumulated a whole pile of these scrapbooks, and there was no room for them. And every time some commission of inspectors visited the school she would brandish her treasures at them. She brandished them so much that she got herself some sort of badge of honour and a citation.

'Then one morning a boy who was the son of a store manager came into school with a whole bundle of pictures of Lenin cut out of hundred-rouble notes. The stupid woman didn't even notice what sort of pictures they were, she just stuffed them into her desk drawer without looking at them, so they could be stuck into a scrapbook later. The boy's mother took him home in the evening, and he never came back to school.

'But the next day the militia appeared at the school demanding to see what pictures the boy had brought. It turned out the boy's father had made quite a pile in his business, and he kept his dirty money in large denominations in a number of different hiding places at home. The boy had discovered one of these hiding places, and after his father had left for work in the morning and his mother was making his breakfast, he had gone into his father's study, pulled out the money and cut out as many pictures of Lenin as he could before his mother called him for breakfast. His father came back from work, saw all the money cut in pieces, and for a long time couldn't understand what had happened. At that moment the mother returned from the nursery school with their son, and the boy immediately boasted to his father: "Papa, I cut out the pictures of Grandpa Lenin and took them to school! Marya Ivanovna was very pleased with me!"

'The mother clutched her heart, and the father lost his temper and started smacking his child's hands, until his wife realized what was going on and took the boy away from him. Poor little mite, he was taken to hospital in shock, with his hands all swollen. The hospital rang the militia, an investigator came, and the boy told him everything. The father was put in prison for embezzlement. And our model teacher Marya Ivanovna is still working at the same nursery school, only now she is the head teacher.'

'No, girls!' begged Irishka, 'let's not have any more of these horrible stories!'

'What can we do if life produces them itself?' objected Galina.

But Emma looked at Irishka and said: 'All right, save your tears. I'll tell a funny story specially for you. It's a bit like the story about the dissident money, but I'm glad to say it has nothing to do with any conspiracy, and I can mention all the names. The characters are quite well-known people. They are unofficial artists and poets, the people that are known in Leningrad as the alternative culture, and who used to be just called bohemians. They're people who live as though there wasn't such a thing as the Soviet government, and the government also pretends – for the moment anyway – that they don't exist either. Listen.'

Story Nine

by the director Emma, about a magic ten-rouble note and the alternative culture.

'After I had travelled round the country working in various theatres I decided to return to Leningrad. To begin with I found it impossible to get a proper job, so I did casual work for radio and television, and put on *The Snow Maiden* for children's New Year parties. Meanwhile my divorce finally came through and my husband very generously gave me a room of twenty square metres. Before the divorce he had a three-bedroom flat, so he exchanged it for a two-room flat for himself and a room in a communal flat for me. Well, at least I had somewhere to live. But life wasn't easy, I can tell you.

'One day I was sitting at home writing an idiotic script for some amateur village group – another way of earning a bit of money – when Kostya Kuzminsky rang me up. "Listen, Emma! I desperately need twenty roubles. I pawned my mother's engagement ring, and the time expires tomorrow. If I don't redeem it I've lost it. I need thirty roubles, but I've only got ten. Can you lend me twenty for a week?"

' "No, Kostenka, I can't. I owe my neighbour for telephone and light, and I haven't got a copeck. I'm afraid to go into the kitchen. Sorry!"

'Kostya hung up, and I returned to my script. A couple of hours later he suddenly appeared in person. I have to tell you that the poet Kuzminsky very rarely got on to his own two feet. Usually he lay on a couch at home in his dressing gown scribbling poetry, while the other poets and artists all gravitated towards him. You could say that his couch was the centre of the alternative culture. Kostya appeared, and handed me a ten-rouble note: "I never did find the extra twenty roubles. I'll lose the ring anyway, so you might as well pay off your debts at least, otherwise your neighbours

212

will kill you and the Russian theatre won't get revived with your new ideas."

'I was delighted, grabbed the tenner and, while we were still standing in the corridor, picked a pencil up off the telephone table and started jotting down on the corner of the note how much I had to pay for the light and telephone, and working out if I had enough to pay for the flat as well. Kostya grumbled something about me not showing respect to money and stumped off back to his couch.

'I worked out that I still couldn't settle all my debts even now, and I was on the point of taking the tenner to the neighbour when the doorbell rang again. It was the young Moscow poet Bakhyt Kenzhiev. "Emma, help me! I need to go back to Moscow urgently and I've lost my money! Have you got a tenner?"

' "You're in luck – I have. Here you are." I handed Kostya's tenner over to Bakhyt, and he went away happy.

'An hour later the artist Yura Galetsky rang. "Emma! You gave Bakhyt a tenner, well he's given it back to me for you, because we had already clubbed together to buy his ticket and we've just been seeing him off. I don't have time to call in today, so I gave it to Shirali to drop in to you."

'I waited for Shirali for a long time, but it wasn't till the next day that he rang up: "Emma! I was on my way over to you with your tenner, honestly, but I dropped in at the Saigon and bumped into Sashka Isachev. And as he hadn't eaten for three days I gave it to him. Do you mind?"

' "Of course not. You gave it to him, and that's that."

'The Saigon is a café on the corner of Nevsky Prospect and Vladimirsky Prospect, and Sasha Isachev was an artist from Belorussia who settled in Leningrad. Actually he didn't become completely one of us: when he got back home the KGB either threatened him or bribed him, but they got him to write a lot of filth in the Belorussian papers about his Petersburg friends. But that's a different subject, in those days he was still a clean kid – like all the others. And like everyone else, always penniless. So that was the end of my tenner.

'About six months went by, and our Kostya started getting ready to go to the West. He had collected poetry by unofficial poets and samizdat prose, but had forgotten to do anything about money, hoping that it would somehow just turn up. A week before his departure he still didn't have the money for the ticket! The word went round our unofficial gang, and we began contributing our threes, fivers and tenners for Sasha's trip. The money was brought in and thrown into a jug someone had put in the middle of the table. The time came to go and get the tickets, and Kostya said to me: "Emma! I just have to finish one page, could you shake the jug and see if there's enough for the tickets?"

'I emptied the money out and began counting. Suddenly among the ten-rouble notes I saw one with familiar figures written down the side!

'"Good heavens, Kostya! Do you remember bringing me a tenner last winter?"

'"I don't recall ever distributing tenners. What about it?'

'"How could you not remember? I stood in the corridor and jotted my debts down right on the note. And you were grumbling that I couldn't find any paper to write on."

'"Yes, I do remember something like that . . . Anyway, what about it?"

'"Just that here it is, that very same tenner!"

'And I told him how our magic tenner had gone full circle.

'Our friends who were in the room were all amazed, and Petya Cheygin said: "We can't give the government such a wonderful tenner just to pay for Kostya's tickets. Let's spend it on booze instead."

'We gave Petya the tenner and sent him off to get some champagne. The poet returned looking gloomy, with no champagne and no tenner: "I met Natashka Lazareva, the artist, in the grocer's. She was about to go on duty at the boilerhouse, and she didn't even have enough money for a package of cheese. So I gave her the tenner."

'I would love to ask Natasha Lazareva if she changed that tenner. Knowing her character, I should think not – she probably met someone else. It's ridiculous, I know, but I still look at every tenner that comes into my hands to see if it has written on it: "tel. – 2.40, rent – 5, light – 2.50". If you ever come across it, think to yourself, that's it.'

Story Ten

by the secretary Irishka, about a cat called Rublik and a boy who lost a rouble.

'This happened a long time ago when I was still at school, in the seventh or eighth year. My mother, father and elder sister were at work all day, and the rule in the family was that I had to do my homework and also the shopping. I also had to go to the laundry and the shoe repairs and do other odd jobs. I was quite a little housewife. We had a happy life, but we had to count the pennies, so my mother would leave me a small amount each day for housekeeping expenses, and in the evening I would do the accounts and give her the change.

'One day I did my homework and went off to get bread. The bread shop was right on our street quite near the house. Just next to the door of the shop I saw a boy of about seven or eight weeping bitter tears.

' "Why are you crying?" I asked him.

' "I lost the money . . ."

' "So why cry about it? Go home, tell your mother what happened, and don't do it again!"

'I felt sorry for the boy, but I also felt proud that I had been going to the shops and doing the housekeeping for all those years, and never once lost any money. Boys! They were all the same!

'I took the bread home, and then set off to get the shoes repaired. As I passed the bread shop the boy was still standing there. It was October, so it was quite cold out. He had been wiping his eyes and his nose with his hands, and they were blue with cold.

' "Why are you standing here? Go home! You'll freeze!"

' "I did. My mother said to go back out again and not come back till I find the money."

' "How much did you lose?"

' "One rouble . . ."

' "A rouble?! You dummy!"

'And off I went to the shoe repairs. I sat in the queue for an hour, and on my way home afterwards I found the little fellow still standing in the same place. He wasn't crying any more, just shivering with cold, and he had pulled his little frozen hands up into his sleeves.

' "Go home, for heaven's sake, I can't stand seeing you there any more! Your mother won't kill you."

' "I know she won't. She's crying because I lost a rouble. How can I go home?"

'I arrived home, but I couldn't get the boy out of my mind. If I had had a rouble of my own I would have taken it and given it to him. But I only had the housekeeping money: three roubles left, and I still had to take the wash to the laundry. There was no way I could help the boy.

'I tied the dirty wash up into a bundle and set off with it. There he was, still standing there!

In the laundry I sat in the queue thinking about my own school problems, and I sort of forgot about the boy. Suddenly I heard a conversation going on nearby. A woman in the queue was getting impatient: "I've been sitting here for more than an hour. How can you work so slowly?"

'The assistant angrily chucked a bundle of washing into the corner and shouted back at her: "So why don't you try doing my job for thirty roubles! And I'll watch how fast you move! We're supposed to have two assistants for each shift, and we only have one. We haven't got enough people, what am I supposed to do about it?"

'And she went on poking about among the dirty bundles. And I thought: "What if that boy's mother gets hardly any wages either? There must be a lot of people like that. And what if the rouble he lost was their last?" And I really began to feel sorry for the boy.

'My turn came, I handed in my wash and paid. I had one-and-a-half roubles left. Then I made a decision: if he was still standing there and hadn't gone home, then I would give him the wretched rouble and somehow square it with my mother. She could give it to me as a reward for never losing any money!

'Yes, he was still there, poor kid. It was dark and I could hardly see him. He was leaning against a drain pipe, and he was absolutely frozen. I went up to him and solemnly gave him my rouble: "There's a rouble for you. Now stop crying and run home quickly. Your mother will be worried about you."

'But he started crying again and wouldn't take the rouble.

' "What's the matter?"

216

' "Mama said I must not ask strangers for the money, I must find it myself because I lost it!"

' "Well, you're not asking for it, I'm just giving it!"

' "I still can't take it. It's not my rouble."

' "Then you tell your mother you found it on the ground."

' "I can't tell lies either!"

'And he cried even louder. What could I do? I stood next to him, crying myself.

' "Why are your crying, a big girl like you?"

' "Because I feel sorry for you."

'We both stood there for a while, sniffing. Then I suddenly had an idea. "I know what you could do. I'm standing here with a heavy load in the freezing cold, all because of you. My hands are absolutely frozen. See, I have no gloves! Now, for that you can help me carry my washing home, you've got nothing else to do."

' "All right, I'll help you."

'We picked up the bundle by the cord and carried it between us back to my place. When we arrived I took out the rouble and said in the most grown-up way I could: "You helped me carry my washing home, now here is a rouble for your work. Your mother won't be angry if you earned the rouble, she'll be proud of you. Yes, she will, I know!"

'How pleased he was! He rushed downstairs without even saying thank you!

'When my mother got home from work that night I told her everything that had happened. I was very worried she might fly off the handle at me for being disobedient. But she quietly listened to my story and said: "You did the right thing. That was clever of you to think up a way for him to earn the rouble by honest labour. He's obviously a good boy."

'About nine o'clock, when our family were all safely home, the doorbell suddenly rang. My sister went to answer it, then came back and said: "Irina! There's a young gentleman with a cat asking for you."

'I went out, and there outside the door stood the boy, holding a little orange kitten in his cap.

'Mama told me to come and say thank you for the rouble you gave me for working for you. She wasn't angry and she stopped crying. She also said the job I did was worth less than a rouble, so the rouble you gave me was really a present. So, thank you."

' "And who have you got there?"

' "That's my present to you. A cat had kittens in our basement, and I took one of them. There's still two left. You don't mind that it's orange?"

' "Very nice! Orange is lovely! Thanks a million!"

'He handed over the kitten and went home content.

'I got into a bit of trouble over the kitten. But the family got used to him in the end. And we named him Rublik, in memory of that little boy and his misfortune.

'So you never did ask where his mother worked?' enquired Valentina.

'Oh, yes, I forgot to tell you! I almost guessed right. There was no father, and the mother was a cleaner at a school. And that's where they lived, in a small room at the school. That means that in those days she would have been earning exactly the same as the laundry assistant, thirty roubles.'

'Well, the minimum wage has more than doubled since then,' said Natasha reassuringly. 'It's up to seventy now.'

'Yes, it's gone up,' replied Emma. 'But prices have gone up so much that it's still worth only thirty, if that.'

'True,' sighed Zina. 'You can't survive on wages if you don't have a profession.'

And everyone understood that she was thinking about her future and how she was going to get a job, and everyone started advising her where to go for help and which jobs had living accommodation. Nelya said she could get a job working at a crèche, then she could keep her son with her.

With this discussion of Zina's future the seventh day of *The Women's Decameron* was concluded.

THE EIGHTH DAY

devoted to stories of

Revenge

The eighth day of *The Women's Decameron* began.

That morning, after the babies' first feed and after breakfast, Valentina turned to Albina: 'Albina! You hinted that you managed to get your own back on that sadist who raped you, and also on the general that said decent girls don't get themselves raped. How about telling us about that today?'

'OK, Valyusha. In which case we could all tell stories about men and women taking revenge on those who have abused them, couldn't we?'

Everybody agreed with Albina, and that evening the stories of revenge commenced.

Story One

by the biologist Larissa, not an anecdote, but a completely authentic story about life in a communal flat, which is anecdotal in itself.

'I shall tell you how a quiet intellectual got his own back on the other people living with him in a communal flat.

'In a particular Leningrad flat an old woman died, leaving vacant a tiny room of ten square metres. As usual, a veritable war broke out among the occupants over this room: one person had applied for an improvement in living quarters and wanted to get it straightaway by adding this room to his own; another wanted to join up with his wife who had an even smaller room somewhere else which could be exchanged for the old woman's room. But the regional accommodation office didn't bother to find out which

220

occupant had the most right to the room, they just gave it to a young engineer. Well, you can imagine the other occupants were not at all pleased to see their new neighbour. All their hatred for each other they poured out on to the poor man. They gave him a hard time in the kitchen and in other communal parts of the flat. If a friend came to see him they immediately sent in a report to the local militia to say the new occupant was bringing in drunks and addicts. And if a girlfriend or female colleague from work should pay him a visit (heaven forbid!), he was just about accused of running a brothel. At first the new tenant tried to defend himself and get into a good relationship with his neighbours, but this only made the atmosphere worse. So he stopped. He tried not to go into the kitchen, he slipped away into his room like a little mouse, and whenever they tried to create a scandal he refused to rise to it.

'In the end all the occupants of that flat had a stroke of luck. The authorities decided to build a super-modern building on that street, which meant demolishing several old houses straightaway. The house with the flat in it was also earmarked for demolition. All the occupants were assigned rooms in new regions, and some even got small individual flats. They were all overjoyed. With the sudden prospect of moving into more decent living quarters everyone seemed to become kinder and better, and human qualities that had long been repressed in them began to show themselves. Basically, it was conscience.

'They said to each other: "Well, now, we've lived together so many years, we all know everything about each other. There have been bad things, but there have also been good things, haven't there? But our new neighbour: is he going to have any good memories about this flat? He's just a quiet intellectual, really, he hasn't done anyone any harm . . ."

'And the occupants of the flat decided to get together and apologize to the intellectual. So they did. They bought cakes, made tea, and invited him to the communal kitchen in the evening. He came, but he stood to one side nervously waiting to see what sort of dirty trick they would play on him as a parting shot. But the other people in the flat said to him: "Dear neighbour, we're very sorry we've been so unfair to you. Now that we're all separating and going to different ends of the town we would like you to forgive us and not bear a grudge against us. And now let's have a farewell cup of tea and drink to peace and friendship, as they say.'

'The intellectual looked at them and was moved to tears. He took his glasses off, wiped his eyes and said: "I gladly forgive you, my dear friends. But I can't drink tea with you, and I'll tell you why. All the time you were waging war against me, trying to get me out of the flat, I never fought back openly – how could I? But you probably noticed I sometimes came into the kitchen with my teapot. The thing was, I made my tea in my own room on an electric ring, using a different teapot, and the other one I used for pissing into. And when none of you were in the kitchen I would empty the contents into each of your teapots and suacepans. So please forgive me, too!"

'And so the good people departed for their new flats.'

The women laughed heartily over the intellectual, if he may be called such, and they recalled other incidents of communal warfare, some of which ended in reconciliation and others in court cases for assault and battery committed by one neighbour against another in the communal kitchen.

The next to tell a story was Zina.

Story Two

by Zina the tramp, and of course yet another story from camp life, about how you can tell murderers from their eyes and about an old woman who murdered her daughter-in-law to get her own back on her son.

'Many of the women in our camp were murderers: some had killed a man in self-defence, some had murdered their new-born baby because they were so poor, and there were also some who had murdered out of revenge or jealousy. And here's what I've noticed, girls: you can always tell murderers by their eyes. They've got strange eyes, sort of white. No, not bright, like children and very good people have, but real

222

white. Even dark-eyed people have this special film on their eyes – they're white, that's all there is to it! And I've also noticed that if they killed someone by mistake – "unpremeditated', as it says in the law – then they don't have that white film. At first I thought I was just imagining it, that it was just me because I hate murderers so much. Well, murder's awful, isn't it? You get people who have a really horrible life with no happiness at all, like these cripples or invalids. You'd think they had nothing to live for, yet they're happy to be alive. We had a war cripple living in our village: no arms, no legs, and shell-shocked. His wife would carry him out into the sun, put him down on the grass, and he would lie there smiling away at everything. He was just smiling to be alive. So how can you take a person's life away from him, if even someone like that enjoys life? So I thought maybe it was something going white in my own eyes when I met a murderer, because they gave me the creeps. Then I noticed that sometimes I didn't know what a woman was in for and I would see her eyes were white and get the feeling she had killed someone. I would quietly ask the other women about her and find out that I was right – she was a murderer. Another sign I noticed, depending on what drove a person to kill. If she killed by mistake she would always repent and feel really sorry and want to be punished. But if it was premeditated murder, those people are the opposite, they hate the people they murdered. Let him rot in the ground, they say, because I'm suffering here in the zone for him, the bastard! That's the way they think.

'Women who have killed out of jealousy don't go around with such white eyes, they just have a bit of a white haze. Sometimes you can only see it from the side, or if the woman loses her temper. And they're often sorry for what they've done, and they usually have something good to say about the husband or lover they murdered. But the ones who murdered out of revenge – they never repent. They're really scary, I always gave them a wide berth. Especially one old woman. She was so small and skinny that people at the zone called her the Grasshopper. She worked at the hot water point, giving out hot water for tea in the morning and evening. I was on duty in my barrack for a while, because I was only in for a short stretch, and I had a hell of a time with that Grasshopper. I needed to collect hot water for every-

223

body, that's six to eight buckets of it, and I couldn't bring myself to go and get the water from her! I had to pay one of the other tramps a packet of tobacco to do it for me. And you know I smoke like a chimney, so that was no joke. I even gave it up so I could afford to send other people to the old woman. Then I started to get curious: what was it that scared me so much about her? She wasn't very frightening to look at: she was small and dry like an old stick, her face was no bigger than your fist, with skinny little arms like a spider's legs – what was there to be scared of? And yet I was dead scared of her. I was scared of her eyes. They were small and dark like bits of a broken beer-bottle, and they had this white light coming out of them that got you right in the heart. Scary!

'I started asking the women: "Tell me what the Grasshopper's in for."

'The zeks tried to put me off at first: "We don't want to remember all that!"

'Then one of them told me, and the others said it was true.

'Her son got married, but her daughter-in-law was a nasty piece of work. They all lived in one room, so they couldn't get away from each other. There were rows and fights. During one quarrel the old woman grabbed a kitchen knife and went for her daughter-in-law. She was a tough girl, so she wrenched the knife out of the old woman's hand and laughed: "Who do you think you're attacking? You better look out, you'll strain yourself waving that knife about!"

She was a pretty unpleasant specimen herself, not the type to pacify her mother-in-law. The son rushed from one to the other, not knowing which of them was right or whose fault it was. The daughter-in-law wanted to report the knife incident to the militia, but her husband persuaded her to have pity on the old woman because she was his mother. Later on he began to take his wife's side when he saw his mother was being nasty to her for no reason.

'Time went by, and the daughter-in-law got pregnant. One day she felt ill at work, came home in the afternoon, lay down and went to sleep. I don't know what had happened between them before that, but the old woman took an axe and laid into the girl while she was sleeping. And not just once: she hacked her into pieces. But she wasn't even content with that. She was determined to get even with her son, so when he came home she gave him a nice bowl of soup and conned him into thinking his wife had gone to the doctor. Then when he had finished his soup she said to him: "How did you enjoy your little wife?"

'When he realized what he had been eating he went berserk straightaway. The old woman was put inside. Our women were amazed she only got prison: "Why didn't they shoot her? Who needs a woman like that?"

'Then one day during roll-call the Grasshopper was missing. All the zeks were kept standing in formation while the guards searched the camp. We were all wondering if she had tried to run away. They found her at the hot water point where she worked. She was hanging from an old electric wire – she hardly weighed a thing. She was full of evil, all right, but in the end her conscience got the better of her. It wouldn't let her rest. If I hadn't known the woman myself I wouldn't have believed all this. I think revenge always hits back at the person who keeps it in his heart. One should forgive and forget, or as the saying goes, he who bears a grudge should lose an eye. Maybe that's something to do with white eyes? Hatred and revenge do make your eyes white.'

'It's hard to argue with you, Zina,' said Emma. 'You have taken us to the very depths of human depravity. But on a more superficial level, what can be more satisfying than paying a rotten man back handsomely for what he's done to you. And that's why your saying doesn't end there. It goes, he who bears a grudge should lose an eye, and he who forgets should lose both.'

The women laughed at this light relief: they had found Zina's story very depressing.

It was now Natasha's turn to tell a story, and she started by saying: 'I don't know which of you is right. I've never got as far as having my eyes go white, but I've had them go dark. Sometimes you get so furious with somebody that everything goes dark in front of your eyes, and your heart feels dark. I don't know how it is with you, but I find it difficult to overcome. Sometimes I start trying to think up ways of punishing the person who has offended me, and I always seem to run short of ideas, they don't seem to match the offence. Then it passes and I'm horrified at how much more trivial it was than my plans for revenge. It's a good thing they don't get further than the idea stage, with me at any rate. But I'll tell you about my friend, who really paid her lover back well, and even managed to keep her nose clean.

Story Three

by the engineer Natasha, about how a certain woman reduced the lover who had insulted her to a state of nervous depression merely by the use of the telephone.

I have a friend called Zoya, and she had a lover. Their relationship was not a success. They were always either separating or coming together again. Zoya was older than Oleg, and more intelligent, and this probably riled him. From time to time they would stop seeing each other, usually when Oleg had found himself a new girlfriend. But he was a dull man, and women soon gave him the push, and then he would return to Zoya. The stupid girl forgave him, and it all began again. Sometimes the question of marriage and children would come up, but Oleg had one very good argument against this – no flat. Then he started saving up to buy a co-operative flat. He asked Zoya to help by saving up some money to lend him. "We'll have our own little place where we can meet in peace," he said.

'Of course, Zoya wasn't thinking about a place to meet so much as that when Oleg finally got his accommodation he would start thinking seriously about having a family. Actually she was already just like a wife to him: she did his washing, his cooking, and if he was ill she never left his bedside. She really loved him. That's why he always came back to her after his adventures.

'A year passed, and together they saved up enough money to buy a co-operative flat. Oleg moved in, and they began making their nest. They both rushed round the town looking for furniture, beginning by collecting old pieces from friends and fixing them up themselves. The only difference was that Oleg was all the time thinking he was making a cosy little bachelor's pad to bring girls to, and Zoya was thinking it was going to be a home she could come to. She was willing not to think of marriage as long as there was some sort of permanency, some semblance of family life. I used to laugh at her. If Oleg wanted flowers she would even steal cuttings from the Botanical Gardens for him and grow them in pots. She learnt to knit, and knitted him a bedspread, a tablecloth and chair covers. In other words, she was feathering her little nest. To all intents and purposes she was living with Oleg, just putting in an appearance at her mother's once a week. The mother accepted the relationship as quite normal and proper. Zoya was a typist, and she brought extra work home so as to get the flat furnished and cosy all the quicker. She didn't have her own typewriter – you can't go far on a typist's wage – but Oleg had one. He worked for a magazine. So they took it in turns tapping away at the same typewriter, earning the money to pay for a fridge or a tape recorder. That typewriter played its own small part in the story.

'One night the telephone started ringing at two in the morning. I picked up the receiver and heard Zoya's voice. It sounded crushed and lifeless: "Can I come and spend the night with you? Oleg's just turned me out on to the street, and I'm in no condition to go to my mother."

' "Of course! Come straight over. Get a taxi in fact."

'Half an hour later Zoya appeared, looking absolutely ghastly and hardly able to stand. "Have you got any vodka in the house?"

'I got a bottle of vodka out and poured her a glass. All this was going on in the kitchen so as not to wake the others. She drank the vodka and sat there without speaking, clutching herself by the shoulders and shaking all over.

' "Well, what happened?"

'No answer. Then she said: "Pour me some more. But not in a vodka glass, in a tumbler."

'She drank a whole tumblerful, continued to sit stock still for a while, then finally she seemed to let go: she dropped her head on the table and burst into tears. Well, thank heavens for that, I thought, things are looking up a bit. I took her in my arms, stroked her head and tried to comfort her. "Tell me about it! Don't try to hold it in."

'And Zoya told me what had happened between her and Oleg.

'She had got back from work first as usual. She cooked the meal, tidied herself up, and sat down to wait for her beloved. When he appeared Zoya noticed immediately that he had something on his mind: he didn't kiss her properly at the door, he didn't sit down to eat straightaway but started pacing the flat, whistling to himself and thinking about something. Then he said to her: "Zoyenka! I have a lot of work for the next few days and I shall need the typewriter the whole time. Why don't you go to your mum for a couple of days?"

'Zoya still didn't realize she was quietly being shown the door. "Why should I go to my mother? I've just finished a big copying order. You go ahead and type. Anyway, I wanted to do some laundry, so I won't be in your way."

'Then he tried a different tack: "Look, darling, I've invited some friends to a housewarming party tomorrow evening. I promised them a long time ago. It would be a bit awkward if you were here."

' "Why should it? Surely I'm not going to be the one friend you don't invite to your housewarming party? And besides, your friends have known me for a long time and they all like me a lot. and I've missed them."

'But Oleg already had an answer to that one: "It would still be awkward in front of my colleagues from the magazine. We're not yet husband and wife, and I don't know how they would look upon it if they thought we were living together. So I thought you and I could have our own private housewarming party tonight, without anyone else. I specially bought a bottle of champagne and some brandy."

'Zoya didn't know what to say to that, but went to prepare some snacks. Then they drew up the armchairs, put on their favourite tapes, and sat enjoying themselves. Zoya felt better and forgot about their discussion. Then Oleg began to bring the conversation round to the various men Zoya had met. This had been during the times he had run off, and she had tried to grasp on to something in order not to feel lonely and abandoned. Zoyka is an intelligent girl, but when it comes to men she's really dim. So now she started confessing everything to him, even though he had already had it all from her before. And Oleg questioned her and pretended to get jealous and provoke a quarrel. But Zoya had enough sense to change the subject. She knew she had a short temper and that Oleg knew how to take advantage of it.

'Oleg waited a little, then he put his champagne glass down, took Zoya in his arms and said: "Zoechka, I have to tell you something. Do you remember I had an affair with a student from the art school? She rang me at work today and said she had almost finished her studies and would like to ask my advice about what to do next. I invited her to supper tomorrow night."

'When Zoya heard this she went numb. And, as she told me, the room took on a horrible transformation in front of her eyes: she saw a pile of soil and broken flower-pots, burnt curtains at the windows, the books from Oleg's beautiful library all torn up, and herself lying dead amid all this chaos. This whole picture flashed before her in a split second, and it was so clear she even noticed she was wearing jeans and a jacket as if she had just come in. And as she looked at this mental picture she quietly said: "No, Oleg, that is not going to happen."

'He leapt up like a scalded cat, went terribly pale and shouted: "Witch! Your voice when you said that! It was as if you slashed my stomach with a razor!"

' "Not with a razor, Olezhenka, with terror. But you really have slashed me with your vileness."

'Then Oleg demanded that she leave immediately: "This is my flat! There's nothing for you here, if that's the way you are!"

'And feverishly he began to collect her things together and stuff them into a travelling bag. Then he shoved her jacket into her hands and started pushing her towards the door. All the time he was shaking with fear and rage and for some reason threatening to call the militia. He had completely flipped. There was nothing Zoya could do but leave. It was a good thing she was able to come to me, and that I had some vodka. I tipped it down her till she was unconscious, then I put her to bed.

'I didn't go to work next morning, I stayed with Zoya; who knows what she might have done to herself in that state? We sat together, both suffering. Most of the time she didn't speak.

' "What are you thinking about?"

' "Revenge."

' "Zoyenka, darling! Forget it! Time will pass and you'll forget that Judas. What did he ever give you? Nothing, he just took and took."

'But she didn't answer, she just shook her head. I sat next to her with my arm round her, and I could literally feel all those horrible thoughts of revenge welling up and swirling round inside her poor head. Suddenly I noticed with horror that she was beginning to smile. That looked really bad! I would rather she cried ... I was afraid for her: there's nothing worse than when a woman gets bogged down in a love like that. Suddenly Zoya said in a completely calm voice: "I need to use the telephone."

'She lay down on the sofa, put the phone next to her and rang – Oleg, of course.

' "Olezhenka!" she said. "You called me a witch last night. Well do you remember what a certain witch in Bulgakov did to the critic Latunsky's flat? She made a bit of a mess of it. Well, my dear, I know you've read Bulgakov, and I know you love your little nest. And although you thought of just about everything yesterday, you forgot to take my key to the flat away from me. Luckily I'm staying with friends quite close by, but it takes you an hour to get back from work. That's ample time to make sure your planned supper with your friend doesn't take place: you wouldn't invite her to a flat that's in ruins, would you? Well, goodbye, dear. No, no, I have no time to talk, I have to hurry! Goodbye!"

'She put the receiver down and collapsed laughing on to a cushion.

'I was frightened. ' "Zoyka! You wouldn't really do that, would you?"

' "I wouldn't dream of it! But can you imagine how he's going to rush home?"

' "I can, and I don't envy him."

' "And that's not all! There's going to be a series of telephone calls. I can promise you a good show, with a scared man taking the lead role."

After that Zoyka got up, took a shower, then came out looking cheerful and asking for something to eat. About two hours later she rang Oleg again, at home this time: "Olezhenka? You know, dear, I felt rather bad after our conversation, and I've just thought things over. I've decided to postpone my little act. Will you be leaving about seven o'clockish to collect your little student? Well, I'll be watching from the street corner, and as soon as you leave I'll pay you a visit. I promise to arrange the cosiest little setting for you that you could imagine! No, there's nothing to discuss. Goodbye, dear!"

'As the evening approached Zoya began acting like a hooligan: every half-hour she dialled Oleg's number, and as soon as he answered she put down the receiver. It would appear that he never did leave home, and his planned meeting fell through. Just before going to bed she rang him one more time and said: "Olezhenka, you're wasting your time trying to change your fate. It means you can't leave home, and I have to waste my time too. You still won't be able to escape what I have for you. Even if you change the lock it'll be no good – your flat is on the ground floor. So just wait. My visit could happen at any hour of the day or night."

'And from then on Zoyka kept ringing Oleg, either at home or at work. If he was home she just put the receiver down. When she rang his work she would ask to speak to him and then put the receiver down when they went to get him. Oleg realized she was checking to see where he was, and completely lost his head: after receiving a telephone call at work he would rush home, and when he was at home he would start screaming down the telephone as soon as he picked it up: "Zoya! Zoyenka! I want to talk to you!"

'But she never answered.

'After a couple of months he moved, but Zoyka immediately found out his new address. This time the flat was on the eighth floor, and so the little bitch said to him: "You think of everything. But I'll think of something too, and then I'll do it. The main thing is, just keep waiting! Wait for me and think of me, dear!"

'Everything gets forgotten in time, everything gets healed. Zoyka got over it. She found herself a nice guy, and they've been living together more than a year now. But from time to time she pops in to have a chat with me and we talk about Oleg. And then she'll pick up the phone and ring him to remind him: "Keep waiting!"

'She once let me listen to his voice. I had seen and heard

him before when he was a bouncing forty-year-old. Now it was the voice of a tormented old man.

When Natasha had finished her story Albina exclaimed: 'Yes, not a bad revenge, and he deserved it! She really got him at his weak point, the flat.'

'Oh, I know so many men whose flat means more to them than anything else in the world! Especially if it's taken them a long time to get it. A boring crowd!' said Emma. 'That's why I prefer our arty set, they're not slaves to a lot of junk.'

'She was wasting her time,' said Zina. 'She should have just got the hell out of it. Shitty little creep. And I can't see why these women don't learn anything from their education. She's got brains, and she has to go and pick the worst sort of man. A simple woman would have left him long ago.'

'You're right, Zinusha!' laughed Larissa. 'The whole problem is that a simple woman will see a pile of shit and say to herself: "Shit". But an intellectual dreams to herself: "Perhaps I could transform that shit into cream." And she won't give up until she finally starts puking. And men like that love to find a woman who is above them, and then drag her down for all they're worth. And once they've dragged her down they trample her in the mud. Sometimes they even trample her to death.'

'But don't you sometimes get women who choose a man they can torment?' asked Olga.

'Sometimes, but not often,' replied Emma. 'We're more easily appeased. And if a woman looks at her victim too long she starts feeling sorry for him. What do you think, Natasha, would Zoya have forgiven her Oleg if she had seen him at work every day? If they had worked at the same place, for example, and she had seen him getting paler and thinner?'

'Of course she would have! She's been getting a bit bored playing this old trick recently. She did it mostly to get the hurt out of her system, and to get him out of her system, too. When a man is as small-minded as that there's no other way to get through to him and show him you can't just trample on other people and get away with it. But if that Oleg was a real man he would have torn his hair in shame at the low-down way he behaved that night, not to mention all the other things he did to hurt her before.'

'What man ever feels shame when he has the desire and the opportunity to sleep with another girl?' laughed Albina. 'All his shame gets turned into sperm!'

'Albinka!' exclaimed Irishka. 'Have you really never come across a man who has treated you well and loved you properly?'

'There was one once. And out of his goodness and love for me he very nearly ruined an innocent girl. I'll tell you about that when it's my turn. Incidentally, that'll be my story about how I got my own back on the rapist. Meanwhile, let's listen to what Valentina has to tell us.'

Story Four

by the bigwig Valentina, being a cautionary tale about how it can sometimes be dangerous to take revenge, even in defence of the constitution.

'When my husband and I worked in the regional committee of the Komsomol we lived in a building that was heated with wood-burning stoves. There were piles of firewood lying around the yard, and the residents had to pick their way among them to get to their doorways. Nobody had a woodshed, and for some reason the basements were always full of water, so they just kept their wood outside in the yard. And, of course, neighbours stole firewood from each other when they didn't have enough of their own. By that time most buildings in Leningrad already had steam central heating, but firewood was still hard to come by. And there were also the clever types who didn't have any firewood of their own and heated their flats entirely on stolen wood. Well, everyone accepted the situation the way you accept acts of God: it was just too bad, you couldn't stand guarding your firewood with a gun. And anyway, the thieves were careful: they only stole at night, and they didn't just steal from one person, but helped themselves from various woodpiles. So everybody was fairly tolerant about it.

'But we had one woman living in our house called Polikarpova, who had fought in the war and was a real pain. She went about in a man's jacket with all her medals on it, and was constantly going on about her war exploits. Especially when she was creating an embarrassing scene with one of the female neighbours. And she loved making these scenes, always fighting for the observance of "socialist legality". She couldn't just say: "Marya Ivanovna, why can't you remember to switch off the light in the corridor?" Instead she would stand with her hands on her hips and shout so that everyone in the flat could hear: "The government is trying to save electricity, and Comrade Petrova is undermining the country's economy by wasting electricity! But Vladimir Ilyich said that communism is Soviet power plus e-lec-tri-fi-ca-tion of the whole country! And it's because of people like her that we haven't been able to build communism yet!"

'You can imagine that poor Marya Ivanovna felt like running away.

'This Polikarpova woman discovered a couple of times that her firewood was being stolen. This caused a new scene for the whole house: "The Soviet constitution is the most progressive constitution in the world, and it even permits private property. Consequently, anyone who steals citizens' firewood is breaking the constitutional law on property and is insulting our Soviet constitution!"

'She made all the residents come to a general meeting on the theft of firewood. The people said to her: "Stop making a fuss about nothing. You only lost a couple of logs!"

'But she yelled: "I'm not worried about the wood, it's the principle that's important! Until recently people in Finland had their hands cut off for stealing!"

'Then one old pensioner, who had also been in the war, said to her: "Don't talk rubbish, Polikarpova. I was in the Finnish war, and I never saw many one-handed Finns. And now they all come to Leningrad to drink vodka every Sunday; have you noticed any with only one hand? You're a war veteran, you should be ashamed of yourself for wishing people to have their hands cut off for your damned log of wood. If you haven't got enough wood, take some of mine.

We'll be getting steam heating next year anyway. We'll have enough till then, and some left over too."

'But there was no stopping her: "If our residential social unit, as represented by an honoured pensioner, refuses to promote the observance of legality, then what can we expect from ordinary citizens? Very well. I shall fight the criminals alone, they will not escape my just revenge!"

'At this point Polikarpova's neighbour, the same Marya Ivanovna that she always hassled more than anyone else, could control herself no longer: "Have you no fear of God, Darya Vasilyevna? Are you really going to try and get your revenge on people for taking firewood? Maybe someone couldn't get any for his stove. You said yourself that they helped themselves to yours only a couple of times. Stop eating out your heart over it, just forget about it!"

'But Polikarpova was not to be thwarted: "I'll show those thieves! They'll learn not to lay their hands on other people's property!"

'The others gave up on her and went back to their rooms.

'Then Polikarpova started to wage a regular war on the thieves. First she lay in wait for them at night, sitting among the woodpiles ready to ambush them. She didn't catch anyone. As if to mock her the thieves started stealing more wood from her than from the others. Then she thought up a plan that was so monstrous that when the others found out about it later they were all amazed that a person could have such a vengeful mind. She got some dynamite from somewhere, gouged out two birch logs and filled them with the dynamite. She carefully closed the ends with wooden plugs and put the logs back on her own pile so that the thief would fall for those particular ones. She took wood from the other side of the pile for her own stove. She walked around the yard looking calm and content, and when she met any of the neighbours she said: "You'll see, soon our thieves are going to get the treatment they would have got in Finland."

'But, of course, she didn't explain.

'Only things didn't turn out at all the way Polikarpova had planned. By a fluke she was the one who lost a hand, punished for her own petty vengefulness.

'One of the neighbours brought in a lorry-load of firewood. The lorry caught the edge of Polikarpova's woodpile as it was turning in the small yard and pulled half of it down. Knowing her bitchy nature, the neighbours rushed to tidy up her firewood and arrange the pile just as it was before. They soon had it all back together again, but the logs that were filled with dynamite got put back in a different part of the pile. So there it was, all nice and tidy. That night Polikarpova just happened to pick up those two logs. And they just had to go and blow up at the very moment she was putting her hand out to shut the stove door. The stove was blown to bits, a fire started in the room, and Polikarpova's right hand was torn right off. And do you know, no one in the house felt sorry for her!'

After hearing Valentina's story the women did not evince any special pity for Polikarpova either, and they turned to Albina: they had been dying to hear how she had taken her revenge on the man who had raped her.

Story Five

by the airhostess Albina, about a cleverly planned revenge and the person who carried it out, revealing certain new and unexpected traits in the character of Albina herself.

'I'll start at the point where I stopped last time when the investigator Anokhin refused to start proceedings against that sadist who had raped me, and the neighbours were afraid to come forward as witnesses, or just didn't want to.

'Life became hell. I suffered day and night thinking about the way I had been insulted and how helpless I was. I wanted to take my life, but I didn't, not because I felt sorry for myself but I was sorry it wouldn't make a scrap of difference to the offenders. They would never even hear about it if some woman called Albina Nadezhdina, who nobody needed and nobody knew, was cremated at the Leningrad Crematorium at government expense without any flowers.

'I decided against death, but life was no better. I just carried on, sort of mechanically. And suddenly I had an admirer, quite unexpectedly and unasked for. This was just not the time! He was a guy of twenty-six who worked as a

236

foreman at a building site. We met by chance: an old friend of mine invited me to her birthday party, and he was one of the guests and fell head over heels in love with me. But I couldn't stand the sight of men. If he'd started making advances I would have sent him packing straightaway. But he had a softly-softly approach: he used to wait for me after work and see me home, and at the house he would say goodbye politely and leave. I never spoke, nor did he. A month went by, and another month. I was used to having this silent shadow waiting for me after work and then trailing home with me. I would walk along thinking my own private thoughts, and he never disturbed me. I didn't even take any notice of him any more, just as though he really was my shadow.

'But one day my shadow spoke. He met me with flowers and invited me to go to a café: "I need to talk to you very badly."

'I was feeling so depressed that day that I didn't care where I went or who with. I could go to the café with him, or I could just as easily jump into the water, I didn't really give a fuck. So I went to the café. We sat eating ice cream and drinking champagne. Then he said: "Marry me, Albina!"

' "Wha-at? You're asking Albina to marry you? Do you know this Albina, do you know her past?"

' "Tell me about it. I really want to get to know you better."

'And he took me by the hand and looked into my eyes ecstatically.

'So, I thought, well, now you're about to get an earful about your fiancée! And I told him everything, starting with Kayur and ending with the sadist. He listened to me without any interruptions, just turning pale or blushing at different points in the story.

' "Well, what do you say to that?" I asked him when I had finished.

'He suddenly kissed my hand and said: "These are terrible things you have told me, Albina. You're not going to believe this, but I had a feeling there was something like this about you. I knew you were a woman with an unusual lot, a tragic lot."

'I laughed in my admirer's face and said: "Well you just take a walk one evening down in Moskovsky Station, to the part where the prostitutes hang about. You'll see quite

237

enough who have a hard lot cruising around there at night! Far worse than me!"

'But he just looked at me, the stupid idiot, and there were tears in his eyes: "Why are you trying to hurt me? I've never hurt a woman."

' "Not one? You've never given a woman the push? You've never slept with a woman? So you're a virgin?"

' "But I have. I slept with my wife. I got married young, when we were both eighteen."

' "So why did you split up? A personality clash, or did she hurt you?"

' "No, she didn't hurt me. She only hurt me once, a year-and-a-half ago – she died in childbirth, and the baby died too." And he gave a pathetic smile, and his face really did look hurt.

'I just sat there gaping at him, my dear girls. What sort of customer was I dealing with? Had I suddenly run up against a real man? I began to melt, and I even took his hand and tried to say something kind. But I couldn't remember any kind words, the sort you say to a man. And I felt a lump in my throat, as if I'd got a piece of ice cream stuck in it that wouldn't go down. I swallowed the lump and was about to say something sensible when I suddenly felt the same old anger burning me up inside. What was I doing? People had trampled on me and walked all over me, and here I was again falling for the first kind words, like a stupid fish taking the bait. What did I know about this Fedya – his name was Fedor – apart from what he had told me himself? Could you trust any of them? Then I had an idea; it was terrible, but it made me happy. I let go of his hand, looked him in the eye and said: "OK, Fedya. I'll marry you. But on one condition."

'He turned pale again, obviously sensing something bad, but he said: "I agree already. Tell the the condition."

' "You have to pay back that rapist for me, and his neighbour, the general, who gave me the biggest slap in the face of all those wretched witnesses."

' "Agreed. I'll do it."

'And he went even paler, grabbed his champagne glass and started swigging it down like water.

' "But the revenge has got to be as serious as the offence. I know you could go and punch them both in the face, but I'm not interested in that – I could get any number of young fellows to do that for me."

'Fedya sat silently for a while, then he said: "Give me the address."

'Naturally I knew that address very well, and fired it off straightaway. He wrote it down. Then he paid the waitress, got up and said: "I'm not going to see you home this evening, Albina. I want to go straight over there and have a look at the place and think about it. I'll come and see you when it's all over. I'll ring you and then come."

' "Agreed!"

'We left the café and went our different ways. I felt bad about it, girls. And I felt empty inside. But I was not being weighed down by all that hurt any more, it seemed to have vanished.

'A week or two passed, and there was no phone call. I was beginning to think my avenger had chickened out and disappeared. But my heart told me that he hadn't, but was looking for a way to pay them back for me, and had perhaps found it already.

'And one evening the telephone did ring. I went to answer it, knowing it was Fedya! I picked up the receiver. "This is Fedor. It's all done. Can I come and tell you about it?"

'I barely managed to whisper "Yes", I suddenly felt so frightened. I couldn't even get up from my chair while I was waiting for him. He appeared almost immediately, so he must have rung from a telephone box nearby. He came in looking all pale, sat down on the sofa and put his head in his hands.

' "Well, tell me about it!"

'I sat down opposite him, trembling all over.

' "Do you know how I avenged you, Albina? I watched everybody there and discovered that your rapist was alone most of the time in the evenings. His wife is a lighting engineer at a theatre and gets back about midnight. General Vasilyev has a daughter called Lenochka who goes to a French course on Wednesdays and Fridays and gets home about ten at night. Have you guessed yet?"

'I had almost guessed. Or rather, as I look back on it I think I guessed. "Well? Go on . . ." I whispered.

' "I found out the telephone numbers of Vasilyev and the sadist Senko. All I had to do was keep watch near the house and ring up, so as to get an evening when that bastard Senko would be alone, the general was at home, and Lenochka had gone to her course. Tonight was one of them. I made sure they were both home, then I went into their entrance and unscrewed the light bulbs on all the floors. Then I sat on the windowsill on the floor above and waited. When I saw Lenochka enter the yard and come towards the entrance I went down to Senko's door and got ready. When the door downstairs slammed I pressed his bell. The only important thing now was that Senko should not open his door too soon or too late. He opened it just at the right moment: Lenochka had reached the landing and was feeling around in her bag for her key. She didn't notice me because I was standing completely still, pressed up against the wall. The moment Senko's door opened I grabbed Lenochka's shoulders from behind and shoved her into Senko's door, right into Senko himself. He stepped back into the flat, and I immediately slammed the door on them both. For a while I didn't hear anything. When I heard Lenochka's first scream I left and came here. That's all."

'We both sat there in silence. Then I started to act – mechanically, as if I was doing it all in my sleep.

' "Give me the general's number!"

'He got out his notebook, opened it to the right page and handed it to me. I dialled. "General Vasilyev, please. This is one of your neighbours speaking. I was going down the stairs just now and I saw the man who lives opposite you drag your daughter into his flat. Rescue her before it's too late!"

'There was a sort of grunt at the other end of the line, a crash, and then silence. I realized the general had just chucked the phone on the floor and run to save his daughter. I put down my receiver too.

'Fedor stared at me. Then he suddenly rushed over to me, buried his face in my lap and cried like a baby. And he kept on saying: "Thank you, thank you for ringing him! I couldn't have lived with it!"

' "Don't get your hopes up! He may have managed to fuck her already."

' "Do you want me to go and watch from the street to see how it ends?"

' "You stay here. You're in no state to go anywhere."

'I put Fedya to bed. With myself, of course. But we didn't do anything, we weren't up to it. We lay there all night without sleeping, waiting for the morning. Next day I told him to stay at my place, and I got myself dressed and set off for the house. I was in luck: as I came along I saw the janitor who had brought my shoe out to me. She was sweeping the pavement outside the gates. I went up and started talking to her: "Hi! Remember me?"

' "Good morning. Who are you, did you use to live in this house? Your face is a bit familiar, but I can't remember."

' "I stayed here one night only while your man from Flat 17 raped me. Do you remember the red suede shoe? You picked it up in the yard and returned it to me. Remember?"

'She threw her broom down and started waving her arms: "Oh, my dear, do you know what? They tied up your rapist just last night and carted him off to prison? He very nearly raped the general's daughter. Luckily someone saw him pull her into his flat and phoned her father, or it would have been bad for the girl. Her father dragged her away all beaten up. Then he got hold of that animal and almost knocked his head off. The neighbours heard the noise and came running along to separate them. If they hadn't the police would have had no one to arrest. But they've taken him away, and they'll try him!"

' "Well, fancy that . . . Say hello to the general, won't you, and tell him from me that decent girls don't get raped."

' "Lord help you, child, you can't go saying things like that to a general!"

'I laughed and went home, feeling very relieved.

'Fedya and I didn't go to the trial. I still haven't married him, and I don't know whether I will. I've had his baby, but as for marrying . . . It was hard for us both after that incident, especially him. I can see his conscience is getting at him and I blame myself – I was the one who put him up to it. So we're dithering about, not knowing what to do. Like, he sends me parcels, and I send them back again. I'm still a pretty good bastard . . .'

Only now did the women realize whom it was that Albina received parcels from and sent them back to again. They began to reproach her for being so cruel and tried to persuade her to change her mind.

But Galina said: 'I understand your Fedor. It's hard for him to live with the knowledge that he almost put a girl into your position. But I really admire you, Albina, especially for saving Lenochka, even though you said you were doing it in your sleep. It means you have a good heart and a strong conscience. How did you manage to hang on to that with all the things you've been through?'

'What things? I've had a fair amount of fun too, and I've seen a lot of things you'll never see through your little glasses, Galka!'

'Oh, stop it! Why do you have to trivialize anything that's noble about yourself?'

'What's noble about anything I do? You'll be calling me a saint soon.'

'Silly! When a saint does something holy there's nothing surprising about it. But what you did was something really holy, if you ask me.'

'A fat lot you know about holiness, you're not a believer!'

'Who said? I was baptized several years ago and I go to church and believe in God.'

'You? But you're a dissident!'

The other women also looked at Galina in surprise. She was rather embarrassed by their stares, but she continued: 'Christianity has also become a dissident movement these days. Many of my friends believe in Jesus Christ.'

'So, do you think your Jesus Christ was a dissident, too?'

'Using modern jargon – yes, of course he was. But let's not get on to that. I want to tell you about a truly saintly woman, my late mother-in-law, and how she took revenge on her rival. Do you want to hear it?'

'Yes, tell us!'

And Galina began her story.

Story Six

by the dissident Galina, about what is perhaps the most unusual and difficult kind of revenge, but which is guaranteed to be one hundred per cent successful and which the author highly recommends to all women if they fall into a similar situation.

'I'm sorry I didn't hear this story direct from Anna Nikolayevna herself, but from her sister Aleksandra Nikolayevna on the day of my mother-in-law's funeral, after the reception.

'Here's the story. Just before the blockade, Anna Nikolayevna managed to get out of Leningrad and take Slavik and her two nephews, Aleksandra Nikolayevna's children, to the country. She took them to the village where she herself came from. She saved those children and kept them fed. She returned to Leningrad after the blockade as soon as her husband called for her and she got a pass to go back to the city. But a lot of evacuees didn't manage to get back again: someone felt it was necessary to change the make-up of the Leningrad population, and a whole lot of people were allowed into the city, but not the native Leningraders.

'Well anyway, she got back, and immediately the neighbours began to gossip to her that when she was away her husband had a mistress, a nurse from the military hospital, and that she lived quite close by. Anna Nikolayevna was upset, had a little cry, as wives do, and then started very cautiously asking her husband how he had got on while she was away. He told her that his old tuberculosis had recurred three months after the beginning of the blockade, and he had begun to spit blood. He couldn't go to work, and started receiving the lowest category of ration cards and almost died.

' "But then by some miracle I got into hospital and they treated me and fed me up. That saved my life."

'After saying that he became embarrassed and changed the subject. Anna Nikolayevna thought about it for a few days – she never did anything in a rush, especially if it was something important – then she set off to visit her rival, having got the address from those same obliging neighbours. They had also told her rival to expect a visit from the injured wife. Anna Nikolayevna arrived, and when the

243

woman opened the door to her she got a fright because she guessed who it was. The woman was beautiful, a few years younger than Anna Nikolayevna, and she looked good even though she had been through the blockade. Anna Nikolayevna saw all this, and it couldn't have been pleasant for her.

' "Why have you come to see me?" asked the woman.

' "To pay my respects," replied Anna Nikolayevna.

' "Pay your respects? How?"

' "In the Russian way, like this." And Anna Nikolayevna bowed down low before her, right there in the doorway.

' "I don't understand..." She really didn't understand, and was expecting something unpleasant to happen.

' "I am bowing to you for saving my husband from certain death. You did not find yourself an officer with good rations or a supplier who had lots of food, but a man with TB who was spitting blood. I realize that if it hadn't been for you he would not have lived long. I don't know whether he will stay with me or leave and come to you because you are young, but you saved a boy's father, and he won't abandon his son. And you saved a man, it doesn't matter whose husband he is. I bow to you for that. And now goodbye, and don't be afraid I'll do anything. Everything has to take its course."

'Anna Nikolayevna bowed once more to her rival and turned to leave. But the woman rushed over to her, took her by the hands and pulled her into the house. Once inside they both had a good cry, as you can imagine, and told each other all about themselves. That nurse had come upon Anna Nikolayevna's husband quite by chance, seen that he was seriously ill and with great difficulty managed to get him into the hospital. Their love affair had begun after he had recovered.

'Do you know how it all ended up with those three? Slava's father did once try to go and see his old mistress again, but she sent him packing. She said she had become firm friends with Anna Nikolayevna and didn't want him rocking the boat. So he laid off his former mistress and began to accept her as a family friend. But he died soon after that, because even after the war it was pretty hard for people with TB, not many of them survived.

The women were amazed at the wisdom and goodness of Galina's mother-in-law, Anna Nikolayevna.

Olga asked: 'Where was she from, your mother-in-law?'

'The Volga, near Rybinsk. Why?'

'Because there aren't many women like that left in the cities. You can't afford to be holy in the crowd, you might get your buttons ripped off!'

'That's true,' sighed Valentina. 'I've gone quite a long way up the ladder, but when I compare myself to my younger sister Lyuba I'm amazed how much goodness I've lost on the way up! I'll tell you about her tomorrow if you like. In fact, tomorrow let's just talk about good people, men and women!'

'A good man is a relative concept,' laughed Larissa. 'I had a friend who thought a man was no good until he had his Ph.D. Before that he was just trash.'

'I hope he's not still a friend of yours?' asked Emma with a laugh.

'Certainly not! So let's define tomorrow's theme in a rather old-fashioned, but accurate way: noble deeds by women and men.'

'Exactly!' laughed Olga. 'You do occasionally get men who are genuine people. But we'll hear about that tomorrow. And now I'll tell about how one of our men paid his woman back so well for her constant jealousy that she wanted to commit suicide.'

Story Seven

by the worker Olga, containing a certain admonition to jealous wives who unwisely curse the object of their jealousy.

'We have a couple living in our house called Nastya and Misha. They were married about ten years ago, and they've had rows every day for the whole ten years, especially at night. Mishenka used to sleep around a bit, admittedly. And like any woman Nastya sensed it and used to throw these wild fits of jealousy that were very embarrassing for him, but just made the neighbours laugh. Misha would come

245

home late, and she would be either hanging around by the gate waiting for him, or leaning out of the window.

'As soon as he showed up the drama would begin, and everyone would hear it. She was so jealous she would just blow her top and scream such awful things at him that the people who had young children would have to shut their windows: "You bloody womanizer! You ought to have them torn off, run over by a car, burnt to ashes! That would put an end to your sinful ways!" Then she would spell out exactly what it was she wanted to have torn off, run over and burnt to ashes. Mishenka would either just take it, or hit her, or try to persuade her not to give these public shows every evening – but it was like knocking his head against a brick wall with Nastenka. She just went on yelling and cursing.

'He was complaining about his bitter fate one evening with some friends, and they advised him to teach his wife a lesson so that she would never be jealous again. One of these friends worked in a meat combine, and he secretly brought Mishenka a ram's prick, or some other animal's prick. And Mishenka also got himself a bottle of red ink. That evening he turned up at home with the ram's prick and a knife in one pocket and the red ink in the other. Nastya was waiting at the window, and when she caught sight of him she screamed: "Have you been running around again, you devil? I'm not letting you in the house, go back where you were. You ought to have them torn off, run over . . ."

'In other words, the same old story. Then Mishenka stopped in the middle of the courtyard in front of the window, and to the amazement of all the neighbours started answering her back. He began quite quietly. "Be reasonable, Nastenka! How could you want anyone to run over the one thing that gives you pleasure?"

' "Pleasure? You whoring dog! Pleasure from your lousy roaming uncontrolled . . ." And off she went, worse than ever.

' "You'll be sorry, Nastenka, you'll be sorry! You'll drive me to do something that will put an end to my pleasure and other women's pleasure, but most of all your pleasure! Then you'll be sorry!"

' "Sorry?! I'll give a whole bucket of vodka to the fellow who tears them off for you in a drunken brawl!"

'The neighbours could hear things were taking a slightly

different turn this evening, so they were all hanging out of their windows listening.

'Suddenly Mishenka unbuttoned his trousers in front of the honourable company and there was a flash of steel. He quickly emptied the bottle of red ink, then waved the ram's prick over his head like a victory torch.

'"There you are, Nastya, my dear former wife. Take it, and don't torment me any more! Now I have nothing to be unfaithful with!"

'And he flung the prick into the window where she was standing. It hit her in the face. She caught it, took one look at the "blood", then started screaming across the whole yard: "Mishenka! Darling! What have you done? O – oh!" And with a shriek she grabbed her hair in both hands, tore it in all directions, then jumped on to the window sill and threw herself down from the first floor!

'Luckily there was a flowerbed below, and Nastya landed on it. She was all right, except that she twisted her foot, and either from the pain of this or the general shock she fainted. Mishenka rushed over to her and the neighbours ran to get an ambulance. Nastya lay there unconscious. She came round when the ambulance men arrived with a stretcher and were loading her on to it. Then she started groaning: "Don't save me! I wanted to kill myself!"

'Then Mishenka ran up to the stretcher, unbuttoned his trousers again and pushed his unharmed penis into her face, saying: "Nastenka, darling! Look, it's all right! I was just joking! Don't die, my treasure! I didn't realize it meant more to you than life itself!"

'Nastenka raised herself up on the stretcher and said quite calmly to the ambulance men: "Hang on a moment, I've got to check this." She felt her precious object to make sure it was completely intact, smiled, sighed and fainted again. They took her off to the hospital. Mishenka brought her home the next day, and in a week she was walking about as if nothing had happened. But the people in our house are still laughing about it to this day. Mishenka earned himself an obscene nickname: the Woeful Prick. In the fairy tale the Woeful Snake gets his head chopped off and grows another, and Mishenka's organ displayed the same abilities.

'Since then Nastya and Mishenka have been living like a pair of love-birds together. He has so much love from his

wife that he's forgotten to look at other women, and
Nastenka never makes a squeak about being jealous.'

The women collapsed in helpless laughter at Olga's
story. Then they settled down to listen to Nelya.

Story Eight

*by the music teacher Nelya, about how the girls at a
music college got their own back on a teacher whose
wisdom did not keep pace with her age.*

'You know, friends, I sometimes think that growing old is a
very dangerous thing for a woman. It's all right if she has a
husband and family: then she has so much to occupy her
mind that she doesn't get any stupid ideas. But if she's single
she's heading for trouble as the years go by.

'We had a single woman teaching us, a widow and not
actually old at all. She taught the history of the Communist
Party, not the most important subject at a music college, as
you can imagine. But since all students, whoever they are,
have to do the history of the Communist Party and political
economy and other subjects which nobody knows anything
about anyway, we had to do them too. Of course no one
would have taken any notice of that course if their stipend
hadn't depended on it: a three in history of the Communist
Party meant you didn't get any stipend. And our history
teacher, Baturina, never gave any pretty student a mark
above three. She couldn't stand anyone who was young and
pretty, because she herself had not been bad at all when she
was young, and now she couldn't come to terms with her
age. The older teachers tried to make her feel ashamed of
the way she carried on, but she pretended not to know what
they were talking about: "They ought to think less about
clothes and more about work!" Of course, by saying that she
gave the game away entirely.

'She once created a really horrible scandal over one of our
best students. The girl had a younger brother who went to
school on the later shift. She once lost the key to their flat,
and so for two weeks, while she was waiting for a new one to

248

be made she would ring her brother from the office before leaving for home. The only telephone we had at the college was in the office. So she would ring him up and say: "Borik! You haven't left yet? Wait for me, I'm just coming." And she would rush home so that her brother could leave for school.

'One day Baturina overheard one of these conversations and put her own interpretation on it: "Zhorik! You're not up yet? Well, stay in bed, I'm just coming."

'I don't know whether she really thought she heard "Zhorik" rather than "Borik", but the girl had a hard time proving that she was actually phoning her brother from the college. One thing that helped was that some of the other teachers had occasionally overheard these conversations, and some of them remembered she had sometimes said "Boryushka". Otherwise the girl could have been expelled from the college.

'After that incident we decided we would have to pay Baturina back properly. For that the students enlisted the help of one violin student, a real tearaway called Dima. Dima was supposed to gaze at Baturina with love-sick eyes, and the girls would take care of the rest. They wrote Baturina a timid confession of love signed by an unknown student. At first she pretended not to take any notice, and maybe she really wasn't bothered. Then she started getting these letters almost every day. Next they began to contain poetry. Baturina started to melt and blush and change her hair-do and clothes. She didn't take any more notice of the female students, and the pretty ones began to get their stipends regularly again. Dima went on obediently sighing during history of the Communist Party, and he didn't have to do anything else.

'One of our girls had a brother who worked for the magazine *Aurora*. Composing a little love madrigal was a piece of cake for our girls, who had talent as well as a wicked streak. They put a dedication on it: "To A.B. – music within music". And they signed it: "D. Unknown". All the letters to Baturina had been signed: "Your unknown friend". Naturally the magazine was sent to Baturina by post before it went on sale at the stands. Later someone noticed her shoving five or six extra copies into her bag. That poem finished her off. She went up to Dima herself during the break between lectures and invited him to go to the White Nights café that evening. Dima came running to his friends: "Girls, help! I'd rather poison myself than go there!"

' "There's no need!" replied the girls.

'That evening, after going to the beauty parlour and the hairdresser, Baturina turned up at the White Nights in a new suit. And what did she see? Her own students sitting at all the tables, fanning themselves with copies of the *Aurora*, the very number with the poem in it.

'A week later the college had a new teacher of history of the Communist Party, a little old man who by contrast adored the pretty students – but quite platonically, I have to say.

'Yes, I agree, revenge is a cruel thing. But remember what a student's stipend is: you can't even buy a pair of cheap shoes with it, and a girl can't just drink tea all the time, she's got to have clothes. It's all right if your parents help out, but what if you don't have that? It meant that girls had to pay for Baturina's change-of-life problems by living off cheap pies and getting stomach pains. I think our students are the greatest labourers. I'm always on their side, so don't try to argue with me!'

No one even thought to argue with Nelya. On the contrary, they smiled to see her sitting there, flushed in righteous indignation: 'Good on you, Nelya! Quiet as a little mouse, but sticking up for your pupils!'

Story Nine

by the theatre director Emma, being a story about theatrical revenge that would be hard to repeat under normal circumstances. Fortunately the powder got damp and the revenge did not take place.

'Girls, you cannot imagine what a stupid crowd of people actors are when they begin to get into their parts! We once put on a stage version of Lermontov's *A Hero of Our Time*. And it just so happened that the two actors playing the parts of Pechorin and Grushnitsky were in love with the actress playing Princess Mary. Up to that point they had kept themselves more or less in check, but as soon as rehearsals began their rivalry flared up with unbelievable force, because every word of Lermontov added fuel to it. Several times they came to blows right in the theatre, in the breaks between rehearsals. Actually the girl playing Princess Mary, Olenka Lapina, preferred our Grushnitsky, and this infuriated Pechorin, especially as it was the other way round in Lermontov.

'One day I got delayed after rehearsals. When I finally came out of the theatre to go home I saw a fight going on in the waste ground behind the building. I looked at them, and saw it was them – Pechorin and Grushnitsky. I sent Grushnitsky home, then took a stroll with Pechorin, because I had decided to have a talk to him. I explained this and that, and that Olenka had a right to choose, but he didn't even hear me, let alone understand me. I got angry with him, because I thought the idiot would go and ruin the play.

'Then I had an idea! I said to him: "Right, I'm fed up with hearing you constantly saying that you're going to kill him. You want to kill him – go ahead! For the first night I promise to get you a working antique pistol and a bullet for it. You can shoot your rival right there on the stage. But just remember, no one's going to pat you on the head for it, and you'll lose Olenka, that's for sure."

'But by that time he was beyond reasoning with, and he took all my nonsense literally. "She'll wait for me!"

' "Fine, we're agreed then. Meanwhile I want you to promise not to disrupt any rehearsals before the first night, and not to stage any extra dramas. Do you promise?"

'He promised, and we parted.

'Rehearsals began to go a bit more peacefully. To be honest, I was hoping that Pechorin would either get interested in someone else before the first night, or would forget about my promise. But nothing of the sort! Just before the first performance he came up to me with a conspiratorial look on his face and asked me if I had forgotten my promise.

' "Everything will be in order," I replied. "Weigh everything up once more tonight and ring me early tomorrow morning in case you've changed your mind. I hope you'll be the wiser for sleeping on it."

'In the morning that blockhead rang me and asked me if

what I had promised was ready. Again I answered that everything was in order. Then I went rushing over to our old props man and told him everything. He laughed fit to burst. He found a special pistol which you could pour powder into and even push in a wad, but when you pulled the trigger it just shot an ordinary cap, like a toy gun. He gave me this pistol and said: "I wouldn't give you this for a normal man. But your Pechorin is a fool and he'll be acting the part all the way. I know these actors!"

'So just before the performance I went into Pechorin's dressing-room and took a shoe box out of my bag with the pistol in it. Putting on a mysterious face, I also gave him a box of damp powder and a wad, explaining how to load the pistol. Then I left him to himself. Poor actors! Nobody takes you seriously! I was delighted to think I was going to have such a genuine Pechorin for tonight's performance. Any director would have given his right arm for such an actor.

'Well, to cut a long story short, my Pechorin acted brilliantly and carried the whole company along with him. Princess Mary trembled beneath his tragic gaze, and Grushnitsky was pale, as though he really did sense imminent death. The duel scene came. Pechorin fired ... and fell.

'Grushnitsky fell too, of course, as he was supposed to according to the story, but he was just acting, whereas Pechorin was lying unconscious. The spectators decided this must be some sort of innovation, and the applause was even more deafening. The curtain came down and I rushed over to Pechorin. So did Princess Mary. We brought him round, and his first question was: "Did I get him?"

'Can you imagine how the poor boy had entered into the part? Well, I shook my head and said quietly: "No, the powder got damp."

'Princess Mary heard this and just gaped at us, not understanding a thing.

'The next day Pechorin himself told the whole company everything, which meant that the props man and I had to tell the truth. Everyone laughed at poor Pechorin, especially Grushnitsky. But Princess Mary, that is, Olenka Lapina, was so impressed that she married Pechorin. They split up after a year, Grushnitsky went to a different theatre, and the whole story was soon forgotten. The things that go on in the theatre!'

Now it was Irishka's turn, and as usual she told the final, tenth, story of the day.

Story Ten

by the secretary Irishka, about how she got her own back on her neighbour, and why the revenge was such a brilliant success.

'We had a really unpleasant neighbour in our flat called Klavdiya Ivanovna, and we also had bedbugs and cockroaches, woodlice in the bathroom, and flies everywhere in the summer. It was a damp flat on the ground floor with its windows looking out on to the courtyard. Klavdiya was the one person who claimed there were no creatures in her room because she was a clean person, but we were all pigs! There was some truth in this: Klavdiya Ivanovna didn't work, she was a widow and her husband had been high up in the army and had been killed during some rocket tests. So she got a big pension. She had a room of thirty-five metres for one person, whereas her neighbours lived crowded together from three to five to a room. The others worked and then came back to their cramped rooms, but Klavdiya spent her whole day cleaning her room, polishing her crystal and china, and walking her dog, a horrible old spaniel. That spaniel had the dreadful habit of howling at night and keeping the whole building awake. We protested, and we asked Klavdiya to take the creature to the vet and get a sleeping pill for it, or something. In the end the neighbours could stand it no longer and told her we were resolutely opposed to her keeping that awful dog. Her ladyship merely laughed at us and said: "You can't prevent me keeping a dog. I don't prevent you keeping bedbugs and cockroaches!"

'She gave a snort and went back into her luxurious abode. We were left feeling humiliated. I even cried. I cried, but then I decided to get my own back on Klavdiya. I went through all the furniture in my room, turned the beds and sofa upside down, felt along the wallpaper in all the corners, and managed to collect a dozen bedbugs in an empty face-

253

cream jar. Then I went to see Klavdiya, as if to ask her again if she could take her dog to be treated for its nerves. And while I was sitting on her wide sofa talking to her I quietly emptied the jar out behind it.

'After that the miracles began. A few days later Klavdiya started to complain for the first time that she was being bitten by bedbugs. The neighbours sympathized with her and said smugly: "Cleanliness is very important!"

'But then the bedbugs completely vanished from our room. Just imagine, we had sprayed and sprayed with all sorts of horrible stuff, and could never get rid of them. And then suddenly they all disappeared, just as if they had packed their bags and left. So I told my sister privately what I had done with the bedbugs. She had a good laugh over that one, and then said: "It's obvious. Klavdiya is juicier and her blood's richer, perhaps even blue blood. Of course, the little bedbugs didn't go hungry with us either. But there wasn't much room for them to sleep, poor darlings! Then the ones that ended up with Lady Muck came and told our fleas that there was lots of grub next door and lots of space to sleep in – so they emigrated." '

The women laughed at Irishka's naïve revenge and her elder sister's amazing wisdom, and began to settle down for sleep. And so ended the eighth day of *the Women's Decameron*.

THE NINTH DAY

in which are recounted stories of

Noble Deeds

by men and women

On the morning of the ninth day a miracle occurred. As usual, the nurse came in with a basket full of parcels from the women's caring relatives and husbands. Parcels for everyone, that is, except Zina the tramp and Larissa. Larissa had only had two visits from colleagues from work, and Zina had nobody at all to visit her. The others were brought parcels every day because the hospital food was insufficient.

Having distributed the parcels, the nurse suddenly pulled out a large package from the bottom of the basket and asked: 'Which if you is Ivanova?'

'That's me,' replied Zina.

'Here's a parcel for you.'

'Not for me. It must be some other Ivanova. I'm not expecting a parcel from anywhere.'

'Zinaida Stepanovna Ivanova, Ward Ten. Right?'

'Right.'

'Well, stop wasting my time!'

The nurse threw the parcel angrily on to Zina's bed and walked away with her basket. The parcel burst open, and several oranges and apples came out, rolled down off the bed and across the floor of the ward. The women rushed to pick them up and arrange them neatly at the foot of Zina's bed. She sat in bed dumbfounded, afraid to look into the parcel to see what else there was. At last she tore the wrapper open, and everyone saw a blue flannel gown, blue slippers, and a white nightdress trimmed with lace. There were also some other small boxes and packages, but this did not interest Zina at the moment: with trembling hands she was going through these gifts, looking for the most important thing. Finally she found an envelope, tore it open, took out a small piece of paper and began avidly reading. When she had finished she buried her face in her pillow and began to sob.

'What is it, Zinulya?' asked Albina, running over to her. 'Why are you so upset? Who's it from?'

Zina silently handed her the note. Albina read it and gasped. 'Zinulya, but that's wonderful! Can I read it out?'

Zina nodded. And Albina read the note out loud: ' "Dear Zinaida, I was not able to forget you and have been looking for you constantly. A miracle occurred, and I found you. I would have found you eventually, in a year or two perhaps, but I am glad it happened now. I am enclosing a dressing gown, nightshirt and slippers, so that my wife does not have to go about in hospital clothes. I have bought everything for our son and will bring it when I come to meet you. I think about you both all the time and am dying to see you, even to catch a glimpse of you. Write and let me know which way your window looks out. Your happy husband and father, Igor." '

'What a miracle!' cried Irishka joyfully, bouncing up and down on her bed.

'How did he manage to track you down, Zina?' asked Natasha in astonishment.

'I've no idea . . .,' Zina answered, perplexed.

'But I know!' exclaimed Albina suddenly. 'Take a look at those two over there, they're looking rather pleased with themselves!' She pointed at Galina and Larissa, who were sitting side by side on Galina's bed trying very hard to look as if all this had nothing to do with them. 'They're the ones who organized this! I saw them composing some letter in the washroom. I thought Galina had got Larissa into the dissident movement again and they were organizing some protest. Well, admit it, it was you who wrote to Igor, wasn't it?'

Galina and Larissa had no option but to confess that they had written to tell Igor about his lost fiancée, and then Galina had asked her friends to make sure it reached him. Larissa and Galina looked anxiously at the sobbing Zina. 'Zinochka! Please forgive us! We thought it was better this way . . . But it's up to you in the end, you can still reject Igor Mikhaylovich!'

Zina raised her head. 'There's no point now!' And she took the blue dressing gown and vigorously wiped away her tears with it.

Five minutes later Zina was arrayed in all her finery, and

the much-laundered yellow shirt with its hospital stamp, the dirty grey dressing gown and the patched-up slippers, one beige and one brown, were returned to the sister.

The morning's events affected the women for the rest of the day: they exchanged whispers, kept glancing at Zina, and were happy. Zina sat silently on her bed, filled with peace and happiness. From time to time she lifted her hand and looked in amazement at the lace cuff of her nightdress. On her dark, coarse hand, with its short broken fingernails, the lace looked strangely moving. Then she would lower her hand, laugh and whisper: 'Well, well! Wonders will never cease!'

Evening arrived, and the women, who were today in a particularly happy frame of mind, began to tell stories about noble deeds performed by women and men.

Story One

by the biologist Larissa, about how a woman who had suffered much from her husband decided against divorcing him and saved his life.

'I have an aunt called Lyudmila. She was still a teenager when I was born, and everyone called her Lyudmilka. But I couldn't pronounce that, so I called her Dilka, and I got so used to calling her that, that I still do.

'Dilka got married at eighteen. It was not a successful marriage: Boris, her husband, was an electrician who drank the whole time and used to beat her up. I remember she was quite puny even as a girl. She had a skinny body, sort of tired eyes without any sparkle, and her hair looked faded. The difficult marriage just finished her off. By forty she looked an old woman already. But then a miracle happened. You know the Russian saying: forty years is a woman's life, but she blossoms again at forty-five.

'It all began when their son went into the army. Dilka had confessed long ago to her mother that she would leave her husband as soon as her son was grown up. Because of his drinking, of course. So when Seryozha went into the army Dilka left home. "That's it! I've had enough!" she said.

258

'She took a room somewhere and even changed her job. She used to work as a cashier at a station booking office. It was hellish work, with long hours, and you know yourselves the sort of things that go on when people are queueing for tickets at the station. Sometimes people wait for days. They're exhausted and on edge, and when they get to the cashier they're ready to crack, and some of them do. Dilka worked for almost twenty years in these conditions, and all for the sake of a few extra roubles because Uncle Borya spent it all on drink. So then she got a job at a travel agency. It was quite a different atmosphere there, with a different sort of customer. People were going on holiday, travelling, and they were happy. Dilka started to travel, too: she would buy herself a cheap travel pass to Tallinn or somewhere down south. People working at the agency got reductions on travel passes. She began to take care of herself. She used to wear her hair in a bun, but now she had it cut short, and it turned out she had lovely thick hair which was an unusual ash colour. Her tired eyes began to sparkle, as if she was anticipating happiness. She even began to walk differently: I observed how from month to month she appeared to be growing taller. And then she got an admirer: a tour guide who used to be an historian. He was a single man. Not divorced, just a bachelor who at well over forty suddenly decided he wanted to get hitched. He was rather old-fashioned, but that suited Dilka perfectly: instead of cursings and obscenities it was flowers and kissing her little hand. He had a car, so he didn't just collect her after work, he took her there, too. Mother and I were absolutely delighted: at forty-five Dilka was enjoying her first spring!

'And then suddenly her happiness was destroyed, almost before it had begun. One day Uncle Borya rang her up at work to say he was going into hospital. He asked her to look in on the room they used to share together from time to time. Dilka asked: "Why? Are they going to keep you long?"

'He quite calmly answered: "I shall probably die there. I've got cancer. So just keep an eye on the room so that Seryozhka doesn't lose his living quarters when he gets out of the army. And if you could just give me a decent burial I won't complain."

'Dilka dropped everything and rushed over: she might have left her husband, but she must at least get him to hospital! He was taken to a cancer hospital, and they got ready to operate. He had cancer of the throat from all the meths and other filth he had been drinking. It's the sort of stuff all alcoholics use. They even extract the spirit from furniture varnish, and they swallow a whole lot of other non-purified industrial spirits as well.

'Uncle Borya was operated on, apparently successfully. Dilka visited him, took him parcels, sat with him, and in general gave him moral support. Then he was discharged with an invalid certificate. Before he was released Dilka had a talk with the doctor. He explained that in cases like this the patient usually developed secondary cancers after the first operation, because the junk they had been drinking would have eaten into their stomach and liver, etc., as well as their throat. "The only hope is if the whole system puts up an active fight. And that depends on how much the patient believes he has a chance of recovery. But usually, when a person finds out he has cancer he gets ready to die."

'Dilka listened to all this, thought about it and then made her decision. She went back to the deserted flat and fixed it up ready for him to come home to. She looked through his wardrobe, saw he had sold everything he decently could for drink before going into hospital, and decided to get him a new set of clothes. She started by buying a good new winter coat. She argued: "If I get him a shirt or a suit he'll think I'm just getting him ready for his funeral. A dead man is always put into his coffin well dressed. But no one has ever yet been buried in his overcoat. He'll see the new coat and realize I'm not preparing for his death."

'She also bought him a suit, new underwear and shirts, and shoes. All this cost her the earth. I helped out a bit, too. She told me later what his reaction was when he was about to be discharged and she brought this bundle of clothes. He put on the shirt and suit and said: "So, this is for me to wear in my coffin. Thanks a lot!"

' "What makes you think you're going to die?" she asked him severely.

'Uncle Borya looked at her sadly, full of self-pity, and answered: "Well, you know I've got cancer . . ."

Dilka stuck her hands on her hips and yelled at him: "Cancer?! So that's your idea, is it? The poor little fellow has cancer, has he? I see what you're driving at! You want me to

260

come back to you, don't you, dearie, so that you can start drinking again and then blame it all on cancer? It won't work! Don't worry, I had a talk with the doctor who operated on you, and I know you had a tiny little tumour. You can fool other people, but not me! I'll come back to you, because you'll need looking after for a few months yet. But only until your first glass, so just remember! And no cancer will help you then! That's it! Put your coat on!"

'Then Uncle Borya saw she was giving him a new coat worth at least a hundred roubles. In one second he had calmed down, believing he was going to live.

'When they got home he had another confirmation that Dilka was not preparing for his death but wanted to start a new life with him. The room was all decorated, with new curtains at the windows and, most important of all, the folding sofa had been replaced by a new double bed. Now he finally accepted that Dilka believed he would live. That made such an impression on him that he gave up drinking and began to make a rapid recovery.

'Well, what more is there to add? After a year his invalid status was reduced and he went back to work part time. He had given up drink. Dilka left her admirer. At first he offered to wait until Uncle Borya died – he knew what the operation was for. But Dilka told him quite firmly she was not expecting her husband to die, and was going to fight for his life. And he is still alive. That's the whole story. One other thing I will say is that Dilka still looks good, though she doesn't have that twinkle in her eyes that had appeared before. She has stern eyes.'

The women listened to Larissa's story and said that basically there was nothing very surprising about it. There were countless examples of selfless wives taking care of sick husbands for years on end.

'But if anyone can tell me a story like that about a husband,' said Albina spitefully, 'I'll give them a prize – a lipstick from Paris.'

'Let's have a look!' said Natasha.

'Here you are. Why?' asked Albina, getting the lipstick out of her bag and handing it to Natasha.

'I wanted to see if it was my colour. It's going to be mine, anyway. It's Zina's turn now, and then, just for you, I shall tell a story almost exactly like Larissa's, only about a man.'

'All right! And now Zina will tell us something else about camp life. Am I right, Zinulya? Or don't good deeds ever happen in the camps?'

'Of course they do, why shouldn't they? If you're not fed up with hearing about the zone I'll tell you a story.'

Story Two

by Zina the tramp, being a story of selfless maternal love.

'I'll tell you about a woman who went to prison for her son and got out early.

'I worked at a building site in the zone. Our camp was a mess because there wasn't room for all the prisoners – the barracks were wooden ones built back in the thirties, and they were all rotting. So instead of the single-storey wooden barracks they were building stone ones on two floors that could hold four times as many people.

'I got a good job, even though it was heavy work. We had no mechanical equipment at all there, you know. It was picks, spades, barrows and the zeks' own hands, unpaid of course. And there was also my horse Seagull who pulled my cement cart. When they marched us out to the site in the morning they would bring Seagull to me from the stable. I would harness her into the cart with the cement box and drive to the store. I would back the horse into the barn and shovel the cement on to the cart. The cement dust was like a thick cloud, and me and Seagull would be completely grey with it: we were both breathing cement and coughing cement. I could at least tie a cloth round my mouth, but Seagull really had it bad. Anyway, we used to load up the cart and take it out to the site. There other zeks would help us unload and we would go back to the barn. We got a bit of fresh air while we were riding along. We would do ten or fifteen trips a day. My arms would feel like dropping off, I had this cough tearing my chest to pieces, but I hung on to my job and wouldn't give it up to anyone else. Seagull was a

262

good workmate: no cursing, no scenes, and if you want to have a good heart-to-heart with someone, you can't do better than a horse. If I was feeling depressed I would put my arms round Seagull's neck and whisper into her ear. Maybe she understood, maybe she didn't, but she wouldn't go and tell on me if I said something about the authorities. And the other thing was that when we went backwards and forwards to the site the only authority over us was the blue sky. And even if it wasn't blue, but cloudly, or rain and snow were falling on us, it was better than gang-bosses and guards shouting at us.

'One day me and Seagull had just brought some cement up and were unloading when a guard came up to me and said: "Ivanova, when you've got that cart unloaded sweep it out and take it round to the hospital. One of your mates has got out early, so you can take her to the Red Hill."

'The Red Hill was the zeks' cemetery. It had grown a lot since 1930 when it was for burying kulaks – the rich peasants.

'I did as he said and drove round to the camp hospital. There was a little group of women standing waiting.

' "Do you know who died?" I asked.

' "Kazakova from Section Four."

' "Kazakova?! But she wasn't even ill. Her son's just about to visit her."

' "Yes, thank God she didn't suffer. She went to bed last night and didn't wake up this morning."

I realized the women had chucked in their work and come to the hospital to accompany Kazakova on her last journey. Zeks don't have funerals or receptions: they take them out and bury them, then stick a post with a number on it in the ground. And that's all the ceremony you get. The zeks will see a coffin going out through the gate and say: "There's another one getting out early."

'Then they'll turn away and forget about it quickly. Everyone knows it might be their turn tomorrow. The ground on the Red Hill is completely full of bones: you can't tell whether you're digging into earth or bones. But Kazakova was a special case. The women were taking a risk coming to accompany her. Of course it wasn't far to the camp gate, but at least it was some sort of procession. That was the kind of woman she was – you had to give her some sort of send-off.

'Kazakova was inside for her son. Here's their story. Her husband was a wild animal. He was a violent drinker and a violent man: he would get drunk and go after his wife with an axe. Of course she would grab the child in her arms and run to the neighbours to get away from him. They would hide her and keep her as long as necessary. She complained to the militia so many times, but they always said the same thing: "It's a family matter!"

There's even a poem about that: "Threats do not concern us. If he kills you, come and tell us." One time he actually did get her with the axe. She did her time in hospital and then came home. She felt sorry for him, so she decided not to press charges. He was scared at first and quietened down a bit. Then he saw he wasn't going to get into trouble, so he went back to his old ways. The son was growing up, he was a youth of fifteen already. He felt sorry for his mother, but he wasn't strong enough to deal with his father. When he was drunk he would knock anyone down who got in his way. The boy got hit several times.

'Then one time when the father started beating up the mother and threatening to kill her, the boy snatched the axe away and bashed his father over the head with the back of it. He fell down. The mother ran up to him and felt him – he was dead. The drunk – it didn't take much! She didn't tell the boy he was dead, she told him: "He's unconscious. He'll lie there for a bit, then he'll start getting wild again. So here's what you'd better do, son. Put your things together quickly and go to your aunt. I'll give you a letter for her asking to let you stay there until the holidays are over. Otherwise your father will get his own back on you when he comes round. Then come back after a month, and by that time he'll have forgotten about it."

'The boy did as his mother said and went straight to the station to go to his aunt. The mother waited an hour or so, then ran round to a couple of her neighbours. She asked one of them for some salt, and she called in on the other on her way home as though she wanted to have a chat. She told both of them she had sent her son to her sister for the holidays, and her husband was drinking somewhere and would soon be home. So she had to make his meal for him so he wouldn't be so angry. And she went home. Then she started shouting as if there was a family row going on. She

264

ran into the yard and shouted there, then went back inside. She held the axe in her hands so as to leave her fingerprints on it. I'm amazed how she planned the whole thing out! And after all that she ran screaming to those same neighbours: "Neighbours! Call the militia – I've killed him, I think . . ." One of the neighbours comforted her, the other went to get the militia.

A month later the lad returned from his aunt to find his father had already been buried and his mother was in prison waiting for her trial. He insisted on seeing the investigator to tell him he had been involved in the whole business, but the investigator wouldn't listen to him: he had the case all buttoned up, the witnesses had been questioned and the accused had confessed to everything. And all the evidence fitted nicely. And the boy really was on the train just when the neighbours and the mother said he was. Well, Kazakova got five years – they saw the dead man had been a monster. Her son was good to her. As he grew up he realized what his mother had done for him. He went to the camp for every visit and sent her good parcels. Zeks who were having meetings at the same time in next-door rooms said that the mother and son spent their whole visit crying and arguing. He would say: "Mama, I'm grown up now! You go home and let me do my time! We'll write a joint statement telling what happened!"

'And the mother would say to him: "They wouldn't let me out, son, or they would have to admit they got it wrong, and then they would get you anyway. I don't have long to do now. Finish your studies, my son, and above all don't drink, don't be like your father!"

'And so they would carry on, crying and trying to persuade each other. And the visit always ended the same way: the son went home, and the mother went back to the barrack to get on with her stretch. She did four years and put in for parole. She and the boy waited for months for an answer from Moscow. In fact everyone in the zone was waiting. We had all sorts of women there, some of them really had hearts of stone, but they all wanted Kazakova to get out, they all felt sorry for her. Partly because they all knew she was inside for her son, though she didn't tell them, and partly because she was a very good person, very calm. And that's unusual in the zone; everyone has such a hard time they're pretty up-tight. She would come back from work in the evening and the barrack would seem to get brighter. The woman had a real soul. And when her rejection came from Moscow she didn't cry or get angry like the others would have done. Yes, hearts aren't made of stone, I suppose. A person can stand anything, but the heart can't always stand it. So she just died, Kazakova did.

'Well, they carried the poor woman out in a simple wooden coffin, not painted, knocked together out of off-cuts from the building site. The women accompanied her as far as the gate, then the gate clanged shut behind us and we drove up to the Red Hill. I rode with the coffin, and two soldiers walked along with spades, and there was a little official with bits of paper: even this last transport had its paperwork. The soldiers buried her, the official wrote on his little bit of paper, they stuck a post in with a number on it, and Seagull and me went back to loading cement.

'A few days later Kazakova's son arrived – they had sent him a telegram. He asked for his mother's body so as to bury it in her home village. They wouldn't give it to him. Against the rules – she hadn't finished her stretch: "Her term will soon be finished. Then you can come and collect her!"

The women were very subdued by the time Zina had finished her story.

Then Albina turned to Natasha: 'Now, who was promising to surprise us with a story of male goodness and nobility? Go ahead, Natasha, surprise us! Otherwise you don't get the French lipstick!'

Natasha smiled and began her story.

Story Three

by the engineer Natasha, recounted with the purpose of winning a Parisian lipstick. It is a story about a truly unusual display of male nobility.

'This happened to my friend Bella. We were in different classes at school because she was three years older than me, but we went to physical education together, and that's where we got friendly. That friendship has lasted ever since.

266

'When Bella was in the first year she fell deeply in love with a guy from a senior year. That was at the polytechnic. There aren't many girls there, they're mostly boys. And of all of them Bella had to go and choose the most self-centred one. He sort of half loved her. Everything was all right for about a year, and then he started seeing other girls. Bella didn't leave him, and he didn't give her the push, but he hardly noticed her love. In other words, it was the usual story: I've known so many couples like that! If only someone could teach women to love a bit less and men to love a bit more!

'The relationship dragged on like this for year after year, almost five years altogether. They had both graduated. Bella got a very good diploma and went on to do postgraduate studies; in another two years she had defended her thesis. I was full of admiration, but she said to me: "Natashka, I'm doing all this for Kirill. Maybe it'll make him appreciate me."

'Kirill just laughed at her efforts to please him: "Do you think if you became world famous I would suddenly give in? I still wouldn't marry you, and that's all there is to it. Be content with what I am able to give you."

'But he was able to give her less and less. The years passed, and the only things that got more beautiful were the trees in the park. Well, the typical moment of truth arrived: Kirill announced he was marrying a young girl. She didn't argue. In fact, she wished Kirill every happiness and even went to the wedding and congratulated the couple.

'I asked her afterwards: "How did you feel during the wedding?"

'And she said: "I felt peace and liberation. I'm only sorry I wasted so many years and so much emotion, but there's nothing I can do about that now."

'And Bella began a single life without even the rare meetings she had been having with Kirill. Occasionally he rang to ask how things were, and she invariably answered that everything was fine. But actually she was like a little candle that was going out. Then we heard she had been taken to hospital. She had been coughing blood, and it was discovered she had an acute case of TB. Just like some pre-revolutionary novel!

'I met Kirill one day at a party. It was someone's birthday, or some other celebration, I don't remember now. We just happened to be sitting next to each other at the table. After chatting about various other things, he asked me how Bella was. When I told him what had happened to her he turned pale and said: "How could that happen? She was always such a healthy person, and very sporty. She never even got flu."

'I swear I never so much as hinted that she started to go downhill right after his wedding. There was no point in tormenting the fellow. I didn't think there was any way of remedying the situation. And he wouldn't have believed me anyway, because the wedding had been two years earlier. And who believes people die for love these days? But Kirill was really upset, and sat there not talking to me or his young wife for the rest of the meal. At the end of the party he suddenly said to me: "I'm coming to see you tomorrow morning, Natasha. We'll go and see Bella, all right?"

'I rather gave myself, or at least Bella, away by saying: "Is that wise? It might make her worse seeing you." But he assured me that if Bella got upset he would leave immediately.

'Next day he turned up, and we went to Pushkin where Bella's hospital was. It was August, and the patients were allowed to walk in the garden. We found Bella in a secluded avenue. She was sitting on a bench looking as small as a little girl. Her face was flushed and her eyes were like saucers. Kirill went up and sat down next to her, put his arm round her shoulders, looked into her drawn little face and asked: "What have you gone and done, little sparrow? Trying to fly away from me? I won't let you go!" I made some excuse and left, so as not to embarrass them, and waited for Kirill at the hospital gate.

'What happened next was totally beyond belief. We suddenly learned that Kirill was leaving his pretty young wife, removing Bella from the hospital and taking her to a fantastic sanatorium in the Crimea. She was given treatment and they came back to Leningrad and Kirill divorced his wife. Then he and Bella got married, and for some reason even had a church ceremony. I was at it. The bride could hardly stand up, and the groom had to support her from behind. But he obviously knew what he was doing, because I've never seen my friend Bella looking so radiantly happy as she did during that sad little service.

'We all thought it would end with her dying anyway, but at least dying happy. But it turned out differently. Kirill worked like an ox, knocking on every door, and got the very best professors to treat Bella. He took her abroad, and even to some sort of witch-doctors in the Philippines. She didn't need to be operated on in the end. And Kirill built up her strength so much that she gave birth to a perfectly healthy child and kept her own health at the same time. Now all our friends consider him an expert on lung diseases, because he read up everything about the subject during Bella's treatment.

'They were round at our place one day. Bella was talking to my husband about photography, and he was showing her his latest works. I quietly asked Kirill how he guessed he could save Bella. He answered: "There's nothing odd about that. I'm an aircraft designer. It was quite simple to work out that Bella was like a plane – she could not fly with only one wing. So when the other wing was removed she went into a tail spin. All I did was to give her back what she had to have in order to fly. A purely technical solution to the problem."

'I never asked Kirill about his first wife. Maybe she's not flying too well either, I don't know. I only know there isn't enough happiness to go round.'

'There's scientists for you!' exclaimed Emma. 'And they always say they're not up to solving emotional problems. But there's something in what Kirill said.'

She and Larissa exchanged glances and smiled knowingly at each other.

'And what does Albina say?' asked Natasha.

'It's not a typical case,' replied Albina with a shrug of the shoulders, opening her handbag with a sigh.

'You didn't ask for a typical case, just a case of nobility. Do I get the lipstick?'

'Yes, yes.'

'Great! My friends at work will go green with envy.'

'Yes, when you finally get back to work! You'll be off for a year with the baby, and by that time the lipstick will be finished.'

'What?! Use up a whole Parisian lipstick in a year? What do you think I am? This is just for very special occasions. I've also got some mascara from England

269

which I've been using for over three years. And I've got some dark-coloured liquid make-up from West Germany. Almost a full set of bourgeois corruption!'

'Yes, they certainly know how to be corrupt! . . .' sighed Irishka. 'I have some American eye-shadow, and when I go out I always have to weigh up whether it's the right sort of occasion to use it. One thing I don't understand: why does our government always buy absolutely the wrong sort of things from the West? I work at a port, and I know what goes to the West and what comes to us. They're always bringing in machinery, and nothing but timber goes out. And of course caviar and other delicacies. But they never think of buying us cosmetics! We want to be beautiful, too. I remember about three years ago you couldn't get any lipstick in Leningrad or Moscow, and they were even writing to the papers about it. We were told that one factory was shut and the other was unable to supply the whole country. Well, surely the West would have sold us some? They've got heaps of it over there, you could paint the walls with it.'

'Technology is more important for us than lipstick,' countered Valentina. 'Especially electronics. It all goes on defence. We can do without lipstick as long as there's no war. You know very well that if it wasn't for our government's defence policy we would have been attacked long ago by America or West Germany. In '68 the West Germans very nearly crossed the border into Czechoslovakia. And if we weaken our defences now we shall be attacked immediately.'

'Yes, that's true,' sighed Olga. 'I can't understand why those Fascists never relent. Germany would never be able to beat us anyway! I remember explaining this dozens of times to Petya. But even though he loved me he pretended that no one in West Germany was getting ready to attack us. Even though he was from the GDR he was still a German. You just can't trust those Germans! Yes, let's do without meat and milk, just as long as we don't have war!'

'Oh, stop this nonsense, girls, or I shall write some leaflets and start distributing them among you!' implored Galina. 'I don't want to listen to you any more.'

'Well, of course you listen to enemy voices, you think differently,' snapped Olga. 'Do you really think they tell the truth on the radio anywhere in the world? I haven't believed any of that for a long time! But I do believe everyone wants to attack us. Otherwise why would our government need so many weapons? For example, we have this shipyard, supposedly on peaceful production, but we all know how much is being done there for the war.'

Nelya sighed: 'I'm probably more scared of war than any of you women. Partly because I've been through some horrible experiences, and partly because I am a coward by nature. I also think our shortages of food and living space are because of the imperialists. And with all your arguments about democracy, Galina, you'll never convince me otherwise. Olga is right: let's do without the essentials, we can stand it, but let's be defended against war. All the same, there's one thing I'd like to get from abroad: some plastic pants for the baby! One family did promise me some. They got them from someone else whose baby had grown up; and now their little boy is a year old already, so they'll soon hand them on to me. They're such a useful thing, especially for going out. I don't understand why they want to attack us when they've got everything over there.'

'The conversation moved from politics to babies' pants, and the tension relaxed. It emerged from the discussion of the shortage of plastic pants, dummies and baby lotion that one could make a very successful baby lotion by sterilizing vegetable oil and that there were lots of good dummies to be had in Tallinn: one could go and get them on one's day off on a cheap tourist travel pass. This improved the general mood, and with that Valentina picked up the thread.

Story Four

by the bigwig Valentina, about a girl who took upon herself a great maternal task.

271

'There were four of us sisters in the family. The eldest, Katya, lived in a workers' village near Krivoy Rog, I had moved to Leningrad, the third sister had done medical school and was practising in Magadan, and the youngest, Lyuba, was a student. Katya, the eldest, had a good husband, but he suddenly came down with phlebitis. He had to have a leg off, and after that he took to drink. They had seven children, which is not unusual in the provinces. Of all four sisters Katya fared the worst. They were very poor, they had this gang of children, and then there was the husband's illness and drinking. The other sisters were doing fine.

'Lyuba was the most gifted of us all. She learned to sew and draw as a girl, and she used to design dresses for herself and us sisters. She would think up a style, draw the pattern and then make it herself. Her dream was to become a dress designer. She started doing a correspondence course at the Textile Institute. She was good enough to go full-time, but she got married young and her husband lived in Pskov. He had his own house there, from his parents. He and Lyuba thought they would sell it eventually and buy a smaller house near Leningrad. But for the time being they were living in Pskov. Lyuba worked at a dressmaker's and did her course for the institute, and Grisha was a driver. Everything would have worked out fine for them in the end, but then a disaster happened to Katya which completely changed the course of Lyuba's life.

'We sisters suddenly received telegrams saying that Katya's husband had died. We sent her money for the funeral and letters of condolence, but it was too far to go there – some of us had work, some had children. And then about a month later we got another telegram, from Katya's neighbours: "Your sister Katerina died suddenly. Come for funeral and children."

'We dropped everything: me, Lyuba, Nina the doctor. We got there and buried Katya. The neighbours said she died of despair – she just couldn't face life with seven children, alone, without a husband to support her. So she gave up. The children were all young: the eldest boy was ten, and then they went down in one-year intervals to the youngest girl, who was only two. After burying Katya we came back to the house for the reception and to decide what to do with the children. They were all huddled together in the other room as if they could sense that their fate was being decided.

'The youngest ones were easy to sort out: Nina and I decided that I would take the little girl and she would take the three-year-old boy. We couldn't manage any more. The older ones would have to go to a children's home. It was just a pity they would have to be split up: the girls going to one home, the boys to another. A boarding school had agreed to take the eldest boy. Nina and I were discussing all this with our husbands, and Lyuba, our baby sister, was sitting in tears. She couldn't take any decision because she had come without her husband. So we understood her tears. Suddenly she got up from the table, went to the door of the room where the children were sitting, took a long look at them, came back into the room and said to us: "Ninochka, Valyusha! We can't split them up! Just think how awful it would be for them, having just lost their father and mother! Let's think of some way not to separate them."

'We were used to thinking of Lyuba as the baby of the family. Nina even got annoyed: "We're trying to decide a serious question, and you come along with your silly ideas. How can they not be separated when something like this has happened? Who's going to take them all? I can't: I've got two of my own, plus a husband and a job. Valentina can't either, she has an important job. Are you going to bring up the whole gang, or something? You haven't even had a child of your own, you don't know what it is to bring up children. Just be quiet while grown-ups are talking about important things!"

Then Lyuba suddenly said: "You're right, Ninochka. I should take all seven of them, since I haven't any children or worries of my own."

' "You're mad! You've only been married a year! Your Grisha wouldn't let you in the door with even one."

' "I shall send him a telegram right now, and he can decide whether he wants all of us together or none of us." The silly girl went and sent off the following telegram: "Have decided to keep Katya's children. If you still want to live with me, come and collect us."

'Grisha couldn't believe his eyes when he got the telegram. He rushed over to the long-distance telephone office and booked a call to Krivoy Rog. Over the telephone she

273

confirmed that she still wanted to take all seven. Grisha thought about it for several days, and on the fourth day he turned up at Krivoy Rog and collected his suddenly enlarged family.

'Nina and I helped out with money, of course, but we didn't think Lyuba would last out long: she would enjoy it for a while, then she would see it wasn't so easy bringing up seven children and abandon her project. We were very annoyed at her, because we would simply have to decide the children's fate all over again, and they would be the first to suffer. But it turned out differently. Two years went by, and Lyuba became more and more attached to the children. And they came to life, poor darlings. Their last few years had been difficult ones, with their father ill and drinking and their mother suffering. And now they had a new young mother, happy and kind. They just loved their "Mama Lyuba", and clung to her from dawn till dusk. The older ones helped about the house and took care of the younger ones. But of course life wasn't easy for Lyuba. She had to give up her studies and her job at the dressmaker's. She got a job as a cleaner at an office near to where they lived. This provided at least some money for the family, and left her time for the housework. Grisha got used to the children too, but he had to work overtime and keep looking for extra work. They got no state aid because they weren't allowed to adopt the children, since they were only just starting out in life themselves. They were made foster-parents and told: "If you can support the children, then support them. If not, take them to the children's home."

'The pension from the children's own parents was not enough even to buy bread for all seven of them.

'Sometimes I look at our Lyuba and think: "What a pity life took such an unfortunate turn for the most gifted one of us. Nina is a doctor, I have an important job, and Lyuba's a cleaner. It's not fair!" But sometimes I think exactly the opposite, that perhaps Lyuba's greatest talent was to give a home and happiness to those seven little children.

'One thing I do regret is that now Lyuba will end up without an education or a profession. What's a cleaner, after all? It's not a profession, it's just a job. The children will grow up and leave the nest, and Lyuba will be left alone with the broken trough. It'll be good if the children grow up to be conscientious and help their "Mama Lyuba". But she'll never have any interesting job with a good income or pension. Nina and I will get a pension two or three times the amount of Lyuba's, and that money will come mostly from Lyuba's children who will have contributed two or three times as much to the pension fund as our four children between us. If you look at it on the government level, it's unjust. It seems that our society sponges on mothers who are willing to bring up a lot of children.

The women were full of admiration for what the young Lyuba had done, and they sympathized with her, too.

'Have you ever thought of discussing this at your party meetings, Valentina?'

'I've tried, but nobody wants to listen. They say: "Every woman should decide what is most important to her, an interesting job and a good pension, or children." That's all the answer I get.'

'What do you think, Galina?'

'What do I think? I think the government wouldn't go bust if they gave mothers like that the chance to get an education while their children are growing up. Instead of spending their evenings mopping dirty floors they could be sitting at home at their books, and then when their children grow a bit bigger they could work two or three days a week at their profession. We don't have that many big families these days.'

'Well I think,' said Olga, 'that working as a mother should count towards a normal worker's pension, that's what I think! As Valentina rightly said, our pension is going to be paid for by the children of those mothers who thought about their children rather than themselves. It's not fair!'

Everyone agreed with Olga and turned to Valentina again: 'Valyusha! Why don't you write to your namesake, Valentina Tereshkova the astronaut? She could raise the matter at the highest level.'

'Yes! And from her highest level she would go tumbling down to the bottom. Have you ever heard of her putting in a single word for women? Of course not, and that's why she's head of the Committee of Soviet Women.'

275

Then Zina suddenly laughed and said: 'Did you know Tereshkova once came to visit our camp?'

'Really?'

'That's right! She got up on the stage at the camp club and announced: "Look at me – see how high a woman can go in our country! And now look at yourselves – see how low you have fallen!" We zeks just gasped. We'd heard a lot of that from our wardens and guards, but we didn't expect anything like that from her. One zek whispered to her friends: "I wonder if those two space-dogs Belka and Strelka turned up their noses at all the mongrels when they got back?" That remark went along all the rows of women sitting there, and they all cracked up and started giggling into their sleeves. Tereshkova just stood there all red in the face, angry that these women who had fallen so low were laughing at her when she had been up in space. I don't know if there was any connection, but after Tereshkova had been round the prisons and camps the women's regime got a lot tougher. They started blocking up the windows with iron grills that were so close together they only had small cracks for the light to get in. They're still called Tereshkova's grills. And you say she could put in a word for mothers!'

Having expressed regret that there was indeed no one to intercede on their behalf, our friends asked Albina to tell them something about noble deeds by women. Nobody expected her to recount anything good about men.

Story Five

by the airhostess Albina, featuring two noble women as its heroines, and an unfortunate man caught in the middle.

'I had two friends, one was an artist who decorated the walls of cafés, and the other worked at the Institute of Russian Literature, Pushkin House. One was hooked on paintings, the other lived and breathed Pushkin. And they never stopped reading books on their subjects. They were the ones I borrowed *Lolita* from. Their names were Lilya and Lyalya, and they had been friends for years, ever since childhood, I think. Well, Lilya and Lyalya both fell for the same guy, and I have to take the blame for introducing them. He was an ordinary airline pilot, in fact a navigator of a TU 104, a completely normal person. He was after me to begin with, but I already had someone, so I chucked him at my friends and said: "Who wants him?"

'The trouble was, they both fancied him. First he had his eye on Lilya, the one who was nuts on Pushkin. She was a skinny aristocratic little type, stuffed full of poetry, old and new. And she wrote poetry herself. I liked her poetry, and Artur was over the moon: the only real live poetesses he had ever seen were on TV. A little romance started up. And since Lilya and Lyalya were inseparable the three of them often sat together and went to all sorts of exhibitions and poetry readings in private houses. Actually, as a woman Lyalya was streaks ahead of Lilya: she was a tall Georgian with passionate eyes and strong hips. And Artur began to notice her too. If he felt like talking he would sit next to Lilya, but if they suddenly threw a dance he would go with Lyalya. The friends talked it over and came to the conclusion he didn't know himself which one he preferred. Lyalya felt she already had a string of men after her, with a couple more round the corner, whereas not everyone would look at Lilya until they got to know her a bit. So she said to Artur: "I don't want to spoil your relationship with Lilya. So let's not meet any more."

'She managed to persuade him. The fellow even seemed glad the matter had been taken out of his hands. He moved in with Lilya for good. But she managed to drag out of him the conversation he had had with Lyalya. And she also decided to act the hero: "I realize you and Lyalya are better suited to each other as man and woman!"

'She invited Lyalya round, put out some wine and said: "You are made for one another, it's obvious! You have nowhere to live, so stay in my flat, because I'm going away to Pushkin Hills for a month."

'No amount of persuasion would change her mind. She placed the key to the flat on the table and left the very same evening, feeling noble and romantic.

'Lyalya and Artur stayed in Lilya's flat. Just before Lilya was due to get back Lyalya started acting the noble martyr: "You stay here and wait for Lilya. She'll be so happy to come back and find you in her house!"

'And she left. Lilya got back, and she really was happy for a week, then she started to get miserable at the thought of Lyalya suffering over Artur.

'Artur came up to me once at the airport and said: "Alka, what am I to do? They're killing me with their nobility!"

'I looked at him, and the poor guy really did look drained by it all. "Stop all this nonsense! You'd be better living all three together than going on with this musical chairs. Just run away, Arturchik, escape!"

'The guy thought and thought, then he dropped both his noble ladies. Later he told me: "No, I want to be with the sort of woman who'll scratch her rival's eyes out, with none of this noble suffering! I don't understand all these refined emotions, Alka, I'm not intellectual enough probably."

' "And a good thing too. Call a spade a spade, I say."

'In the end my two noble friends had a row and fell out, though not over a man, but over a remark Lilya made about one of Lyalya's pictures. Lyalya got her own back by calling Lilya a Pushkoholic. Neither of them could forget that, and they split up.'

The women laughed at the sufferings of Lilya and Lyalya, and then prepared to listen to Galina.

'I shall tell you about a real miracle that happened to one of my friends. It'll be another camp story, but not as horrible as the ones Zina usually tells.'

Story Six

*by the dissident Galina, asserting that one person
may perform the most incredible miracle for another.*

'A certain dissident artist from Leningrad was recently released from camp. She brought out with her some amazing pencil drawings done on various scraps of paper and cardboard. I was at her place with some friends once,

278

and she was showing them to us. They were all sombre realistic sketches. But on one small piece of cardboard there was a picture of a flowering branch of marsh tea with the caption: "For an hour of your freedom I would give my life." I looked at the drawing for a long time because it was so different from the others. Masha – that was the artist's name – noticed and asked: "Would you like to hear the story of that drawing?" And this is what she told us.

'In the criminal camp, where Masha was the only political prisoner among fifteen hundred criminals, there was total tyranny by the authorities and guards. They treated the women like cattle, and they bullied them, beat them up and sometimes even raped them. But there was one young officer there – the women nicknamed him Lieutenant Nazansky (after seeing a film at the club based on Kuprin's *Duel*) – who didn't arouse either fear or hatred in the zeks, but only universal respect. Perhaps it was just because he was the only one to use the polite form of "you" when talking to them. He had been sent to work at the camp as a punishment for some misdemeanour at the rocket base nearby. He had to do two or three years at the camp. He hated every minute of it and drank heavily.

'So when Masha turned up at the camp he noticed her straightaway and tried to get into conversation. But Masha operated on Griboyedov's principle: "God spare us from the worst of woes, the master's wrath, the master's love." So she avoided all private conversations with the authorities.

'About a year passed. Suddenly, while Masha was working in the field with all the other zeks, Lieutenant Nazansky came up to her and said: "I heard a programme about you on *Voice of America* yesterday. It was called: 'For an hour of freedom I would give my life.' Can you explain the meaning of that title?"

'This time Masha decided to answer, because the man had confided in her first: he had admitted that he, an officer guarding the camp, listened to forbidden broadcasts.

' "That was the slogan we used to use when staging a demonstration. It's a quote from one of the Decembrists."

' "Do you really value freedom so highly?"

' "Yes, certainly."

' "Then why do you do things that land you up in camp? I just don't understand the logic. Now you've lost absolutely all your freedom, haven't you?"

' "No, not all of it. I still have my inner freedom," replied Masha.

' "No! It's beyond me! And I suppose when you get out of here you'll do something else, and they'll put you back in a camp?"

'Masha didn't answer this question – it could have been a provocation. She merely smiled, but the Lieutenant understood the smile.

' "Would you like me to tell you what else they've been saying recently on *Voice of America*?"

' "Tell me if you want to."

'And Lieutenant Nazansky told her all the news he had heard on the American radio. And from then on he got into the habit of coming up to her once or twice a week while she was working and telling her the news from the big world.

'Another spring came round, and Masha was still in the camp. For days on end she thought about home and pined. She began to suffer from severe vitamin deficiency. Her gums started bleeding and her teeth became loose. The lieutenant noticed that Masha was fading and tried to persuade her to accept apples and other normal food. But Masha refused the food. The only thing she took from him was vitamins. Her gums became less painful.

'The May Day holiday arrived. That is a good time for zeks: the authorities all drink for three days non-stop, and the zone is left to the prisoners. During those days the women are able to get some rest and tidy up their modest clothing. Masha also made some time for drawing. She installed herself in a secret nook behind the barracks and started drawing the little hillocks that were pink with marsh tea and that she could see over the camp fence. The Lieutenant came upon her there. He went up to her and said: "I think I've understood your slogan about freedom. I've thought about it a lot. And now I'm going to ask you to do something. Don't say anything and try to get to the guardhouse without being noticed. Walk quite calmly past the sentries, and I'll meet you there. Only not a word to anyone!"

'And he quickly walked away.

'Masha thought about it, and then decided to risk going out through the camp gate. She wondered what Lieutenant

Nazansky had cooked up for her. She got to the guardhouse, where the soldiers on duty silently opened the gate in front of her. Outside there was a small Gaz with the Lieutenant sitting at the wheel. He opened the door for her and said: "Get in quickly and put your head down until we get through the settlement. Hurry!"

'Masha realized there was no time to ask questions and got into the car. About fifteen minutes later the Lieutenant said to her: "You can sit up now."

'Masha lifted up her head. They were driving along a forest road among hillocks covered with flowers. Soon the Lieutenant stopped the car near one of them, got out and opened the door on Masha's side.

'Masha got out of the car. The smell of the forest air made her head spin and she nearly fell over. The Lieutenant took his watch off his wrist and handed it to Masha, saying: "I would love to have a talk with you here, outside the barbed wire, but I'm sure it is more important for you to be alone. I shall come to collect you here in an hour. Don't go too far or you'll get lost."

'With that he got back into the car and drove off.

'Masha thought to herself: "What a fool I am. This is just provocation!"

'She knew that shortly before the end of their term political prisoners were subjected to various forms of provocation so that they could be tried in camp and given another term. This always happened just before they were due to be let out, and Masha had only three months to go. She realized then that the noble Lieutenant Nazansky was most probably carrying out an assignment for the KGB so as to earn their forgiveness more quickly.

'She listened. No, she couldn't hear the barking of dogs yet. Obviously the hunt was to start later, when they reckoned she would have gone deep into the forest. And Masha began to rack her brains for a way of out-smarting them. Suddenly she had an idea. She threw off her shabby zek coat, spread it on the ground right beside the road, lay down on it and started to sunbathe! The watch she hid in her bra. When the hunt caught up with her, there she would be, calmly lying in the sun. What fool would start sun-bathing half an hour away from the camp if she's trying to escape? The watch she would have to keep hidden until she was questioned by the investigator, and she would tell the Lieutenant she had left it on the ground by the road. The watch was her most valuable alibi: if it came out that all this had been a provocation, she had nothing to fear.

'Masha lay on the ground, thinking what a bastard the Lieutenant was. The heady smell of spring filled her nostrils. Tiny inhabitants of the forest crawled along the blades of grass nearby, birds sang overhead, the marsh tea was everywhere in bloom, and there was a smell of young birch leaves. Spring! Masha looked at the watch and saw that the hour was already coming to an end, there were only ten minutes left. And she was lying by the road like a fool, waiting for the sound of the dogs! She jumped up, picked up her coat and ran up the hillock, snatching at a few twigs of marsh tea as she went. She stumbled, exhausted, on to the soft moss, picked herself up again and ran on. Now she was at the top, and she could see the three large cedars she had admired from afar in the camp. She looked back, and there, far below, beyond the little river and beyond the settlement, lay the zone. Masha could even make out the roof of her own barrack. She leant against one of the cedars and wept into its warm bark. She had forgotten how wonderful freedom was, what it smelt like.

'Then she looked at the watch and gasped: she had exactly three minutes left. She rushed headlong down through the undergrowth towards the road. She thought as she went that she wouldn't be able to take the marsh tea into the zone. So she quickly buried her face in it, pressed it briefly to her breast, and threw it away. Just one small twig she kept, deciding she could smuggle it in inside her sleeve.

'No sooner had she reached the road than she heard a car coming round the corner. The Lieutenant drove up precisely on the dot. Masha was relieved to see he was alone. He got out of the car and came over to her. "Well? Did you have a nice walk?"

' "It was a miracle!" replied Masha. "It was even more than a miracle. I don't know what to call it."

' "Call it an hour of freedom for which one would be willing to give one's life. Now it's time to go. Get in the car."

'They arrived without incident at the camp. As he ushered Masha through the guardhouse, the Lieutenant said quietly: "I have modified your slogan slightly: 'For an hour of *your* freedom I would give *my* life.' Goodbye."

' "Goodbye. Thank you."

'It was only later that Masha realized the Lieutenant had risked far more than she had: he could have been court-martialled for her "hour of freedom". It was in memory of that hour that she did the drawing of the marsh tea.

'That's the sort of miracle one person can give another. Actually, I don't know who got more out of it: Masha, who was given an hour of freedom, or the Lieutenant who gave it to her.'

'And what happened afterwards with the Lieutenant and Masha? Did they meet up after Masha's release?'

'Of course not. Masha wanted to send him some sort of present, but we talked her out of it, because she would have been endangering his freedom. Can you imagine what an officer would get for helping a dissident in camp? And if Masha sent him some small gift they would be able to accuse him of taking bribes as well. But Masha said she would paint a picture of him from memory one day, and that would be her way of thanking him for her hour of freedom.'

After Galya, Olga began to recount her story.

Story Seven

by the worker Olga, about how the noble deed of an abandoned husband was rewarded by fate the day after it had been performed.

'I shall tell you about a boy from our yard, and what happened to him and his wife. We had two young workers who got married – Yevgeny and Yevgeniya. So we had Zhenya the husband and Zhenya the wife. As soon as they were married the yard gave Zhenya the husband a one-room flat, a real stroke of luck. But soon after that Zhenya the husband was called up to the army. Up till then he had had a white ticket, because he'd had TB as a child. But now there weren't enough people for the army and they were taking everyone. People were having fewer children, I suppose. So

Zhenya the husband went away for two years, and Zhenya the wife meanwhile met a sailor and fell head over heels in love with him. But she never said a word about him in her letters to her husband.

'Zhenyha the husband came back from the army and found his flat had two unexpected occupants: Zhenya the wife's new man and their baby. Zhenya the husband stood in the doorway wondering what to do: whether to chuck all three of them out or whether to leave himself. He felt angry at being robbed while he was out defending his country. He stood thinking about it for a while, then said to them: "OK, it can't be helped. Stay here. We'll arrange the divorce later."

'Zhenya the wife didn't want to let him go: "Where are you going? This is your flat, isn't it? Just wait a month, we'll find a room."

' "Where? Who's going to have you with a baby?"

' "Well, at least take your things! Most of these things are yours anyway."

' "And where am I going to put them? All along the street? I'll go to my mates in the dormitory. I'm coming back to work in the yard anyway. I don't suppose they'll chuck me out of the dorm."

' "Zhenechka! At least take some money from us! You're ending up with nothing, I feel awful about it!"

'The new husband was so embarrassed and ashamed he didn't know what to do. So he offered Zhenya the husband his wallet and said: "That's all we've got. Take as much as you want."

'Zhenya the husband looked at the open wallet: it had a few tens and a lottery ticket. He laughed and took the ticket. "I'll take this as a souvenir. If you really wish me well, maybe I'll win a tape recorder or a radio as a consolation prize. Then I can listen to music." He took the lottery ticket, turned and left.

'The next day the newspaper came out with the winning numbers. Zhenya the husband checked his ticket against the numbers and couldn't believe his eyes – he had won a Zhiguli! He felt awkward at first and decided to take the ticket to his wife. Then he changed his mind. If fate had dealt him a blow, then maybe now it was sending him a present. He was a good man, but he wasn't an idiot. He didn't go and collect the car, but instead went to Kuznechny

Market and offered the ticket to the Georgians who sold fruit. They brought him to the right person, and he sold him the ticket for 15,000 roubles. With this money he bought himself a co-operative flat and some furniture, and still had enough left over to get a motorbike. We were all very happy for Zhenya the husband, especially Zhenya the wife and her sailor.'

Everyone was delighted to hear that justice does indeed sometimes triumph very quickly. But Zina observed: 'Usually while the good people are waiting for this justice to be done, the bad people kick them around so much that they think themselves happy if they get through the day without being shoved by someone in the tram or sworn at by the cashier in the shop.

'That's true, especially about cashiers!' sighed Irishka. 'Oh, girls, I've been scared of them ever since I was a child! Now I'm a grown-up woman, supposedly, but I tremble every time I go to pay the cashier in the shop, wondering if she'll swear at me or not. Unless something drastic happens to change the cashiers and shop assistants of this world, I shall have a heart attack in a shop one of these days and drop dead. I just can't take the way they swear at me.'

'Well, you shouldn't spend so much time queuing for things!' advised Emma. 'Do you know how I take care of my nerves? By never queuing for anything, even pineapples! You couldn't get me into a queue even if you stuck a gun in my back. If I see a crowd of people in the milk shop I say to myself: "Today we do without milk!" If there's a crowd in the vegetable shop, I get by on bread and sausage. It's a great saving for the nerves! And you've got to understand these shop assistants too: they have to spend their whole day looking at a queue of hungry animals, so it's not surprising they become like animals themselves.'

'It's true,' commented Nelya. 'Shop assistants aren't rude by nature; it's just that our way of life is enough to make anyone bitter. I'll tell you about a shop assistant like that. Do you mind if it's another old war story?'

'No, go ahead!'

285

Story Eight

by the teacher Nelya, about how a rude shop assistant saved a young man's life.

I heard this story from relatives. Uncle Aron, the one who saved our whole family from the Fascists by taking us underground, had a son called Rafik. He was twenty at the time. Rafik didn't want to go down into the sewers with everybody else. He wanted to get through to the forests with a group of Ukrainian and Polish friends and join up with the partisans. But their expedition didn't come off. By the time they got back to Lvov, Rafik's family had gone: some were dead, others had been taken to camp, and some had escaped with us. Rafik was afraid to go home, and he started wandering the streets in search of shelter. Old friends were afraid to hide him, even the ones he was with when they tried to get through to the partisans. It was winter. Not a very severe frost, not like in Leningrad during the siege, but bad enough to be dangerous to Rafik, who was homeless, poorly clothed and hungry. Sometimes people would take him in for the night, but they would push him out the next morning. One time Rafik went for four nights in a row without getting into a warm place, just hiding from patrols in barns and basements. On the fifth night he took refuge in the attic of a house and kept warm by sitting with his back against the stove pipe. He was just dozing off when he heard shots, and he realized a raid was going on. During these raids the Nazis always searched attics and basements very thoroughly for Jews. He knew he had to get out of the attic straightaway. He went down to the street and started making his way towards the outskirts of the town. But as he reached the area where he used to live he suddenly heard the sound of the raid going on again, and he stopped. He knew there was a bread shop nearby, and that round the back by the service entrance there was always a pile of empty wooden bread crates. He decided to hide among them. He got to the yard just in time: he could tell by the noise that the raid was going along the very streets he had just passed. He hid among the empty boxes and fell asleep exhausted, despite the cold.

'He was woken up by someone shaking him by the

286

shoulder. He opened his eyes. It was just beginning to get light, but he recognized the face bending over him: it was the woman from the bread shop, the rudest shop assistant in the whole region. "That's done it!" thought Rafik. "She's bound to hand me over!" He wanted to run away, but his feet had got frostbitten during the night and he couldn't take a step.

' "So, look who we've got hiding here!" said the woman after she had examined him. "How did you manage to survive? There are none of you people left here! Well, up you get, let's go. It'll be light soon and the Germans will find you as soon as they come from their barracks to get bread. Get up!"

'She lifted Rafik up and took him back home. Dusya they called her. She kept Rafik in her flat right up until the liberation of Lvov, cured him of his frostbite and fed him. When the Red Army arrived Rafik came out of hiding, thanked the "rude shop assistant" Dusya and went off to fight.

He returned to Lvov after the war and went to see Dusya again. She was not at home. Then he decided on the off chance to look in at the bread shop where she used to work. He heard her voice as soon as he opened the door: she was swearing at a customer. Rafik got into the queue, and when he reached the counter he quietly asked her: "Could you give me a roll for free?"

'"Wha-at?!" she bellowed at him. But then she suddenly recognized him and gasped. Without even a second thought she immediately bundled all the customers out of the door, hung up a sign in the window saying: "Gone to base", and took Rafik home.

'He looked at the humble abode where he had been hidden so long from death, and he saw that Dusya was still single, and not well-off. Then he said to her: "Dusya, I came to thank you, but I haven't got anything. I have nothing and no one in the world except myself. So that is all I have to offer as thanks. Will you marry me, Dusya?"

'The rude shop assistant Dusya was frightened at first. She was quite a bit older than Rafik, and she didn't look a year younger than her age. But seeing that Rafik felt the deepest gratitude and tenderness for her, she decided that maybe that was enough to make them happy.

'They have a happy marriage. Dusya stopped working at the shop long ago, because Rafik became an important surgeon and it was embarrassing to have his wife standing behind a counter arguing with customers. They have two lovely children, and they're deeply in love with each other. There's not a trace of rudeness left in Dusya, she is the tenderest and gentlest wife and mother I know.'

Nelya finished her story and Emma began hers.

Story Nine

by the director Emma, in which an explanation is given of the Gospel saying: 'Greater love hath no man than this, that a man lay down his life for his friends.'

'This will be another story from the life of our bohemians, the people that are known as the alternative culture, since they are not connected with official art. The KGB is not very fond of this giddy uncontrollable group, and sometimes puts one of them behind bars as a warning.

'Well, a small group of unofficial writers and artists got together and decided to put out a humorous journal, complete with Soviet-style name. There are collective farms called Red October and Red Ploughman, and even a brewery called Red Bavaria. So these jokers called their journal *Red Dissident*. And of course, a lot of the humour was aimed at the KGB. They even had their own meaning for the initials KGB: Kommunist Gangsters and Bandits. We split our sides laughing at every number that came out. But the KGB did not laugh, it took measures. Soon the whole editorial board had been tracked down and taken. The investigation quickly revealed the ringleaders behind this bit of samizdat: two artists, Yuly and Oleg, and two poetesses, Yuliya and Natalya. The were arrested, but the women were soon released, which surprised even them. But when the artists were put on trial everything was made clear: they took upon themselves the entire responsibility for having published the journal. That wouldn't have been so unusual. We knew them, they were wonderful kids. Both incredibly talented, and both totally fearless. But at the trial they both suddenly started to repent and claim they had put out their journal purely from motives of hooliganism. Natalya and Yuliya, who were in court at the time, were terribly ashamed of their friends and kept saying: "What is this? Why are they talking like that? Why?"

'We all expected they would give the boys a suspended sentence and let them go – clearly a confession like that would have delighted the KGB. But they got an unexpectedly severe sentence – six and seven years in strict-regime camps. And they cited precisely the confession of hooliganism. They must have thought: well, if they want to admit that their journal was not political, but just hooliganism, let them suffer for it! And they both did their terms in criminal camps where they had to fight not only the authorities in order to survive, but the criminals as well.

'One of their defence lawyers told us much later how this had all come about and why they had behaved the way they did at the trial. Apparently, at the beginning the boys had taken a very independent and arrogant line, as one would have expected of them. They were threatened, then they were offered freedom in exchange for a confession, but they refused to talk.

'Then one old investigator said to his colleagues: "You're approaching this in the wrong way. You have to bear in mind the psychology of the defendants. This calls for different methods, a different approach."

'And he explained what methods he had in mind. After that the boys were brought back for questioning and told approximately the following: "How could chivalrous artists like you drag women into this business? They've already caught colds in the damp prison cells, so how do you think they'll survive camp?"

'In other words, they began to work on their consciences. The boys really did begin to suffer at the thought that they had brought women on to the editorial board. The investigators let them sweat it out a bit, then made them an offer: if they repented and removed the political halo from the affair themselves, they would still get the same sentence, with no favours. Even worse, in fact: they wouldn't go to a political camp, but to a criminal one. But on the other hand, the KGB would free the women immediately. The artists wavered. They were given a private meeting. They conferred together and decided to sacrifice their honour in order to save their friends. If they had been offered freedom or a lighter sentence in exchange for a confession, they wouldn't have budged an inch – that's the sort of kids they were! But now they wavered. From the very start the KGB showed they were going to fulfil their side of the bargain. As soon as the artists began writing down their evidence in the prescribed style, the women were immediately let out of prison. The boys were shown the order for the women's release. Then, after they had given more evidence against themselves, they were shown the order closing the case on the women. They believed it and did everything as agreed. But they had forgotten whom they were dealing with. After the trial one of the women was arrested anyway, without the artists' knowing about it. It was on a different matter, admittedly – they found anti-Soviet poetry in her possession. They would have put the other inside too, but at that moment she had a baby. The KGB decided against risking the scandal of putting a mother in prison with a new-born baby.

'The artists had a difficult time. Not many people wrote to them or helped them. Everyone condemned them for their unworthy behaviour at the trial. Only when the truth came out did the tongues stop wagging.

'And you know, that's when I understood the meaning of that Gospel saying: "Greater love hath no man than this, that a man lay down his life for his friends." I always thought it was just about people dying for their friends, and that used to surprise me because I thought: what's so special about that? Surely there are worse things in this world than death? But since Oleg and Yuly's trial I understand the saying completely differently. They gave up their honour, their very soul, and went off to camp for six and seven years not as proud dissidents, but as despised hooligans. Even their friends didn't understand this at first, and when they were let out they didn't know the price that had been paid for them.'

Galya had been listening to Emma in amazement, and when she had finished, exclaimed: 'So that's how it really was! I've heard so many different stories about that case. I could never understand why people spoke so highly of those artists, when they had behaved so disgracefully at their trial. What's happened to them now?'

'They all got out. Yuliya and Natalya got married, and afterwards Yuliya went over to the West. I think the four of them are still all good friends. Yuliya is writing a book about her friends to thank them for the sacrifice they made for her. Well, it's getting late, let's hear what Irishka has to tell us.'

Story Ten

by the secretary Irishka, describing her own heroic deed performed during a time of great food scarcity.

'I was walking along Nevsky Prospect one day, when I saw a huge crowd outside Yeliseevsky's. I asked what was being sold. "Bananas!" they answered.

'So I immediately got in the queue and started dreaming of bananas. I had only had them two or three times before, and I had really liked them. I used to dream a lot about the various exotic fruits. I would read about mangos and avocados in travel books and try to imagine what they tasted like. My dream about bananas was a bit different: I didn't just want to taste one little banana, I wanted to eat three or four at once and really stuff myself on them! And suddenly there was this stroke of luck – bananas being sold, up to a kilo per person! Well, I thought, congratulations, Irishka, your dream is about to come true. Just as long as they don't run out before I get there.

'I stood for two-and-a-half hours, and then the happy moment arrived. I squeezed my way out of the shop carrying a paper bag with a kilo of bananas! I wanted to eat one on the way home, but decided against it. Somehow it didn't seem very good manners to be walking down the street, munching away on such a rarity in front of everybody. It wasn't just an ice-cream!

'As I was walking along my street I met my friend Liza. She looked upset and angry, and the sparks were flying out of her eyes.

' "Hello, Lizaveta! Why are you looking so angry?"

' "Hi, Irishka! My twins are getting out of hospital tomorrow after their scarlet fever, and I wanted to shoot something tasty for them. But the hunting is terrible today, I haven't seen it so bad for a long time!"

'I ought to tell you that my friend Liza came to Leningrad from Altay, in Siberia. She had been living with her father, a famous hunter, and she had come to Leningrad to study. But when she finished at the institute she stayed and got a job. And she would always say about our food problems: "You have it just the same here as we do in Altay. If you want some meat, you take your gun and go into the taiga to track an animal or a bird. The only difference is that here you don't take a gun, you take your shopping bag, and after that everything depends on hunter's luck. You have to have the same patience, too. There you sit in a hide waiting for a grouse, here you stand in a queue for hours waiting for a chicken. And you've got to have intuition too, so as to go into the very shop where the meat or sausages have just appeared. Just like in the taiga, where you'll be going along and you suddenly get a feeling you ought to have a quick snoop in that dip over there!"

'And whenever Liza talked about food shopping she always used hunting language. For instance, she would ring up and say: "Irishka! Do you need any pork sausages? I've just shot two kilos, one for each of us. When can you come round for them?"

'Liza's hunter's intuition helped her a lot. Not one of my friends could shoot food the way she could. But this had obviously been a bad day for her. "Just imagine, I waited two hours for oranges, and they ran out just as I got to them. I went to another shop and was told the apples had run out an hour ago, while I was wasting time queuing for the oranges. And while I was running from shop to shop the market closed. To hell with it, I would have used up five times as many cartridges if I could just have got some nice apples or even mandarins for my little ones."

"Cartridges" was Liza's word for money. She would say: "Irishka! My cartridges have run out. Could you chuck me ten or so till pay-day?" And I would lend her money until pay-day. Our wages fitted very conveniently: she got hers on the first and fifteenth of the month, and I got mine on the tenth and thirtieth. So we would bale each other out if we were running short.

'Liza's twins weren't five yet. They had been coming down with illnesses ever since they started going to nursery school. It was a good thing they always got ill together, or she would have been completely worn out by it all. She was already getting dirty looks at work because the children were ill so often. Her husband was a good man, but he couldn't help. They don't give fathers medical certificates for looking after children, only mothers get those. I looked at Liza and saw how exhausted and upset she was over her shopping failures. And then a great heroic feeling rose up in my breast, and I had this noble impulse to give her the bananas! People shared their bread during the siege, but this was just bananas! We'd survived without them so far, we could survive without them another hundred years! First I wanted to divide the bananas up, but then I decided to give her the whole kilo. There were only seven bananas, anyway, and you couldn't divide seven equally. Let the twins really eat this rare fruit, not just taste a little bit of it. Triumphantly I asked her: "Lizaveta, have your twins ever tasted bananas?"

' "Not yet. They hadn't even heard about them until I read them Kipling's Mowgli books. They asked me what a banana was like, and so as not to whet their appetites too much I said it was like potato with sugar.'

' "Well, Liza, here are some bananas for your little ones! A kilo. Give me a couple of roubles for them!" – and I handed her the bag.

'Liza took the bag, opened it and gave a squeal that could be heard half-way down the street: "Irishka! This'll mean so much to them! It'll make them get better straightaway and they'll be hopping like rabbits right up to the ceiling. Wait a moment, have you kept some for yourself?"

' "No, there's no point, they only gave us a kilo each. Anyway, I'm not that keen on them."

'That was stupid of me to go and say that, and I regretted it for a long time afterwards. If I hadn't said I was not so keen on bananas I could have asked for one for myself, but after that I felt embarrassed to. But I felt very good inside when I pictured how happy the twins would be. Liza and I went our own ways, highly satisfied with the day's hunting.

293

'Well, what do you think? Would you say that was a noble deed? I'm so fond of bananas!'

All the women agreed that without a doubt Irishka had performed a really heroic deed.

And Emma said: 'You see what a happy life women have in this country, Galina? We manage to get something special and it makes us happy for three days. And you're always grumbling at the government. Do you think women in the West have any concept of the joys of life? Can they understand the delight of the girl who has managed to buy a bra in her own size by skipping the queue, or the joy of the housewife who has "shot" a kilo of smoked sausage for the holiday? Of course not! I think they have a poor life. It lacks substance.'

'Yes, they don't experience our joys!' laughed Galina. 'I wish we didn't have to either!'

'I often wonder,' said Natasha thoughtfully, 'if there's a single item of food or anything else that has never been in scarce supply in this town.'

'Let's have a competition,' suggested Larissa, 'and see who can name an item which has never been missing from the shelves, and which we have never had to go chasing about for. I'll begin: matches!'

'No! The factory was closed for repairs last year, and they never thought of bringing matches in from other towns. We were rationed to two boxes each. Kettles!'

'Forget it! I've had to go to Moscow to get a kettle.'

'Irons!'

'Five years ago you couldn't even get those solid smoothing irons our grandmothers used to use.'

'Soap!'

'Don't talk about soap! A few years ago I gave my mother-in-law a piece of household soap for New Year, apart from the usual cake, and she was over the moon . . .'

The women laughed as they listed item after item, only to find that every one of them had been unavailable in the shops at one time or another. They mentioned wallpaper, clothes pegs, hair-curlers, towels, saucepans, teacups, plates, washing powder, nappies, stockings, thermometers and the most basic medicines, babies' bottles, shoe-laces, toothpaste, bed linen, knives and forks, pens, school exercise books and textbooks, sports clothes, children's and women's underwear, nails, floor polish, brushes and brooms for the floor, school ink, carbon paper and typing paper, cigarettes and vodka, contraceptives, hairpins, flower pots, needles and thread, and a host of other items.

Olga won the competition. She suggested salt, and the women agreed that at no time since the war had salt been unavailable in Leningrad. True, Zina observed that sometimes even salt was not to be had in the provinces.

'See how lucky we are!' joked Emma again. 'We have constant scarcity, but think of the potential happiness it brings! If you get something on the black market at three times the price you're satisfied, and if you manage to pull some strings and get it at the right price, that's pure happiness!'

The women laughed at Emma's definition of female happiness. Then they started to think of what to talk about tomorrow.

'How about happy women?'

'Well, Emma's already dealt with that one so well there's nothing to add. But there's a lot left to be said about women's troubles and misfortunes.'

'You bet there is! That's an inexhaustible topic . . .'

'I'd rather talk about something more cheerful,' said Irishka. 'Let's stick with the theme of happiness. There are so many different sides to happiness – everyone can find something to say about it!'

And so it was agreed.

THE TENTH DAY

devoted to stories of

Happiness

Story One

by the biologist Larissa, offering her own formula for happiness.

'When I was a child the most miserable day of the week was Saturday. That was the day my mother and I went to the bath-house. We always went to the same one, on the corner of Mayorov Prospect and Griboyedov Canal. We would get there and start queuing on the street. Then the queue would move into the courtyard, then ever so slowly, even slower then a funeral procession, up the stairs to the second floor where the women's section was. Then we would go into the changing room, hand in our coats, get a metal disc with a number on it and go and find the locker which had that number. All that took from one to three hours.

'By the time we finally got down to washing, we were both exhausted. We were so tired we didn't even talk to each other. My mother would give my hair a thorough washing. At that time I wore long pigtails, and my mother took very good care of my hair because she was worried I might get lice. There were lice everywhere in those days, and you could even pick up something nasty in the bath-house. Then she would wash my back, and after that I could do myself and she could do herself. After we had washed and rinsed I would just sit beside my mother on the stone bench and splash myself with a basin of cool water. And of course I would look around me. Sometimes I would recite lessons set for school on Monday, so that I would have less to learn on Sunday.

'We were once set a poem to learn about our happy childhood. Something about how, if Lenin was alive,

He would take us on his knee,
And ask us with a smile,
"How are you, little children?"
And we would say to him,
"We're the happiest in the world,
So your will has been fulfilled."

'As I sat mugging up these unpretentious verses I was watching the woman sitting next to us. She was a nice young woman, and she was covered all over with tatoos. There were several on her back: a sailing boat, an anchor with a snake wound round it and various inscriptions. When she turned to face me, I saw a smiling picture of Lenin on her right breast, and a motto on her left: "There is no hapiness in life." I thought that was a very wise saying, and I liked the picture of Lenin too. But, being a bright schoolgirl, I couldn't resist saying to her: "Excuse me! You've got a mistake on your left breast! 'Happiness' should have two p's."

'She laughed and replied: "What difference does it make? It doesn't matter how you spell it, there still isn't any happiness!"

'My mother gave me a slap and told me not to bother people.

'I went back to learning my poem, but I kept looking at the tattooed lady. I was wondering if I could do something like that on myself. I really liked the picture of Grandpa Lenin.

'Then the torment was over and we went to get dressed. After we had put on all nice clean clothes, Mama took me to the buffet where you could get fizzy drinks. This was the happy moment that made up for all my sufferings. First Mama would buy us each a glass of fizzy water without syrup, then she bought me another glass, this time with syrup. And I had the right to choose the syrup: raspberry, cherry or strawberry. And when I lifted the glass to my lips and caught the smell of the fruit and felt the tiny bubbles splashing my face – that was happiness!

'I grew up, went to university, and had many good and bad experiences, many successes and failures. But whenever I managed to get through a disaster or finish some important but unpleasant job, I would say to myself: "Well, now you

298

can have your glass without syrup." In other words, I could relax. And if it was to be a glass with syrup, that was real luxury! And at such times I often think about that woman in the bath-house and wonder what has happened to Lenin's face after so many years. Is there anything left of his smile? And the letters forming the sacred phrase, "There is no hapiness in life", must have got a bit stretched. But no doubt this merely emphasizes their sad significance.

'And you know, my dears, when they brought me my new-born baby I clearly felt the little bubbles splashing my face, and I caught the scent of raspberry – the symbol of happiness in the midst of sufferings.

'There. Now let Zina tell us if she's ever met any happy people during her wanderings.'

Zina said nothing for a while, then smiled to herself. 'You know something? You get some happy people even in prisons and camps. Our whole barrack was once happy for nearly a month. By some miracle a kitten got through the security fence and wandered in. We kept it in the barrack and played with it. A clever little beggar he was, bright as a button. You'd shout: "Vaska! The pigs are coming!" and he would pop behind the stove and lie snuggled up right in the corner.

'Then a guard shot him for fun when he strayed into the forbidden zone. And he joked about it: "I shot a zek trying to escape. I'll have to ask for extra leave!"

'Sure, there's some happiness in the zone. And in the tramp's life, too. I'll tell you about an old tramp whose whole business was her old man. She's been fighting the government for years for this happiness of hers.'

Story Two

by Zina the tramp, similar to the story of Philemon and Baucis, but in a modern variant.

'I was once taken off a train in Lvov and brought to a special reception centre. From there people are sent to all different places: some are let out, some are sent into exile, some are sentenced and put in prison. I sat there and waited to see what would happen to me. There was a whole bunch of riff-raff like me there, all people without passports. Two gipsies, a thief, a tramp and one little old lady with fluffy white hair like a dandelion. She never said anything all day, just sat on her bunk praying. But every evening she would ask the guard on duty: "Let me take a look at my old grandad! Please, dear!"

'She would beg and cry till the guard gave up and brought this grey-haired, bent little old man from the men's cell opposite. The old woman would look through the slit at him and be satisfied: "Grandad's still here, they didn't take him away anywhere today. Please God, they won't separate us tomorrow. Now I'm happy, everything's all right." And she would go to bed.

'We called those old people Grandad and Grandma. They were quiet, harmless folk. We gradually got Grandma to talk, and she told us their story.

'They lived in a hut on the outskirts of Moscow. They had no pension, because they used to be collective farmers, and in those days collective farmers didn't get any pension. How did they live? Grandad painted icons, and Grandma took them to the market and quietly sold them. They didn't get rich, but they got by. Then their region started being developed. The other people there were moved to new flats, but these two had no one to help them. So the authorities decided to flatten their hut and move them into an old people's home. They wouldn't give them a flat because they had no pension and they couldn't pay the rent. So that's what they did. Sent them to separate homes for old people and invalids: him to a men's home, her to a women's one. They couldn't care less that these people had spent all their lives together and got to be like one person, like when two trees grow together as they get old.

'Grandad was so unhappy he got ill and took to his bed. He wanted to die. But Grandma had more guts. She saved up a lot of bread from her dinners, dried it, put it all in a pillow-case and took off one night from the old people's home to look for Grandad. She travelled on buses without paying, she begged for money, and she searched all the areas round Moscow till finally she found Grandad. She pretended she was visiting him. Sometimes those homes allow relatives to visit at weekends. So she arrived and told him: "Let's get out of here, Grandad. You'll die without me." And she took her beloved away.

'They became tramps, begging outside churches and sleeping where they could. They saved up a bit of money and rented a hut in a half-derelict village. Grandad started painting icons again, and they lived together happily again. But then the militia jumped them. They'd left their passports in the old people's homes! They were taken back, him to one home, her to the other. That was winter time. Grandma waited a couple of months, then took off same as before and went to fetch Grandad. Then it started all over again, with them begging in the name of Christ, looking for a place to rest their heads and end their days together. But the militia was after them, and soon the police on all the railways knew about the couple. They used to hunt them like criminals and then lock them up again in the old people's homes. Only not in the same ones as before, but further apart. But they always had a way of sending messages to each other. And Grandma was always the first to get out, and she would go and rescue Grandad. He was her happiness.'

'What a nightmare!' exclaimed Nelya. 'Do we really still have such open, hopeless poverty?'

'Open poverty isn't so bad,' answered Natasha. 'I think the worst of all is the poverty that's ashamed of itself. I once saw a respectable old lady in a café finishing up other people's scraps. I asked her why she did it and she answered: "My pension isn't enough, dear. I only get an old-age pension of twenty roubles. Not enough to live on, too much to starve on." So I advised her to go to an old people's home, and she just laughed. I'm so ashamed I said that now, after Zina's story! Well, let me tell you a more cheerful story about happiness.'

And they all prepared to listen to Natasha.

Story Three

by the engineer Natasha, about a meeting with her first love and how she discovered she could run along the clouds.

301

'I once had what promised to be a really bad day. The people at work had started some unpleasant campaign against another colleague, and I didn't feel like going in to work. My husband was complaining that I didn't know how to run a household – it's true, as a housekeeper I'm no great shakes – and that we would never save enough money at this rate to buy a co-operative flat. But I ask you, how are we supposed to save when our expenses come to 260 roubles a month? We barely make it to pay-day. I was feeling so lousy that, without saying anything to my husband, I took a day off work at my own expense and went to the Kirovsky Islands just to look at the green trees and blue sea. I always found that a help. The weather was indifferent, which suited my mood. Sometimes there were clouds rushing past, and it even drizzled; sometimes the sun broke through and made the raindrops shine and sparkle, and that cheered me up.

'I made my way to a quiet corner down on the beach, a place where very few people came because there were no amusements or cafés nearby. And that was just what I wanted – to be alone. I found a dead tree on the beach, sat down on it and looked out at the bay, the islands, the reeds growing along the shore. And my anger, depression and irritation gave way to quiet sadness and peace.

'As I was sitting on my log, lost in thought, a tall man suddenly walked past in the blue uniform of a civil airline pilot. He looked intently at me as he passed – I could feel it without raising my eyes – and then walked on. Thank goodness, I thought, at least he's not going to stop and chat me up, I certainly don't need that right now. But no sooner had I thought that than he turned sharply round and started marching towards me in the most determined manner. I got a scowl ready, made a sour face and started preparing a speech to get rid of him. But he stopped right in front of me and said: "Hello, Natasha! Somehow I always knew I'd meet you one day, and I was even thinking about it today. Don't you recognize me?"

'I looked up, stared at the pilot's face, and suddenly saw in those adult lines the features of a long-forgotten young boy.

' "Amiran, is it you?"

' "Of course!"

'We shook hands and I invited him to sit down next to me.

' "So tell me, how's life with you?"

' "Fine. I'm flying. I'm married and I've got two sons. And I want a third. I have a beautiful wife. Do you want to see?"

' "Certainly!"

'He showed me a photograph of a Georgian beauty with two fine boys.

' "And what about you?"

' "Married. No children yet, but we will have. My husband's good-looking, too, but I don't carry any photos around. How did you recognize me, Amiran? Have I changed so little?"

' "You know, I see you while I'm flying, and I often try to imagine how you might have changed over the years. I was always afraid you might have got fat, and when I see you like that in my mind's eye you're not able to run along the clouds. But you didn't get fat. Thank you."

' "What do you mean, you see me when you're flying? And how could I run along the clouds?"

'All this surprised me, and I thought: I just hope he doesn't go and tell me he's in love with me! But he smiled and said: "You see, when I'm flying I often go back over my life and remember all the nice things that have happened and people I've been fond of. The sky is very conducive to that. When I fly in a sunset or a sunrise I nearly always see my wife Natela putting the children to bed and singing them a song. I see her every day. But sometimes I see people I've loved in the past. Including you, my first love."

' "And how do you see me?"

' "It's very simple; I see this mischievous girl running gaily along the clouds waving to me, or diving off a steep cloud and swimming in the blue. Sometimes she flies right up to the window and makes faces at me and teases me. Do you remember how you teased me when you climbed that cypress tree and I couldn't reach you? And when there's a thundercloud nearby I often see you as you were on that first day, floundering about in the waves. Do you remember how I had to save you?"

' "Of course I do! What else! How else do you see me?"

' "Sometimes I've seen your face through the mist, and it was a grown-up face already. But it was always difficult to make out the features – I didn't know how much you had changed when you grew up. Now I shall see you as you are."

' "How interesting, Amiran! You were romantic when you

303

were young, and now you've turned into a poet."

' "Poet? Rubbish! That's only in the air."

' "And are there a lot of us living up there in the clouds with you?"

' "O-oh, a whole harem! On the ground I love my Natela and no one else, but in the sky I have everyone I ever loved and that ever loved me. And even just pretty girls I remember passing on the street. But I see you most of all: you were just the type to go running along the clouds! You probably don't remember what you used to be like, but I see you on almost every flight."

'I stared at Amiran and couldn't get over the idea that I existed in some other world, unknown to myself.

' "What about the way I insulted you when we were young? Do you see that too?"

' "Oh, come on, Natasha! How can there be any insults in heaven?"

' "In that case, would you like to come home with me and meet my husband?"

' "No, Natasha, I don't want to do that. Let's part here. I know I shall see you on my very next flight. And I guess it will be a sad, grown-up Natasha sitting on a solitary cloud, and then she'll see me and smile. And she'll wave her hand and drift on."

'We parted, and we shall probably not meet again. But here's the strangest thing about that incident: I went home completely happy. And ever since then, whenever I feel sad, or petty worries get the better of me, or someone hurts me, I think of that meeting and say to myself: you can say horrible things to me and hurt me, but you don't realize that at this very moment I might be running along the clouds, while somebody watches me with loving eyes and waits for me to wave to him. Then in my mind I wave to Amiran and feel happy, and I feel beyond the reach of those trivial disappointments.

'So that's the happiness that a long-forgotten boy from Georgia gave me.'

'I understand that very well, Natasha!' said Valentina. 'You were given that happiness, but I had to learn it for myself. Shall I tell you about it?'

'Of course!' cried Irishka. 'We too want to learn how

to be happy all the time.'

'You can't complain!' laughed Emma. 'You're always bursting with happiness! It's us unsettled ones that need to hear the story.'

Story Four

by the bigwig Valentina, being a tried and tested recipe for happiness.

'There was a period in my life when I was so unhappy I could have hanged myself. It was shortly after Andryusha's departure abroad, after our one and only night together. I knew he would never come and see us again. I knew that night would never be repeated, and I didn't want it to be – yet I was very depressed. As I was walking along the Nevsky Prospect one day I passed a vegetable shop that's in a semi-basement. And I saw a woman of unusual beauty coming up the steps – a perfect copy of Raphael's Madonna! I even slowed down to look at her face. Her face was the only thing I could see to begin with. But when she reached the top and stepped out on to the pavement, I saw that she scarcely came up to my waist and that she was a hunchback. I quickly lowered my eyes and walked on! And I felt so ashamed of myself . . . Valyukha, I said to myself, you've got your arms and legs, your face is OK, you can't complain about your health, so how dare you call yourself unhappy? Pull yourself together! There's real unhappiness, see it hobbling past . . .

'I couldn't forget that hunchback with the face of the Madonna, and I probably never shall. And whenever I feel inclined to grumble at life or feel miserable, I think of her.

'So that's how I learnt not to be unhappy. But it was an old woman who taught me how to be happy. Soon after that incident I began to feel rather down in the dumps again. But this time I knew how to fight it, and I went to the Summer Gardens to calm my troubled soul. And so as not to sit doing nothing, I took some embroidery to finish, a tablecloth for special occasions. I put on the simplest dress, did my hair in a single pigtail and just let it hang down. After all, I wasn't going to a ball, I was just going to give my soul an airing.

'I arrived at the Summer Gardens, found a free seat, sat down and started sewing. As I worked I said to myself: "Get a grip on yourself! Calm down! You know you're not unhappy." This did calm me down a bit and I got ready to go home. At that point an old woman got up from a seat opposite and came over to me.

' "If you're not in a hurry," she said, "may I sit down and tell you something?"

' "Certainly!"

'She sat down beside me, looked at me with a smile and said: "You know, I've been watching you for the last hour, and I've enjoyed every moment of it. You so rarely see this nowadays."

' "See what?"

' "Everything! In the centre of modern Leningrad suddenly to see a pretty young woman with a dark pigtail, wearing a simple white linen frock, and even doing embroidery! You can't imagine what a wonderful sight that is to see! I'm putting it in my happiness basket."

' "And what is your happiness basket?"

' "Oh, that's a secret! But I'll tell you about it. Do you want to be happy?"

' "Of course! Everyone does."

' "Everyone wants to be happy, but not everyone knows how. But I'll teach you. As a reward for what you have given me. Happiness, child, is not success, luck, or even love as you probably think now because you're young. Happiness is the happy moments when a peaceful heart smiles at someone or something. I was sitting on a seat, I saw a pretty girl opposite, busy at her embroidery, and my heart smiled at you. I have made a note of that moment so as to re-live it again and again. I have put it in my happiness basket. Now, if I feel sad, I shall open my basket and begin to go through my treasures. Among them will be a moment that I shall call 'A girl in white embroiders in the Summer Gardens'. As I touch it the moment will immediately come to life, and I shall see a girl with embroidery on her lap against a background of dark summer foliage and white marble statues. I shall remember that the sunbeams fell on your dress through the leaves of the lime tree, that your pigtail was hanging over the back of the seat and almost reached down to the ground, that your sandals were pinching you a bit and you had pushed them off and were sitting barefoot, turning your toes in slightly because the ground was cold. Maybe I'll remember something else, some other detail that I'm not aware of now."

' "That's fantastic!" I exclaimed. "A basket of happy moments! Have you been collecting them all your life?"

' "Ever since a certain wise man taught me to. You know him, you've read his books. It was Aleksandr Grin. We used to be friends, and he told me that personally. And you can find the same idea in a lot of his stories. And you will realize that a person who is wise and generous in heart is able to forgive and forget all the bad things in life, and retain only the good things in his memory. But for that sort of memory the heart has to be trained. So I invented my mental basket of happy moments."

'I thanked the old woman and set off home. On the way I began to recall happy moments from my earliest childhood, and by the time I got home my happiness basket already contained its first treasures.'

'Oh, how well I understand!' exclaimed Irishka. 'Me and Seryozha often think about a certain frog we knew. It lived in a pond at the Tavrida Gardens, and we were sure it had got fond of us and that we were seeing it every time we went there. Actually it was probably lots of different frogs, but we thought it was the same one. We always tried to get it to admit it was the Frog Prince from the fairy tale and to show us its little crown.'

'Everybody has memories like that, it's true,' said Emma, 'only we don't appreciate them, we're always waiting for some huge, weighty happiness. But perhaps happiness only consists of happy moments. Well, what will Albina tell us about happiness?'

'I shall tell you a story of earthly happiness, even though I came across it in the air, like Natasha's Amiran.'

Story Five

by the airhostess Albina, about why a diplomat chose himself a Russian wife.

'I was on a flight to London one time. There weren't many people on the plane: a few foreigners, a couple of Soviet embassy personnel and a troupe of actors on their way to tour England. There was also an English diplomat, a good-looking young man with a Russian wife who was pregnant. Of course, you can't expect every pregnant woman to be beautiful, but this one really did look dowdy beside him. Me and my friend said to each other: "That scarecrow certainly hit the jackpot."

'An hour after take-off the young diplomat's wife started her contractions. We transferred her to our section and laid her on the couch, but what else could we do? The rule in such cases is to look for a doctor among the passengers. Well, we made an announcement just in case, but we knew there was hardly likely to be a doctor in a passenger list like that. Sure enough, there wasn't. The diplomat's wife was lying there moaning. She kept asking us: "Will we be crossing the frontier soon? I don't want to give birth over Soviet territory!"

'We tried to reassure her: "We'll soon be across!" But we knew that until they got off in London all the passengers were still on Soviet territory – it was an Aeroflot plane!

'The young husband sat next to her holding her hand and trying to soothe her in Russian and English. Sometimes he called her Katenka, sometimes Kate. She was also switching from one language to the other, complaining of the pain. I saw she really might have the baby on the plane, and I wondered who would deliver it. We needed to calm her down, but I was afraid to give her a sleeping pill – there was nothing in the rules about it, and I didn't know enough about it myself.

'Then I had a brilliant idea about how to calm her down and delay the birth. Only I couldn't do it without the husband's agreement. I called him out of the compartment for a moment and explained the idea to him in the corridor: "Your wife is very nervous. If it goes on like this she won't make it to London. And there's no one to deliver the baby.

But we do have some actors on board. Why don't I ask some elderly actress to play the part of a doctor and calm your wife down? Then perhaps she'll go to sleep and we can get her safely to London. We've already radioed ahead and a doctor will be there to meet us."

'David – that was the husband – was so scared he was ready to agree to anything. I sent him back to Katenka and went back to speak to the actors. One of the actresses agreed: "All right, I'll improvise in an unscheduled performance!" And she came through to our section. She began to get into her part while we were walking down the plane, and when she spoke to Katenka her voice had even changed: "Well, my dear? What's the big hurry? Let's have a look at you!"

'She sat down next to Katenka, felt her stomach, then turned to us and said: "Please leave us alone for two minutes!" Her tone was so bossy that me and my mate and David immediately did as we were told and left.

'When she let us back in she said very impressively: "There's no need for panic. She won't give birth just yet. But to be on the safe side, please get ready some hot water, clean towels, surgical spirit and scissors. Let me see your first aid kit." She examined it professionally and said: "That's all right. If the worst comes to the worst our friend can have her baby here if she's in such a hurry. But on the whole, dear, it would be better for you to sleep. Get some rest, you'll have enough work to do later."

'It all sounded so natural that not only Katenka calmed down, but so did David who knew this was not a doctor. The mother-to-be went to sleep, and we all sat around biting our nails.

'So what happened? We got Katenka safely to London where an ambulance was waiting for her. David was so nervous he forgot to thank us for our troubles. I thanked the actress myself: "I hope your tour goes as well as it has begun!" I said. "It's just a pity we were the only ones to see how brilliantly you acted that part! What would you have done if she really had started to give birth?"

' "My dear, I was so much into the part I probably would have delivered the baby. I've had babies of my own!"

'We said goodbye, and I didn't think I would ever see any of those people again. But a year later David was on that same plane. I recognized him straightaway, but I didn't let on. We also have our rules about that sort of thing: maintain the high calling of the Soviet citizen, and avoid striking up acquaintances with foreign passengers! David stopped me himself as I was wheeling the drinks trolley past: "Hello! Weren't you the person on the flight when my wife nearly had a baby on the plane? I didn't have time to thank you. Thank you very much from me, Katenka and little David!"

'And I answered, still according to the rules: "I merely did my duty." And, giving him a toothy smile, I moved on with all the dignity of a Soviet citizen. But of course I was delighted. Every cat likes to be stroked!

'As I was taking round the lunch David handed me a large handsome package and said: "This is a denim suit. I was taking it to Katya's sister, but you have the same figure, I would say. I think it will fit you, and Katenka will be glad I met you and gave you a present."

'Our damned rules strictly forbid accepting presents from passengers, so I had to refuse the suit. I would have taken it, of course, but you never know who else might be travelling on the same plane. If they saw me and reported it I would fly out of that job at supersonic speed.

'But David knew the form himself. When I came to collect the dishes he quietly pushed a note into my hand. It said: "Ring me this evening at this number in Leningrad." And there was a telephone number. Well, that was quite a different kettle of fish!

'I rang David that evening and we met at a café. He brought the denim suit. We sat together and he told me how he had met his Katenka. "When I came to work in the Soviet Union I left a fiancée behind in London, the daughter of a high-up diplomat. I thought we loved each other enough for a happy marriage. My fiancée made the condition that after my tour of duty in the USSR was over I should get myself assigned to a West European country, and then she would marry me. I considered that a perfectly reasonable demand and agreed to it.

' "I once came to Leningrad on business from Moscow, and a colleague from the American Consulate introduced me to some young nonconformist artists. Katenka was among them. We got into an interesting conversation about the directions modern art was taking, and I suggested continuing the conversation some other time. So without any fear she invited me back to her place for supper. So I went there. She lived with her mother and brother pretty well by Soviet standards: they had their own flat. Katenka's mother was very hospitable. She had made *pelmeni* that day, and they were fabulous. As we were sitting at the table a frail voice suddenly came from the next room: 'I'm hungry! You forgot me again!'

' "Katenka jumped up from the table and ran to the other room. Her mother said to me: 'That's Katenka's grandmother, my mother. She's been bedridden for five years. She's become very difficult and won't let anyone look after her except Katenka. The poor girl is sometimes worked off her feet: she has the institute, her work, her painting, and on top of all that a difficult sick grandmother to take care of.

' "A few minutes later Katenka came back to the table looking calm and happy. 'Gran smelt the *pelmeni* and got hungry again. I had already fed her before. Now she's gone to sleep.'

' " 'So have you been looking after her the whole five years, Katenka?' I asked her.

' "She answered rather sadly: 'I was her favourite granddaughter. Now she's forgotten everyone else, and she doesn't even recognize Mama, her own daughter. I'm the only one she remembers.'

' "And they told me how Katenka and her brother carried their grandmother out into the street in an armchair every day – that was her outing. They didn't have the sort of wheelchair that would fit into the lift, and they hadn't managed to change their flat for one on the ground floor. I suggested it might be better to put her into an old people's home, where they had all the facilities for taking care of old people like that. But the whole family jumped down my throat: 'How could we take grandmother to an old people's home when we're all perfectly happy ourselves! What would people think of us! She has earned the right to die in her own bed.'

' "Katenka looked at me in horror: 'David, surely you wouldn't get rid of the grandmother that brought you up?' Then I remembered that my fiancée's own mother had been in an old people's home for several years, let alone her

311

grandmother. She felt it was better for her there, more convenient. And for some reason it occurred to me that if something happened to me and I became an invalid, my fiancée would just as easily get rid of me as she got rid of her mother when she had her stroke. I think I decided that evening deep down that I would marry Katenka. But it only happened several years later, after her grandmother had died. I had to go through all the rumpus with my fiancée and her parents, and then there was a lot of trouble getting permission for the marriage. The KGB put so much pressure on Katenka not to marry me that it just strengthened her resolve to leave the country. She said it was stupid when the authorities decided who should marry who, and how each person should live. She didn't even want to have a baby here, she was afraid it might be bad for him in the future. So I got a wife with whom I can calmly face sickness and old age."

'So, my dears, that Katenka was lucky! Yet when you think about it, Russia is full of women like that, and David didn't know! I know so many families that have their sick old folks living with them in the same room as the rest of the family, and nobody ever thinks of getting rid of them.'

'It's strange that David should reason that way,' observed Galina. 'Of course, basically old people's homes in the West are nothing like ours. Apparently the old people are given individual rooms and they even get pocket money for spending on small things.'

'You're laying it on rather thick, Galina!' laughed Olga. 'There's no way they could give the old folks separate rooms. And as for pocket money, that's absolute nonsense! If the state is keeping them, how can they possibly get pocket money as well? That's just bourgeois propaganda.'

'No, maybe it really is like that,' said Emma. 'But even so, a state-run home is not the same as one's own. Even if they did have their own rooms and all the facilities, it's still hard without your family, your grandchildren. We've got an excellent old people's home for actors, but I hope my boy will never shove me in there! I can see from his eyes that he would never do a thing like that!'

'It's a bit early for you to be reading his thoughts!'

laughed the women. But everyone agreed that it was a dreadful thing to have to spend one's last days away from one's own home.

Then Galina began to tell her story. 'You remember Emma told you about how two young artists sacrificed their dignity in order to save their friends. Today I shall tell you how a "lucky dress" enabled a certain incredible coward to keep going in similar circumstances with amazing courage.'

Story Six

by the dissident Galina, which she herself entitled
'The Story of the Lucky Dress'.

'I had a friend called Marina. She was an excellent typist and an unbelievable coward. Her parents were arrested in 1949 and died in the camps, so she felt it her duty to do something for the democratic movement. But whenever she was brought some samizdat to copy she would always warn the person: "For heaven's sake don't tell me where this comes from or where it's going to! I'm so weak that I'm afraid I would break down under questioning. And don't mention any names to me! I won't betray the people I know because I love them, but if they start questioning me about people I don't know personally, I won't hold out."

'She was petrified of informers, hidden microphones, and everything else to do with the KGB. But she still asked to be given work: "I must do something. But I don't want to know any more than is necessary."

It was rather difficult dealing with her. Some people tried to calm her fears: "Why should they arrest you? If they arrested all the typists who copy samizdat the prisons would burst!"

'Others tried to avoid having anything to do with her. "If she's warned us herself," they said, "it means she knows her own weaknesses; she'll crack if she's interrogated."

'Marina was not well off. Her one ambition was to have a black velvet dress made for herself trimmed with black Vologda lace. That dress was an *idée fixe* with her, and she

313

saved up for it for several years. Finally she bought the velvet and the Vologda lace at enormous expense, and took it to the dressmaker's. She wanted to appear in it at a New Year's Eve party. I should add that she was secretly in love with one of our friends, and her dream was to appear before him in this amazing dream-dress. But she didn't manage to come to our New Year's Eve party in her fabulous dress: she was arrested just before.

'The investigation went on for months. When we first heard about Marina's arrest we remembered what she had said and assumed she would start giving damaging evidence, and that more arrests would follow. But time went by, and nobody was even summoned for questioning. That was bad in a way, because it was impossible to get any idea how the investigation was going. Marina had an elder brother, and they allowed him to get a lawyer for her and told him when the trial would be. Of course we all came to the trial. The lucky ones got into the courtroom, the rest crowded the corridors and stairs. It took place at the Municipal Court.

'So we sat in the courtroom, waiting. Suddenly the door opened, and two guards with guns escorted Marina in. The whole courtroom gasped: she was wearing her luxurious velvet evening dress! After several months locked in a cell the poor girl looked pale, of course, but she was as beautiful as a princess in a fairy tale. I don't know how she managed it in her cell, but her hair was done up in the most ornate Empire style and tied with a velvet ribbon. She had a similar ribbon round her open neck, with a cross hanging from it. This was the first sign that Marina had not been broken: the right to wear a cross in prison is not easy to win.

'As the trial proceeded we saw that Marina had not implicated anyone. Only her two neighbours came forward as witnesses. The KGB had forced them to testify that they had seen people coming to visit Marina, and that they had brought her certain papers and taken papers away. Marina herself did not deny she had been typing samizdat. She said: "I don't see anything wrong in this. People must know the whole truth if they're to get some idea about truth. But if people are to be persecuted for this, why should I help the persecutors?"

'That was all she said to the court. For the rest of the trial she hardly looked at the judge. She sat in the dock half-facing them and calmly looked at her friends in the courtroom and sometimes smiled to us. She looked as if she had got tired dancing many waltzes and was resting, "in the middle of the ball sitting down in the dock", as one person put it jokingly. Meanwhile the person she was secretly in love with couldn't take his eyes off her.

'Marina was given a light sentence – three years in a general regime camp under the article about spreading slander against the Soviet system. When the address of her camp became known I wrote her a letter asking her where she had found her strength, being such a coward, as she always maintained. Marinochka wrote back: "Galka! How could I possibly lose my dignity wearing a dress like that? I had to conduct myself properly. I was so hurt when they came to arrest me. I had just that day got the dress back from the dressmaker, and I couldn't get over how beautiful it was. I was imagining how I would wear it to see the New Year in, together with X. And suddenly they came for me and I realized there wouldn't be any party for me. So in desperation I put my dream-dress on and went to prison in it. And in my thoughts I was with X on New Year's Eve. It was all because of the dress. I still am a coward and a weak person, as you know."

'I took the letter and showed it to X. He immediately rushed to the camp to get a meeting with Marina. Everything's fine with them now and Marina is very happy. And all because of the lucky dress!'

When Galina had finished, all the women competed to tell stories about lucky and unlucky dresses of their own. It turned out that buying clothes or hats can not only change a woman's mood, but her whole life!

Emma, for example, shared a secret: 'When I was quite a young student at drama school my dream was to buy a beautiful green hat to go with my red hair. And since then, whenever I feel miserable I say to myself: "I think it's time I bought a green hat." I go to a shop and spend a long time choosing. If they don't have green I try others on, then I buy one and go home content. I've got so many of these hats I don't know what to do with them. I've got about a dozen green ones. Maybe some of you need a green hat? Come and choose, you can have one for free!'

But nobody was interested in a green hat, so Olga began her story.

Story Seven

by the worker Olga, about two mothers whose sons were swapped by mistake in the maternity hospital, and how they resolved the situation.

'I shall now tell you a story that has been on the tip of my tongue since the first day. I didn't tell it earlier because I was afraid to scare you. But now I can see you have all had a good look at your little babies and none of you thinks you have been palmed off with someone else's. Because my story is about just that.

'Two women were in the same ward of a maternity hospital. One was local, from Leningrad, an engineer, and the other was from the country. She had come in to buy food and her contractions had started while she was in the queue. They were lying next to each other in the delivery room, both gave birth to sons at the same time, and afterwards were in the same ward and got friendly. They were very different types, like us here, but women always find something to talk about once they've had time to get to know each other.

'Later they were discharged, and they said goodbye forever, as they thought. Five or six years went by, I don't remember exactly, and the engineer went to market one day to buy potatoes and suddenly saw her old friend behind the stall. They recognized each other and were very pleased to see each other again.

' "So how's your little son?" asked the peasant woman. "Did God give you another child?"

'The engineer had been having treatment for infertility, and she had waited many years for that boy. She hadn't had any more. "He's a good boy. My husband and I are delighted with him. But we haven't any more children. My husband can't get over our Edik having red hair. Everyone in our family is dark. Perhaps he takes after some grandmother."

316

' "And our Kolya is as black as a beetle. My husband even gave me funny looks at first. He said: 'Who could that black one take after? He doesn't even look Russian.' "

'The engineer was Jewish. So she took a photo of her son out of her bag and showed it to the peasant. She grabbed the photo, stared at it and in a low voice asked: "What did you say you called your son?"

' "Edik."

'Then the peasant woman let out a scream that could be heard right across the market: "My son, my darling little son! How could they give you such a horrid name! And how could you end up in someone else's family, my darling?"

'She went on screaming and wailing until it brought the militia on the scene. By now she wasn't making any sense, she was just poking her finger at the photo and pointing to the engineer and wailing: "She's taken my son away and put him in her own family!"

'Suddenly it occurred to the engineer why the woman was screaming. She turned as pale as death and fainted. Luckily there was a first aid post at the market, and a nurse was sent for. She brought her round, and they were both taken to the militia to sort things out. The militia took their addresses and told them to go to court over the matter, because it was not something they could solve.

'Well, before going to court they calmed down a bit and decided first of all to take a look at the children to make sure they really had been swapped round. So the engineer immediately got a taxi and took the peasant back to her home. On the way she made her promise not to say anything to the child, but just to look at him.

'They arrived. The peasant took one look at the boy, this Edik, sat down and burst into tears. But silently, as they had agreed. They went out on to the street afterwards and the peasant said to the engineer: "That's it, Sofa, definitely a swap! Your Edik is the image of his father, my husband, I mean. He's a redhead, like all our children. Now here's my address. You come and have a look at your real son. But with the same agreement: don't say anything."

'The next day the engineer bought a whole lot of presents for the peasant's children and set off for Lodeynoye Polye, about three hundred kilometres from Leningrad. What did she see when she got there? Five little children sitting on

317

benches – four of them with flame-red hair, and the fifth dark. She could hardly stop herself rushing over to this dark-eyed, curly-headed little Kolya – he was an exact copy of what she was like as a child, and looking at him was like looking at a childhood photograph of herself.

'When they had put the children to bed that evening the grown-ups sat round the table and began discussing what to do next. The women wept buckets of tears, as you would expect, and the husband sat thinking. Here's the idea he came up with: "Sofya Aronovna, let's swap boys just for a time and see if they recognize their own mothers and fathers. Of course, you've probably given ours lots of chocolates and spoilt him a bit ... and Kolka has got used to an open-air life, he runs around barefoot, spends the whole day down at the river, drinks about a litre of milk a day. How's he going to survive without fresh air, on nothing but chocolates? But the boys need to go back to their allotted fate."

'The mothers thought about it, and then decided to try solving the matter peacefully. Sofya Aronovna stayed another three days in Lodeynoye Polye and tried to make friends with Kolya. She bought him some hooks and a fishing rod in the village shop. In other words, she did her best. The little boy seemed to feel something and be drawn towards her. And then on the agreed day she suggested to him that they go and stay with his 'cousin' in Leningrad. That was an idea the mothers had had – to tell the boys they were cousins, so that they wouldn't feel strange in each other's family.

'So Sofya Aronovna and Kolka set off for Leningrad, and Vasily Vasilyevich went with them to have a look at his son Edik and take him to stay at Lodeynoye Polye if everything worked out.

'Kolka liked it in Leningrad and became firm friends with Edik on the very first day. He was the youngest in his family, and Edik was an only child and was glad to have a friend. Meanwhile Vasily Vasilyevich was working on him, telling him all about the fishing boat and hunting. That was all the boy needed. By the second day he was saying: "Uncle Vasya, when are we going looking for squirrels in the forest, and fishing?"

'A few days later they packed up and set off. Kolka stayed

with his real parents. Of course, Sofya and her husband spoiled him no end, taking him to the circus and the zoo and children's theatres. They bought him books and, most exciting of all, they bought him a bike! The boy was delighted and became attached to them. He asked Sofya Aronovna to read aloud to him at night, because he said he didn't get such nice things at home. But after a week he began to think about leaving. "It's time to go back to Mama and Papa. They'll soon be lifting the potatoes, and I have to help."

'His parents were horrified! But they had to get him ready to leave, because the agreement was not to upset the children or tell them anything for the time being, but just to do what seemed best for them.

'And Sofya Aronovna and her husband decided to take their holiday and go to Lodeynoye Polye with Kolya so as to be near him, so he wouldn't forget them. And that's what they did.

'When they arrived Edik met them looking healthy, suntanned – and barefoot. He had learnt to swim in the river and fish. A typical boy, in fact. Of course, he was very pleased to see his parents, and especially his new cousin Kolya. After all, they were the same age, to the very hour!

'And what do you think happened? The whole business was resolved without a court case. Each boy got two sets of parents: Mama Sofa and Mama Nyura, and Papa Lyova and Papa Vasya. And each one had five brothers and sisters. They put the two boys into an English-language school in Leningrad, and for the holidays they spend the whole summer in the country. And during the summer, so as not to get too lonely, Sofya Aronovna and her husband have all the "cousins" to stay one after the other – that's the brothers and sisters of Kolya and Edik. It's an odd family set-up, but they're closer than many families and everyone envies them. The main thing is, the boys are both happy. I mean, anything could have happened. People are so different, after all – at first sight anyway.'

'God, it's nice when people behave like human beings!' exclaimed Zina, after the story was over.

And everyone agreed with her.

Nelya began her story next.

Story Eight

*by the teacher Nelya, in which she describes the
happiest day in her mother's life.*

'I told you on the first day that my earliest childhood
memory was of my mother in a white dress, looking young
and tender and playing the piano by an open window. For a
long time I thought that was just a dream, because I often
did dream about it. I never told my mother about the dream,
because when I grew older we lived in a sort of darkness: my
mother was ill the whole time, we never had enough money
even for food and clothes, let alone music! For a long time I
didn't even know she played the piano.

'Then one day we went to visit some distant relatives,
very rich people. They usually avoided us, but this time for
some reason they invited us to the birthday party of their
daughter Ella, who was my age. We spent a whole week
getting ready, but I didn't have any shoes. Until late autumn
I would go to school wearing rubber slippers over my
woollen socks. My school dress had been mended a
hundred times, and the apron was from the lining of my
mother's coat. During term I would come home from school
and immediately take off the dress and put on an old
dressing gown so as to save the dress. I didn't have any other
dress, either a party one or an everyday one. So what was I to
wear? But by the end of the week Mama had literally worked
miracles. She collected up remnants of old woollen things –
single mittens, a torn scarf, the sleeves of an old sweater
that she had converted into a sleeveless jumper. For two
days we sat together picking that whole pile of things to
pieces and rolling the used wool into balls. Then my mother
wound all that wool into one skein, dyed it a dark colour
and knitted me a lovely skirt. She made a blouse to go with
it out of her nightie, using the parts that were least worn.
And most important of all, she managed to make some
shoes for my outfit! She took the goloshes that I used to put
over my slippers in rainy weather, and she knitted little
covers for them with straps and buttons. The result was a
delightful little pair of shoes. But my mother told me not to
wear them at all before the party, because she didn't think
they would survive being worn more than once.

'Mama didn't forget about herself either. Her sister, who was a doctor, gave her an old medical gown, and Mama made an elegant summer dress out of it, and then she embroidered it with little blue flowers so that no one would see it was very simple material. I don't know why she put such a lot of effort into all this, but I guess it was because poverty has its own pride, and she didn't want to look poor in front of her rich relatives. But perhaps it was just that she hadn't been out and had a good time for ever so long. After all, she was still young!

'So we arrived at the relatives' house, all dressed up and excited. They had a huge flat, full of polished furniture and crystal. The large round table was laid with foods that I had never even heard of, let alone tasted. I didn't know any fruits beside apples, water-melon and wild berries, and here they had grapes, peaches and honeydew melon. Ella was wearing a smart delicate blue velvet dress with a large lace collar. But I looked just as good, honestly! At least, that's how it seemed to me. The only thing that disappointed me was Ella's loud question: "What's that on your shoes? Are they home-made?"

'I felt a pang of shame. But then I immediately thought my mother would be hurt if I was ashamed, so I got a grip on myself and said: "Yes, Mama made them specially to go with this skirt. Do you like them?"

' "Oh, I know! That's called an ensemble!" said Ella, trying to show how clever she was.

'It felt like a real holiday as we sat at the table with our hosts and all the guests. There was so much beautiful tasty food that I didn't even feel hungry after a while. Like the other children I spent most of the time drinking lemonade. At the end of the meal we were all given ice cream in little cups. That was just like a fairy tale! In fact I felt like Cinderella at the ball – only the prince was missing.

'Then the miracle happened. When the table had been cleared away and the grown-ups had danced a bit, the hostess suddenly said to my mother: "Basya, you used to be a wonderful pianist. Play something for us."

' "Oh, come on, Rufochka, I haven't touched a piano for years! I forgot everything long ago. Oh well, I'll have a try. If it doesn't work, it doesn't work." And my mother went over to the corner where there was a large black piano. I hadn't

321

noticed it till then, it had just been part of the furniture in the flat.

'She sat down on the round stool, opened the lid, put her hands on the keys and closed her eyes, trying to remember. Then she smiled and ran her hands lightly over the keys without even looking. And she began playing a happy, simple little melody. It was some well-known song, and all the guests began to sing along. Afterwards they applauded but she had already started to play something serious. Everyone listened quietly, and I just held my breath, I was so proud of her. She looked so beautiful in her white dress at that shiny black piano, and the music was so solemn and beautiful. How could anyone compare this to the crackling, dull sort of music that came out of our radio at home?

'Suddenly Mama began to play a rather sad, incredibly beautiful tune, and I knew instantly that it was the tune from my dream, when Mama played by the open window and I danced in my cot. My dears, I'm afraid I spoilt my mother's evening out! I suddenly had the feeling that our whole life was just a splinter, a tail end, of a wonderful former life that was now only a dream for me. I kept back my tears as long as I could, but finally I burst into sobs. Mama was frightened: she rushed over to me and tried to calm me. The hosts and guests gathered round me, too, and somebody put a glass of lemonade to my lips. But I couldn't even drink. Then my mother made her apologies to everyone, quickly got our coats and took me home. She put me to bed without asking any questions. She gave me a pill and I went to sleep.

'The next day I told my mother about my dream and how I had recognized the music she had played. "That was a waltz by Godard,' she said. "I used to be very fond of it. But how could you remember that? You weren't even one!"

' "That was the music I always heard in my dream. Shall I hum it to you?" And I hummed Godard's waltz to her. It made her cry. She told me much later that that had been the happiest day of her life.

'What sad stories we're telling each other for the last day,' sighed Emma, 'even though they do have something to do with happiness. My story isn't particularly cheerful either, but it's quite funny.'

And she began her story.

322

Story Nine

by the director Emma, about a sad parting and a happy find that saved all Emma's friends who were suffering from the Romanov experiment in Leningrad.

'There came a time in my life when I was constantly saying goodbye to people. One by one my friends were leaving and going to all four corners of the earth. Now half my close friends are abroad, the other half are here. People leave in order to be free to write books, paint pictures, play music, produce films and plays. Sometimes I feel that Russia herself is leaving! But why? That's just the thing: nobody knows why this exodus of creative talent from Russia is taking place. Each farewell is an ocean of tears, and the memories left afterwards are like the dry sand.

'The most difficult farewell for me was when we saw Kostya Kuzminsky off. I've already told you about him. His home was one of the most interesting in Leningrad. The most varied group of people would meet there every day. But the people were always either artistic or just very interesting, unusual people. Kostya and I had been friends since he had been studying in the history of theatre faculty at our institute. What sort of person was he? Well, he was the sort that you would call on and chat about this and that, and then you'd go home and find you had all sorts of new artistic ideas and plans. From the artistic point of view he was incredibly stimulating.

'But then Kostya left, too. We saw him off, and then I went back to his flat to help his mother, who was staying behind, to sort everything out. After Kostya left the government took one of their two rooms away from her, as one would expect, so his room had to be cleared out. It was so sad collecting up the remaining few books, and taking the pictures off the walls that Kostya couldn't afford to take abroad with him. The newspapers had described those pictures as "untalented daubs by pathetic imitators of the West". Yet now the government was demanding huge prices to take those same pictures out of the country. As I was busy doing this job I was listening to the music coming from the window opposite. Some kids were playing the same Abba record over and over again, and I swayed to the music to stop myself crying.

323

'One day Yevdokiya Petrovna, Kostya's mother, asked me to sort out all the junk that had accumulated over the years in the attic. I climbed up into the attic, bending double because the space was so cramped, and began going through the things, calling them out and showing them to Yevdokiya Petrovna below. She sat on a chair down below like an empress on her throne, giving appropriate instructions: "That's to be thrown out. That you can keep as a souvenir of Kostya. That can stay."

'In the far corner of the attic I found a sack. I untied it, and inside there was an old pillowcase, but very clean like everything else belonging to Yevdokiya Petrovna. I put my hand in – it was some sort of grain. Wheat perhaps? "There's a sack up here. It's got a pillowcase in it with wheat, I think."

'Yevdokiya Petrovna jumped up from her chair: "What? A pillowcase with wheat in it? It couldn't be! Is it still there? Good gracious! Do you know what that wheat is, Emma?"

'I immediately crawled over to the hatch and put my head down. Yevdokiya Petrovna always had fascinating stories to tell. "Towards the end of the war, long after the blockade was over, but when food was still very scarce, I managed to get a sack of wheat. I ground it in a coffee mill and made cereal and even muffins for Kostya and me. That wheat was a real godsend. Then things got better and we stopped eating the wheat. Someone suggested I take it to the peasants at the market and exchange it for something else. But I couldn't bring myself to do that. "I hope to God we'll never need it," I said, "but I'll keep it. Just in case. So it's been there all this time. Since 1944."

'I sat listening to her story, letting the grain run through my fingers. "So what shall we do with it? What do you say this time?"

' "The same as before. I hope to God I'll never need it, but let it stay."

' "Right."

'And I dragged the sack over to the pile of things to be kept. I was about to tie it up when I suddenly noticed another small linen bag underneath the pillowcase of wheat. I looked into it – and started to laugh so hard I nearly fell out of the attic. I was speechless. Yevdokiya Petrovna was getting worried down below: "Now what have you dug up, Emma?"

324

' "Dear Yevdokiya Petrovna! What's your phrase? 'I hope to God I'll never need it, but I'll keep it just in case'? I've found something else here that's been waiting 'just in case', and this is the time to use it. Dried onions!" And I threw the bag of dried onions right down on to her lap.

'Now Yevdokiya Petrovna started laughing too, and the tears began to roll down her cheeks as if they were fresh onions, not dried ones.

'This was back in 1974, when our mayor Romanov had just announced his latest "Leningrad experiment". He announced that the Leningrad region could supply the city with vegetables itself, and he imposed a strict ban on bringing in vegetables from other regions and republics, even to the market. The result of one year of this experiment was that he was able to move up a bit more in the Politbureau and the city ended up with no potatoes, cabbage, carrots and, worst of all, no onions. If they did appear at the market they were snapped up immediately. And the prices were crazy – eight to ten roubles a kilo! Of course, Yevdokiya and I hadn't had a whiff of onions in our kitchens for a long time. And then these riches all of a sudden!

'We divided the dried onions into separate little packages, then I sat down by the telephone and began ringing round all our mutual friends. "Hi!" I said. "How are you off for onions? How long have you been going without? One month? Two? Would you be interested in some onions from the harvest of '44? Then come and get them."

'The people started to come, and they also laughed when they heard the story. So those are the happy onion tears I associate with our farewell to Kostya. And our kitchens smelt of onions, to the envy of our neighbours. Wartime onions."

As one might have expected, after Emma's story all the women, including even Valentina, had a few hard words to say about that 'Kremlin Leningrader', Grigory Romanov. But the author is afraid to quote their utterances, lest she be accused of 'spreading knowingly false ideas slandering the Soviet state and social system'.

Then they all turned to Irishka: 'Well, take it away, Irishka! You have to finish our *Women's Decameron*. Don't disappoint us!'

Story Ten

by the secretary Irishka. It is a story about a woman nicknamed Lucky Mariya, with something about happy women in Russia in general.

'Since I have to finish our *Women's Decameron* I would like to tell you about a particular happy woman. She lives in our house and everyone just refers to her as Lucky Mariya. She's retired, and she drinks. When she's had a drink she totters out into the yard, sits down on a bench and tells anyone who has time to listen how lucky she is. I've heard the story of Lucky Mariya several times, so I can tell you it exactly.

'Mariya's luck began the day they came to arrest her parents. Just before the knock on the door Mariya, who was then the five-year-old Masha, was playing hide-and-seek with her father. She was hiding, and her dad was looking for her. Masha thought up a wonderful place to hid – she crawled under the bath. She lay there waiting for her dad either to find her or call to her and say he was giving up. She lay there so long that she fell asleep. During that time the flat was searched, her parents were hastily questioned and then taken away. The mother and father were expecting Masha's grandmother to come that day, so they decided not to mention they had a child in the flat. They were afraid Masha would be taken and put into a children's home, since that's what usually happened to the children of people who were arrested. So Masha was lucky. Her grandmother did come that evening. She arrived just as Masha had woken up, crawled out from under the bath and started to cry because she couldn't find her mum and dad. The grandmother had been through a lot herself, and when she saw the mess in the flat she knew immediately what had happened. She grabbed her granddaughter and the first items of clothing she could find, took the photos of Masha's parents down off the wall and escaped from Leningrad into the country. That was Mariya's first stroke of luck. Many children in those days didn't just lose their parents, they lost their own names. They were given new names so as to speed up the "re-educaiton process".

'Just before the war, when Masha was already a teenager, her grandmother took her away from the Leningrad area to some distant relations in Siberia. That was Mariya's second stroke of luck, because at that time people were running into Leningrad from the outlying areas and then starving to death. But she and her grandmother went to Siberia and survived.

'Masha grew up like every other Soviet child, joining the pioneers and then the Komsomol, and learning to recite with all the others: "Thank you, dear country, for our happy childhood!" As for her parents, she assumed they were dead. Only just before her death did her grandmother tell her about her father and mother. That was during the post-Stalin era. Mariya rushed off to make enquiries and they told her: rehabilitated and living in such and such a place. She went straight off and found them, alive but not well. They, too, had started to try and find her as soon as they got out of camp. They both died in her arms, one after the other. But Mariya considered herself happy to have seen them, and that they died at home in a warm bed, and not on a camp bunk.

'Mariya was married to a good-looking guy, but it was not a successful marriage. He was a heavy drinker and used to beat her almost to death. When she started talking about divorce he actually did threaten to kill her. Mariya was scared, so she hung on. But again she was lucky: her husband took up with a pretty neighbour and left her himself.

'Mariya worked as a guard on a train. The wages were small, so she augmented them the way all guards do on long-distance trains: she brought fruit up from the south, and from Leningrad she took various clothes, car spares, radios and other things you couldn't get in Georgia and Armenia. One time her train was searched to see what the guards were taking with them, to check whether they were speculating. Mariya had a bag of mandarins. She decided to hide it on the platform between two coaches. She opened the door of the coach while the train was moving, went out on to the platform and started to hang the bag on it. At that moment the train gave a jolt and she went flying. But she was lucky. She didn't let go of the bag, and the bag got caught on a bolt and held her. She was badly maimed, but the bag saved her life. Someone saw what had happened through the window and pulled the emergency cord.

' "Another minute," said Mariya afterwards, "and I would have let go of the bag and gone under the wheels. I was already losing consciousness."

'In other words, lucky Mariya.

'She was taken to hospital. As she lay there she thought that if they found out how she had had her accident – all because of a bag of mandarins she wanted to sell – she wouldn't get any pension. But a friend of hers who was also a guard whispered to her that in the general confusion a quick-witted passenger had stolen the bag of mandarins, so Mariya was safe. And she got a good pension because of a disability incurred at her place of work. And because of that disability the railway gave her a room in Leningrad, eight square metres! Lucky Mariya!

'Mariya was a pensioner, she tippled a bit on the side, she didn't hurt anybody and nobody depended on her. And suddenly the neighbours went and denounced her to the militia, saying she was an alcoholic and ought to be thrown out, and her room given to "honest, sober workers in straitened circumstances". Mariya was taken to be examined and was declared an alcoholic. But as she was a disabled worker they started giving her treatment, rather than throwing her out.

'She spent three months in hospital, then was pronounced cured and sent home. She got back to find three months of pension waiting for her untouched. Well, she immediately bought herself a good winter coat and drank the rest of the money the same day. So all that treatment was a waste! But since then, whenever Mariya needs to buy something or is just short of money she calmly goes along to the drug addiction office and tells them: "I want to be treated for alcoholism! Put me in hospital!"

'And they do. And her money keeps coming. So that's our Mariya. She's quite a sight to look at, but if a person says she's been fortunate from birth, how can you not believe her?

'And as I look at you and listen to your stories, and mine too, I think: there's good things and bad things in all our lives. And we ourselves are a mixture of each too, we might as well admit it! And we've all had happy moments in our lives. Yes, each one of us has her happiness. Albina has taken quite a knocking in her time, but look at her, women

– she's beautiful! Well, isn't she? A real doll! We think it a great happiness to see one foreign country, and she's seen the whole world! So, is she fortunate? Of course she is!

'And what about Larissa and Emma? They've grown head and shoulders above their menfolk, so they'll have a job finding someone now, it's true. But they've decided to have their own babies and make their own families. And they're doing the jobs they love, and people respect them for their work. Aren't they fortunate? Of course they are!

'I don't even have to mention Zina. What she's going through now is the most real happiness there is. No one knows how things will go with her and Igor, what difficulties they'll have to face. But she has a new life beginning today, or tomorrow at least. We can only envy you, Zinusha: you're having two good fortunes at once – you've had a son, and you're marrying the man you love.

'I'll say something about Valentina. I've always been petrified of women like you, Valyusha. If I have to go to some office on business I always look in to see if it's a man or a woman sitting there. Bureaucrats are frightening, but the women are a hundred times worse than the men. But you've managed to stay human. And if you like, that's your greatest fortune, that with your sort of job you're still a human being. Even better – you're still a woman!

'Natasha has a good husband, her own flat, and she's a warm-hearted person herself. Olga's got her feet firmly on the ground. She's the sort of person Nekrasov wrote about: "She would stop a galloping horse, she would go into a burning hut." Not that it's so great that our women have to do things like that. But there's Olga, working all three shifts and fulfilling the shipyard's plan, side by side with the men. And if there should be a war or some other disaster, it'll be simple women like that who'll save us.

'What shall I say about you, Galina? Your happiness isn't everyone's cup of tea, certainly not mine. I don't understand your dissident point of view. What's the point of it, and where is it going? But one thing is clear to me: you are standing up for the truth. And that must be happiness, too.

'Nelya, you yourself probably know what your happiness is. But I'll just spell it out: it doesn't lie in your music or your pupils, or even in your good husband, but in the fact that you have an unusual soul. It is quiet, deep and pure like a forest lake. That is perhaps the most difficult happiness to attain.

'Well, I've said something about all of you. Now I'll say something about myself. My friends, I am disgustingly happy, unforgiveably happy! I can't remember a single day in my life when I didn't feel loved by the people I lived with – my mother, my sister, my husband Seryozha. I'm never itching to go anywhere, I have no wings and no special talents. I shall have as many children as possible and then be absolutely drunk with happiness. But one thing I will say: no matter how happy I've been, I still wish life here could be civilized. I think we women deserve to have life get a bit easier; and I don't just mean us who have been sitting here telling each other various stories, but all the women in this country. That's all. And forgive me if I said the wrong thing about anyone. You're not angry, are you?'

Nobody was angry at Irishka. On the contrary, Larissa rushed over to her, hugged her and said with great feeling: 'Our little Irishka, how wise you are! You're right. We can be happy in the life that has been given to us. But we would like life to be more civilized as well. I think we could end our *Women's Decameron* with those words. Don't you?'

All the women agreed with Larissa. After thinking it over a little, the author agreed, too, and decided to place a full stop after it. Here it is.